* * *

Mark to Murder

* * *

MARK TO MURDER

Death in Budapest

A Mark Kent Mystery

MORIS SENEGOR

ISBN: 1976099072
ISBN 13: 9781976099076
Library of Congress Control Number: 2017915565
CreateSpace Independent Publishing Platform
North Charleston, South Carolina

ALSO BY MORIS SENEGOR

Appassionata: and other stories of lovers, travelers, dreamers and rogues

Dogmeat: A Memoir of Love and Neurosurgery in San Francisco

To the boys and girls of English High School, Istanbul.
We have dispersed all over the world, yet we are still in Nişantaşı.

Chapter 1

* * *

He took the elevator down to the Royal Suite wearing a luxurious white bathrobe and flip-flops, enjoying cool air after the hot sauna. Pulling out his iPhone from the robe's side pocket, he pressed its home button, checking for time. Five-fifty p.m. More than an hour to prepare for his rendezvous. His eyes lazily drifted to the ornate elevator panel, lights changing slowly on floor markers, as he thought about Olga, the masseuse. Older now, plumper, but it didn't matter. She had skillfully handled his impressive erection, her lips soft, her mouth velvety smooth. He had wanted more but this would certainly do for now. The vigorous massage she followed with had eased all the tension of the past days. She had particularly concentrated on his muscular thighs, which, according to her, were all knotted up. It provoked another erection that she deftly covered with a nearby towel as she carried on, responding to his broad grin with a slight curl of her meaty lips, now free of lipstick. The sauna at the end was brief but divine. As the elevator door opened on the second floor, he thought he had enough time to finish himself off again before taking a shower and getting dressed.

The suite was chilly, a light snow outside dusting windowsills facing an ornate, spacious balcony. A March sun was setting over the Danube, traffic on the Chain Bridge heavy with Tuesday evening commuters. The bridge and its colossal columns were already lit. In another hour, when full darkness fell, the graceful columns would glow in floodlight, casting long glimmers onto the wavy surface of the river. He walked toward one of the picture windows to take in the scene, emptying the pockets of his gown onto a coffee table in the middle of the capacious living room, next to a house phone. There were only two items, his iPhone and the business card Olga had given him with her private number scribbled on the back. The view was spectacular, scattered clouds bright pink in the sunset, Buda Palace, grand and noble, dominating the skyline to the left of the Chain Bridge, small boats gliding slowly on the river like lit swans.

He was of medium height, balding atop and wore round wire-rimmed spectacles, like those John Lennon once wore. Over the years he had maintained a lean, athletic physique through regular exercise, although he could no longer play soccer as he had for so many years, his knees having failed him. Fortunately, his prowess in bed was still intact. He thought of Olga's ample breasts, her cleavage, generously revealed though the top of her white uniform, and felt another erection beginning. He would call her at the first possible opportunity for a better encounter elsewhere, away from her workplace.

A chill went through him as he realized how cold the suite was. He had to find the thermostat before disrobing. He headed from the luxuriously upholstered living room, through a small dining area with a bar and microwave, to the bedroom. He thought he had spotted something on the wall there that looked like a thermostat. It was to the right of the entrance, an old-fashioned, round, dial-up deal, surprisingly mismatched against the modern appointments everywhere else. It was set to sixteen degrees. No wonder it was so cold. He adjusted his spectacles. They had a tendency to slide down his nose. He leaned closer to the dial.

Suddenly a frosty feeling in the back of his neck sent a fresh chill through his body. It was the muzzle of a gun. He jolted and his glasses fell off. The muzzle pressed harder. He let out an instinctive whine.

"*Tăcere*," he heard a menacing grunt, *hush*. Romanian.

He tried to turn and look. The muzzle was now pressed against the side of his chin, stopping him. "*No spune nimic!*" *Don't say a word*. He recognized a distinctly Moldovan accent.

Suddenly his arms were jerked behind him, causing the front of his gown to open. The gun was still pressed to his chin. His pulse rose as he realized that there were two of them. He felt the frigid metal of handcuffs first on one wrist, then the other. They rattled as they clamped tight around his flesh, his palms touching together behind his waist, his arms pulling painfully on his shoulders.

"*Deschide-ti gura*," ordered the same voice, gun back on his neck, at the nape of his skull. *Open your mouth*.

He did as told. He saw a blurry, lean figure facing him. Without his glasses he may as well have been blind. The man shoved a piece of cloth into his mouth. It tasted bitter. Duct tape soon followed, locking the stuffing tightly inside his lips.

As the gun withdrew, he stood, facing the thermostat he could no longer see, eyes wide with fear, his erection long gone, his unrequited member exposed and shrunken. It would no longer come to life.

Chapter 2

* * *

"Gresham Palace," confirmed the taxi driver in Hungarian-tinged English. He fiddled with a small tablet computer mounted on his windshield, and soon the modern new terminal at Ferihegy was a distant spot in the rear window of the yellow Škoda. Mark checked his watch: five p.m. Dusk was already settling outside.

"How long is the ride there?" he asked the driver.

The taxi had circled away from Terminal 2 and was waiting behind several cars at a railroad crossing. Mark saw two large businesses, a furniture store, and a car dealership, plus several single-story, motel-like airport lodgings.

"About half an hour," said the driver tersely. A lengthy freight train slowly lumbered by. The driver stared at it silently.

Mark removed a typewritten itinerary from his shoulder bag. Passport control in Munich had taken too long and he'd missed his connection that should have brought him in earlier. No worry, he was told at the Lufthansa counter, the airline ran a frequent schedule to Budapest. They placed him on the next one, the flight only about an hour and fifteen minutes. But now, Mark figured he barely had enough time to get settled in before his rendezvous with Ahmet. He was much excited by the prospect.

The taxi crossed the railroad and started up a small, two-lane road lined by rickety apartment houses with faded paint. Mark looked out and read *Üllői út* in large black letters on white street signs. He didn't know how to pronounce the word. He thought about asking the driver, but the man, older, with white hair and beard, seemed in no mood to talk.

Mark leaned back, closed his eyes, and thought about the resurrection of Ahmet. What a grand surprise it had been, and so peculiar. A few Turkish words scribbled behind a Romanian radiology report. It was of a CAT scan of the abdomen. *Merhaba*, said the message, *beni hatırlıyormusun? Hello, do you remember me?*

How could Mark forget?

The message included an email address that Ahmet said was secure. After several back-and-forths, Mark was now here, in a country he had never visited, for his first encounter with his old Turkish mate since their high school days.

They passed a prominent stadium to the left on a rapidly widening boulevard, as the landscape became more densely urban, the buildings more stately. Two yellow trams crossed each other to their right, on rails that paralleled the road. The taciturn driver was skillful and seemed confident in his chosen route.

By the time the taxi reached the Danube, it was dark. The driver turned right onto a riverside road near an old, steel suspension bridge with towers that resembled minarets. He sped along river cruisers docked by the shore. The vista across the river, on the Buda side, was captivating, with an illuminated statue high atop a hill, of a woman with her arms up, a Hungarian lady liberty. Ahead was a modern white suspension bridge glowing magnificently. At the foot of the bridge across the river, a solitary building complex fronted a sheer cliff side. It was a series of different styled buildings, old and modern, fused to each other side by side.

Mark took a chance and asked the driver what it was. In a fit of generosity, the old man pointed to the bridge and said, *Erszébet*, then to the building complex. *Rudas*. "It's a bath house," he added.

What a strange bath house, thought Mark. It looked nothing like the Turkish bath houses of his childhood. Maybe he'd get a chance to visit it.

Soon after passing the Erszébet Bridge, Mark was struck by another one up ahead, a beautiful replica of the Brooklyn Bridge, its concrete towers ablaze, its roadway and cables gracefully glittering. Across the river from it was a colossal building atop a hill, with a giant domed tower, radiant in floodlight. It had to be some sort of palace, Mark guessed.

The taxi turned out of the riverside drive onto a small plaza, curved around, and seemingly jumped a curb onto a narrow drive. It stopped in front of an imposing arched door with a glass awning. A young, uniformed attendant rushed to open Mark's door, effusively welcoming him.

As the attendant collected his luggage, Mark stared at the single column of the Brooklyn-like bridge across the plaza, all that was visible from this new perspective, and at the giant building filling the horizon to its left. As the taxi sped off, Mark pointed and asked, "What is that?"

The young attendant, bent over Mark's luggage, straightened up and smiled. "*Széchenyí Lánchíd*," he said. He grabbed the bags and started toward the door. "We all know it as the Chain Bridge," he added. His English was good. "That building to the left is the Buda Palace."

They entered the hotel through a Romanesque doorway, all glass, intricately ornamented with ironwork, and walked on a marble-tiled hallway with convoluted patterns inlaid in black. Mark stopped short of the check-in counter ahead, overwhelmed by an Oriental-style arched glass dome, crisscrossed with ironwork, adorned with striking stained-glass patterns around its base. A strangely compact, gilded chandelier hung down from it, slicing the magnificent space with an arrow-like tip. Ahmet had not lost his appetite for ostentation, Mark gathered, choosing as he did this luxurious hotel.

They put him up on the fourth floor, in a so-called Gresham Room overlooking a courtyard. It was spacious, elegantly accoutered, and had a king size bed with an ornate spread. It had been expensive enough. Mark wondered how much one of the suites with a Danube view would cost. More than what he would be willing to pay, for sure.

By now it was six p.m. He took a shower, put away a few items from his suitcase, and decided to take a short nap before meeting his old friend downstairs.

* * *

Mark sat at a stylish bar to the side of the reception desk, nursing a martini, and stared at the spiky chandelier spearing the vast ceiling space. A skillful pianist was playing renditions of American oldies, singing into a microphone in accented English that gave familiar lyrics an exotic touch. Two stylish, leggy women sat on stools near the piano, enjoying the music. The pianist kept his eyes mostly on them.

There were few others at the bar. Mark noticed a solitary man at a poorly lit far corner. He was dark-haired and dark-complexioned, with a long, pointed nose and shaggy moustache that concealed his upper lip. He looked vaguely familiar, Turkish maybe, but Mark could not make him out. The man seemed to be eyeing him, although Mark wasn't quite sure.

Only the good die young, sang the pianist. The women joined in on the Billy Joel refrain. *Only the good die young*, all three bellowed, out of phase. The pianist improvised a virtuosic Jazzy solo that drew delighted squeals from the women.

Mark anxiously looked at his watch. Seven-fifteen. Ahmet was late. He no longer knew his old friend's habits. Was he punctual or, like most Turks, chronically late to everything? Mark walked out of the bar to the reception desk, throwing a surreptitious glance toward the piano. The man in the dark corner had disappeared.

* * *

The young blond receptionist was impeccably dressed, with a perfectly knotted silk tie, his well-pressed jacket featuring a stylized Christmas tree on its breast pocket, insignia of the Four Seasons hotel chain. After a few clicks of his mouse he looked up at Mark with a smile.

"Mr. Radu is staying in our Royal Suite," he said in a German accent. Ahmet had instructed Mark to keep their rendezvous a secret and to ask for him under the name of Nicolae Radu.

The receptionist took a plastic card from a nearby drawer and inserted it into an encoding machine. "He left us instructions to have you sent to his suite." He handed him the card, explaining that Mark would need it to access the second floor.

The elevator stopped only at whatever floor the card was programmed for. It was modern but sluggish. Its interior was recently renovated to reflect the glory of the old building, itself extensively renovated after decades of Communist neglect. Mark lazily eyed the lights of the elevator panel as he wondered if Ahmet had assimilated into Romania, his current home, as well as Mark had into the U.S.

Mark recalled how Ahmet had displayed an affinity for Romania in their high school years, in those days a backward, Communist country. Ahmet had regaled him with exciting accounts of escapades with sexy, older Romanian women. Romanian women were a well-kept secret, Ahmet had said. They were gorgeous.

Mark wondered what kind of trouble Ahmet was in. His note had betrayed a touch of panic, with its message secreted inside a CT report. Then there was his Romanian alias. *Nicolae Radu*, thought Mark, shaking his head in disbelief.

Mark recalled the first hint that his old chum was leading a troubled life. It was in a hastily arranged high school reunion for which he had flown to Istanbul. Almost all his classmates had been there, except for Ahmet. By then he had lost touch with him, as it had been nearly two decades. Disappointed, Mark had inquired where Ahmet was, only to be told by various irate classmates that he had swindled them years ago and then disappeared, leaving a wife and young children behind. In the years that followed, Mark would periodically ask about his old buddy and always received the same answer. Searches on the internet were also useless. Thus, when Ahmet's unexpected message arrived, Mark was both excited and curious.

It had been an inauspicious time for Mark to abruptly depart from San Francisco. On the cusp of pending divorce litigation, he had distressed Joel, his lawyer and friend, with news of his impromptu trip. His short notice had not gone over well with his fellow radiologists at Kaiser, either. His boss, Ben Allen, the chief of radiology, was irate about losing Mark when two others were already on vacation and another out on sick leave.

But Mark could not refuse his old mate's invitation. He was eager to get reacquainted with Ahmet and reminisce. Besides, with Angie gone, and his second marriage crumbling, he felt a need to get away. He should have done the same when his first marriage ended in a disaster, but he had worked on, his solitary, monotonous days in dark rooms, reading endless streams of X-rays a solace back then. This time, however, he found his job cumbersome, painful. He looked forward to a European break and immersion in nostalgia.

The elevator opened to a lushly decorated foyer, bedecked on one side with a table bearing a vase of fresh flowers, and on the other, a full-length mirror. A long, boxy security camera above the vase, aimed at the elevator doors, disturbed the otherwise tasteful decor. *Shades of Communism past*, Mark thought to himself.

He stopped by the mirror and examined himself. He was tall and lanky, just as he had been in his teenage years. But his face—still robust and square-jawed— betrayed wrinkles, mostly around the obsidian-dark eyes that Megan, his first wife, had called "bedroom eyes." His thick charcoal black hair, which he still kept long in a seventies style, had grayed at the temples. He finger-brushed his hair off his broad forehead and wondered if Ahmet would recognize him after all the years. He had no doubt Ahmet would still be his old short, wiry, muscular self. The John Lennon glasses he favored in the old days, if he still wore them, would certainly give him away, no matter how he had changed otherwise.

The narrow hallway was empty. Mark had no trouble finding his way to the Royal Suite. It was well marked with hallway signs.

He knocked on the door of the suite several times. No answer. He checked the room number against a pocket guide of the hotel the receptionist had given him. He was at the correct door. He toyed with the key card he had received to operate the elevator. Would it open the door? Should he try?

Oh, what the hell, he thought, it was Ahmet after all, his best friend from his teenage years. Mark placed the key card in the door slot and heard a quiet swish in response. A green blinking light by the doorknob beckoned him in. He hesitated for a split second, then entered the room.

Chapter 3

* * *

Günsu anxiously eyed her cellphone. It was an old-fashioned flip phone. She opened and closed it several times, staring at its blank screen. Outside, a *Lodos* was raging across Istanbul with fierce winds, promising sheets of rain. She approached her living room window and stared at a few pedestrians being blown about in the wind. She wondered why Ahmet had not called.

Günsu's spacious apartment was in Nişantaşı, a swank, Westernized, up-market neighborhood in the European part of the city. It was not far from the English High School where she had met Ahmet years ago. In those days, the school had a separate building for girls in Beyoğlu. That's where she had attended grade school. Günsu and her girlfriends joined the boys in Nişantaşı when their school decided to go co-ed in high school. She was an industrious student, as were the other girls. They spent three years with the boys, most of them rowdy and academically uninterested, and injected a semblance of civility into their lives by their presence. Günsu and Ahmet became part of a clique of girls and boys who hung out together.

Günsu left the windowsill and moved to her bedroom at the back of her apartment. It was only eight p.m., too early to go to bed. Even if she did, she was too jittery to fall asleep. She looked at a desktop computer that Tarık, her son, had placed on a bureau she kept there. It was too old now, unused for years.

She wished she had kept up with computers. All her friends seemed to be on social media while she was stuck communicating solely with an old flip phone. She decided to call Tarık.

"Hi, Mom. What a storm, eh?"

"Hello, my love."

"What's wrong?" He had instantly detected dread in her voice.

She hesitated before answering. "It's Ahmet."

"Not that asshole again. Are you still in touch with him?"

"Please," she pleaded, "hear me out."

"I thought you two had broken up...." He paused for a moment. "What, two years ago?"

"Well, yes and no," she answered sheepishly. "We're still in touch."

Tarık was silent.

"He was supposed to travel to Hungary and call me when he arrived. He never did."

"So, what else is new?" Tarık was indignant. "He's probably out screwing some Hungarian chick."

"No, no, it's not like that."

"Mommm!" he said impatiently. "Are you ever going to learn?"

"Look, I think he is in some kind of trouble. I am not sure what. This trip... to Hungary. He hastily arranged it. He sounded panicky when we last spoke."

"So what do you want me to do?"

"Can you search around on your computer, like in Facebook, and see what you can find?"

Tarık sighed. "Okay."

Günsu hung up, embarrassed. She turned on her TV and tried to get her mind off Ahmet with the soap opera. After what seemed like an eternity, her phone rang.

"There is no trace of Ahmet on social media, as usual." Tarik was matter-of-fact.

Günsu's heart sank.

"But I found this guy. His name is Mark Kent, but I think he changed it when he moved to America. His Turkish first name was Metin."

“Oh, I know him,” said Günsu, excited and surprised. “He was one of our classmates, Metin Özgür.”

“Well, whatever.”

“How did you find him?”

“He is Facebook friends with many of your old classmates.”

“I haven’t seen Metin,” Günsu thought for a moment, “since our twenty-fifth high school reunion.”

“Well, this Metin character. He is in Budapest. He put up a Facebook check-in post from Ferihegy Airport. Do you think that’s a coincidence?”

“I have no idea,” said Günsu, intrigued.

“I got his phone number. Maybe you should call him.”

“How did you manage that?”

“Not too difficult,” said Tarık. “This guy is a doctor in America, a radiologist, in San Francisco.”

“Yes, that’s right. He’s the only one from our class who became a doctor.”

“American doctors have huge internet footprints.”

Günsu had no idea what that meant.

“He was easy to find. It is daytime in San Francisco right now. He works at some hospital called Kaiser. His secretary was kind enough to give me his personal cellphone when I told him I represented an old classmate of his from Turkey. Apparently she has instructions to do so for his old Turkish friends.”

“Oh, my God, Tarık. You’re a genius. I’m so proud of you.”

“Never mind. It’s nothing. Do you have a pen on hand?”

Günsu took the number down, profusely thanking her son. Outside the heavy rainstorm had begun, pelting the windows of her apartment. She had a hunch that Tarık was right. Metin’s presence in Budapest could not be a coincidence. He and Ahmet were best friends years ago, both in the clique that Günsu and her girlfriends hung around with.

“I hope that fucker is dead,” said Tarık as he hung up the phone.

Chapter 4

* * *

Metin approached the center of the muddy soccer field with apprehension. He was not accustomed to being there, defense near the goal being his more common position. In scratch schoolyard games, he was usually chosen last by the captains who picked teams. They invariably assigned Metin to insignificant positions where the ball rarely came near him. Today, however, the teams were picked randomly by their gym teacher, a fearsome, ill-tempered Australian named Mr. Ryan, who did not know the aptitude of the new kids. Ryan had assigned Metin to the all-important center forward position.

It was 1968, and the boys were in their *Hazırlık* (preparatory) year in the elite English High School. They were a select few, offsprings of wealthy, westernized families who had secured entrance to the expensive school through a rigorous exam. In this, their first year, they were to be immersed in everything British—language, customs, and culture—before they moved onto a much coveted bilingual education through grade school and high school, all in the same compact, four-story building in Nişantaşı. It was located in a densely populated section of the quarter, with rows of low-rise apartment buildings all around. The school was walled off from the neighborhood and had a small dusty side yard with a single miniature soccer goal, in front of which the boys played their schoolyard games. Inside, on the ground floor, indoor sports were conducted in a gym that also served as a theater and assembly hall.

Neither the gym nor the yard was sufficient for a proper British sports program suitable for a prep school of its caliber, so the school had acquired a spacious plot of open land near Okmeydanı on the periphery of the urban center, where most P.E. classes were conducted. The boys were bussed to this facility, changing into their sports outfits in a rickety wooden hut that served as a field-house. It had a stove that never worked, and showers that never ran. No lockers, just hangers. Outside on a crumbling porch, rotting wood peeking through peeled paint, kids could observe games in a vast, muddy soccer field encircled by a running track. At the end of each class the boys returned to the decrepit field house, sweaty and dirty, changed back to their school uniforms without cleaning up, and were bussed back to Nişantaşı.

It was in such a P.E. class, early on in his *Hazırlık* year, that Metin now found himself about to play center forward, a striker position he had no talent for. The field, a patch of uneven mud with vague white lines outlining boundaries, was soft and gooey amid a chilly, late-autumn drizzle. Metin's shoes were already muddied to his ankles. He tensely eyed three opponents on the opposite side of the dividing line eagerly watching him, predators about to pounce. They were some of the best in his class.

Metin looked at the opposite goal, three pieces of moldy wood assembled into a rectangle with no net behind. A hard, well-aimed kick would easily bring it down like a house of cards. Not by Metin. Only Rahmi, one of the boys facing him on the opposing center, could kick that well. Still, Metin fantasized about scoring a goal that day, something he'd never done. Wouldn't it be wonderful?

Mr. Ryan blew the starting whistle and Metin kicked, ushering the ball into play. It was a hesitant kick that sent the ball only a few paces ahead, across the dividing line between the two teams. Mr. Ryan again blew the whistle. Rahmi picked up the ball and returned it to Metin. Metin kicked the ball forward again, this time more assertively.

Another loud whistle. Mr. Ryan rushed toward Metin and bent down, bringing his red face perilously close to Metin's. "Goldmanite," he shouted, flecks of spit flying off his mouth. "Do it properly."

Metin winced and momentarily closed his eyes, expecting a slap on his face. He had never been beaten by Ryan, but he had witnessed classmates getting roughed up. When he opened his eyes, he was relieved to see Ryan walking back to his position as a referee, several paces away. One of the boys who flanked him on his own team brought the ball to Metin, holding it up in his right hand. As Metin reached for it the boy whispered, "You need to kick the ball backwards, toward us, not across the line to the opponents."

At that moment Metin felt a sense of comfort that he had never experienced in sports. No one had explained any rules to him before. The boys were presumed to have acquired their knowledge from street play. Metin hadn't. His parents demanded that he study at home and do his homework. They kept his street play to a minimum. Metin's awkwardness in the field had made him a sports pariah. This was the first time any mate had come to his aid.

Metin gave the boy a thankful stare and the boy nodded back. The two had never spoken before. He knew the boy's last name, Gürsen, from daily morning roll calls that their British teacher Mr. Lewis pronounced in a funny accent, unable to utter the "ü" in his name. But what was his first name? The whistle blew again and this time Metin lined up to the side of the ball, aiming his gaze backwards. He kicked.

Another loud whistle. Another rushing Ryan. More spits and shouts. Metin braced for the worst.

"Get out, you lunatic!" yelled Mr. Ryan, pointing to the sidelines. The Gürsen boy gave him an *I'm sorry* expression, displaying open palms at the side of his hips.

As Metin trudged through the mud, downcast, Ryan ran after him and handed him a small flag. He was to be a line referee, another position he knew nothing about. Metin had intended to kick the ball backwards but he had accidentally sent it flying forward, his strongest kick thus far, the ball landing deep in opponent territory.

At the end of the class, Metin sat on the fieldhouse porch, his legs drawn up, his arms wrapped around his knees in a futile attempt to keep warm. His clean soccer uniform was wet from the drizzle. He watched his classmates approach, their hair knotted with sweat, their bare legs and clothes blotchy with mud. The boys entered the changing room without giving him a glance, as did Mr. Ryan. The Gürsen boy, however, came and sat next to Metin. He chuckled.

"Good game," he said, smiling. He had a charming smile that erased Metin's angst.

"He called me a *lunatic*," Metin said.

Gürsen laughed. "Yeah, I heard. Everybody did."

"Do you know what it means?" asked Metin. He knew that *luna* referred to the moon. Why would Mr. Ryan call him a person from the moon?

Gürsen shrugged. "No," he said. "But it sure was funny."

His smile was infectious and Metin began laughing. They both got up and headed in to change.

"What is your first name?" Metin asked as they passed the door ledge.

"Ahmet," said the boy, extending his hand. Metin shook it, firmly.

Chapter 5

* * *

The Royal Suite was chilly and dark. Incoming city lights from a bank of windows gave Mark a sense that he was in a well-accoutered space. Drawn by the scenery, Mark approached a window. The Chain Bridge that he had seen earlier still dominated the view, dazzling and luminous, Buda Palace to its left a regal partner. The Danube shimmered with reflections broken by an occasional boat idly drifting by. Mesmerized, Mark momentarily lost his sense of whereabouts and stood motionless, staring.

The room was quiet. It seemed empty. Mark turned his attention inside and noticed that there was no bed. As he walked back toward the door he was startled by a loud, electronic sound, a cellphone ringing. Suddenly the room was illuminated by the flickering light of an iPhone on a coffee table nearby. He instinctively picked it up and looked at the screen. *Iancu*, announced the top of the screen. Mark held the phone against the wall, using the lit screen as a makeshift flashlight, and found a light switch.

He was in a smartly furnished living room, now brightly lit. The chic furniture was in perfect order, as if no one had been here. On the coffee table was a cordless house phone with a business card next to it.

There were no bags or clothes in the room. Where was Ahmet? Could he be downstairs looking for him, while Mark was up here?

"Hello," he said, loudly. "Ahmet!" No response.

He sat down on the loveseat, facing away from the picture windows, and picked up the house phone, examining its various shortcut buttons for one that might ring the registration desk. The iPhone rang again. Mark had placed it back where it had been. He looked at the screen. Iancu! Mark waited for the iPhone to stop ringing before he dialed the house phone.

While waiting for an answer, Mark absentmindedly picked up the business card next to the receiver. It had the Four Seasons insignia on it, with the word Spa in prominent black print. Under it was a name, *Olga Kaminesky, Masseuse*. A few words were listed beneath in Hungarian. Mark presumed they were services offered at the spa. He turned the card over and noticed a phone number scribbled in blue ink. He turned it forward. The spa's phone number was clearly stated in easily visible print. He looked at the back again. This was a different number.

"Hello, reception desk." Mark tossed the card back on the table.

The receptionist politely offered to take a look around the lobby if Mark didn't mind. Mark rubbed his eyebrows and waited with the phone to his ear. With his other hand he reached for the iPhone and pressed its home button. It lit with a series of four missed calls in small print, the two on top from Iancu. The other two caught his attention. He picked up the phone and brought it closer to his eyes. Günsu.

Could it be the Günsu he once knew? *No way,* he thought. He tried to check for more information but the phone required a passcode. He set it down and wondered. To his knowledge Günsu lived in Istanbul. He recalled catching up with her at the same high school reunion where he discovered that Ahmet had disappeared. Since no one knew his whereabouts then or subsequently, how could she be contacting Ahmet?

The receptionist returned and interrupted his thoughts. Mr. Radu was not in the lobby area. Yes, the receptionist remembered what he looked like. He had checked him in earlier.

Puzzled, Mark stood up. He turned back to the scene outside, the floodlit highlights of a historic city, calm in darkness. A sense of dread descended on him. Why, he wondered, would Ahmet have him sent to a dark, empty suite? Should he remain here? Was he trespassing? Maybe he should return to the lobby and enlist the help of the sympathetic receptionist. But what could he do? After all, the only way to reach Ahmet, his mobile phone, was lying right here, on the coffee table. Mark was certain that this was indeed Ahmet's phone. Who else would get calls both from a Turkish woman, possibly an old classmate, and an Eastern European name that he presumed was Romanian?

Mark looked about the empty suite. This was not what he had flown all the way to Budapest for. He decided to give the place a complete look-over before returning to the lobby.

* * *

Mark crossed a dining area and entered a capacious bedroom. He quickly found a light switch. A king-size bed to his right dominated the room, with a luxuriously shiny, dark headboard rising regally along the wall. Beyond the bed was an arrangement of tall bay windows jutting out of the room, framed by the main façade wall as though the windows were a stage. An armchair and coffee table were tucked near the windows affording a convenient view of the Danube. The curtains were open. Mark ignored the now familiar outside view and looked around.

This room appeared more lived in. At the foot of the bed was a stylish black leather bench with a pile of small pillows on one side and a small carry-on bag in the middle, unzipped but closed. On the other side of the room another armchair was littered with casually tossed clothes, pants that had almost slid to the floor, a long-sleeved shirt, all wrinkled, socks on the armrest, white briefs on top of the pants. A pair of shoes lay near the opposite wall, as if they had been kicked out directly from the feet. Mark recognized his old friend's modus operandi. Ahmet's childhood room in Şişli had been a bigger mess than this. Raised with a spick-and-span upbringing, Mark had always been fascinated with Ahmet's mess and the way his parents allowed it.

The bed was well made, the cover unwrinkled. The nightstand by the bay windows was empty. The other, closer to the entrance, had a wrist watch, a few foreign bills and some coins. Mark did not touch them.

To the right of the nightstand was a round, dial-up thermostat. It clashed with the generally modern décor of the suite. As Mark stared at it, something glistened on the carpet below. He knelt down and picked up a pair of round, wire-rimmed spectacles, realizing as he did, that the right side of the pair was cracked. He also noticed that his fingers were wet. He examined the carpet more closely. There was a prominent wet spot where the spectacles lay.

The glasses were familiar. Mark knew that Ahmet would be nearly blind without them. Where could he be?

He laid the glasses on the nightstand and smelled his wet fingertips. An unmistakable aroma of ammonia filled his nostrils. Urine. His sense of dread resumed, now with more fervor.

There was only one area left to explore. A luxurious suite such as this had to have an opulent bathroom to match. Mark looked at the other side of the entrance, at an open door with darkness beyond. He walked over to it and felt the wall for a light switch.

* * *

It was indeed an impressive bathroom, spacious, with a walk-in-shower lined in white Carrara marble, and two side-by-side sinks with wide mirrors and towels neatly arrayed nearby. It looked sparsely used except for some toiletries on one of the sinks. Mark noticed two flip-flop sandals near the entrance, askew and far from each other.

Then he saw Ahmet.

His old mate was sprawled in the cavernous bathtub, his back upright against the side, his eyes closed as if he had fallen asleep there. It was a white, square tub, equipped with whirlpool outlets. There was no water in it. Ahmet wore one of the hotel's lush bath gowns, open in the front, revealing a lean, athletic body, still youthful for his age. His right leg was spread out, bent at the knee, his left leg straight. The back of his gown behind his open legs was prominently stained by a colorless wet spot. It looked like he had passed out in the tub.

At the top edge of the bathtub, near Ahmet's slumping head, were two passports. One was upright and had been bent backwards so it would remain open.

It was burgundy colored, had an impressive coat of arms on its front cover with the words *Uniunea Europeană România* emblazoned atop. It looked brand new and was open to the identification page featuring a mature photo of Ahmet. He had gone bald and looked like his father, Latif. The name in it was Nicolae Radu. To its left was the other passport, unopened. It was a Bordeaux-brown Turkish passport with a gold crescent and star on its cover. It looked well worn.

Mark stared at the passports and wondered why Ahmet would bring them to the bathtub. He reached for the Turkish one and just before touching it, thought better and stopped. He turned his attention back to his old friend lying in the bathtub.

Mark now realized that Ahmet was not breathing. His face was dusky, his cheeks bruised in thin lines that ran from his nose to the edges of his lips. There were strange parallel lines on his upper arms and bare chest, down to the belly button. He reached over and took Ahmet's left wrist, searching for a pulse. There was a thin, circular bruise on it, like a bracelet. As Mark lifted the wrist, Ahmet's elbow and shoulder easily gave way. His body was not stiff. Mark couldn't find a pulse. He then searched for a carotid pulse, his eyes on the strange passports behind Ahmet's head. Once again, no pulse.

Puzzled, he stood over the bath looking his friend over. Did he have a heart attack? Some drug overdose? His right wrist also had a bracelet-like bruise. What were these? Mark noticed the same parallel lines as on his torso along Ahmet's legs, extending from mid-thigh to ankles. He had no idea what these were.

Did Ahmet fall into the bathtub drunk? But there was no disorder in the bathroom that a drunk person might produce, nor was there any blood anywhere.

The doctor in him momentarily took over, his perplexity suppressing his shock over the calamity he had walked in on. He knelt again and opened Ahmet's left eyelid. The pupil was dilated and the white of his eye, his sclera, was full of petechiae, tiny spots of blood. He quickly inspected the right eye and found the same. There was no doubt.

He stood up and quickly exited the bathroom, leaving the lights on. He needed to notify the police, but he had no idea how to do that. He returned to the living room of the suite, to the same spot that he had occupied minutes ago on the loveseat. He sank his face into his palms and, head bent down, reflected on what he had just witnessed. His old friend, his best friend from his teenage years, was dead. Images of a lively young Ahmet, mischievous, charming, all smiles, filled his mind. He let out a muffled sob, then collected himself and picked up the cordless house phone.

As Mark waited through two rings, the business card from the spa caught his attention again. He picked it up and held it in his free hand while he calmly described his dreadful discovery to an increasingly alarmed receptionist, asking that police be summoned. He then sat back and waited for hotel staff to arrive, the business card still in his hand. It appeared to him that Ahmet may have visited the spa this same evening. If so, this Olga, a masseuse according to the card, would have been the last person to see him. Why had she given him this card with a phone number jotted on the back?

Mark knew Ahmet's allure with women. He needed to find this woman and talk to her about what Ahmet had been like. She would be the only one who could describe to him that which he had flown all this way to seek. Mark pocketed the card.

Chapter 6

* * *

Metin sat in his aunt's apartment with a small math exercise book on one lap, a notebook on the other, while his mother and aunt played a smoky card game with two upstairs neighbors on a nearby dining table. He was in one of two spacious armchairs facing each other along bay windows overlooking Kodaman Caddesi, a small side street in Nişantaşı, not far from his new school. It was lined shoulder to shoulder with five- or six-story apartment buildings.

Metin's *Hazırlık* year math consisted of the British Imperial System of Measurements in weight, distance, currency and so on, and conversions to metric equivalents, the Turkish standard. It was all very confusing, these inches and yards and pounds and stones, most based on the dozen. Worse yet, British currency units were also related in equivalents of twelve, making exchange calculations cumbersome. Metin was floundering in this class, as were many others. His father, a mechanical engineer with a consulting business, who was also a professor at ITÜ, Istanbul's prestigious Technical University, urged him to study harder and pay more attention to details, but did not offer any help. Metin had to solve his own problems himself.

"A baker's dozen of notebooks costs two pounds," began the math question. "You have a pound note with you, two half crowns and seven tuppences. How many notebooks can you get and how many coins do you get back if the storeowner gives back only hay pennies?" Metin stared at the question, his mind blank. Little did he know that, soon the British would change their monetary system to a decimal-based one, making all his angst for naught.

A loud "aaah" drew his attention to the card table, where Meliha Hanım slapped her hand of cards on the table with typical swagger. She had just won the round after drawing only one card. She eyed her opponents with delight as she took a puff from her cigarette. Her fellow players flung their cards and tossed coins in her direction. She scribbled the residual value of their cards onto a score sheet.

A slim, alert woman with flashing eyes and a stern countenance, Meliha swiped her new earnings into the large pile of coins in front of her. She was a wizard at *konken.* Füsun, Metin's mother, and Nilüfer, his aunt, resentfully accused her of counting cards. Regardless, they continued to play with her regularly.

"I have blind luck today," said Füsun, as she gathered the scattered cards and deftly arranged them into a pile. A proper housewife, cheerful and outgoing, Füsun was a slim, petite woman who wore her walnut brown hair in a stylish beehive. Metin wondered if his mother ever had a chance when she played Meliha and Fevziye, her sister's neighbors.

Metin looked at his watch. The weekly card game was a boring ritual on Thursdays after school. He walked over to his aunt's apartment and waited until the end of the game before he and his mother took a *dolmuş* (shared taxi) back home to Kurtuluş. Tea and snacks, served after the game, was the only event he looked forward to.

As Füsun shuffled the deck of cards, Fevziye Hanım said, "Meliha my dear, is there anyone who can top you in this game?" She was older, prematurely wrinkled and overweight. A spinster, she lived alone on the top floor with two cats. She spoke slowly and with a slight lisp.

"Sedef Hanım would," chimed in Nilüfer, Metin's aunt, who looked different than her sister. She was tall and chubby, with closely cropped raven hair curled in a 1930s style. She lived in the spacious second floor apartment with her husband, who ran a wholesale coffee business in Eminönü, at the Spice Bazaar.

"Who is she?" asked Füsun, while rapidly dealing cards with machine-like precision.

"Latif Gürsen's wife," said Nilüfer, "the industrialist." She fanned her cards and examined them with a grim expression. "They live on Halaskârgazi Caddesi in Şişli."

"I've played with her," said Meliha, reordering her hand of cards. "She's good."

"She has nothing else to do but play cards," said Fevziye, her hand of cards closed, waiting for the new round to start, "with that *çapkın* husband of hers."

The word *çapkın* caught Metin's interest. It meant a playboy, womanizer. To his knowledge there were no fathers among his classmates with such a reputation. His own father, Sadık Bey, was a dedicated family man, reliable yet boring, a homebody who mostly read in his free time. Metin usually had a deaf ear to the gossip at the card table. Now he listened keenly while looking out of the window, pretending to not pay attention.

"Isn't he that rich guy who owns Gürsen Industries?" asked Metin's mom. "I think he has a son in Metin's school." She then looked at her cards and sighed. "Another terrible hand."

"Yes," said Meliha, drawing a card from the covered stack spread on the table and rapidly discarding it. "Big textile manufacturing business. I heard that he will soon be making French-style frilly underwear for women. What do they call them?"

"Lingerie," said Nilüfer, who spoke fluent French.

"*Tövbe, tövbe,*" responded Fevziye, *let us repent*, as she contemplated wholesome Turkish women contaminated by skimpy Christian underwear. It was her turn to pick a card but she didn't, disturbing the fast rhythm of the game. What was their world coming to, she added.

"Pick a card," Meliha ordered. She took a last drag from her cigarette and forcefully extinguished it.

The game resumed and they briskly played several rounds without speaking. Each time Füsun picked a new card she uttered a delighted "hah!" as her fortunes improved. "There," she said finally, unloading her hand in two pairs of three and one series of four, throwing another card into the pile. She had won.

Meliha Hanım quickly added the value of the residual cards and announced that this was the end of the game. Despite Füsun's last-minute performance,

Meliha had won the day, collecting yet more coins from her tablemates. Nilüfer put away the cards while Meliha and Fevziye lit new cigarettes. Füsun got up and headed to her sister's kitchen. Metin eyed the table expectantly as the women cleared it. Snacks from Rio Patisserie, a small basement bakery in nearby Rumeli Caddesi, were soon to arrive.

They silently partook in the miniature éclairs, profiteroles and millefeuille sweets that accompanied tiny *böreks* filled with cheese or sausage, washing them down with hot tea served in tulip-shaped glasses. Metin had the most items on his plate.

"This Latif Efendi," said Meliha Hanım, bringing the old subject back, "spends a lot of time in bars, nightclubs and bordellos." She carefully used a Turkish euphemism for the last word, mindful of the young boy at the table. The other women nodded. "The word is that he also brings his son with him to these places. A young boy, like Metin here, exposed to all that smut at such a tender age."

The other women shook their heads and made disapproving "tsk, tsk, tsk" sounds, clicking their tongues.

"I feel sorry for his wife," said Fevziye as she opened up an éclair and licked the custard off the middle. After loudly swallowing, she added, "The poor woman, left alone at home, has nothing else to do but play cards."

Meliha turned to Metin. "Do you know his son?"

"Yes," he answered, holding a particularly fat *börek* in one hand. "He's my classmate."

"What is he like?"

Metin took a bite of the *börek* and wondered about visiting a nightclub. It sounded glamorous. But it might as well be the moon. Metin's parents were homebodies and did not pursue any nightlife. A bordello? That was totally beyond his imagination.

"His name is Ahmet. He is nice."

"Well," said Meliha, "if his father keeps it up, he will not end up so very nice."

Chapter 7

* * *

The call came right after Mark had returned to his fourth-floor room, still reeling from his discovery of Ahmet. He kicked his shoes off when his mobile rang, the screen lighting with *No Caller ID.* Mark collapsed onto a stylish chair by the entrance and eyed his neatly made bed, wondering whether to answer. The hotel had come alive with the news he had conveyed to the reception desk, a big commotion raging on the second floor. Mark needed a brief respite, another power nap perhaps, before meeting the police. He let the phone go to its last ring before answering.

"Metin," he heard, a woman's voice. He did not recognize her. "This is Günsu," she said in Turkish, "from high school."

Stunned, Mark did not answer. He took the phone off his ear and stared at the screen, as if it held some hidden clue.

"Do you remember me?" Still in Turkish.

Here we go again, Mark thought. It was the same line Ahmet had used in his own first contact. How could he forget?

"Of course," he said, in English. His Turkish was rusty. "How did you get my number?"

"It's a long story." She switched to English too. It was a familiar routine from their old high school days, this freestyle back and forth between two languages.

"Are you in Budapest?" she asked.

"Yes, how did you know?"

"Have you run into Ahmet there? Are you..." Her voice was jittery. She paused and collected herself. "Are you there to see him?"

An image flashed in Mark's mind of Günsu, giggling at Ahmet's jokes, touching him, always touching him, while Ahmet remained aloof, carrying on with his easy charm, vying for maximum impact upon the whole group, unaware of Günsu's adoring eyes. Mark kept his own eyes on her, admiring her smooth, radiant long hair, her pouty lips, the slight chip in the corner of her front tooth when she smiled, wishing he held the same sway with her as Ahmet.

"How do you know that Ahmet had been here?" asked Mark.

The thought of Günsu knowing Ahmet's current whereabouts had been gnawing at Mark ever since he saw her name on Ahmet's iPhone. Her strangely well-timed call was astonishing.

"Oh, my God!" she nearly shouted. "Is he all right?"

Mark realized he should not have referred to Ahmet in the past tense. But it was too late. "Look, Günsu," he said as calmly as he could. "I don't know what's going on between you and Ahmet. But yes, I came here to meet him. But we we could not meet."

He didn't know how to say it without being blunt. "He's dead." He heard a loud cry and then sobbing at the other end.

After collecting herself, she asked, "When? What happened?"

"I don't know," said Mark. "It happened tonight. Looks like he was murdered. I found him." He was interrupted by more loud sobs.

"I knew it," she cried, "I knew something like this would happen to him."

Mark wanted to ask her why she had called, and tell her that he had seen her name on Ahmet's phone, but this was not the right time. "Günsu," he said instead. "I can't talk right now. The police will summon me soon for questioning. Give me your phone number and I'll call you later. Probably tomorrow."

"Can you come to Istanbul?" she asked. "And tell me what's going on?"

"I only took a few days off to come to Budapest. I am not sure I can extend my time off work."

There was a knock at Mark's door. He muted the phone and yelled, "A minute, please!"

"For old times' sake?" Günsu pleaded. "It would be so nice to see you again. You know how I was fond of you."

Really! He wanted to say. "It's a sad night for both of us," he said. "*Başımız sağolsun.*" It was the standard Turkish expression of condolence, *may our heads remain healthy.*

"*Başımız sağolsun,*" she echoed, whimpering, and she hung up.

Mark opened the door to find the blond hotel receptionist, who tried to stammer a greeting, his demeanor jittery. He was here, the young man said to Mark, to escort him to the Royal Suite. Together they headed to the elevators.

Chapter 8

* * *

Mark reentered the Royal Suite with the receptionist in tow. Two officers in navy blue jumpsuits and tilted caps, bearing *Rendőrség* (police) insignia on their shoulders, stood at each side of the door and nodded them in. The young receptionist's professional demeanor had melted away amid panic after Mark's call. He eyed the policemen with fear and shuffled hesitantly behind Mark.

Inside, the living room had shed its earlier darkness and quiet. It was well lit and abuzz with activity, officers here and there, one dusting for fingerprints, another rushing out of the room, brushing by Mark. The windows reflected images within, rather than the beguiling ones outside. There were two men in the central area, amid the loveseats and coffee table, one sitting, the other standing, both eyeing Mark.

The one who stood, a short, beady-eyed man with red nose and cheeks, approached Mark peremptorily and firmly shook his hand. He had rumpled clothes that looked hastily thrown on. His eyes had streaks of red and bags underneath.

"Dr. Kent?" A faint smell of alcohol wafted from his breath. Mark nodded.

"I am Imre Kárpáty, Criminal Investigator, Budapest Police." He pointed to the empty loveseat facing the windows and gestured for Mark to sit down.

Mark slowly settled, leaning on one armrest. It was past ten p.m., and his long trip, along with all that had happened since, bore down on him, negating his brief rest in his room before Günsu's phone call interrupted it. He noticed the other figure facing him silently across the coffee table, where he himself had previously sat while calling the reception desk. The man was older, tall and slim, pale, with thick, brown-rimmed spectacles. His white goatee elongated his ovoid, expressionless face. Mark nodded to him. He did not nod back. The cordless house phone was still atop the coffee table between them. Ahmet's iPhone, however, was gone.

The German receptionist said something unintelligible and rushed out, his mission complete now that he had accompanied Mark up the elevator with a universal access card. A young, blonde woman in civilian clothes rustled behind Mark's sofa and hastily left the room. Mark caught a quick sight of her, enough to notice cameras dangling from each shoulder. Mark looked toward the bedroom, stretching his neck behind the seat. He saw no one else.

"Is he still...in there?" he asked Kárpáty. The inspector nodded.

"The forensic unit arrived late, just recently. They are examining the scene," he said. "This unfortunate event caught us all at a most inopportune time." His words dripped with disappointment.

Mark wondered precisely what Ahmet's demise had interrupted for the detective. "I'm sorry," he said.

"About what?" Kárpáty approached Mark but did not sit down, preferring to look down on him from a height too slight to be imposing.

"I don't know," Mark mumbled, "about whatever you were doing." Mark paused. "About..." he turned back toward the bedroom. "About my friend."

Kárpáty pulled out an envelope with the Four Seasons insignia from his side pocket, stuffing a rumpled paper that came out with it back inside. He removed a document, unfolded and read it.

"Mr. Mark Kent," he said, still reading. He then looked at Mark. "Doctor," he corrected himself. Mark realized that the inspector was examining his own hotel manifest.

"What are you doing here in Budapest, in the hotel room of Ahmet Gürsen?" He pronounced Ahmet's last name atrociously, reminding Mark of their British teachers back in Istanbul.

"I came to meet him. He left instructions with the hotel to have me brought up to this suite."

Kárpáty folded back the document. "And you found him dead?"

"Yes, in the bathroom."

"When was the last time you saw Mr. Gürsen alive?"

"In 1974."

Kárpáty and the silent man exchanged glances. "But you are good friends?" He sounded incredulous.

"Am I a suspect?" asked Mark.

"No, sir, you are not. Not at this stage." He tucked the hotel document into a side pocket on his jacket. "Doctor, we will need your passport. Do you have it on you?"

Mark did. He had brought it along in case he was asked to show his identity. He handed it to Kárpáty. The inspector briefly reviewed the passport, stopping to eye Mark, then his photo. He then placed the passport in the inside pocket of his jacket, where he had pulled out the hotel envelope.

"We will keep your passport for now. I hope that does not inconvenience you, Doctor."

"Why?" Mark tried to conceal his alarm.

"Run some background checks."

It seemed to Mark that they could do that simply by taking down the information in the passport. There was no need to confiscate it. He thought about raising an objection, but then he reminded himself that he was in a foreign country and had no idea what their procedures were. Besides, any protest might work against him.

Mark decided to change the subject. "How come I am not a suspect?"

"At this time I am not prepared to fully answer that. We'll have to wait for a forensic report first. But let's just say that we've checked the hotel records and security camera recoding for this floor, and that's our conclusion for now."

Mark was impressed with Kárpáty's efficiency, his appearance having betrayed no hint of it.

"Do you have any idea who did this?"

"We cannot divulge that," replied the inspector. Mark felt stupid for asking the question.

Kárpáty then took Mark through every activity he had engaged in after checking into the hotel, asking in great detail about what he had done in the

Royal Suite. Mark made sure to tell him he had touched Ahmet's phone and spectacles, and his body. When asked why, he told them that at first Ahmet appeared possibly passed out, so he took a pulse and found none. He added that Ahmet's arm moved freely. There was no rigor mortis.

"Thank you, Doctor, for your forensic tip." Kárpáty sounded sarcastic rather than grateful. "What about the other items—why did you touch them?"

The eyeglasses were lying on the floor, Mark recounted. He omitted the wet spot, also on the floor. The phone, because it was ringing. Bypassing these, Kárpáty asked him about the passports by Ahmet's head at the tub. Did Mark know about Ahmet's Romanian alias? He explained that he did. Why did Mark suppose the passports were left that way? Mark had no idea.

"Did you answer the ringing phone?"

"No, I didn't."

"Did you see who had called?"

Mark figured they would already have checked the phone. "Yes," he said, "but I have no idea who it was."

Mark preferred to keep Günsu to himself. He was still reeling from her phone call.

"Did you rearrange anything else or take anything out of the room?"

"No." Mark felt strange about lying, but there was no way he could convincingly explain why he had removed the business card from the spa, the one with the name of Olga Kaminesky. He was intrigued by the handwritten phone number in the back and curious about his old friend's allure on women, if it was the same as when they had been together years ago. Mark doubted Kárpáty would understand that.

The inspector changed his tack, apparently satisfied with Mark's curt answers. "Doctor, why do you suppose Mr. Gürsen was using an alias?"

"Well, I don't know for sure." Mark hesitated, wondering if he should divulge old news. He decided to go ahead. "Years ago, when I had my first reunion with my classmates, I discovered that Ahmet had swindled many of them and then disappeared. No one knew where he was."

"What do you know about this swindle?"

"Not much. I was not one of the victims."

The inspector remained silent as Mark paused.

"Anyhow," Mark concluded, "under those circumstances, a guy in hiding, I wasn't surprised that he was using an alias."

Kárpáty then took Mark through the reason why he had traveled to Budapest. Mark answered truthfully that he didn't quite know. His old friend, with whom he had lost touch, had unexpectedly contacted him and asked for this rendezvous. He sensed that his friend was in some kind of trouble, but Ahmet had not divulged what it was. Mark had expected to hear the details tonight, in this room.

"Are you returning to the United States?" asked the inspector.

"Yes, but my reservations are not until Saturday. I had planned to spend four days in Budapest."

"Good." Kárpáty turned away and took a few steps toward the windows. He then turned back and faced him from behind the opposing loveseat. "May I suggest that you stay here and enjoy our beautiful city." It was more a command than a suggestion.

"When can I get my passport back?"

"Soon," said Kárpáty. "Certainly before you depart. In the meanwhile I am afraid I will have to ask you to visit our District V police station tomorrow morning to give us fingerprints and DNA samples. I hope that is not too much inconvenience."

"Sure, no problem."

"We'll send a police officer to pick you up from this hotel."

Mark stood up. "May I go back to my room now?"

"Thank you, Doctor." Kárpáty pulled a small notebook from his inside pocket and began jotting something down.

* * *

As Mark headed to the door, he noticed that a light snow had begun, snowflakes lazily drifting outside his window, illuminated by the floodlights of the city. Inspector Kárpáty's interrogation had worn him out. He looked forward to his own room and much-needed sleep.

"One more minute, please." The strange figure who had sat silently until now, spoke. His thick French accent caught Mark by surprise. Mark locked eyes with Kárpáty.

"Oh, my apologies," said the inspector, shuffling from around the back of the sofa. "Allow me to introduce Commissaire Jean-Claude Gérard, the local liaison officer from the French National Police and Interpol Europe."

Mark looked at the man in disbelief. Gérard took his glasses off and rubbed his eyes. They looked squinty without the spectacles.

"I'd like to ask you a few questions as well, if I may." Gérard put his glasses back on and gestured for Mark to sit back down. Mark obeyed, hoping his annoyance was obvious.

"Doctor," said Gérard, "you practice in America, is that correct? In San Francisco?"

"Yes."

"And you are a radiologist? You read X-rays?"

"Well, not just X-rays; CTs, MRIs, and other studies."

Gérard ignored the comment. "We understand that Mr. Gürsen first contacted you via a radiology report." He pronounced the last name well, rolling the "r" with his French accent.

The question caught Mark by surprise. He had not told anyone about this. The Commissaire continued in a monotone. "A report with a Regina Maria letterhead."

Mark recalled a logo of a five-edged star made of the letter M, which encircled a white cross. "Yes," he said.

"It was from their Braşov Clinic, a radiology center."

"That I didn't know. I don't read Romanian."

"Do you recall what the report was?"

"A CT of the abdomen."

Mark remembered the curious two-page report that had slipped into a pile of paperwork he needed to sign off on. He was accustomed to an occasional foreign report, mostly from Mexico, of patients who had received treatment abroad and then came to Kaiser. But this one caught his attention, a totally foreign language. The report was two pages. The letterhead announced the address of the radiology center as being from Romania. Skimming the letter, he had surmised that it was a CT of the abdomen.

"Doctor, if you don't read Romanian, how could you come to such a conclusion?"

"It was a Latin alphabet and the medical terms in the report, you know, the anatomy...it was similar to English." Mark recalled being struck by how similar such medical terms were across different languages.

"Who was the patient?"

"I did not pay attention to that because I discovered Ahmet's message on the back."

The message was on the back of the first page, easily spotted, handwritten with a pen in large, uppercase Turkish. When he turned over the first page to read the second, it had taken his attention away from the report itself.

"I'll get to that in a second," said the Frenchman, facing him stiff and still. "Could you tell what the diagnosis was?"

Mark found Gérard's interest in the medical information of the report curious. To him the report was an obvious ruse, a vehicle for clandestine contact. He had not paid any attention to the substance of the report.

"No, sir. This was not a patient we were treating. I did have that checked with our records. We have an extensive inter-hospital electronic record system. Kaiser is a very large organization. The patient was not ours. So I had no interest in the content of the report."

"Do you still have the report?"

"Yes. Back in the States. Filed away." Mark kept meticulous files on everything. He had started one titled *Ahmet* after receiving the report.

"We'd be very interested in seeing it. Is there any way you can get it to us?"

Mark thought for a moment. It was a workday back home in San Francisco. He could easily have a secretary email it to his phone. But he wanted to examine the report again before handing it over. "I can have my office fax it here in the morning," he said. "But it would be a copy, obviously."

Gérard nodded. "How about if I arrange for us to pick up the original? Our liaison to the FBI in San Francisco can do that for us."

"Yeah, sure." Mark was relieved that the Commissaire did not insist on an immediate handover. It did not occur to him that an FBI visit to his office might cause some alarm back home.

"Can you please see to it that it stays safe, that it's not tampered with?"

"No worry. My files are locked away. Only my assistant can get to them."

Kárpáty shifted, taking a sideways step from his vantage point where he had been quietly listening to the conversation. He leaned back on a small mahogany writing table by the wall, where he could continue observing Mark and Gérard in profile. He crossed his arms and yawned.

"Now, Doctor, let's get back to Mr. Gürsen's message."

Mark was distracted, watching Kárpáty. The Hungarian seemed uninterested.

"Doctor." Gérard was more firm.

Mark snapped back. "Oh, sorry."

"This message. What did it say?"

"It was very brief. It announced that he was Ahmet and asked if I remembered him. He said he would like to get in touch with me. He gave me an email address where I could contact him. He said it was secure."

"Do you remember that address?"

"No, not offhand. I'll have my office copy it and fax that too."

"And you contacted that email?"

"Yes, and so, I'm here."

"Yes," said Gérard, thoughtfully. "You're here." After a brief pause, he moved on. "Can you tell me exactly why?"

Mark looked at his watch and wondered if this would be going on until the morning. He decided to get it all out in one swift summary. He told Gérard that their email exchange was brief. He responded to Ahmet with a message about himself, where he was, what he was doing, that he was disappointed to have missed him at their high school reunion. Ahmet's message was curt. *Can we meet,* he asked, *in Europe*. Mark said he'd love to. The response was swift, with a seeming sense of urgency: Ahmet asked if Mark could come to Gresham Palace in Budapest. When Mark wondered what it was about, Ahmet responded that he would explain it face-to-face. So Mark hastily made arrangements for a rendezvous.

Gérard listened quietly. "Thank you, Doctor," he said. "You look tired and I appreciate your cooperation with us. Now, if you don't mind, I'll ask you a few more questions. It'll be brief. Formality."

Mark nodded in resignation.

"Doctor, do you practice anywhere else?"

"I did when I was younger, during my training, but not now. I've been with Kaiser for over twenty years."

"You don't ever " Gérard hesitated, groping for the right word, "moonlight?" He uttered the idiom with difficulty. "Say, in other countries?"

"No." Mark was uncertain what he was referring to.

"Doctor, do you interact with other specialists?"

"Of course. I am a radiologist. I interact with every specialty in my hospital."

"How about outside your hospital?"

"No. Kaiser is a closed-system HMO. We don't deal much with outside physicians."

"Doctor, have you heard of or have you had any interactions with Regina Maria before you got that message from Mr. Radu?"

Gérard's switch to Ahmet's alias caught Mark by surprise. He thought for a moment before he answered. "No."

"Have you ever heard of Clinica Santa Maria in San Jose, Costa Rica?"

"No."

"How about Elita Clinic in Kosovo, near Skopje?"

"No," answered Mark, his voice growing impatient. He again gestured to rise from his chair.

"Doctor, bear with me for one more moment." Gérard's voice was flat, unemotional. "You were born and raised in Turkey, correct? Istanbul?"

"Yes."

"Do you have any contact with Turkish doctors?"

"Yes, I meet some in international radiology conferences."

"Have you ever visited or worked in a Turkish hospital?"

"No."

"Have you ever heard of a Turkish doctor named Mahmut Erkan Gazioğlu?" Mark was again impressed by the Commissaire's Turkish pronunciation, despite his French inflections.

"No, is he a radiologist?"

"No, sir. But he is much wanted. We have an Interpol Red Alert in his name."

"Why are you interested in all these hospitals and doctors?" asked Mark, not necessarily expecting an answer.

"Never mind, Doctor," Gérard responded. "Thank you very much," he added. "You're free to leave."

Neither inspector offered any handshake, both staying put where they were. As he made his exit, Mark nodded to the two *Rendőrség* officers guarding the door. They smiled back, friendlier than those inside. In the elevator he pulled out his iPhone and entered the Turkish doctor's name into his reminders app. He had already forgotten the obscure clinics the strange Frenchman had mentioned. He would have to look up this Gazioğlu. He had no idea what a Red Alert was. He'd have to look that up, too. But first he had to get some sleep.

Chapter 9

* * *

Mark stretched out over the bedcovers with his clothes on, trying to make sense of it all. What was that peculiar Frenchman getting at? He couldn't imagine why he would persistently question Mark's outside affiliations when he had none. What did this have to do with Ahmet's demise, anyway? He also wondered why the French officer was there to begin with. Ahmet had obviously been involved in some serious international mischief. Still, how had a local Interpol liaison discovered his death so fast? Who had invited him to the scene?

The Hungarian officer, Inspector Kárpáty, seemed unsavory, inebriated, and as disheveled as Mark was—rude and abrupt, too. Mark wondered if, in this country, law enforcement was routinely intoxicated while on duty. He was miffed that Kárpáty had confiscated his passport. It seemed more an intimidating gesture than a true need to run a background check. But why? Kárpáty had already told him he was not a suspect.

The image of Ahmet's body returned, his face peaceful, as though he had fallen asleep in the bathtub. There was clearly no evidence of forced entry into his suite. How had the killer received access? Mark remembered the security camera aimed at the elevator doors. Had the killer evaded them? If so, how? Was it a he or she? Was there more than one?

Mark wondered what those parallel marks were, the ones on his torso, arms and legs. Ahmet had been killed with almost no sign of struggle. Well, not quite. He had dropped his glasses and peed on the carpet at the same spot. Some struggle must have occurred, but not much. The bruises on his wrists and cheeks suggested the same. Mark couldn't figure the wrists, but the lines on Ahmet's cheeks were the same shape as medical oxygen masks, common plastic ones. Mark was unsure what this meant.

Ahmet surely would not have allowed them to kill him like the sacrificial sheep of *Kurban Bayramı*, the Muslim Feast of the Sacrifice. Mark had vivid memories from childhood, when, during this holiday, men openly slit throats of sheep on every street corner. Ahmet, a sacrificial lamb! He certainly had none of the innocence that the image evoked.

Mark felt a deep sense of disappointment for not having seen his mate sooner. Whatever Ahmet had done, he surely did not deserve to die. He tried to wipe these thoughts out of his mind and force himself to sleep. But his mind was racing. He bolted out of bed and undressed, neatly tucking his clothes into the closet on hangers. He pulled the curtains ajar and looked out into the night. His room was facing a courtyard and was not as well illuminated as the Royal Suite. All he saw were lazy flakes of snow swimming by his window and a few distant lights of other windows. It was well past midnight. He wondered what thoughts kept other insomniacs awake at this hour. Surely they were not as troublesome as his. Mark headed to the bathroom to brush his teeth.

When he returned and pulled back the bedcovers, he caught sight of the business card he had removed from Ahmet's suite on his nightstand. He examined it front and back as though seeing it for the first time. He needed to meet this Olga. He would call the front desk in the morning and book a massage with her at the spa.

He closed his eyes and tried to calm down. His head felt heavy, his body achingly tired. He needed some sleep but it was only around four p.m. back home. His cellphone rang.

"Mark, how the hell are you?" It was Joel, his divorce lawyer, in his *friend-of-Mark* voice.

"Don't ask," he answered wearily.

"Yes, my friend. I understand."

Mark did not answer, wondering how Joel knew.

"These damn asset splits can be a real grind," said Joel, now with his professional voice. "We have a court appearance tomorrow. Remember?"

"Fuck!" Mark sat up in bed. He had totally forgotten.

"Yeah, yeah, I know."

"No," said Mark. "Actually, I'm in Europe, in Budapest."

"No way!" Back to *friend-of-Mark*. "I love that town. We visited it twice with my car club, touring along the Danube. I loved driving my new pre-War Bentley across that Chain Bridge. What a sight!"

Joel was an antique-car nut; his newly acquired Bentley dated to 1924. Mark had had some interest in antique cars years ago and had met Joel on the circuit, the two of them becoming friends. Fortunately, Mark's interest faded and he never acquired one of these vintage cars. They sucked up an enormous amount of money for upkeep.

"What are you doing there?" Joel was upbeat.

"I came to meet an old friend. A last-minute rendezvous."

"I hope she's hot." Joel made an *mmm* sound. "Those Eastern European women!"

"I wish." Mark wondered if he should tell Joel about Ahmet. He decided not to. "Listen, I can't make it to that hearing. Can you do it by yourself?"

"Sure," said Joel, "but you need to approve the new compromise our accountant reached with Angie's."

At this point Mark no longer cared about assets. Financially he was getting raked over the coals, but his upcoming divorce from his second wife was not nearly as painful as the end of his first marriage. Mark gave Joel the fax number of his hotel.

After hanging up, Mark remembered that he needed another fax sent to him. He called his San Francisco office just in the nick of time, before the secretarial staff left for the day, and left instructions about the Romanian radiology report, making sure that they copied the back of the first page as well.

Mark pulled the covers over his head and tried a different tack to calm his mind down, thinking of the old days back in Istanbul. It was mostly a happy time. He thought of Ahmet's car, a sleek, sporty Murat 124, the Turkish version of a small, boxy Fiat. It was silly to think of it as glamorous by today's standards, but in the Istanbul of the 1970s, owning a car was a rare luxury for most households, let alone a high school student. Latif Bey, Ahmet's father, indulged his son. They had cruised around in that car with countless girls, Mark usually in the front passenger seat, enjoying the benefits of being Ahmet's friend.

Various girls paraded through Mark's mind, giggling, competing with each other for Ahmet's attention. Mark's memory froze on an image he had stared at for years. It was a photo he himself had taken with a Canon SLR he had acquired as a gift. He was proud of that fancy camera that impressed his classmates. He always kept it handy, becoming a shutterbug every chance he found. The photo was a black-and-white shot that he had taken in Büyükada, an offshore resort island in the Sea of Marmara. In those days, black and white was all there was.

She smiled at him with long, thin lips, slightly curled. Her dark eyebrows soared like wings, her eyes squinting in the sun. She lay prone and faced the lens with one cheek resting on the wrinkles of a beach towel. Her straight, jet-black hair, pulled back, was in partial disarray in a light wind, strands hanging down her forehead and temple. Mark had snuck up on her, camera in hand, while she was tanning by herself. The others in their group were at the water's edge, screaming and laughing, kicking sea water on each other. He had whispered her name in the last minute, and when she opened her eyes, she had instinctively smiled at the lens. It was an intimate portrait of a beautiful girl on the cusp of becoming a woman.

Mark didn't show that shot to Günsu. For a long while he kept a small copy of it in his wallet, the larger original in his neatly organized files. As years went by the photo became timeless, frozen in a bygone age. Mark married a college sweetheart from the University of Chicago and relegated Günsu to the same nostalgic corner of his mind that Ahmet occupied. Her photo disappeared from his wallet but remained firmly imprinted in his mind. He didn't see her again for decades, and he preferred not to. It was better to remember her as in that photo.

He wondered if he should go to Istanbul.

Chapter 10

* * *

Mark walked into the Gresham lobby, his traveler's bag on his shoulder, his steps echoing in the vast emptiness of the dimly lit, high-domed reception area. A solitary receptionist came to attention, looking up from her computer screen.

"Breakfast?" Mark asked.

The receptionist looked at her watch. "Not until another hour, sir." She was accustomed to early risers. She pointed behind Mark and to her right. "Kollázs," she said. "It serves a good breakfast, but not until six-thirty."

Mark looked around for coffee. There was none. Sensing his quest, the receptionist offered, "If you go out the main door and take two right turns, there are coffee shops on Zrinyi. Some are already open."

Mark thanked her and headed toward the grilled inner gate at the entrance of the lobby. He admired the intricate ironwork of twin peacock figures flanking a stylized globe. An alert doorman bowed and opened the gate, then the outer door. It was still dark outside, and the columns of the Chain Bridge glowed like jewels. A cold breeze was blowing from the direction of the river, swirling the dusting of snow. It sent him straight back in.

Kollázs was immediately to the left of the inner gate, its reception counter dominated by a prominent brass espresso maker. Inside, lights were on and shadows skittered around, preparing the eatery for the day. Mark settled into a plush armchair across from the elevator bank and toyed with his cellphone, waiting for the restaurant to open.

Mark's brief sleep had been restless. Between thoughts of Ahmet and the police, and the room's heating system that left his mouth dry, he had awakened frequently. By three a.m. he was wide awake, tossing and turning in bed before finally sitting up, supported by several soft pillows, and opening his laptop.

He first ran a Google search on Ahmet Gürsen. He had done this before and it had yielded little, a few news articles, now over a decade old, from Turkish gossip columnists about how he had abandoned his wife, now a stylish, overly made-up socialite and TV newscaster. Mark found nothing new. Ahmet had a negligible internet footprint.

Mark then searched Mahmut Erkan Gazioğlu, the doctor the French officer Gérard had mentioned. The screen, still set to Images, popped up with photos of a gaunt face, cheeks sunken, cheekbones protruding. He was completely bald and had an elongated face with narrow, angular eyes that gave him a vaguely Asian look. A thin dark moustache curved down from lips to chin, completing the picture of a modern-day Genghis Khan. There were several photos of him in surgical wear, his green scrubs and surgeon's cap somewhat softening his features.

Mark switched from Images to Web. He was stunned by the top hits, several similar photos in their midst. "Organ Trafficking in Moldova: Mahmut Gazioğlu found in the..." was the first, a headline from moldovantimes.org. Scrolling down, Mark read, "Trafficking Investigations, Organ Theft, Organ Smuggling, The Doctor at the Heart of The Moldovan Organ Scandal." Mark paused and closed his eyes. Why would international police associate him with such a character?

The next hit was even more captivating. It was headlined "Mahmut Gazioğlu – Interpol." Clicking onto it, Mark opened what was in essence a wanted poster, with more photos of the Genghis Khan face and identifying descriptors, name with no aliases, birthdate, age and place of birth. He was Turkish and about the same age as Mark. His crimes were listed as "trafficking in persons, organized crime, unlawful exercise of medical activity." The page instructed those with any information to contact their local or national police.

Mark scrolled to an American newspaper article about Gazioğlu among the hits. It was five years old and featured an interview with the man while he relaxed in his seaside villa in Istanbul. "Trafficking Investigations Put Surgeon In The Spotlight," read the headline. A photo of Gazioğlu, sitting in his garden at night, partially illuminated by lawn lights, displayed him modestly dressed in a simple shirt and slacks, wearing a pair of spectacles that gave him a professorial look. He boasted to the reporter that he was the best transplant surgeon in the world. He had worked on innumerable cases and had taught the procedure to many foreign doctors. Unconventional as his mission was, he was in the service of humanity, giving new life to unfortunates who had lost their kidneys. The way he described himself, one would think that he was another Albert Schweitzer. Yet the article also stated that the Turkish government had closed down several clinics he owned and arrested him several times. It also mentioned that Interpol was interested in him.

Gazioğlu was a typical cutting surgeon, cocky and arrogant, a man who made no mistakes. Mark knew the type well. He wondered how he could give such an open interview and not escape the law. Mark's curiosity was aroused. He decided he would ask the police, Kárpáty or Gérard, about this character and what it had to do with his old high school friend.

The lights in the lobby brightened as a large group of Asian guests arrived to check out, their luggage neatly assembled by a bellman. They seemed to be waiting for an early ride to the airport, quietly chatting with each other. Mark looked up from his cellphone and scanned the group. They were unaware of the tragic event last night while they enjoyed their last evening in Budapest. For them, Gresham Palace was the ultimate lap of Eastern European luxury, the glitz of the old Austro-Hungarian Empire updated for modern times. For Mark, it would be something altogether different.

A young woman appeared at the Kollázs reception counter. Mark pocketed his phone, shouldered his bag, and approached her. *Jó reggelt*, she said. *Good morning*, he replied.

Mark curiously eyed a glass of pumpkin juice with sea buckthorn oil that the waitress recommended. He took a sip of the strange blend. It was slightly sweet and cinnamon flavored. He chased it down with a sip of strong coffee.

He needed some stimulation this morning. This pumpkin-buckthorn concoction was not it. He split a piece of Hungarian brioche with sour cream and goat cheese, and waved to the waitress for a newspaper.

The restaurant was vast and multi-purpose. The section he occupied was a coffee shop. It had a counter with sweet pastries, breads, and rolls. Behind it was a display of different bread loaves. Farther down was the main restaurant with plush seats. The two areas were separated by a large, backlit, stained-glass sign with the restaurant's name, framed by a display of wine and cocktail glasses.

It was still dark outside and traffic was scarce, a few taxis and a bus or two passing by. Inside, Mark noticed two more tables occupied by sleepy-eyed customers in casual clothes. Americans. Probably jet-lagged like him, he thought, and could not help but rise early. He examined two newspapers the waitress brought, the International Herald Tribune and something called Magyar Hírlap, which he could not understand. He scanned them for news about Ahmet and found none in the English one. Checking for photos or Ahmet's name, he found none in the Hungarian either.

As he put the papers down, Mark had a strange sense he was being observed. He looked around and realized that the Gresham lobby was partially visible through an open side door. He recognized the dark, mustachioed face sitting in the bar area beyond the reception desk. He was fiddling with his cellphone. Mark raised the Hungarian newspaper, the larger of the two, to his face and played peek-a-boo for a few seconds. He was not mistaken. The man was directly staring at him. When he put the paper down and stared back, the man rotated his chair and, picking up his phone, stood up, disappearing farther inside.

Wonderful, thought Mark. He had a tail, just like in the movies.

Mark quickly signed his breakfast bill and exited the restaurant, abandoning the strange juice and leaving the brioche half consumed. The overnight clerk at the desk had been replaced by a fresh young woman, chipper in her crisp outfit. She looked at him with bright blue eyes. Mark asked if any faxes had been received in his name.

He waited while she disappeared into a back room, and scanned the spacious lobby. The dark man was in a far corner by the closed gift shop, ostensibly browsing through newspapers left by the door. The man picked one up and scanned it, throwing split-second glances toward the reception desk.

"Here you are, sir."

Mark inspected two documents, the radiology report and Joel's one-page summary of the financial settlement. He tucked the documents into his shoulder bag. "Thanks," he said. "I wonder if you can do me one more favor."

Two couples had lined up behind him for the solitary clerk. Mark gave them an apologetic glance and turned back to the young woman. "I wonder if I can book a massage at your spa."

"Yes, sir. For when?" The woman turned to her computer screen.

"Actually," Mark hesitated, searching his pocket and pulling out the business card. Holding it up, he said, "I'd like a special masseuse." He read out Olga's name.

"I am sorry, sir, we cannot do this from the lobby. To book that you'll have to do it in person at our spa. It's on the sixth floor." She pointed in the direction of the elevators.

"Thanks, I'll do that." Mark nodded to the guests waiting in queue and headed back to the elevators.

The dark man was gone.

Chapter 11

* * *

"It's a short drive to the station," said the bespectacled young woman in a sky-blue jumpsuit. Her English had a mix of Hungarian and British accents. Mark unzipped his coat. It was warm in the car.

"Is this your first time to Budapest?" She took her cap off and placed it on the dash.

"Yes," he said. "I arrived yesterday afternoon. Not even twenty-four hours yet."

After straightening her hair in the rearview mirror, she pulled her patrol car, a white subcompact Audi with a narrow light bar on its roof and blue *Rendőrség* signs all around, out of the Gresham driveway. She looked to be no older than thirty, slim, with angular features. Her dusky hair was tucked behind her ears, hanging loose over her open uniform collar. The small car aimed north along the river, the Chain Bridge receding behind.

She glanced at him and said, "Not a very nice introduction to Budapest. This weather, the snow…." She halted, searching for the right word. "And that nasty business at the hotel."

"You're telling me!" said Mark. "The last place I expected to be on my first morning here was a police station."

The road curved inland by a plaza that fronted an enormous riverside building, white with a red roof, its façade an array of sharp vertical columns that flanked arched windows, reminiscent of Westminster in London. A tall red dome with a spire atop peeked behind the roofline. "Our Parliament," she said.

Mark craned his neck, admiring the magnificent building until it was out of sight. "Will Kárpáty be at the police station?" he asked.

"Yes," she said. "He is the one who summoned you."

The station was a drab eight-story building with a plain beige-brown façade. It sat on a narrow street across from a more somber, lofty, brick building with an arched entrance topped by flags. The young officer pointed to the more august building and said, "This is the back of our courthouse."

She double-parked in front of the plain, unimposing station door, under a sign that read *Belváros-Lipotváros Rendőrkapitányság* and motioned Mark out of her car. Mark zipped up his coat and looked around, surprised at the paucity of police cars and lack of activity in the street. This looked nothing like any American police station he knew.

Inside, a musty odor permeated the hallways. Uniformed officers milled about, chatting over plastic coffee cups; others sat at desks, peering at their computer screens. She took him up a dank staircase into an area that looked more like a business office. She ushered him into a dark, low-ceilinged room, lined with cameras and stools – for mugshots, he figured – and a fingerprinting station. There was no one there except the corpulent older officer who also swiped Mark's mouth for a DNA sample.

Kárpáty's office was one floor up, in a poorly lit hallway with walls that needed a fresh coat of paint. Mark's driver exchanged a few Hungarian words with a secretary in a cramped antechamber and bid Mark a temporary goodbye. Mark sat on one of two uncomfortable chairs across from the secretary's desk while she notified her boss that he had arrived. He noticed a wrinkled newspaper on the next chair, *Metropol,* quickly picked it up, checked its date and scanned it for news about Ahmet's murder. Nothing.

Soon Kárpáty appeared, escorting a young woman out of his office, his arm around her shoulders. The woman was strikingly pretty, slim but buxom, dark-complexioned yet with blonde hair, her stygian eyes alluringly wide set. She looked up at Mark and they momentarily locked eyes. Hers were bloodshot, and she clutched a wrinkled tissue in one hand.

"Ah," said Kárpáty, disengaging from the woman. He was different from the night before, clean and fresh, his clothes crisp, his face and eyes no longer red. He briskly shook Mark's hand and thanked him for coming. He then ushered him into his office after showing the woman to Mark's chair.

It was a spacious room rendered claustrophobic by a large desk and several chairs, all stacked with files and paperwork. Several large bulletin boards all around were also full of paper. Two windows faced the gray brick courthouse across, adding to the closed-in feel. The room was starkly lit by fluorescent lights. By now Mark had grown accustomed to the moldy smell, also present here. Kárpáty cleared a chair and offered it to Mark, then positioned himself partially sitting on the edge of his desk. He drew a notebook from his inner pocket and readied a pen.

"That was his wife," he said, nodding toward the antechamber. Mark looked back but the door was closed. "Romanian," he added. "Do you know her?"

"No," said Mark. "Unfortunately, Ahmet and I did not get a chance to catch up with each other." An uneasy silence followed. "Do you have new ideas about who might have done this?"

"No, not yet," said Kárpáty. "It looks professional," he added. "A clean hit."

"How did they kill him?"

Kárpáty shook his head. "We'll have to wait for a preliminary forensics report to determine that."

"He looked so strangely peaceful," Mark murmured.

Kárpáty did not respond. There was a brief moment of silence, the inspector staring at Mark, whose eyes drifted toward the pattern of gray bricks on the courthouse building across.

"What did you know about the activities of your old friend?" asked the inspector, ignoring Mark's comment.

"You mean business?"

"Yes, you might say so."

"Nothing about what he did nowadays. Back in the seventies he was to inherit a successful textile business from his father. I assumed that he was still in textiles."

"What do you know about his activities in Turkey?"

"Nothing more than what I told you last night," said Mark. "You know—what I discovered about him swindling our classmates."

"Can you give me the names of these classmates?" Kárpáty began writing into the notebook.

Mark rattled off a few names, those whom he recalled, spelling them. "I can't imagine that any of them would come after him after all these years."

Kárpáty nodded without looking up from his notes. "What do you suppose he wanted from you?"

"I don't know," said Mark. "He didn't tell me." Mark decided to switch roles and become the inquisitor. "How come there is nothing in the newspapers about him?"

The question caught the inspector by surprise. "Do you read Hungarian?" he asked.

"No, but I can draw enough clues from your papers that the news is not there. In America a mysterious murder in a fancy hotel such as the Gresham Palace would draw instant, splashy headlines."

"Well," said Kárpáty dismissively, "this is not America." He seemed annoyed. He placed his notebook aside and eyed Mark. "And may I suggest that you not play detective? Leave the investigation to us."

The threatening tone in his voice surprised Mark. After all, Mark had merely scanned a few newspapers. He wondered how Kárpáty would react if he knew that Mark had swiped a piece of evidence from the crime scene.

"Now, Doctor," Kárpáty said briskly, picking up the notebook again, ready to write, "I want to once again take you through exactly what you did in that Royal Suite before you notified the hotel's reception desk."

Mark realized that this was the real purpose of the interview, to seek a second account and check for discrepancies with the first.

Mark calmly answered his questions, repeating all he had said the night before. It was still fresh in his mind, so consistency was not a problem. He again mentioned Ahmet's iPhone and Ahmet's spectacles. He didn't mention the wet spot on the carpet, figuring the forensics team would have taken note of it. He said that he had touched the body, looking for a pulse. Olga's business card, however, was now Mark's secret.

"I have a question," Mark said afterwards, annoyed at the trepidation in his voice. Kárpáty stood up and looked down at him. "Why are you interested in this Turkish doctor, Gazioğlu? I looked him up. The man is into black market kidney transplants."

Kárpáty let out an exasperated sigh. "Dr. Kent," he said, his irritation obvious. "We, Budapest police, have no interest in the person you mentioned."

"So it's Interpol who is pursuing him?"

Kárpáty did not answer but maintained a stern gaze.

"That means that Ahmet—Nicolae—somehow had some connection with this doctor." Mark was puzzled.

"Your friend and whoever he was collaborating with are outside agitators. They come to our country and stir up trouble. We have enough work with our own homegrown criminals. We don't need them here."

Mark nodded silently, deep in thought. He understood the inspector. Local police had a different agenda than Interpol. Why, then, was Gérard at the crime scene so fast? Mark opened his mouth to utter the question but was cut short by Kárpáty.

"May I repeat myself," he said, his voice more emphatic, "maybe in a different way." He paused and waited for Mark's attention. "Do not investigate this! We don't need another foreigner, an American amateur," he spat out the last words in contempt, "meddling in our affairs."

There was nothing to do but accede. The inspector motioned for Mark to get up. The interview was over.

"By the way, are you finished with my passport?" Mark asked before leaving the room.

"No, Doctor. We will notify you when we are."

On his way out, Mark approached the young woman who was still sitting in the antechamber, dabbing her eyes, tapping into a cellphone. He introduced himself to her in English and she looked at him quizzically. Mark stood over her, stooping, while she sat, facing him.

"*Türkçe konuşurmusunuz?*" she asked in Turkish, with an accent that Mark did not recognize. *Do you speak Turkish?*

Surprised, Mark answered back in Turkish, telling her who he was, using Metin, his Turkish name, and shaking her hand. She recognized him, she said, from old photos Ahmet had kept of their teenage days. "He spoke fondly of you." Her name was Miruna.

Mark offered condolences. She broke into light sobs and dabbed her eyes with fresh tissues from her purse.

"Will you be here in Budapest a while?" he asked her.

"Just overnight. I am taking an early afternoon flight back to Bucharest tomorrow."

"I would like to speak to you some more. Do you think we can meet?"

She stared up at him, helpless.

"I need to know why Ahmet contacted me. It won't take long. Breakfast tomorrow maybe?"

Mark felt a shadow behind him and looking back, met the harsh gaze of Kárpáty observing them. Miruna nodded okay.

"Give me your phone number," Mark whispered, afraid that he would be cut off any moment.

"I believe we have no more business with you, Dr. Kent." Kárpáty was eye to eye with Mark, who was still stooping over the bereaved woman. Mark looked at him and then back to Miruna.

She was holding her cellphone toward his face with a phone number on its screen. Mark gazed at it and nodded. He stood up and hastily exited without saying anything to either of them. He walked briskly across the hallway, silently reciting the number he had just read over and over. He entered the staircase, skipped two steps at a time down one floor and stopped. He tapped the number into a reminder in his own phone.

Downstairs they called for the young female officer to take him back.

"I hope that wasn't too bad," she said, as she opened the passenger side of her patrol car for him.

"No, not at all," said Mark. "A bit like visiting a dentist."

She closed his door, smiling. She was pretty in her own way. Mark thought that if Ahmet were here, he would surely make a pass at her.

She took him back to the hotel through a series of confusing side streets and asked him what he planned for the rest of the day. Mark didn't mention the masseuse. She suggested he explore Andrássy út. It's a fancy street, she said, with some pleasant surprises, not far from his hotel.

"Do you know Inspector Kárpáty well?" asked Mark.

"Some," she said.

"What's he like?" Mark wasn't sure if he was overstepping.

She was unperturbed. "Experienced," she said, as she pulled into the Gresham driveway. "He's considered very competent." She stopped and turned off the engine. "And very eccentric." She took her blue uniform cap from the dash and put it on, adjusting it just so, using her rearview mirror.

"So I gather," Mark replied, "from what I've seen of him thus far."

She accompanied him to the hotel door and politely bade him goodbye while handing him a card. It had the official *Rendőrség* insignia, with her name and number. Mark studied it.

"Jasmin," he said. "Pretty name."

She beamed at him. "Enjoy your stay in Budapest," she said. "Maybe we'll meet again."

Chapter 12

* * *

Mark walked down a narrow hallway with a slanted side wall and entered a wider area with a glass bottom floor reflecting ornate tiles below. Floor-to-ceiling slanted windows lit the interior with bright sunlight. An older couple in white bath-gowns passed him by, speaking German. They smiled and nodded to him. Mark moved on to a large room with a remarkably long, infinity pool. The same tall, slanted windows lined the room. The pool was empty, its calm surface reflecting wispy clouds and blue sky. He stood admiring the scene. On the other side of the pool a solitary guest sat in a chaise longue, absorbed in a book.

"*Segíthetek?*"

Mark was startled by a female voice behind him and turned to face a strikingly beautiful blonde, her full, wavy mane bundled behind with a simple but elegant red-and-white band. She had hazel eyes highlighted with makeup and sultry red lips, puckered. She wore a dress uniform with the hotel insignia bulging forward from an ample bosom. She was tall and curvaceous, most likely in her late thirties.

"Oh, I was admiring your pool," said Mark, his gaze fixed on her chest.

She turned and looked at the solitary guest on the chaise longue. "Not many guests here this early on a Wednesday," she remarked.

Her accent sounded Russian, her well-proportioned face vaguely Slavic. She had full thighs emerging from a white skirt well above the knees. Mark scanned them up toward her shapely behind, well defined by the tight skirt.

"May I help you?" said the woman, abruptly turning back to face him.

Mark continued gazing down, now at her equally alluring front, before snapping out of it. "I would like to book a session…" he said hesitantly, "a… massage."

"Please follow me." She started across the large room, walking toward the pool.

"Not now, later." Mark stood still, uncertain that she understood him. He took advantage of the opportunity and stared unabashedly.

She stopped and turned. "Come with me, please." She seemed accustomed to being gawked at.

They left the pool area for the other end of the spa, where she sat down at a small desk and showed Mark to a chair on the side. She opened and examined a large appointment book, sitting with crossed legs that revealed more of her voluptuous thighs. They continued down to well pedicured, sandaled feet.

"We have several slots available later this afternoon," she said, eyeing him with a professional smile.

Mark rifled through his pants pockets and drew out the card he had removed from Ahmet's room. "I had a specific masseuse in mind," he said. He flipped the card back and forth, holding it aloft, looking for the name. "I'd like it with Olga. Olga Kaminesky."

He did not notice a change in her attitude upon seeing the card. There was a pause as she studied the appointment book with some intensity. Then she looked up at Mark, her smile gone, her lips more puckered than before.

"Olga no longer works for us," she said brusquely.

Mark looked at the card again, puzzled. "But," he said falteringly, "didn't she work here just yesterday?"

The woman reached for the hem of her skirt and stretched it toward her kneecaps, partially covering her thighs. She stared at her lap. Mark looked away, embarrassed that he'd been gaping. He turned toward the small, sterile foyer of the spa.

"She called in this morning and told us that she quit," said the woman. "A shame," she trailed off. "She was a good worker."

Mark slid the card in his pocket and tried to collect his thoughts.

"May I offer you Helga?" said the woman. "A German girl. Gives a dynamic massage. Invigorating." Her professional smile returned. "She's available at two or four-thirty this afternoon."

"No," he muttered, standing up. "I only wanted Olga."

The woman closed her appointment book.

* * *

Downstairs, Mark checked his watch. It was near noon and he was not hungry. The morning had wasted away with an unpleasant police interview and a fruitless visit to the spa. He sat on the same lobby chair as earlier and tried to decide what to do next. Jasmin, the young policewoman, had recommended he visit a glitzy street, a name he had already forgotten. He opened his shoulder bag and felt inside for the Budapest guidebook he had brought along. There were some papers inside as well, and he pulled them out instead. *Damn*, he thought. He had forgotten about them.

He first eyed Joel's fax related to the asset division in his upcoming divorce. Angie would be getting the E-class Mercedes and their small getaway in Carmel. Mark would get the Telegraph Hill Victorian, their house, and a Fiat 500, a winsome, tiny car that reminded him of Ahmet's old Murat. The Carmel place was worth more. He glanced over the division of retirement assets and a few other investments impassively and stuffed the document back in the bag.

Then he unfolded the Romanian CT report and examined it more keenly. Kárpáty had not asked for it, and now Mark knew why. He would have to somehow deliver it to Gérard, the French officer.

Mark stared blankly at Ahmet's handwritten message. His staff had sent it as a separate page, as instructed. *Do you remember me?* Ahmet's handwriting was slanted to the left. Mark's eyes teared up. For a moment he looked away and examined the busy lobby, uniformed bellmen walking about, guests gawking at the splendid décor, the reception desk buzzing with activity. He contained his emotions and turned to the first page, scanning the body of the report in Romanian script. He stopped on occasional Latinate words that sounded out anatomic terms. He returned to the top of the page and stared at the five-edged star logo of Regina Maria. He wondered what sort of a clinic this was. He would have to look it up later. Looking farther below, he was suddenly startled.

There, under the letterhead of the clinic, was a standard listing of the patient's name, I.D. number, birthdate, date of exam, and type of study being reported. The patient's name was Cezar Kaminesky 58. He wasn't sure what the number fifty-eight was. Looking at the birthdate, Mark figured it was not the patient's age. But the name! Could this be a coincidence?

He took out the business card still in his pants and placed it next to the CT report: Olga Kaminesky.

Until now he had regarded this radiology report as nothing but a suitable ruse with which Ahmet had concealed his message. He had no idea why his old friend had chosen a medical document to do this, nor did he know how Ahmet had access to such reports.

What was the likelihood that Olga in Hungary knew of Cesar in Romania? He figured Kaminesky was a common last name. It had to be a coincidence. But then why had Olga quit her job so suddenly? It surely had to be somehow connected to Ahmet's murder. Mark folded the papers thoughtfully and went in search of the hotel manager.

* * *

The day shift manager was an older woman with an obvious facelift and heavy makeup, wearing a stylish skirt suit with a prominent silver brooch on her left lapel. She peered at Mark from across her desk. Her open laptop screen projected to her neck and chin with a spectral glow.

"We don't know why she quit," she said, looking back at her screen. "Ms. Kaminesky's abrupt resignation is a surprise to us too." She had a British accent. "She'd been with us for quite some time and she was popular with our clients. She will be missed."

She studied her screen again and looked up at Mark with slightly raised eyebrows. "I see that you checked in with us last night. Your first time at the Gresham Palace. Correct?"

"Yes," said Mark, "and let me offer you my congratulations."

She accepted the compliment, nodding gracefully.

"I have stayed in many luxury hotels in America and abroad, but this is certainly a cut above the others."

"Thank you," she said, taking her glasses off and closing her laptop screen. "We try hard to maintain ourselves that way." She leaned back in her high-backed chair. "Do you know that this building was erected as the European headquarters of a British insurance company?"

Mark shook his head no, surprised.

"Yes," she continued proudly. "Gresham was its founder. His bust is carved on the front façade of the building, over the fourth floor, in the center."

"I didn't notice," said Mark. "I'll have to look for it."

"It fell into disrepair during Communist times." She paused. "Didn't everything!"

"Well, you've done a magnificent job of restoring it."

She acknowledged the remark with a gracious bow of her head. "Tell me: how did you know about Olga? Did someone recommend her to you?"

The question alarmed Mark. Did she suspect something?

"You have not been here long enough to know about her through us," she added, "unless someone in our staff mentioned it. If so I need to know. They are strictly instructed not to…how do you say it?" She paused to think of the American expression. "Hard-sell any of our services, especially with particular employees."

"Oh, no…no." Mark was relieved. "It was nothing like that. I received the recommendation back home from someone who had stayed here recently."

"All right then." She rose and took a step toward the door. Mark followed suit.

As they shook hands at the doorstep, she said, "I am still not quite certain how you discovered Olga's resignation so fast."

He looked at her quizzically.

"I got the call from the spa, not too long ago." She looked at her watch. "It's only been about half an hour."

* * *

Mark walked back to the lobby slowly, deep in thought, trying to make sense of what the manager had just said. The concierge desk was separate from reception, to the right of the main entrance facing the elevator bank. There were two people staffing it. One was occupied with a Dutch couple. Mark approached the other, a middle-aged man wearing the same hotel uniform as the receptionists.

"I wanted to ask you about your spa." Mark stood across the counter, facing the man who listened politely with a smile. He gave Mark a brief exposition about the hours and services, and handed him a list of prices to peruse.

"I was interested in a massage," said Mark, after the concierge finished. "I wonder," he paused. He wasn't quite sure how this would go over. "Do you have a photo list of your masseurs?"

"Why, yes, certainly." The concierge pulled out a slick brochure and leafing through it, halted at a photo catalog of the massage staff. "Here, you can look through them."

The photos were alphabetically arranged. Mark spotted her quickly, her strikingly attractive visage standing out among the others, lips puckered. It was the same woman Mark had met at the spa earlier. Mark pointed to the photo as he returned the book to the concierge.

"Oh, yes," said the man. "Olga." He gave Mark an appreciative glance, approving Mark's choice.

"She's quite popular. Would you like me to book a session for you with her?" The concierge had obviously not heard the news yet.

"Thank you," Mark said as he got up. "I'll get back to you on that."

Chapter 13

* * *

"Hey," Ahmet whispered from behind, "do you want to go to a soccer game at Mithatpaşa?"

Metin did not respond. He eyed their teacher, Mrs. Irma, who stood by the blackboard, following the recitation with an open book in hand. They were in Orta II, second year of grade school, reading out loud from a novel called *The Wooden Horse*. Mrs. Irma had started at the other end of the class and was going front to back, calling on the boys one by one. Metin figured that she would not get to him or Ahmet during this session. He was not sure if he should answer Ahmet and risk a conduct card signature from this rather imperious English teacher.

The boy Mrs. Irma had called on was reading poorly, with a heavy Turkish accent and countless mispronunciations. She frequently interrupted him to correct his mistakes, carefully enunciating each misspoken word. A slim woman with dark hair and a courtly countenance, Mrs. Irma was unique among foreign teachers in the school, having assimilated to Turkey by way of marriage. She spoke fluent Turkish. The boys, generally less respectful toward the small handful of female teachers, maintained a robust esteem toward Mrs. Irma.

Metin took a risk. "What soccer game?"

"*Milli takım*," said Ahmet with relish, *national team*.

"Against USSR?" Metin was incredulous.

Home games of the Turkish national team were singular events, almost like national holidays. Most were played in the old Mithapaşa stadium at the foot of a hill that descended to the Bosporus by the splendid seaside Ottoman palace at Dolmabahçe. It was a small stadium. Tickets for such games were rare and precious.

Ahmet nodded yes.

"How did you get tickets?" Metin blurted out excitedly, loud enough for all to hear.

"Mr. Özgür!" Mrs. Irma interrupted the session. "Are you paying attention to what we're reading?"

The novel was actually quite interesting, an adventurous World War II account of British prisoners of war who hatched a scheme to escape their German prison camp by digging a tunnel in the prison yard under a wooden horse that they used for gymnastics, a sort of Trojan horse in reverse.

"Yes, ma'am," Metin answered firmly.

"Well then." Mrs. Irma approached Metin. "Why don't you pick up from where he left off?"

Metin was a good reader, fluent and with few pronunciation errors. He was therefore picked upon infrequently by English teachers, the weaker students being more commonly targeted. He looked at the open page and realized that in his excitement over Ahmet's proposal, he had lost track of where they were. Metin took a chance and started somewhere. He was soon cut short by his teacher, who arrived at his desk with her palm extended.

"Your conduct card!"

As Mrs. Irma ceremonially signed the card, Metin received appreciative glances from his classmates for having broken the monotony of the class. Ahmet looked on with a wide smile.

Mrs. Irma handed the card back to Metin and turned to Ahmet. "Mr. Gürsen"—she pronounced the last name correctly—"wipe that silly grin off your face."

* * *

Later, during an afternoon break at the yard, Metin found Ahmet in the small basement commissary at the end of the dusty side yard buying a *gofret* and *gazoz*, a Swiss chocolate wafer-bar and Turkish ginger ale.

"You were joking, right?" said Metin.

Ahmet took a bite of wafer and walked out to the yard, Metin in tow.

"If you were lying and I got that signature for nothing, I'll be really mad," he added.

"I wasn't joking," said Ahmet with a smile. "And get this." He paused dramatically.

Metin took the *gazoz* bottle from Ahmet's hand and took a swig.

"We can watch it from the VIP stands, in the covered area."

Metin's eyes widened. He let out a loud burp. Not to be outdone, Ahmet took multiple swallows, draining the bottle, and burped louder. A pair of soccer players chasing a ball nearly knocked them down. Ahmet took Metin by the arm and led him toward the entrance of the school building, where they sat atop the steps and watched the soccer game.

"My parents won't let me go," said Metin pensively.

Soccer games at Mithatpaşa attracted unruly, belligerent crowds. Brawls broke out frequently. Crowd-control police, always at hand, were quick to bring down heavy batons on anyone, guilty or innocent. Metin's parents forbade him from going to the games with his friends. He had to be accompanied by an adult, and there were none in his family interested in soccer.

Ahmet smiled. "No problem," he said. "My father can vouch for your safety."

"Why? Will he be there too?" Metin had never met Ahmet's father, and was curious.

"No, he's busy that day."

At the foyer was a prominent staircase that rose high from the first floor to the second, under which boys frequently congregated to observe the underskirts of female teachers. Ahmet headed toward a small crowd with their necks craned. Before joining them, he turned to Metin.

"We'll be guests of the police chief," Ahmet said. "Is that good enough for your parents?"

Surprised, Metin hesitated. An ominous stir nearby caught his attention. Boys entering the foyer were scattering about. Realizing the cause, Metin reached for Ahmet and tugged him away from his group.

Mr. Ryan, the fearsome gym teacher, lumbered by them, a burly bear zeroing in on helpless prey. The boys under the staircase did not stand a chance. Mr. Ryan was a one-man police force. His slaps and blows landed with adroit, artistic precision. The boys scattered to the floor like bowling pins. Their howls were drowned by Mr. Ryan's growls.

Ahmet gave Metin an appreciative glance. They climbed the stairs in haste. As they entered their classroom, Metin asked, "So what's with this police chief? Is he a friend or relative?"

"No," said Ahmet. "He works for my father."

Chapter 14

* * *

Mark walked out of the Gresham Palace and onto a colonnaded, covered sidewalk on József Attila, reminiscent of Rue de Rivoli in Paris. It was a sunny but chilly afternoon, although the snow that had fallen overnight was melting. Mark removed his Budapest guidebook from his shoulder bag and sifted through the pages for directions. He much preferred a good, detailed guidebook, old-fashioned as it was, to impersonal iPhone apps. After locating the street in a walking tour that the book recommended, he continued along to a park, a quiet oasis where the noise of the traffic-laden street was muted. A Renaissance fountain stood in the center, Neptune atop ruling the world, three bent female figures along a lower fountain supporting him on their backs. He sat on an empty bench and read from his guidebook: Danubius Fountain, Neptune representing the Danube, the females its three main tributaries.

His thoughts drifted to Olga and how her poise had fleetingly faded when he brought that business card out. She clearly was not some random masseuse that Ahmet had engaged. Not after she abruptly quit her job once she met Mark. Her card was still in his pocket. He pulled it out and examined her handwritten phone number. Would she answer if he called?

Mark rose up and continued along József Attila to a large intersection of wide boulevards. Two neo-Classical buildings, redolent of Paris, with faded but resplendent façades ushered him onto Andrássy út. He entered an obviously affluent, narrow avenue, lined by trees that obscured elegant, high-arched windows of stately old buildings. He passed by chic clothing stores, a restaurant or two, and the ubiquitous coffeehouses.

Soon he came upon a lavish building that looked like the Paris Opera. He stopped and pulled out his guidebook again. It indeed was an opera house, its second-story balcony populated with statues of famous composers. As he looked up from his book, a curious figure caught his eye, pacing along a lengthy bus stop across the street. Mark had the distinct sense that the man was observing him, but when Mark gazed back, the man turned his attention down the street as if anticipating a bus. Mark recognized the dark face, prominent nose, and thick moustache, despite dark sunglasses and a low-lying baseball cap that concealed the rest of his face. Mark pretended to read his guidebook and followed the man with his side vision. He was staring directly at Mark.

Mark walked around the opera building, examining its baroque façades. When he returned to his original spot at Andrássy út, the bus stop was empty. He scanned both sides of the street. The man was gone.

Mark strolled away from the Opera, farther into Andrássy út, vigilant of his surroundings. He spotted an array of rental bicycles on the next block, their light green color contrasting with the dark hues of the buildings lining the street. In the middle of the block was an Art Deco building, its narrow façade featuring a giant, five-story rounded arch that enclosed its windows. Strong vertical gashes on the façade flanked the arch. Lower down, a smaller, angular arch framed a majestic entrance at the sidewalk, on which were inscribed the words *Parisi, Nagy, Áruház* in capital letters.

The sign meant *Paris Department Store*, according to the guidebook, what the building used to be before World War II. Mark crossed the street and entered the building through automatically opening glass doors under a simpler *Alexandra* sign. He found himself in a bookstore. A white marbled grand foyer was lined with tall columns, the bases of each surrounded by circular displays of books. To his right, Mark was surprised by a black marble wall displaying bottles of liquor under Hungarian headings. To the left, a similar wall was filled with bookcases.

Looking up, Mark gaped at a magnificent five-story atrium with a glass roof that let in ample sunlight. The various floors of the building were visible as balconies that lined the soaring emptiness, each connected by a bridge redolent of the Rialto in Venice. The effect of these bridges, lined by glass balustrades, stacked on top of one another, was dazzling. Mark realized that the smaller, angular arch on the outside façade of the building reflected the same Rialto shape. The place had to have been luxurious and expensive in its department store days.

Ahead, a grand staircase beckoned him. To Mark's surprise, amid the 1930s splendor, this was actually a modern escalator. It took him to a more mundane second story also lined by bookshelves—a regular bookstore. His eyes immediately went to a short stack of stairs leading to a high arched entrance, a third floor where, through the arch, all he saw was gold. This had to be it, *the* Lotz Terem Café that he had read about. It was listed in his guidebook as the most beautiful café in all of Europe. He climbed up and entered a new world, a fantastically ornate Neo-Renaissance ballroom.

It was taller than the first floor and with colossal arched windows. The walls curved toward a high ceiling that dwarfed visitors within an immense space. Two grand chandeliers hung down in the middle of the room, symmetrically spaced, adding more light to a vast space already bathed with bounteous sunlight. There were massive mirrors at each end of the room, grandiose replicas of the tall windows, reflecting yet more light.

Mark saw a small stage ahead, by the windows, with a grand piano. To his left was the café counter that zigzagged beyond a cash register next to the entrance, extending toward the far wall, with two refrigerated glass displays of food and a serving counter. It would have been spacious in any other coffee shop but was eclipsed by the splendor of this grand room. He realized that it was past noon, and that he had eaten practically nothing all day.

As Mark took a step toward the food displays, he looked up and discovered a ceiling resplendent with murals, painted by—according to his guidebook—Hungarian artist Karl Lotz, after whom this café was named. There were an endless series of multicolored paintings separated by golden crown moldings, each with its own unique geometric pattern. It was a ceiling that belonged in a grand palace, Versailles or Schönbrunn maybe, not in a narrow building tucked within Andrássy út.

Mark examined the first refrigerated counter that offered cheeses and colorful rillettes in Mason jars. The next one, set at right angles, was larger, and filled with a variety of dazzling pastries. Mark counted over thirty, some with recognizable names such as *tiramisu* or *Sacher torte*, others alien, *rigó janzsi, répa torta, somlői revolúció*. The serving bar beyond had two baristas in beige uniforms patiently eyeing him.

As Mark stared at the glittering pastry case, silently deliberating over the ravishing choices, he heard a gravelly voice behind.

"May I suggest the *dobos torte?*" The English was Turkish accented. "It is the house specialty."

Mark turned around and was startled to see the dark man who had been following him, his cap and glasses off. He stood beside Mark, holding up a tray on which was a cup of espresso and plate of dark chocolate sponge cake, edged with nuts and topped with golden and orange caramel.

"Who are you?" asked Mark, annoyed yet curious.

Chapter 15

* * *

They settled into a secluded corner of the vast coffee shop, sitting under one of the majestic side mirrors. It was mid-afternoon and the café was meagerly populated. The man looked younger up close than Mark had imagined from a distance. He had thick black hair, disheveled without his cap, dark eyes under a thick unibrow, and a long nose that would have protruded awkwardly were it not for his dense, bushy moustache.

"I am Mustafa Ersoy," he said, extending his hand.

Mark hesitantly shook hands. "Why are you following me?"

Mustafa took a sip of espresso and waited for its impact. "Let me first explain my mission."

"Are you some sort of secret police? MIT?" asked Mark. MIT was the Turkish equivalent of the CIA.

"No, no…I'm a private citizen," he replied, and added, "although I do have a police background."

Mark spooned a bite of *gesztenyepüré*, trying it without the whipped cream that had been generously heaped on edges of the glass bowl. The young woman at the serving counter had told him that this was a unique Hungarian treat, chestnut purée. It was creamy and nutty, not too sweet, the chestnut flavor more prominent in the aftertaste. He tried another spoonful with cream.

"I work for Meltem Pekün. Have you heard of her?"

The name sounded familiar. Mark thought for a moment and remembered the countless Google searches he had run on Ahmet. This name appeared frequently in news articles related to Ahmet's disappearance.

"Ahmet Gürsen's ex-wife?"

"Not quite," Mustafa sounded official. "They're still married."

Mark tried unsuccessfully to hide his surprise.

"Is there a problem?"

Mark wasn't sure whether this man was aware of Miruna, Ahmet's Romanian wife. He decided not to bring her up quite yet. "It's just that I had read various newspaper articles on how Ahmet left her years ago. I figured that..."

"Yes, I can see how you would."

"What about her last name? How come it is different?"

"That's her public name. You know that she's a famous journalist and TV personality, don't you?"

Mark had gathered that from his research. Meltem was a strikingly attractive socialite, with a father who had been a senior politician in Ankara. Mark had seen photos of her from an era when she would have been dating Ahmet. She was just the kind of woman he imagined Ahmet with—glamorous, alluring, and intelligent. She seemed to have a successful solo career, first as a newspaper columnist, then as a TV personality, appearing on news and gossip shows. Mark had seen a video or two of hers on YouTube, an older Meltem, aging well, sharp and alert in front of the camera, articulate in her Turkish.

"So what do you do for Meltem Hanım?"

"I used to work for Gürsen Industries, for Latif Bey and then Ahmet himself, years before she hired me."

"Is Latif dead?"

"No, retired. He lives in Bodrum, with a young girlfriend."

"What about Sedef Hanım?"

"Ahmet's mother passed away a few years ago. She lived in Istanbul for many years, by herself, after divorcing Latif."

Mark did not know any of this. While curious about the details, he was more eager to hear the remainder of Mustafa's account. He took another spoonful of *gesztenyepüré* and listened.

"I was in charge of security at Gürsen's office buildings and factory," said Mustafa, "a job I inherited from my own father."

Mark's face lit up. He finally realized who this man resembled, as old images of an exciting afternoon in Mithatpaşa stadium flooded his memory. "I knew your father," he said excitedly.

Mustafa raised his eyebrows in surprise as he sipped more espresso.

"I attended a *Milli takım* game at Dolmabahçe with him years ago. He had a large entourage."

"Yes," said Mustafa. "The seats allocated to him made my father quite popular, especially in international games."

Mark recalled the man. He was shorter than Mustafa and more corpulent, but with the same dark, hairy features, same protruding nose and bushy moustache. He had been cordial to the boys but distant, paying more attention to his adult guests. They had sat in the covered portion of the stadium facing midfield, the only time Metin ever sat there, observing the game from a perfect vantage point. The stadium was filled to capacity and the faithful crowd was well behaved, loudly supporting the Turkish team despite the 3-1 loss inflicted upon them by a vastly superior Soviet Union. Nevertheless, Ahmet and Metin had enjoyed it immensely.

"I also met him at his office once, at Gürsen Industries," said Mark.

It had happened about six months later, on a Saturday morning when Ahmet took him to his father's sprawling factory complex near Çekmece on the outskirts of town. They were on an errand for Ahmet's mom, to pick up a large batch of lingerie that she would distribute as gifts. Ahmet's father, Latif Bey, was away on a business trip. So his chief of security had greeted the boys. They followed him through a series of single-story low-rise buildings at the edge of the factory campus and into a nearby warehouse. The man treated Ahmet with a fawning attitude that Metin found strange for someone of his rank and stature. Saturday was part of the Turkish work week, a half day, and he was there for work. The campus was calm and didn't seem in need of such lofty security. Metin had wondered exactly why Latif had hired this man but did not know how to ask Mustafa the question.

"Unfortunately, my father passed away young," said Mustafa, "in 1981."

"*Başınız sağolsun.*" Mark expressed condolences in Turkish.

"I was a young police officer then. Latif Bey was very good to us. He supported my mother financially and took me under his wing, assigning me my father's position in his business. He also helped me rise in the police ranks."

The *gesztenyepüré*, by now nearly consumed, settled into Mark's stomach like a heavy weight. He began feeling tired and sleepy. He looked at his watch and realized that jet lag was creeping in. But this conversation was too interesting. He straightened in his seat and willed himself to be more alert, pushing his bowl away.

"Tell me," said Mustafa. "What was your relationship to Ahmet Gürsen?"

The question surprised Mark. "We were classmates through grade school and high school," he answered. "Don't you already know this? I figured a private detective of your caliber would have investigated this already."

"I am not officially a private detective." Mustafa took a bite of his *dobos torte*. "M'mmm," he said, "delicious." He pointed to his plate. "You must have a bite. You can't come to this place and not leave without trying this."

Mark picked up his fork but did not reach for the generous serving of cake on Mustafa's plate. "So, what exactly are you?"

"I just do private jobs for certain select clients, whatever they need. You can call me an *iş bitirici*."

Mark had heard that term before. Translated literally, it meant *business concluder*. It was a shady profession, conducted behind the scenes by people with legitimate professions as a front. Mark knew some family friends who had smuggled foreign currency into Swiss bank accounts using such intermediaries.

"Meltem Hanım hired me to track down her husband and recover assets that she feels are owed to her."

Mark was reaching toward Mustafa's cake when this revelation stopped him. He looked at Mustafa with a puzzled expression.

"You don't know the background, do you?" said Mustafa.

"Not much," admitted Mark. "You see, after I moved to the U.S., I lost contact with all my friends in Istanbul. Ahmet had gone to England for university. We exchanged a few letters. Then that was it. When I reestablished contact twenty-five years later, my old mates told me that Ahmet had disappeared. I have not known his whereabouts since."

Mark omitted the story about Ahmet swindling his classmates. He didn't know Mustafa well enough to bring this up. Yet the man seemed sincere, enough for Mark to shed his ire about being tailed by him and continue with the conversation.

Mustafa took a final gulp of his espresso. "Ahmet's business went bankrupt in the mid-1990s. Gürsen Industries was no more. I lost my job there at that time. By now he was married to Meltem Hanım and they had two young girls. They lived a fancy lifestyle, a *yalı* near Bebek, European trips, summer house in Büyükada, a boat in Tarabya, another house in the Mediterranean near Antalya. After his bankruptcy he continued spending the same way. How, I don't know. Then he disappeared amid a financial scandal, leaving his wife in a lurch. He never paid her any alimony or child support."

"But you said they are not divorced. He shouldn't owe her any." Mark figured basic divorce laws were similar in Turkey as in the U.S. He recalled that Joel, his lawyer, would have already made a court appearance back home, on his behalf.

"Legally, true. But that's not how Meltem Hanım feels. For her it is, for all practical purposes, a divorce. Only worse." Mustafa paused to gauge the impact of his statement.

"I can see that."

"She has been searching for him since. She knows that he probably started a new life abroad, with new prosperity. And she wants her own share that is due."

Mark finally took a bite of the famed torte. The nutty, chocolaty caramel sweetness heightened his alertness, now further flagging under jet lag. He took another bite.

"Good, eh?"

Mark nodded.

"Anyhow," Mustafa said. "I finally tracked Gürsen to Budapest. Then you stumbled into my investigation."

Chapter 16

* * *

A low-lying sun cast orange beams through the grand windows of Lotz Terem, the moldings of the splendid ceiling radiant in golden glitter. There was a late afternoon swell in the crowd gathering at the café counter. Mustafa continued his hushed account amid an audible din, causing Mark to lean in closer. To any stranger, they looked like a pair of old chums catching up.

"I couldn't track down Gürsen by his location. So I did it through his bank accounts. He kept several in reputable banks like Iş Bankası, Yapı ve Kredi Bankası, and HSBC. Then I came across a large account in a little-known, rather shady bank. Silivribank. Have you heard of it?"

Mark shook his head. He was fighting a growing lethargy, but he forced his eyes open. "How can you do that?" he asked. "Isn't that sort of information confidential?"

"Nothing is confidential if you have the right contacts," Mustafa looked around him, "and you know how to motivate them." His thick moustache parted into a toothy smile, revealing an out-of-line canine tooth on one side of his mouth. "Do you get it?"

Mark knew the way things worked in the old country.

"It's not all that different here in Budapest. Everyone has their price," Mustafa added, confidently.

"It doesn't quite work that way in America," Mark objected.

"In certain circles, it probably does." Mustafa spoke with assurance. "America is no different than anywhere else. It's just that you don't mingle in those circles."

Mark let the comment pass. "So who's your contact?"

"I don't have a single contact. Different ones in different banks. The one at Silivribank was fairly high up, a chief financial officer. I had some information on him—sexual indiscretions with young boys—that he could not afford to have revealed."

Mark smiled thinly. "It figures." He took another bite of *dobos torte*. "How did you get that information?"

"Let's just say it was a by-product of another job I had been hired to do."

A young man ascended the podium with the piano. He plunged into a spirited recitation of a Chopin Polonaise, the music reverberating magnificently around the spacious enclosures of the café. They stopped and listened.

"Anyhow," Mustafa resumed, "my Silivribank contact had informed me that Gürsen was doing business with Gránit Bank. Hungarian. It's a pretty respectable institution."

The name meant nothing to Mark. Mustafa continued.

"I then received a tip from him that Gürsen was coming to Budapest and had arranged a meeting with a Gránit representative at the Gresham Palace Hotel."

Mark pondered this news. Ahmet must have been preparing to make funds available to himself for whatever he had planned, while at the same time summoning Mark for assistance. "So, did they meet?"

"It was to happen today or tomorrow." Mustafa paused, his expression darkening. "Now everything has gone to pot. Ahmet's death was a nasty surprise."

"How did you find out?"

"Contacts at the Gresham hotel," said Mustafa. "They informed me of your call to the reception desk that Ahmet was dead."

The pianist finished the Chopin and took a brief applause.

"What a disaster," said Mark.

"Yeah. It brought my best lead to a dead end." Mustafa skipped a beat and then added, "Sorry." He had not intended to make a pun. "Then, all of a sudden, you appeared. And here we are."

The pianist launched into a sweet recitation of a popular Brahms tune. Mark recognized it as the Hungarian Dance No. 7. They once again paused to listen.

"Do you know who killed Ahmet?" Mark broke the silence after the pianist finished.

"I have no idea," said Mustafa. "I suspect it's somehow related to his business activities."

"Textiles?"

"Yes, of course. We all know that textiles have been his bread and butter. But there has to be more."

"You know," said Mark, "when I walked in on the scene of Ahmet's murder in his suite, it was strange."

Mustafa sat up, piqued by the revelation. "How so?"

"No violence, no disorder, no bloodshed. I am not sure how he was killed."

"How did you happen to be in his suite?"

Mark recounted the events that preceded his discovery. He then described the bathroom with Ahmet in the tub. "The only signs of violence, and they were subtle, were thin bruises on his cheeks." Mark moved his index finger in a diagonal line from his nose to the edge of his lip to demonstrate. "And circular bruises on his wrists."

"Handcuffs," said Mustafa.

"Handcuffs?"

"Those wrist marks. They happen commonly if anyone struggles against tightly cuffed wrists. I have seen it in countless arrests."

"What about the cheeks?"

Mustafa played with his fork, thinking. "That, I'm not sure about." He put the fork down and leaned back. "Did you notice anything else?"

Mark described the strange parallel lines on the body and limbs, and the petechiae in the eyes.

"The small blotches of blood in his eyes indicated strangulation or asphyxiation," he said.

"But he wasn't strangled, right?"

"I don't know," Mark said thoughtfully. "There were no marks or bruises on his neck. But then, I'm not a forensics expert."

"It's all pretty strange."

"What do you think those lines around his body and limbs were?"

Mustafa pondered for a moment. The pianist had launched into a lengthy Schubert sonata, but the two no longer paid attention to the music.

"I don't know," said Mustafa. "We would have to see a forensics report from the police."

"Do you have any police contacts here?" Mark asked.

"No."

Mark paused for a moment. "I have already had contact with police investigating the case," he said quietly, almost mumbling. "One is a local Budapest detective, the other a Frenchman from Interpol. Maybe I can get it from them."

"What—now you want to be an investigator?" Mustafa had a mocking tone that irritated Mark.

"Ahmet was an old friend," Mark said firmly. "Do you know what a shock it was to find him that way? At the very least, I am willing to try."

Mustafa shook his head. "Good luck."

The pianist changed styles, playing an animated, virtuosic jazz piece. He was good. Mark stood up. "Do you want another coffee? I am really fading," he said. "Jet lag, I think."

Mustafa looked at his watch and nodded in agreement. "Sure."

They stood in line behind some animated Hungarians who were enjoying the music.

"If you have reliable contacts at the hotel, can you do me a favor?" Mark had spoken too loudly. A couple standing in front turned and eyed him, no doubt thinking, *American.*

Mustafa placed his index finger on his lips in a universal hush sign. "Let's talk at the table," he whispered in Turkish.

They returned with more espressos. Mustafa dug into his half-eaten *dobos torte* and devoured it in three large mouthfuls. "So, what did you have in mind?"

Mark pulled out Olga's business card from his pocket and handed it to him. "Can you get me an address for this person? She works at Gresham Palace."

"What is it to you?" Mustafa wiped flakes of cake from his moustache as he examined the card.

"Probably nothing. But I want to talk to her."

"Try calling this number." Mustafa displayed the back of the card. "Looks like it may be hers."

"I'd rather not. I'd rather talk to her in person."

Mustafa gave him a skeptical look. He placed the card on the table, next to Mark's espresso cup. "Why don't you catch her at the hotel? Book a massage with her or something."

"She no longer works there."

Mustafa silently pondered the proposition. "Okay," he acquiesced. "If I find anything useful I'll let you know."

Mark smiled in gratitude. They both pulled out their cellphones, Mustafa jotting down the name. "Should be easy," he muttered. "What's your number? I'll text you." They exchanged numbers and tapped them into their respective phones.

The pianist finished to loud applause. He took a bow and stepped down.

"What are you going to do now?" asked Mark.

"I'm not quite sure," Mustafa said. "Meltem Hanım doesn't know the news yet. I suppose I'll inform her and get instructions on how she wants me to proceed."

"Do you think she'll be upset?"

Mustafa gave a sly smile. "Yes and no. She won't be upset that he's dead. But our mission is incomplete. I don't know how she'll take that."

Mark recalled YouTube images of the elegant Turkish TV hostess, poised and articulate, impeccable in her diction, every bit the epitome of social grace. One could not fathom the poison she harbored.

"What about you? What will you do?" asked Mustafa, in a friendly tone.

Mark felt a sense of kinship toward him now, relieved that Mustafa was no longer a sinister figure lurking around. Mark pushed his spent espresso cup and gathered his cellphone. "I am leaving three days from now," he said. He picked up Olga's card and pocketed it. "I'll see the sights."

Mustafa eyed the card as it disappeared. "I hope you don't plan to investigate Gürsen's death on your own."

"Do I look like a detective?"

"You certainly don't." Mustafa was stern. "And you probably should not be meddling with that woman." He pointed to Mark's pocket into which Olga's card had disappeared. "Or anyone else."

Mark avoided his gaze.

"I mean it!" Mustafa sounded like Mark's old Turkish headmaster back in the English High School, who bore the same name. "Whoever did this to Ahmet Gürsen," Mustafa added, "they are dangerous."

"I realize," said Mark quietly.

"Not the kind of people you're used to dealing with in your civilized life." Mustafa paused. "In America."

Mark nodded uneasily.

"Just see the sights. Enjoy the town." Mustafa was giving sound advice, same as Kárpáty. "There are a lot of things to do here. Do you know they have amazing *hamams* in Budapest?"

Mark had not been to a bath house in decades. It would be interesting to try one. He looked at his watch. It was past five p.m.

"You look tired," said Mustafa. "Are you going to walk back to the hotel, the way you came?"

Mark had forgotten that Mustafa had tailed him the entire way, accidentally revealing himself only once.

"May I suggest the Metro?" Mustafa stood up. "The Oktogon station on the yellow line is a block down from here. Get off at Bajcsy-Zsilinszky, two stations down. It'll be near your hotel."

They took the escalator down to the bookstore, silent.

"Budapest is a memorable city," said Mustafa at the sidewalk on Andrássy út. Shoppers swinging fancy bags passed them by. "Your first time here, right?"

Mark nodded. They shook hands.

"You'll never forget it," said Mustafa.

Chapter 17

* * *

"Ha, ha....!"

Ahmet laughed with delight as he moved his last piece, a white one, out of Metin's territory. He slammed it onto his side of the board. Metin stared in dismay at the dice Ahmet had tossed. A double-six! His third in the game. Ahmet looked at his mate with a wide grin. Metin hesitated before picking up the dice. The game was lost. Still, he had to go through the motions to prevent a *mars*, a double loss, if Ahmet removed all his pieces off the board before Metin had a chance to remove any of his.

It was late Saturday afternoon and, there being no good movies in the theaters, the boys were hanging out in Metin's Kurtuluş apartment. A game of *tavla*, backgammon, was an obligatory accompaniment to any such gathering.

Metin tossed the dice. Three-two. He groaned.

"It'll be a *mars*," said Ahmet, with glee.

Metin moved his pieces methodically. Ahmet's reckless style fascinated him, the way he left his pieces open to hits, his herky-jerky momentum. Yet he always found a way to win. By contrast, Metin played a cautious, defensive game with conventional moves, mindful of doubling up his pieces, avoiding singles vulnerable to hits. Ahmet had uncanny luck, the dice rolling in his favor.

"Who's winning?" Sadık Bey, Metin's father, approached the boys, newspaper loosely hanging in one hand, reading glasses in the other. He examined the backgammon board.

"We were even," said Ahmet. "Three-three. But now it looks like Metin is headed to a *mars*." They were playing a sequence of best of five. If Ahmet's prediction was correct, the game would end soon.

Sadık folded his newspaper and sized up the board with a quick glance. "Luck of the dice," he said. "You never know who it'll favor."

"It's rarely me," Metin complained as he rolled a two-two.

"Well, son," said Sadık Bey, "if you don't like how the dice are treating you, then you should stick to chess." Chess was Sadık's forte, and he had taught the game to his son at a young age. Metin, now in his first year in *lise* (high school), was already a rising star in the school's chess club.

Ahmet rolled the dice and began removing pieces from the board. "I don't know how to play chess," he said to Sadık Bey.

"Then you don't live by your wits." Sadık replied to Ahmet as if he were addressing his own son.

Metin tucked the dice into his fist and shook them for an extra long time. He needed a large double, five or six, to bring his sole piece back home in a hurry. He forcefully flung the dice onto the board. They crashed against the opposite edge and rolled back, one of them whirling like a top. All three eagerly looked on.

Double-twos. Again!

"You're going down!" Ahmet taunted Metin.

Metin scrambled all the pieces with his hands. "Okay, I accept the *mars*."

Conceding defeat before the game ended was a chess move, foreign to backgammon. Metin could not bear any more dice rolls, each slapping him with more ignominy. Ahmet closed the board and extended his hand to his mate.

"Maybe I should teach you chess," said Metin.

"I don't think so," Ahmet replied. He knew about Metin's prowess in the game, occasionally winning against senior, veteran players in the school. "I have no use for all that thinking and strategy. I like to play with my instincts. It serves me better."

* * *

"Charming boy," said Sadık after Ahmet departed. He sat at the same table where the boys had played backgammon and stared at the view of the old Roman aqueduct at Unkapanı far in the distance. Their apartment had a commanding hilltop view of the old city beyond the Golden Horn. "But he is a bit unruly, isn't he?"

"He has his moments at school," said Metin, taking a last swig from his Coke bottle. "But he never gets caught. He rarely gets signatures on his conduct card."

"Somehow I guessed that about him. Your mom has told me some rumors." Sadık paused for a second, deliberating whether to bring the subject up with his son. "About his father—have you met him?"

"I have," Metin said. "He's a pretty casual guy, funny. Cracks a lot of jokes."

Metin recalled the first time he encountered Latif Bey, Ahmet's father, a couple of years ago. Metin had come over to pick up Ahmet on a Saturday afternoon for an outing to the movies. Latif opened the door wearing a partially buttoned white shirt, black socks in slippers, and boxer underwear. No pants. His face was lathered and half shaven. He cracked a joke at the expense of his son while Metin stared at him, mouth agape. His own father—tall, thin, aloof, a speaker of impeccable Turkish who never used slang—would never have answered the door in his underwear. Metin admired Latif Bey's easygoing informality, so different from his own formal and methodical father.

"From what I hear, he is a bit too casual with his family," said Sadık.

The comment surprised Metin. His father was not one prone to gossip. His veiled reference to Latif Bey's *çapkın* ways, his rumored womanizing, was a subject Sadık would have kept off limits with his son. Sadık was a devoted family man, and infidelity was a concept about as foreign to the family as eating pork.

Darkness was falling. Father and son stared quietly at the lights of the old city as they came up, the flow of traffic under the Roman aqueduct a distant river aglow. Sadık fell into one of his frequent thoughtful spells.

He finally broke the silence. "Your friend Ahmet reminds me of my great-uncle Nurettin."

"Did you know him?" Metin had heard some stories about this ancestor and his adventurous life.

"No." Sadık pulled a Meerschaum pipe out of his pocket and bit into its lip. It was a stylish pipe with a curving, black stem and an ivory white statue of Barbaros Hayrettin, the grand pirate admiral of the Ottoman Empire, as its bowl. He took it off his lips, inspected the bowl, and patted down the tobacco already loaded in with his fingertip. "He died way before my time."

"Wasn't he a soldier?" Metin vaguely remembered this fact.

"Yes," said Sadık. "He died with Enver Paşa in Tajikistan." Enver was among the Young Turks who led Turkey into World War I. In 1919, after the ignominious Turkish defeat, he fled the country.

Sadik lit a match and turned the flame down into the pipe. He took several puffs, filling the room with an exotic aroma. Through the half spectacles that he routinely balanced on the bridge of his nose, he stared at the dark distance beyond the moving lights of the boulevard at Unkapanı. "Nurettin was a young man when he died, thirty-two. A waste." He fell silent, lost in thought, puffing his pipe.

Knowing his father, Metin waited patiently. "What about Nurettin?" he finally prompted him. "How is he like Ahmet?"

Sadık took a final puff from his pipe and asked his son to go fetch the miniature eclairs that Füsun, his wife, had purchased that morning. They each popped the tiny pastries, some chocolate, others custard, into their mouths and silently enjoyed their delight.

Afterwards, Sadık continued. "Nurettin was handsome and charming. A dashing adventurer. A ladies' man. He had been to Europe many times and his tastes were exotic. He especially liked French and Russian women. I think a Russian woman may have been behind his disastrous decision to follow Enver into the USSR."

"Ahmet is very good with girls," Metin remarked. "They are naturally attracted to him."

His *lise* had gone coed, and the boys were still transitioning from their unruly all-boys middle-school years to more proper behavior with girls among their midst. It was awkward for them, especially Metin. Ahmet was one of the few who seemed at ease.

"I can see that," his father replied. "I also see an adventurer in him. You heard what he just said, at the end of the *tavla* game."

Metin nodded and did not reply. He could not tell his father that he was jealous of Ahmet's ease with girls. Already resigned to a stolid but secure career in the footsteps of his family—his father was an engineer, his grandfather a lawyer—Metin nevertheless wondered what adventures Nurettin must have experienced in his short but eventful life. He had to keep this from his father, too.

"Watch out for women," said Sadık emphatically. "They can lead you down the wrong path."

"Yes, Father." His father need not worry, Metin thought to himself. Those sorts of women were unlikely to cross his path.

Chapter 18

* * *

Mark awoke from a deep sleep, disoriented by darkness all around. For a moment he thought he was back in San Francisco and wondered what his work schedule would be that day. Then he recalled the busy subway car, the rush-hour crowds, and returning to Gresham Palace. He had looked up at the façade of the building from the green plaza across and noticed the bust of a square-jawed, bearded man carved into the ornate Art Nouveau decorations along the roof line, the name *Gresham* inscribed above it.

Mark sat up suddenly. His bedside clock glowed nine-ten. Was it a.m. or p.m., he wondered. His curtains were closed, effectively restricting incoming light.

Dazed, he stumbled out of bed and opened the curtains. It was dark outside. He sat down by the entryway desk and tried to clear his thoughts. Could he have slept more than twenty-four hours? The way he felt after leaving Mustafa, it was possible. An email chime on his iPhone brought him back to reality. It was on the bedside next to the hotel clock. He took steadier steps toward it.

The phone announced nine-twelve p.m. Same day. Mark was relieved. He had merely slept away the rest of the afternoon and early evening. He quickly erased several useless emails. Then he noticed a single text message, from Mustafa: an address. Mark stared at the screen, now wide awake.

* * *

The hotel lobby was busy with well-dressed guests. A private party was gathered at the piano bar where he had first spotted Mustafa. Young, attractive men and women were loudly mingling with each other while the same pianist sang the same oldies Mark had heard the evening before.

Mark went to the concierge desk, where a middle-aged man politely looked up the address Mustafa had given him.

"Are you sure that's where you want to go?" the man asked skeptically, as he studied his computer screen.

"Why, what is it?"

"A nightclub, sir," said the concierge. "There is a warning about it from the American Embassy in Budapest." He read it. "'Expats are strongly urged to avoid the following establishments due to multiple bad reports received....'"

He eyed Mark with more curiosity. "Your address is among several listed underneath this warning. It's a gentleman's...um...a strip club."

Mark took his phone back. "Is it far from here?"

"No sir. District VII. Ten or fifteen minutes by taxi."

"All right, thank you very much." Mark took a step away from the desk toward the entrance nearby.

"Sir!" The concierge waved him back over. He leaned into Mark and whispered. "May I suggest that you be careful with...you know...women who might offer to accompany you?" He hesitated and continued awkwardly, "Your bill... it might turn out quite high."

Mark gave the man a nod of appreciation and proceeded to the driveway, where an attentive bellman called for a taxi.

The cab went through numerous quiet side streets and onto a wide Parisian boulevard with a streetcar line in the middle, modern yellow trams crisscrossing. Mark observed stately buildings lining Erzsébet körút as they passed by lively sidewalk cafés and diverse businesses, some still open—a magic shop, a Lego shop, an Ergoline tanning salon with prominent pink signs.

The cab turned left onto Dohány utca by the Boscolo Hotel, passing the famous New York Café that was on the hotel's first floor. Mark had read about it in his guidebook, another beautiful café like Lotz Terem. The sidewalk was busy here. Mark anticipated the remainder of the street would be the same, but as the taxi advanced farther into the one-way street, it turned dark and desolate. Apprehensive, Mark pulled out Olga's card from his pocket and examined it. Was she worth the trouble?

Ahmet's lifeless body flashed in his mind, and his sorrow momentarily returned. Memories flooded in, of fun with his old friend in high school, of outings to movies, of incessant *tavla* games. Even though Ahmet mostly won, now, after all these years, they seemed so enjoyable. Olga may have been the last person to see Ahmet alive, except for whoever killed him. Mark's desire to know what his mate had been like in those last moments was as intense as when he first spotted Olga's card in the Royal Suite. Mark needed to know how Ahmet had come to deserve her private number.

The taxi slowed down by a well-lit beer bar alongside a triangular building, the only open business on the isolated street. Mark noted a prominent *Colorado Sörbár* sign brightly lit above the door. The bar had outdoor tables on the side of the building that faced a pedestrian mall, a few customers the only sign of life in the area.

The driver stopped farther down, at the end of the block, and pointed across to a series of arched windows, all curtained. It was the first floor of yet another Parisian building. Varying colors of light faded in and out from behind the curtains. A dimly lit sign announced *Mercy Club and Lounge*.

* * *

The sidewalk was desolate, except for an old man walking an equally old, shaggy dog. The club had its own door, separate from that of the building. There were no attendants. Mark entered through a red velvet curtain and into a dimly lit, hazy space with a loud techno beat reverberating inside. He saw a few silhouettes seated at tables, darkened by two bright stage-light beams that illuminated waves of smoke. They were aimed at a small, slightly elevated stage where two young women were kissing each other as they danced in synch to the beat, naked except for G strings, their oversized breasts squeezed against each other.

"*Segíthetek*," he heard a male voice behind him. It startled Mark. He had heard that word before, uttered by Olga upon their first encounter.

"English," he answered.

"Please," said the man, "this way."

He was seated at a round bistro table close to the stage. The young women were sweaty, their hands caressing each other's hips and thighs, their crotches glued and grinding. One was slim, tall and blonde, the other darker complexioned, more buxom. The blonde slid her partner's G string off.

"May I offer you a drink?" Mark could hardly hear the waiter amid the loud music. It was the same man who had seated him.

"Not quite yet," he shouted back. "After this set, maybe."

The blonde began simulating oral sex on the dark girl. An audience member approached the stage and threw bills at the women. An attendant, tall with prominent gold earrings, stood by the stage and watched him carefully. He motioned another spectator who came too close to the stage to back away.

The show ended with no applause and the women scrambled around the stage collecting money before they disappeared. The stage lights went off and house lights came on. Mark looked around the cabaret-like room. It was compact, sprinkled with bistro tables and with a prominent bar at the far end, opposite the stage. Few tables were occupied, all men, some sitting with scantily clad women who obviously belonged to the establishment. Several tall, stocky men were stationed in various corners of the room, keenly observing the guests, including the one by the stage who stood motionless at his spot, his hands folded by his groin.

Olga was nowhere to be seen. Mark wondered if Mustafa had given him a wrong address.

The two strippers who had just left the stage reappeared through a side door, now adorned with colorful, skimpy gowns that revealed ample cleavage and thighs, strutting on high-heeled platform shoes. The dark, buxom one spotted a table far back where she recognized two men who had approached the stage and sprinkled her with money. The other one, the blonde, came by Mark, pulled up an empty chair next to him and sat.

"Hello," she said, slurring in a heavy accent. "American?"

She looked young up close, in her late teens maybe. Her deep blue eyes were half-mast and bloodshot. Her blonde wavy hair, freshly combed, was still wet with sweat. Mark nodded yes.

She motioned to the waiter. "Will you buy me a drink?" she said to Mark, and to the waiter, "Champagne."

Mark noticed the bouncer with the gold earrings, still standing by the stage, carefully watching his table. He was tall and dark, with rumpled black hair that covered his forehead and ears, all except for the prominent earrings that protruded down. He wore a dark suit, dark shirt, and brightly polished black shoes with long pointed tips.

"What else do you have?" Mark asked, sending the waiter to fetch a menu.

"Hannah," said the blonde, extending a slim, delicate arm. Her fingernails were long and bright red, her perfume heavy, with a strange scent of roses and lemon. She smiled, revealing two crooked upper teeth, one on each side of her mouth. The waiter returned with a glass of champagne and a menu. She took a sip and leaned back in her chair, crossing her legs. Her gown slid back, revealing lanky legs. Mark had already seen them earlier, on stage. He paid no attention.

"Hello," said Mark, shaking her hand lightly, not knowing quite what to make of her.

"Would you like a friend?" Hannah asked, her lips resting on the edge of her champagne flute.

"Yes, I would," Mark replied.

Hannah smiled broadly and rested her glass on the table.

"But not you, I'm afraid."

Her smile faded.

"You're very pretty, but...I was looking for...for someone a bit older." Mark pulled out Olga's card from his pocket and handed it to her. "I want *her* as my friend."

Hannah examined the card front and back and threw a quick, anxious glance toward the bar before turning to Mark, forcing a half smile. She read the card again.

"Is she here?" asked Mark.

She paused, her expression subdued, unsure how to respond. She looked at the card again and this time, without meeting Mark's eyes, said, "She doesn't do this kind of work."

"So you know her?"

No answer.

The waiter interrupted.

"Single malt Scotch," said Mark. "Do you have any?"

The waiter opened the menu for him. Glenfiddich and Lagavulin. There were no prices. Mark tapped the Lagavulin.

"Yes, sir."

As he turned around, Mark spoke more loudly. "Get me a whole bottle of that, will you?"

The waiter exchanged glances with Hannah, both surprised. Hannah's smile returned.

"Okay," said Mark in a tone he usually reserved for subordinates at his hospital. "Now go and see if she's here."

This was going to cost him dearly. He hoped Olga would be worth it.

Chapter 19

* * *

She sat behind a small desk in a moldy back office, her face illuminated by a faint table lamp. Her wavy golden hair hung loose, her face more radiant than at the spa despite meager makeup. The room was chilly and she wore a wool V-neck sweater over her dress, unbuttoned at the top, her ample bosom conspicuous. She extinguished a spent cigarette, forcefully squeezing it, and gave him a weary look.

"What do you want from me?"

Mark played with the straps atop a plastic bag containing his bottle of Lagavulin. He sat awkwardly on an uncomfortable wooden chair in front of her desk as if he were interviewing for a job.

"First," he muttered, "let me tell you that I am not a policeman, or detective, or anything like that."

She let out a hoarse chuckle. "That's obvious," she said.

Mark felt foolish. He stroked his bottle as if it were a pet. The Scotch had been effective, attracting sufficient attention from the bar. Still, he had had to wait over an hour, suffering through two more strip performances. When they presented him with the bill, Hannah long since gone, Mark realized that he would indeed pay dearly for a tête-a-tête with Olga. Eventually, after his credit card cleared, one of the bouncers that stood guard led him to the back of the bar and through a narrow, dark hallway into this office.

After a pause to collect himself, Mark began. "Why did you not tell me who you were at the hotel?"

"Is this why you took all the trouble to come here? To ask me that?" She was disdainful.

"No, no...." Mark tried a fresh start, a bit more assertive. "It's just that Ahmet was an old friend of mine, a dear friend...at one time."

"Who?"

"Nicolae," Mark corrected himself. "Nicolae Radu."

She reached over to a dark corner of the desk and slid a pack of cigarettes toward her. She shook one out and looked at him. Her hazel eyes were captivating.

"Did you know Nicolae?" Mark asked.

She nodded. "I saw him from time to time."

"You mean, he came here to Budapest and got massages from you?"

She lit the cigarette, leaning into the lighter in a seasoned move. She squinted as she let out her first drag. "No. Mostly in Romania."

Mark tried to contain his surprise.

"This was our first time in Budapest," she added.

"I wanted to know what he was like." Mark hoped he sounded nonchalant, the news of their Romanian relationship reverberating in his mind.

"He was a good lover," she said. She took another drag from her cigarette and was momentarily lost in thoughts. "He was funny. Jovial."

"Yes," said Mark.

"It's a shame," she whispered, looking down at her cigarette, avoiding Mark's eyes.

"But he was naughty too, wasn't he? Prone to trouble?"

"He didn't talk about any troubles with me. That's what I loved about him. We all have our troubles." She placed her cigarette on the ashtray and rubbed her forehead, her eyebrows raised. She looked tired in the harsh chiaroscuro of the table lamp. "He made me forget mine."

For a moment Mark thought she would tear up. Instead, she picked up her cigarette and took a longer drag.

"So how did you know him...back in Romania?" Mark felt like he had a thousand questions to ask this woman.

She suddenly sat up, alert, like a guard dog that sensed something. "You shouldn't have come here," she said.

He opened his mouth to respond and she raised her hand, shushing him. They both listened. Mark heard it too. Faint footsteps in the hallway.

"We don't have any more time," she said anxiously. "They're coming for you."

"Who?" Mark was incredulous.

Olga sprang to her feet. "Come on," she said hurriedly. "Come here, quick!"

She moved toward a dark corner behind the desk and opened a different door that Mark had not noticed. "Follow this hallway all the way. It has a few turns. It'll take you out to a back street."

Mark hesitantly got up. The footsteps outside were getting louder, sounding like more than one person. Mark came around the desk.

"Hurry! If they find you, they'll kill you."

"But I have more questions," Mark protested.

"Not now!" She was almost in a panic.

He was by the door, his face inches from hers. He could smell fresh lavender and musk in her hair. He stopped, momentarily enthralled by her. Why, he wondered, was he drawn to Ahmet's women? How could he, after all these years, feel like the awkward teen he was in Istanbul? He leaned in toward Olga.

"When you get to the street, run!" She did not notice his quandary. "And don't look back. Don't come back."

"Can I call you?"

The footsteps were almost at the door, loud, reverberating from the walls of the main hallway.

"I don't know," she said, and she shoved him out the door. "I'll be leaving soon."

The door slammed behind him.

The hallway was cold. Mark took a few nervous steps in pitch darkness. He imagined whoever they were bursting into the room, Olga holding them off for a brief while. Alone now, and free of Olga's allure, Mark came to his senses, a sudden fear swelling within. He briefly lit up the hallway with his phone screen. It was around thirty feet straight, unobstructed, then a left turn. He thought about running for it but his footsteps would be too loud. Besides, he was afraid to do that in darkness. He walked fast, trying hard to muffle his feet, his heart pounding.

After taking the left turn, he lit the corridor again and found it blocked by a door up ahead. He shoved the door open into what seemed like another building. It was warmer here, and harshly lit by one bare bulb. It smelled mustier. The door loudly clanked shut behind him. Damn!

He ran, breathless, almost slamming into a wall as the hallway took a turn. He heard the door opening. He ran faster toward another door up ahead. He could hear the same footsteps approaching behind. He slammed his body into the door and found himself in crisp, fresh air, a short set of stairs leading up to a sidewalk. He took the stairs two at a time.

He was on an empty, narrow, one-way residential street. He randomly took a right turn and ran again toward a nearby corner where he took another right turn. It was a slightly wider street, still one way, and Mark recognized it. The entrance to the strip club was only a few paces away. Traffic was scant. A man who appeared drunk stumbled on the opposite sidewalk, past a shadowy figure who stood still under a dark doorway. A couple, arm in arm, walked toward him, their eyes on the pavement.

Mark stopped for a minute and looked around the corner to where he had come from. No one in pursuit. He broke into a massive sweat. He felt a weight bearing down on his right arm. He lifted it and was amazed to see the bottle of Scotch, still in its bag, that had survived his flight. He unzipped his coat, tucked it into his chest, and zipped back up. He began walking at a brisk but steady pace, past the entrance of the club, still desolate, and toward the next corner. It was brightly lit on his side of the street. Mark recalled the *Colorado Sörbár* that he had spotted from the taxi earlier.

The building bearing the bar curved around into Almássy utca, a pedestrian mall that cut diagonally across Dohány. Mark relaxed and turned into Almássy, walking toward the sidewalk tables set up by the beer bar, well lit and occupied by a few customers. Mark intended to continue down this mall, unsure about what he would encounter farther down. He figured heading away from the nightclub was the safest move. Then his heart skipped several beats.

Two shadowy silhouettes broke out of the dark, directly approaching him at a fast pace from the opposite end of Almássy. It had to be them. They must have taken a left turn out of where Mark had emerged and circled around the opposite direction. Mark quickly ducked onto an outdoor chair of the Colorado Bar, facing away from the pair of pursuers. He forced himself to be calm but his heart raced.

They ran right by the bar without taking a look at its patrons. Mark got a quick glimpse of the two. One was tall and heavy-set, dark and greasy, with a bushy moustache and what looked like a week-old beard. The other was short and athletic, also dark complexioned, pacing slightly ahead of his partner, his hands swinging by his sides like a track athlete. Mark saw a gun in his right hand moving swiftly up and down with his arm motions. He contained his rising panic.

As the pair disappeared into Dohány, Mark felt stunned stares directed at him. Two young men and a woman sat around the table, hands on beer mugs, regarding the sweaty intruder who had suddenly occupied the only other free seat at their table. Mark smiled sheepishly and nodded hello to them. He quickly wiped his brow with a paper napkin set at his spot on the table. He stood up so abruptly that he almost knocked over his chair. After saying good night in English, he walked as nonchalantly as he could into the darkness of Almássy, away from Dohány.

The street was lined with old apartment buildings and had waist-high wooden planters down the middle, empty benches between each. Silhouettes of young trees protruded from the planters, supported by poles. Beyond the bar there was not a soul on Almássy. Mark came upon a triangular plaza where the street forked into a Y, its extensions no longer a pedestrian mall. A small park was tucked between the two diverging roads, walled and fenced, its entrance straight ahead, shuttered. There were cars parked along both streets, all facing one way, toward him. A street sign announced Almássy tér. Mark realized he was at one edge of a small, triangular square with a park in the middle. The area was dim and desolate.

Mark stood and hesitated. Should he go left or right?

He heard faint footsteps and looked behind. He recognized the shadowy figures of his two pursuers backlit by the lights of the beer bar walking quickly toward him. They must have gone back to where they started, and now backtracked.

Mark instinctively took off, running fast toward the left, tripping into the street across a step where the pedestrian mall ended. He ran along the fenced wall of the park, not looking back. Suddenly he spotted a break in the wall, an alcove, and he dove into it. He stopped, panting hard. A wooden hut was built into the alcove as a public toilet. Mark was in a narrow space between the fence and the entrance to the ladies' room, hidden from view. Trying to catch his breath, he wheezed loudly as he exhaled. The sound scared him. He held his breath and listened. No footsteps. Had they gone down the other side of the fork?

Despite his terror, Mark collected his thoughts. He could not hide here forever. Sooner or later they would discover him. He listened attentively, and hearing nothing, slid out of the alcove and onto the street.

"*Állj meg!*" The yell startled him. He stopped and looked behind. He saw the solitary figure of the tall, stocky pursuer who repeated the order in English. "Stop!"

The man was standing at the end of Almássy út, where Mark had stood minutes ago, in front of the park entrance. He turned to his right and yelled at his partner. Mark realized that the two had split there, each searching one side of the fork.

Mark dashed forward. A shot rang out. Mark instinctively ducked and tumbled, the bottle of Scotch thumping painfully against his ribs. He almost fell down. As he recovered his balance, he realized that he was not hit. He heard loud footsteps approaching. There was an intersection fifty feet up ahead, a faint headlight of a motorcycle far beyond. A left turn there would bring him to a busier quarter, Mark hoped, back to Dohány maybe, closer to the New York Café. They could not openly shoot at him there. Could they?

Just then he was blinded by bright headlights. Mark froze and almost fell again, this time backwards. A car had come to a sudden stop at the intersection, then slowly turned into the street, facing him. The sound of footsteps behind him disappeared. They must have frozen, too. The car stood still, engine running, lights on, blocking Mark's way.

Mark panted, sweat pouring out of his forehead and neck. Was there an accomplice in this car? Is that why his pursuers had stopped? Terror, rising within, threatened to overwhelm rational thought.

Maybe it was just a random vehicle, someone lost, stopping to figure his location. Maybe that's why his followers had stopped, too. They did not want any witnesses.

The car did not budge.

Mark had two choices. He could run forward and take his chances with the car, or he could run back, into the arms of his chasers. *Goddamnit*, he thought. How would they take the news of his death back home, not far from a seedy strip club in Budapest? What would they think he had been up to? He couldn't believe he had gotten himself into this predicament.

Mark broke into a run, toward the car. He heard a commotion behind him as his pursuers also took off. Soon Mark was upon the car, a mid-sized sedan. As he tried to bypass it, the passenger door suddenly opened and he slammed into it, his arms flying through its open window.

"Get in!" A shout from within. It was too dark to make out the driver.

Breathless, with sweat-blurred eyes despite the cold, Mark turned behind and saw his followers, now within a few feet, the tall guy stationary, the short one sprinting toward him.

A loud order rang out again. "Get in! Fast."

Chapter 20

* * *

As Mark dove into the front seat of the car, a shot rang out, followed by the sound of shattered glass. The car jolted as it backed into the intersection, tires screeching. The passenger door was still open, with Mark ducked inside. The car stopped for a split second. Mark righted himself and saw the short, dark one positioned directly in front of the car, standing still, his legs apart, both hands firmly grasping his upraised gun. His stocky partner hurried toward him, panting.

Suddenly the car accelerated, rear tires smoking as they emitted an ear-splitting shriek. The door slammed shut against Mark's right shoulder, dropping him toward the driver's seat. When Mark righted himself, they were racing down a narrow street with parked cars all around. The two pursuers had disappeared.

"Fucking gypsies," he heard Mustafa utter with disgust. He turned into a wide boulevard with a tram line in the center. Mark soon recognized Erzsébet körút, still lively with traffic, sidewalk cafés and other open businesses. They were headed in the opposite direction from where Mark had come from. Mustafa slowed down to a normal speed.

Mark wiped the sweat off his brow, rubbed his right shoulder, and looked for a seat belt. He couldn't locate it.

"Oh," said Mustafa, taking his eyes briefly off the road. "Now you're concerned with your safety?"

Mark found the belt and awkwardly brought it around his chest.

Mustafa suddenly ducked the car into an open spot by the sidewalk. Mark watched as flashing blue lights raced toward them on the opposite side, across from the streetcar tracks. Mustafa turned off his engine and lights. Two police cars whizzed by, lights ablaze, sirens off, toward Dohány.

"*Pezevenk*," snarled Mustafa. *Pimp*. "That gypsy shot off my headlight on your side."

Mark craned his neck toward the back window and followed the silent haste of the diminishing police cars.

"Here come some more." Mustafa pointed forward. Three more pairs of flashing lights sprouted up, growing rapidly. "Congratulations. They're all looking for you."

Mark did not answer. He undid the seat belt and unzipped his coat, pulling out the plastic bag he had tucked in there earlier. He drew out the bottle of Lagavulin and looked at it in amazement. It was still intact.

Mustafa let out a coarse laugh. "How much did that cost you?"

Mark smiled sheepishly.

"Do you know what kind of a place you went into tonight?"

"Have you been following me?" Mark sounded hurt.

"You better be damn glad I did." Mustafa took the bottle from him and examined its label in a corner of the dash illuminated by a dim streetlight.

"I could have gotten this for you at the black market for just seventy-five dollars," he said, turning it this way and that. "It goes for over a hundred in the stores."

"They charged me around a thousand," said Mark.

Mustafa shook his head. He handed the bottle back. "These bars, around here," he said in a lecturing tone, "are full of women who will run up bills that will rob you blind and who you can't even fuck."

"Let me tell you," said Mark. "I wouldn't fuck the women I saw there even if they paid me."

"Not even that masseuse you were seeking?"

Mark looked ahead and did not answer.

Mustafa restarted slowly and soon turned into dark, quiet side streets.

"Why are we going this way?" asked Mark.

"I don't want to draw any attention with my headlight shot off. We're still close to where you had your little adventure."

They were on a very narrow, residential, one-way street with a wall of parked cars on each side. It opened onto a wide boulevard, where Mustafa took a left turn. Mark soon recognized Andrássy út as they came upon Oktogon circle, where he had taken the subway earlier in the day. The intersection was busy and they blended into the crowded traffic.

"Who were those two guys?" Mark asked.

"I don't know. Hired hands, probably."

"Do you think they're the ones who killed Ahmet?"

"Maybe. Maybe not. There are plenty of gangs in this city who'll do anything for the right price."

"How did you know where to find me?" Mark suddenly realized how uncanny Mustafa's timing had been.

"I knew you'd go to the address I'd given you. So I parked on Dohány several blocks ahead of that strip joint and staked it out on foot. When I saw you coming around the corner in a hurry and duck around that Colorado bar, I headed back to my car to catch you where I figured you were heading."

Mustafa pulled the car into a well-lit spot near the opera house on Andrássy. He looked at Mark and his bushy moustache parted into a smile. "I arrived just in the nick of time, huh?"

"Did you hear the earlier gunshot?"

"I sure did," said Mustafa. "It's a quiet neighborhood. So did, I am sure, those who live there. Why do you think the police are heading out there so fast?" He opened his door. "I speeded up when I heard that shot. To tell you the truth, I expected to find you sprawled on the ground. I was surprised when you appeared in my headlights."

Mustafa got out and inspected the damage, the intact left headlight casting angular shadows on his face.

"Goddamnit!" He slammed the driver's door shut as he plopped back into his seat. "This is a rental car," he said. "I'll have to get that fucking light fixed before I turn it back in."

"Why don't you just take their repair charge and turn it in the way it is?"

"Are you kidding me?" Mustafa looked astonished at Mark's remark. "And have them create a damage report?" He shook his head. "'What happened to our car, sir?'" He mimicked a rental agency attendant with a mock Hungarian accent. "Oh, some gypsy thugs shot it out!"

Mark felt foolish all over again.

"'Sir, did you report it to the police?'" Mustafa continued with his monologue. "No."

"'Well, then, no trouble. We'll report it ourselves.'"

"Okay," said Mark testily. "I get it."

Mustafa pulled back out onto Andrássy. "I don't know," he said, throwing a side glance at Mark, "how you became a doctor. I thought you had to be intelligent to do that."

He took the same route back to Gresham Palace that Mark had walked earlier in the day, past Erszébet Square on József Attila and into the plaza of the hotel. It was now nearly one a.m. The sidewalks had a smattering of people, some single, a few couples, some languid, others livelier, returning from bars and cafés. Mark was fully alert despite the late hour. It was four p.m. back home in San Francisco, of the day before. No wonder.

"This Olga of yours." Mustafa interrupted Mark's thoughts. "She may not be just any ordinary masseuse."

"What do you mean?"

"The scuttlebutt among the hotel staff was that she may have had something to do with the murder."

"How so?"

"I don't know. The rumor was that it had to be an inside job. The killer had to bypass the security they have there at that hotel."

"I wonder what the police think of that," said Mark.

"That, my friend," said Mustafa, poking Mark's chest with his fingertip, "is up to you to find out."

"How do I do that?"

Mustafa reached for the bottle of Lagavulin on Mark's lap and lifted it up, smiling broadly. His crooked canine tooth protruded beneath a thick moustache. "Hungarian police love good whiskey," he said.

"Scotch."

"Whatever." The car jumped onto the curb-like driveway of the hotel. "You met the Hungarian investigator already, didn't you?"

"Yes."

"Well then. Tomorrow..." Mustafa corrected himself. "Today, after daybreak, you pay him a visit with that thousand-dollar bottle and see if it'll buy you some information." Mustafa stopped several car lengths beyond the entrance, avoiding the doorman. "Did you get to meet Olga?"

Mark was wondering when Mustafa would ask this. He nodded yes.

"What did you find out?"

"Not much. We got interrupted by those two guys. But she did tell me that she had a prior relationship with Ahmet. In Romania."

"It figures." Mustafa turned off the engine.

"There's one thing that I don't get," continued Mark. "If she is guilty, an accomplice, as you say—and I do think that the way she abruptly quit her job is indeed suspicious—why did she help me?"

"She helped you?"

"Yes, she hurried me out of the building through a back door. She seemed concerned for my safety. Now, why would she do that? She could have handed me over to them and let them kill me. I was trapped."

Mustafa thought for a moment, then shook his head, giving Mark a *who knows* expression.

"I'll have to call her and talk to her some more."

Mustafa shook his head again, this time in a disapproving gesture. "Bad idea."

Mark made a gesture to open his door and exit. Mustafa grabbed his arm and stopped him.

"I told you," he said, looking directly into Mark's eyes. "I warned you not to investigate this case. This woman is trouble. Here you are. You had a brush with death. And you want more?"

"I can't help it."

Mark felt exhilarated at that moment, enlivened by what he had just been through.

Mustafa released his grip and sat back in resignation.

"Do you know that Ahmet has another wife?" Mark asked. "A Romanian one. I met her. She is here. She speaks Turkish. I have her number."

Mustafa shrugged. "No, but I am not surprised. Two wives, one in each country, a masseuse girlfriend..."

"And a mistress in Istanbul," added Mark.

Mustafa did not know about Günsu. He didn't seem interested either. "Just like Latif Bey," he said.

"Yes," affirmed Mark. "He turned out like his father."

"All right, Mr. Investigator!" Mustafa was mockingly ceremonious. "So you contact the police today, and then maybe visit this Romanian wife, see what you can find out. And I will call Meltem Hanım for more instructions, nose around that bar where you almost got whacked, and pump the hotel staff for more information."

He extended his hand to Mark. It was Mark's turn to grin. They shook hands firmly.

"Thank you," said Mark, "for saving my life."

Chapter 21

* * *

The four boys set out from Nişantaşı after the Friday afternoon recitation of the national anthem. They had sung with gusto, as they always did before a weekend, all except Metin, who had butterflies in his stomach. It was a warm April afternoon and they decided to walk the fifteen-minute distance toward Taksim Square. They still wore their school uniforms, gray slacks, white shirts with open collars, striped blue and yellow ties askew. Their navy blue sports coats with school insignia on the chest pockets flapped in a light breeze as they briskly climbed Valikonak Caddesi in the direction of Harbiye.

Ahmet was leading the way. He turned around and gave Metin a big slap on the back. "It's his big day," he announced to the others. Metin's initiation was long overdue. He was one of the few in the Lise II class, second year of high school, who was admittedly still a virgin.

Metin did not know the other two boys well, both soccer teammates of Ahmet. One of them, Aram, a brawny Armenian boy said, "It's about time."

Metin cowered and speeded his pace, trying to walk ahead of the group, even though he wasn't quite sure about the precise location of their destination. He ignored the idle banter behind him, frequently interrupted with laughter.

As they passed the old war school in Harbiye, now a military museum, they bunched closer on a wide sidewalk. Metin overheard Cengiz, the other boy, ask Ahmet, "How often do you go to Varol?"

Cengiz was tall and lanky, a good all-around sportsman, better in basketball than soccer.

"As often as I can," said Ahmet proudly.

Metin knew this, for the subject had come up before, frequently. Ahmet was fond of describing his peccadillos in math class, whispering to a group of boys bunched together, when they were supposed to be engaged in solving trigonometry problems. Their teacher, Mr. Surry, a tall Scotsman with a dark goatee and laissez-faire attitude, ignored them.

"Heck," said Cengiz, "I can't afford that."

Varol was an expensive establishment, illegal and luxurious.

Metin could afford it, but was afraid to cross a threshold into a foreign, forbidden world and sample its mysterious pleasures, so colorfully recounted by Ahmet.

"I usually go to the ones on Abanoz Street," said Aram. "Much cheaper."

Aram favored the legally sanctioned bordellos, regulated by the government.

"Yeah, but the women are butt-ugly and you can catch shit there," Ahmet retorted.

"I did," said Aram. "Twice."

The rare few who contracted gonorrhea wore their misery like a badge of honor. It was the ultimate proof of their virility.

"It's a wonder your dick hasn't fallen off," said Ahmet, his eyes gazing at Aram's crotch. They laughed.

Metin just chuckled, trying to conceal the fear rising within. He did not know precisely what the illness entailed, and the prospect of explaining such a predicament to his parents bothered him more than what he might suffer. He walked on anxiously, with eyes on the pavement.

Ahmet noticed Metin's silent quandary. He sidled up to his mate. "Don't worry," he said, "Varol is a ritzy place. The women are clean. You won't catch anything."

They crossed Cumhuriyet Caddesi near the luxurious Hilton Hotel. It was a wide boulevard connecting Taksim Square to Harbiye. They dodged busy traffic in one direction, caught their breath in the dusty median strip, and made another dash onto the opposite sidewalk at Notre Dame de Sion, a bilingual French girl's *lise.*

"I know a really cute one that goes here," said Aram, pointing to the school. "I think she's ready to put out. You know what I mean?"

All the boys sought dates with girls, most in vain. Reputable girls did not openly date boys, and they certainly did not have sex with them. The boys had only one recourse for sex. They had to pay for it.

"Who?" Ahmet quipped. "Your little sister?"

Aram gave Ahmet a gentle slap on the back of his head. "*Amcık*," he growled, *little cunt*, as Ahmet ducked. He squealed with delight as he avoided a second blow.

"He fucks his sister." Ahmet laughed and pointed his index finger at Aram. Metin and Cengiz joined in the laughter.

"No," said Aram, "I fuck your mother." He guffawed.

"Okay, children," Cengiz took charge. "Let's forget about who fucks who and focus on our mission."

"Yeah." Ahmet put an arm around Cengiz's shoulders. "Listen to him."

He motioned them all to a small downhill street off the boulevard, taking hasty steps and waiting for his mates to catch up.

The bustle of Cumhuriyet Caddesi suddenly vanished. They were in a quiet, cobblestoned street lined by dilapidated wooden buildings, some askew as though about to tumble. They turned left and a few doors down, Metin saw a neon sign on what looked like a small hotel, a building in better shape than its neighbors, with the word *Varol* on it. Ahmet opened the door and motioned them in.

They climbed a few steps and entered a small hotel lobby with an American bar to the side. It was dimly lit, with a greenish hue, and devoid of customers at this early hour. Metin was momentarily nauseated by a pervasive smell of cigarette smoke and stale perfume. They entered the bar and stared at women lounging on barstools and bistro tables, smoking, chatting, filing nails. They all wore negligées, some more revealing than others. There was no bartender.

The boys' arrival provoked amused interest from the women, as they examined them in their disheveled school uniforms. One of them recognized Ahmet and walked over to him, planting a kiss on his cheek.

Ahmet put his arm around Metin's shoulder and quietly announced that his good buddy was the guest of honor. Metin blushed as all eyes turned to him. He looked down at his feet, avoiding the women's gaze. Oblivious, Ahmet ceremoniously invited Metin to go first.

"You choose," he said, his arm tight around his shoulders. "Whoever you like best."

Metin lifted his eyes and gingerly eyed each woman. The boys remained silent, also scanning the women, curious about whom he would choose.

* * *

Metin was last to finish. He returned downstairs to find his companions waiting for him at one of the tables in the bar, Ahmet chitchatting with the women. Aram and Cengiz were quiet, daydreaming.

"Let's go," said Ahmet, as soon as he spotted Metin. He nodded to a short man with a scruffy beard who occupied the previously empty bar. The man nodded back. "I paid the bill," said Ahmet as he stood up. He had collected money from his mates soon after Metin made his choice.

They climbed the narrow uphill street back to Cumhuriyet Caddesi.

"So how was it?" shouted Ahmet, over the din of traffic.

"Very good," said Aram, "well worth the money." Aram had chosen a full-figured woman similar to the one Metin selected.

Flustered by Ahmet's offer to have him go first, Metin had chosen hastily, picking the bustiest of the bunch. She wore a pink negligée with a black bra beneath that barely contained the flesh bursting at its edges. She was older than the others, probably in her thirties. Her name was Pembe. As they climbed the stairs, Pembe led the way, holding him by the hand. Metin wondered if this was her real name. It meant pink in Turkish.

"We'll have to do it again," said Cengiz. Metin had not seen his choice. By then he was on the second floor, in a rundown hotel room with Pembe, sitting on the bed, nervously eyeing her as she removed her negligée.

They jaywalked across busier traffic on Cumhuriyet Caddesi and headed back toward Harbiye. As they crossed the old war school Ahmet proclaimed, "Mine was amazing." He had a noticeable bounce in his step as though he were dancing. "The best!"

Ahmet had made a quick selection before Metin departed with Pembe, a choice that Metin found surprising. She was short, slim, and flat-chested. Greasy dark hair fell on her shoulders, framing a light-complexioned, pleasant, but mousy visage. She had kept to herself when the boys entered, sitting at one of the tables with her legs folded under her, preoccupied with her lit cigarette, making no eye contact. Upon Ahmet's call, she rose up, and Metin saw that she was just a teenage girl, an unripe fruit among older, more voluptuous offerings.

"Her name was Yıldız," said Ahmet cheerfully. "She was phenomenal, a real star." *Yıldız* meant star.

Cengiz and Aram gave him a skeptical look. Metin once again stayed ahead of them, hoping to avoid the conversation. He wanted to reach a *dolmuş* station up ahead, and leave his comrades for home. It was past six p.m. and his mother would be wondering where he'd been.

"I slipped it into her ass," Ahmet proclaimed effusively. "She actually let me do it."

The revelation stopped all four boys. Metin turned back, stunned.

"You're a liar," roared Aram.

Ahmet adjusted his glasses and swore to God, *vallahi, billahi*, trying to convince the others that he had actually done it.

"Did she charge you extra?" asked Cengiz, skeptically.

"No way," said Ahmet. "Why would she? She enjoyed it."

They walked on, Metin increasing his pace. He did not want to listen anymore.

"I came twice," he nonetheless heard Ahmet from a distance. "From now on, it's no one but Yıldız."

The boys picked up their pace and caught up to Metin. It was impossible to tune them out.

"I thought about picking her," said Aram. "But I have a weakness for breasts. You know..." he made a gesture, rounding his arms over his own chest. "Big ones."

"You should have." Ahmet was proud. "You missed out on a great performance."

Finally convinced, Aram relented. "Next time, I'll try Yıldız."

Cengiz turned to Metin. "How was yours?"

"Oh, pretty good."

"You sure took your time," Cengiz continued. "Did you come twice too?"

"No. Not really."

In fact, Metin had not climaxed at all. Scared and nervous, he could not even mount an erection. Pembe gave him extended service commensurate with her fee, trying every possible trick to stimulate him, all the while chattering about her life and gossiping about the other girls. It was distracting and annoying. Eventually she gave up, put her panties back on and slipped her pink negligée around her shoulders. She had never removed her bra, leaving her alluring breasts a mystery that by then, Metin did not care to uncover.

"I would have chosen yours," said Aram, addressing Metin, "if you hadn't gone first."

"You would have chosen everyone else's but yours," Ahmet mocked him.

Aram gave Ahmet an obscene gesture with his hand in a fist, the tip of his thumb sticking out between his index and middle finger. They all laughed.

They came upon a Y intersection where a small crowd of people were assembled by the curb, shouting their destinations to *dolmuş* drivers, who slowed down their taxis with their front passenger windows open.

Aram and Cengiz bade them goodbye and continued on to Valikonak toward Nişantaşı. Ahmet and Metin joined the crowd of *dolmuş* seekers, Ahmet destined for Şişli, Metin to Kurtuluş. Just before they, too, began shouting their destinations, Ahmet closed in on Metin.

"Pembe told me what happened," he said.

Metin stared at his friend, wide-eyed in embarrassment. Ahmet gave him a pat on the back.

"Don't worry about it," said Ahmet. "It'll be better next time."

Chapter 22

* * *

Mark luxuriated under the large nozzle, letting the hot, powerful stream massage his body. Invigorated by the evening's events, he felt more alive than he had in years. It was nearly two a.m., but he was wide awake. It had been foolhardy to ignore Mustafa's advice; Kárpáty's, too. But he had survived, and he craved more. He realized now, more than ever, what a rut he had fallen into back home. He turned off the water and stepped out to a marble-tiled bathroom. He took a towel and exited the steamy bathroom into crisp, cool air in the bedroom, the chill further refreshing him.

He flung his wet towel on a chair and examined his clothes. He had thrown them haphazardly onto an armchair. Wrinkled and in disarray, they looked like Ahmet's clothes in the Royal Suite. He picked up his shirt, still damp with perspiration. It stank. He would need to have it laundered.

He plopped on top of the bed naked and picked up the bottle of Lagavulin he had tossed there earlier, stroking its fat neck with his fingers. He examined the regal coat of arms embossed on the side of the bottle, a vertical lion silhouetted under an oversized crown. He would check in with Kárpáty first thing in the morning and see if Mustafa was right, if this bottle could extract information from the cantankerous detective.

Back in the bathroom, the steam had cleared. He brushed his teeth and combed his hair, examining himself in the mirror. He still looked young for being in his fifties, no wrinkles, no jowls, just a bit of gray at the temples. His day-old stubble made him look a bit older. Mark had always favored a clean-shaven look, shunning moustaches or beards that were emblematic of masculinity back in the old country. He thought of Mustafa, with his dark, bushy moustache, and chuckled. He had given Mark quite a ribbing during their drive back to the hotel. Mark knew he deserved it. He had been *acemi*, as they would say in Turkish, green and inept. Annoying as Mustafa had been at first, Mark was growing to like him.

Mark donned one of two luxurious white bath gowns the hotel provided, the same as the one he had found Ahmet in, and checked himself in the mirror again. He did not have Ahmet's athletic physique. He was tall and bony, his torso flat, his legs awkwardly lanky. Despite his shorter stature, Ahmet had always displayed a more alluring masculinity that, together with his charm, was irresistible to women. Mark, on the other hand, had always been uneasy, incapable of breaking the ice with the opposite sex, content to be monogamous. Now, with Angie no longer there, he was resigned to a fate of drought in his love life. Mark tightened the belt of his gown and turned away from the mirror.

He lay on top of the sheets, gown on, legs crossed, and closed his eyes. His thoughts drifted to Olga. He regretted not getting an opportunity for a massage with her. He was surprised at how she had been more attractive in the dim, unpleasant setting of that seedy office. It was her more authentic self, devoid of the fake formality of the spa, that Mark found enticing. There was a hard edge to her that was alluring. Mark wanted to call her but it was too late now. Maybe after daybreak. He began drifting off, images of her shapely figure and sexy legs floating in his head.

* * *

Mark was not quite asleep when the hotel phone jolted him awake. The room lights were still on. The bedside clock read three-ten a.m.

"Mr. Kent, sorry to disturb you at this hour," he heard a cordial receptionist, "but there is someone here at the reception desk who insists that we call you, a police officer."

Still in his hotel gown, Mark reluctantly greeted Kárpáty at the door to his room. The detective looked haggard, bags under his eyes, his face badly in need of a shave. His clothes, the same ones he wore when Mark had seen him in the police station, were rumpled. Kárpáty scanned the room, his eyes briefly resting on the Lagavulin bottle that Mark had placed at the desk near the entrance. Mark gestured toward a chair by the same desk and the inspector sat down.

"What brings you here at this hour?" For once Mark was looking down on the diminutive detective, standing over him.

"Doctor," Kárpáty sounded irked, "do you know that you managed to stir up an entire neighborhood tonight?"

"What do you mean?"

Kárpáty shifted in his seat, uncomfortable with his lower perspective, and lifted himself slightly. Then he changed his mind and sat down.

"Citizens of Budapest," he said in a condescending tone, "do not appreciate gunshots in the middle of the night." He paused and stared deep into Mark's eyes. "This is not America, where that sort of thing is routine." He eyed the Scotch again.

Mark picked up the bottle. "May I offer you a drink?"

Mark searched for a drinking glass among those in his bathroom, welcoming the break it afforded. How was he supposed to answer the inspector? Why was Kárpáty here, questioning him now, rather than at daybreak, during regular working hours, at the police station? He returned with a glass, apologized that he had no ice, and poured the inspector a generous serving. He pulled another chair by the table and sat across from him while Kárpáty savored a first gulp.

"Doctor," said Kárpáty, his tone softer, "I clearly warned you not to get involved in the Radu matter, as I recall."

"Yes."

"Why, then, did you go to *Erzsébetváros* tonight?"

"Where?"

"District VII. The area where you caused a disturbance. What was your interest in Olga Kaminesky?"

The question caught Mark by surprise. How did the inspector know about Olga? The gunshot reports would have been reported to the police from an area far from the Mercy nightclub building where Mark had met Olga. No one had observed him and Olga together. The police could not have discovered his encounter with her through witnesses.

"I was jet-lagged and wide awake. I decided to explore the nightlife of Budapest." Mark tried to sound calm. "Isn't that what you advised me? Enjoy the town?"

Kárpáty gave Mark an annoyed look and took another sip of the drink.

"Do you like it?" asked Mark, hoping to divert the conversation.

"Yes," said the inspector, "very good."

"More?" Mark reached for the bottle and poured another generous serving. "I don't know any Olga."

Kárpáty seemed to be ignoring him, looking at the drink in his glass.

"I was approached by some pretty women at that club, but they were a bit too young for me."

"That club," said Kárpáty, "is not for American tourists."

"So I discovered."

"Doctor," Kárpáty exhorted, "you stirred up a hornet's nest with what you did tonight. Those two men who chased and shot at you are nasty, dangerous characters."

Mark was once again taken aback by the inspector's revelation. How did he know about his pursuers? Almássy tér and the park had been deserted. He could not imagine anyone reliably witnessing what had happened. Some residents in nearby apartments might have spotted the chase, but how could they have identified his pursuers in the dim light of the small square? And so soon. And how did Kárpáty know they were dangerous? Mark considered asking him but held back, waiting to see what else the Scotch might reveal.

Mark pushed the Scotch bottle toward the inspector. "Would you like the whole bottle? Consider it a consolation for disturbing you."

Kárpáty grabbed the bottle and brought it toward him, inspecting the regal label with a glint in his eyes. He shifted his chair away from the table, threw an arm over the back of the chair and crossed his legs. He eyed Mark silently.

"My sincere apologies, Inspector, for any trouble I may have inadvertently caused."

Kárpáty took a last sip of the Scotch and nodded in approval.

"I assure you that I have no intention of playing detective." Mark put on an assuaging attitude, one that worked well with irate colleagues back home. Clearly, Kárpáty was not going to offer anything more. "Now, it is very late and we should all be in bed. I'll be happy to continue this discussion later today at any place of your choosing."

The inspector nodded, his eyes glassy. He grabbed the Scotch and stood up unsteadily, knocking his chair to the floor. Mark rushed him and grabbed his arm as he righted himself. The man smelled of stale tobacco and sweat. He freed himself from Mark and took a couple of steadier steps toward the door as Mark straightened the fallen chair.

"Do you know how Radu died?" asked Mark, walking after him.

"Not yet," said the inspector. "We expect a preliminary forensics report this morning." He sounded listless, with a hint of slur in his speech.

Mark wondered what it would take to pry that report from him once it was available.

The inspector fumbled with the doorknob. Mark opened the door for him. At the hallway, Kárpáty turned around.

"We ran the plate on that vehicle that extracted you. It is a rental. This morning we'll find out who you were collaborating with." Kárpáty belched, then swallowed. "Let's hope, Doctor, that it doesn't turn out to be anyone in any of our wanted lists."

He turned around and began stumbling down the hallway, the bottle of Scotch held low by his waist. Mark called out after him. "Inspector!"

Kárpáty swayed as he turned back.

"My passport. Can I have it back?"

Kárpáty turned around and began walking. Just as Mark's heart was about to sink, he heard the policeman grumble at a distance, but audibly.

"We'll send it to you later today."

* * *

Mark locked and latched the door and collapsed onto his bed, his heart racing. What the hell was that all about?

He ran the encounter over in his mind. What had this seasoned policeman expected to extract from him with a personal visit at an ungodly hour? When Mark had clearly lied to him about not knowing Olga, Kárpáty had not called him on it. Surely he wasn't that gullible. It now occurred to Mark that the inspector's visit was not for the purpose of interrogating him. It was a warning—or a threat— partially placated by the bottle of Scotch. It had been pricy but worth it.

How had Kárpáty discovered so much, so fast? The inspector's last comment in particular, about the license plate of Mustafa's rental, spooked him. Mustafa had been discreet during their flight and had skillfully evaded police attention. The only witnesses who would have noted that plate would have been Mark's pursuers.

Mark checked the clock. It was half past four. Would this night ever end? He needed to talk to Mustafa, let him know that the police were on to him, that something fishy was going on between Kárpáty and the thugs who aimed to kill him.

Mark dialed Mustafa twice and got no answer. He then left a text message: "Late night visit from Inspector Kárpáty, Budapest police. He seems to know too much about our little adventure tonight. Call me when you get this."

He stared at his phone for a couple of minutes, waiting for an answer. None came. He then added another message. "Be careful," he tapped on the screen. "They are on to you."

Chapter 23

* * *

"I'm all right," she said, her voice weary, her Eastern European accent more pronounced. "And you?"

"I barely escaped," said Mark. "You were right. Those guys were out to kill me."

Kárpáty's visit had rattled Mark. He could not sleep, running the night's events over and over in his mind. After debating whether he should or not, he finally took a chance with Olga's number. He was surprised by a prompt answer. Olga was also awake.

"Were they the ones who killed Nicolae?"

"I can't talk about that." She had a pleading tone.

"There are rumors here in the hotel that you were somehow involved." Mark knew he was playing with fire. She could hang up any minute.

"I did not know that this would happen." She sounded despondent, as she had when he met her earlier that night. "I am as upset about it as you are."

She seemed willing to talk. Mark pushed on.

"How come these guys did not harm you?"

"Let's just say that I have my own protection."

Mark didn't doubt that. By now it was obvious that Olga was no ordinary masseuse. He posed another question that had bothered him from the very beginning.

"Why did you give Nicolae a business card with your private number?"

"We were going to meet later, outside the hotel. It is a new number."

She paused for a moment, then added, "That number will be dead soon. I am leaving later today and the phone will be deactivated."

"Where to?"

No answer.

"Are you going back to Romania?"

"I can't tell you. Don't look me up." She had an imploring tone. "If you do again, this time you might really get yourself killed."

"Who is Cesar Kaminesky?" Another burning question that had preoccupied him.

"How do you know about him?" She sounded alarmed.

"His name was on a Romanian X-ray report. Same last name as yours. Are you two related?"

"You know too much," she said. "Don't go there. He is a nasty, dangerous person."

"But are you related to him?"

"In a manner of speaking." She was curt. Mark could sense that they were nearing the end of the conversation.

"Look, I can't talk much more...." Olga's voice was fading.

Mark cut her off. "There is this Inspector. Kárpáty. Hungarian police. He has some peculiar methods of investigation. Do you know him?"

"Yes," she said. "Be careful with him."

"Why?"

"You already sensed it. Trust your instincts." She was getting curt. "I really have to go."

"Olga!" He almost shouted her name, looking at the screen of his phone, hoping she hadn't hung up yet.

"What?"

He breathed a sigh of relief. "Thank you for saving my life tonight. I owe you for that."

"You don't know how much trouble you stirred up by visiting me," she said wearily, echoing Kárpáty's message. "I suggest you leave Budapest as soon as possible. Go back home to America and forget about all this."

It was sensible advice.

"I can't quite yet."

"Suit yourself." She clearly thought he was foolish. "But watch your back," Olga added. "You'll be safe in that hotel. But when you're out, they'll be looking for you."

The message had a chilling effect. Mark did not answer.

"Goodbye now."

Chapter 24

* * *

The sailboat rocked as the wake of a passing tanker hit the coast of Tarabya. Accustomed to this regular disturbance, Metin and Ahmet held on to the foremast and stood steady while they laughed at Leyla, an overweight, awkward girl who splattered onto the deck with a loud thump. Ever vigilant with his camera, Metin steadied himself and took a shot of Leyla, still down, her arms and legs flailing.

Günsu had been sunning prone near the bow and was unaffected by the disturbance. She gave the boys an evil eye as she extended a helping hand to her hapless friend. Leyla was a tack-on that the boys tolerated in order to hang out with Günsu and her better-looking friends.

"I'll go check on Mari," said Ahmet. Mari, the prettiest of Günsu's friends, was the only other one there. She was inside when the wave hit, resting in the aft cabin behind the galley.

Günsu examined Leyla's thigh. There was a small cut in a spot Leyla could not see, bleeding. She asked Metin, still by the mast, to quit taking pictures and fetch a first-aid kit. Metin obediently headed inside, to the galley.

Blinded with the sudden change from bright sunlight to dim galley, Metin groped for the first-aid kit. He wasn't sure where it was. He heard Ahmet giggling in the aft cabin, its door closed. As the cabinets of the galley became more visible, Metin searched again, to no avail. Another, smaller wave rocked the boat and he stumbled toward the aft cabin, barely avoiding a fall.

Metin had never needed to search for a first-aid kit in Latif Bey's sailboat. The sixteen-meter vessel was anchored at the small, scenic cove of Tarabya, along the European shore of the Bosporus. An imposing white building curved along the seashore at the north end of the cove, the Tarabya Hotel. The cove served as a summer playground for Ahmet and his friends. Metin presumed that Latif Bey sailed the vessel, but on lazy summer afternoons when he visited with Ahmet, the boat was free of adults and always anchored. The teenagers sunned themselves on deck, played games, and swam in the crisp waters of the cove, safe from the steady sea traffic of the Bosporus.

His search having failed, Metin decided to ask Ahmet about the first-aid kit. He opened the aft cabin door and stuck his head in. Ahmet was lying on his side on a small round bed staring at Mari, who lay next to him in her bikini. A striking dark-haired, dark-eyed Armenian, Mari was short and shapely, with wide hips and an ample bosom. Ahmet lavished much attention on her but so far, he had not managed to break through her wall of virtue. Mari stared at the ceiling, seemingly uninterested in Ahmet's chatter. Ahmet leaned in closer to whisper something to her ear. Neither noticed Metin poking through the door.

Presently Metin heard footsteps in the galley. "Where have you been?" he heard Günsu ask impatiently.

Before he could answer, he felt Günsu's one-piece swimming suit pressing against his back as she pushed the aft cabin door wide open. Metin almost fell forward into the cabin. Ahmet and Mari sat up and looked toward the door, surprised.

For a brief moment no one spoke. Günsu stared beyond Metin, into the cabin, her face downcast. Her body was still pressed against his, squeezing him toward the door, giving Metin an awkward thrill. He turned to look at her and admired Günsu's dark eyes up close, her slim eyebrows upturned. She had a strange smell of lilacs and suntan lotion, intoxicating nonetheless. She parted her lips as if about to say something, but didn't. Instead, she abruptly pulled back and rushed out of the galley, back to the deck.

Metin steadied himself against the doorknob as another wave rolled by. He still felt Günsu's swimming suit on his skin and her fragrance in his nostrils. Ahmet and Mari continued to stare curiously.

Metin finally snapped out of it. "Where is the damn first-aid kit?"

Afterwards Metin and Ahmet were back at the foremast, watching Günsu and Mari tend to Leyla's injured rump with tincture of iodine and a bandage.

"She looks nice in a swimming suit, doesn't she?" Ahmet whispered into Metin's ear.

Metin examined Günsu, so slim and girlish compared with Mari's voluptuous curves. Günsu abruptly shook her head every so often to get her straight, black bangs out of her eyes, a gesture that Metin loved. "Yes, she does."

"Damn," Ahmet exclaimed. "She won't give me the time of day."

Ahmet grinned. Mari may have been a tease, resolute with her barriers, but Ahmet did not mind. He enjoyed the chase.

Metin wondered whether Ahmet was oblivious to Günsu, or if he was just pretending.

* * *

They all sat on the aft divan that curved with the stern of the yacht, savoring *helva*, round wafers the size of 75 rpm records, containing sweetened sesame paste within paper-thin pastry. Veli, a historic shop across the street from the marina, served excellent ice cream with it, a *helva* sandwich.

"Thanks for fetching these," said Ahmet to Metin, wiping off melted vanilla ice cream streaming down his chin, as he leaned on a nearby table that stretched across the divan.

Metin nodded and did not answer. Fetching ice cream was usually his errand. He stared beyond a line of boats and yachts moored along the cove, at the majestic Tarabya Hotel curving out of the cove along the coastline. He took out his camera and shot photos of the hotel, ignoring his own *helva*.

He then turned his lens on the girls, who placed their arms on each other's shoulders and posed, smiling.

"Nice camera," said Leyla, her lips black with melted chocolate. "He is so sophisticated, isn't he?" she said to her girlfriends. Her ungainly fall was all but forgotten. Metin saw Leyla's admiring eyes in his viewfinder. He turned his lens on Günsu.

"And so gifted, too," Leyla continued. "Don't you think Metin is the brightest boy in our school?"

Ahmet laughed. "That's not saying much. Compared to you girls, us boys are all fuck-ups."

"That's right," Metin confirmed. "None of us could even come close to Günsu." He gazed at Günsu, who stayed silent. She did not need to respond. Metin's statement was common knowledge.

Mari changed the subject. "How are your plans for America coming along?"

This was the summer before Lise III, their senior year, and Metin had already begun investigating universities in the U.S.

"So far all I have is information. I'll be taking two tests this fall, the SAT and TOEFL, and then I'll apply."

"What about you?" Günsu asked Ahmet.

Ahmet shrugged his shoulders. "Textiles," he said, "somewhere in England, most likely Manchester." His fate was pre-determined.

Günsu turned to Metin. "I hear it is hard for foreign nationals to get into medical school in America." They all knew about Metin's desire to become a doctor.

"Yes," Metin confirmed. "I've already heard that from the attaché in the American Embassy. I think I'll shoot for a degree in biochemistry and hope for the best afterwards." He paused and stared at his uneaten *helva,* ice cream melting at its edges. "That is, assuming I get accepted somewhere in America."

"Oh, of course you will," said Leyla. "And we will miss you when you're gone." She turned to her friends. "Won't we?"

Günsu nodded. Mari stared at the hills of Asia on the opposite shore of the Bosporus. "You're doing the right thing," she said to Metin thoughtfully. "Your future will be so much brighter than if you stayed here in Turkey."

The comment gave everyone pause. Metin detected a tone of jealousy in her statement.

* * *

"Drinks," said Ahmet. "We need drinks." He looked at Metin and Günsu. "Can you two fetch some?"

They were inside again, in the galley, peering into the small refrigerator where Latif Bey kept mostly beer. They managed to scrounge up two Coca-Cola bottles to share among all. Günsu searched the cabinets for cups. Metin came behind her and pointed to where they were. When she turned back, they were face to face under the low ceiling of the dim galley. She paused and waited for Metin to give way. Metin stood still, in a fit of fearful excitement, immobilized by her scent.

Günsu waited patiently, her dark eyes on his. Metin mustered enough courage to lean in and touch his lips onto hers. It was a light, timid kiss, and for a split second she let him.

"Günsu," he whispered.

She placed her palm against his mouth.

"Please," she said, and wiggled away from him.

As she ascended the stairs to the deck with cups in hand, she turned back. "Bring the Cokes."

Disappointed, Metin was relieved nonetheless that she had stopped him from further embarrassing himself. It was hopeless anyway. Günsu was beyond reach.

Out on deck he found a commotion on the gangway leading to the boat. Latif Bey had stepped on deck with a stunningly pretty young woman whom the teens immediately recognized. A man dressed in a faux navy uniform followed after them, his dark captain's cap pulled low on his forehead.

Latif looked dapper in a double-breasted, navy-blue jacket with a golden silk scarf tastefully bulging from the open collar of his white shirt. A newly lit cigarette extended from a long, dark holder between his lips. He took a puff and nodded hello to everyone. The young woman, a well-coiffed blonde whose hair curled right above her shoulders, looked around the yacht, fluttering her long eyelids.

"Hello, Father." Ahmet was peppy. "These are my friends." He introduced the girls, each of whom received an exaggerated bow from Latif.

Latif recognized Metin and shook his hand. The blonde had moved over to the opposite side of the boat and observed the scenery, leaning on a low gunwale, Latif's captain a few paces behind her.

"Is my son treating you well?" asked Latif.

The girls affirmed effusively. Even Mari, captivated by Latif's aura, shed her supercilious attitude.

"Is that Güneş Yumlu?" asked Günsu, composing herself, pointing to Latif's guest.

Güneş Yumlu was a famous singer and starlet in Turkish movies. Her baby-doll face regularly graced the covers of gossip magazines and tabloid papers.

"Yes," said Latif, taking his spent cigarette out of its holder and extinguishing it beneath his foot. He turned to Ahmet. "I am afraid I'll have to take over the boat. We'll set sail soon."

"Sure." Ahmet was not annoyed. "Shall we go to the movies?" he proposed to the girls. "I'll drive."

Ahmet and the girls hastened below deck to gather their belongings. Metin stayed on deck, near Latif Bey, who stared at the three girls as they went in.

"So, which one of them is Ahmet's girl?" he asked Metin.

Metin pointed to Mari. "That one," he said. "But she plays hard-to-get."

Latif examined Mari's shapely body. "H'mmm." He seemed to approve.

Metin then pointed to Günsu, who had bent over as she climbed down the steps. "That one," he said, "is in love with Ahmet."

Latif watched Günsu as she disappeared. "I prefer the other one," he said firmly.

Güneş Yumlu returned and placed her arm in Latif's. She smiled at Metin. She had a sexy gap between her two front teeth. As Latif introduced her, Metin maintained his composure and did not gush. This seemed to go over well with the famous star.

"Have you seen me perform?" she asked Metin.

The three girls had gathered their stuff and were bunched a few paces away. They watched with fascination as Metin carried on with the celebrity.

"No," said Metin.

Güneş Hanım turned to Latif. "Maybe you should bring him to Maksim some time."

Maksim was a swank night club in Taksim Square that booked the most famous singers. Metin's parents did not pursue a night life and did not frequent such places. Metin knew of the club mainly from magazines and gossip columns.

"I will do that," promised Latif as he petted Metin's hair in a fatherly gesture. He then approached the girls, who loudly gushed as they were introduced to the starlet.

Ahmet came up from the opposite side and stood by Metin as he waited for the girls.

"What's your dad doing with Güneş Yumlu?" asked Metin.

"Who knows," said Ahmet impassively. "Fucking her, I hope."

Chapter 25

* * *

Miruna sipped her cappuccino, eyes downcast. Her bleached hair was pulled into a tight bun, starkly revealing its dark roots. Her carry-on luggage stood next to her with a dark leather Hermès purse on top. She looked up at him.

"He was scared," she said in Turkish. She wore glasses with stylish brown rims that exaggerated her hazel eyes. They were clear now, no tears.

"Of what?"

Mark's curiosity about Ahmet's Romanian wife was momentarily overcome by her beauty. She wore almost no makeup, just a hint of lipstick on her fleshy lips. She stroked the edge of her coffee cup with a long, red fingernail as she pondered his question. Despite her gloom, she exuded radiant sex appeal.

"I don't know," she said. "He wouldn't tell me."

Mark took a sip of espresso and tried, in vain, to release himself from her captivating presence. She was impossibly young.

"One minute things were fine, the next, he was in a hurry, packing. He told me he'd be going away for a few days, he wasn't sure where. He'd contact me later about his whereabouts."

Mark was thankful for her heavily accented Turkish, her only feature that drew away from her magnetism.

They sat at an upstairs table for four, just the two of them, by a terrace that overlooked the first-floor café counter and small dining area. A prominent gold painting depicting a stylized African woman topped an equal-sized blackboard announcing the day's specials on a wall between the counter and terrace. It was an eclectic, modern café inside a classic Parisian building.

Mark looked at a small, rectangular menu card, few items, all in Hungarian. Toward the bottom, between the price list and food selection, somebody had painted a colorful Tinkerbell in miniature, buxom and curvaceous, with luxuriant crimson hair, wearing a green miniskirt and green boots, rays radiating from her wand. Mark was hungry but didn't know what to order.

"Then I got a call from the hotel. The day after he left." A tear ran down her left cheek, slowly curving around her nostril. Mark had the urge to reach over and wipe it, but he held back.

"Do you want something to eat?" Mark turned the menu toward her.

Miruna shook her head no. She eyed the menu. She noticed Tinkerbell and her lips parted into a slight smile.

"The concierge at my hotel said that this place is good. Popular with locals." Mark was awkwardly trying small talk.

He had slept little, yet he was not tired. At around eight in the morning he had dropped in at Kollázs for coffee and, running the events of the past day in his mind, had remembered that this morning was his only chance to meet Miruna. She had been agreeable, but was checking out of her hotel, waiting for a ride to the airport. She suggested that they meet at the Csiga Café, near her hotel. Cognizant of Olga's admonition, Mark was apprehensive about leaving his hotel, but nothing untoward had happened on the taxi ride over.

"I am not hungry," Miruna said.

Downstairs, a steady stream of customers flowed in and out, creating a background of Hungarian buzz that clashed with the muffled Turkish voices on the terrace. Two young men, college students by their appearance, climbed the staircase, their backpacks loose in their hands as they chatted amiably. Mark and Miruna stopped and eyed them cautiously. They were both on edge. Though it remained unspoken between them, they both knew their meeting would have met with disapproval by Kárpáty, and perhaps by Ahmet's killer.

"He asked to meet me," whispered Mark. "Here in Budapest."

A waitress followed the young men up the stairs. She looked like another college student, wearing a tightly wound white apron around her waist.

"Do you know why?" Mark continued.

"No," said Miruna. "But he talked often of getting away from here." She paused. "Romania, I mean." She did not notice the waitress approaching their table. "He dreamed of taking us to America. Leaving it all and starting new."

"Don't we all," said the waitress in Turkish, in an accent Mark couldn't place.

Mark and Miruna looked at her, startled. She was tall and had round hips that emphasized her apron. Her dark hair, braided on both sides, gave her a childish look even though she had to be in her twenties. She held up a notepad and pen.

"Pardon," she said, as she realized the effect she had caused.

Mark eyed her curiously, then gazed at Miruna. *What am I doing here*, he thought, *with this young woman*? Did he really think he could unlock Ahmet's secrets? He was out of his mind.

"*Nerelisiniz*?" he asked the waitress. *Where are you from?*

She was from Rize, on the Black Sea. Mark now recognized her accent. Her name was Zeynep. Could she recommend something to eat?

Zeynep tapped *vöröslencseragu citromos rizzsel* on the menu, slightly above Tinkerbell. "Red chicken with lemony rice," she explained. "It is good."

Miruna ordered another cappuccino, ignoring the recommendation.

"What was he like?" asked Mark after Zeynep left. He had ordered the dish.

Miruna took her glasses off and looked deep into his eyes. He avoided her gaze, following the waitress down the stairs.

"He was funny," she said, "charming."

Mark met her eyes, shrunken without the glasses, yet somehow more hypnotic. He regretted asking the question.

"He was a great lover."

There it was again. First Olga, now her.

Miruna teared up.

"Do you know anything about his business?" Mark handed her his cloth napkin. She sobbed and buried her face in the clean white cloth. "Was he involved in some kind of medical venture?" He knew he was pushing his luck.

Miruna put the napkin down and tried to regain her composure. "He was a good businessman," she said. "He provided well for us."

Us! Mark realized that there was more than just Ahmet and Miruna. He was embarrassed for not asking earlier.

She produced photos, a young boy with glasses, spitting image of Ahmet, no more than ten, and a little girl about three or four years, cute, with a toothy smile, resembling her mother. Miruna broke into more sobs.

"What are their names?"

"Nazlı," she said, pointing to the girl. Then the boy: "Latif."

Now it was Mark's turn to tear up. It saddened him to see the connection between this boy and his grandfather, with Ahmet, who should still have been between them, now gone.

"Did you meet his father, Latif Bey?" he asked Miruna. He used the honorific, *Bey,* to indicate his respect for the old man.

"Yes," she said, still staring at her photos. "He visited us regularly. He is old now, walks with a cane."

So Ahmet had not completely cut off his Turkish connections when he disappeared. It was a surprising revelation, but Mark was glad to hear it. Mark had fond memories of Latif.

Zeynep returned with Mark's food and Miruna's coffee. "*Buyrun,*" she said politely, *please help yourselves.*

The chicken was good. Mark stopped speaking and attacked his plate. Miruna drifted off, sipping her coffee, examining the African woman on the painting in front of them.

"What will you do now?" Mark wiped his lips. His plate was totally clean.

"I am not sure," said Miruna. "Move back to Bucharest, maybe. Closer to my family. Nicolae had moved us to Constanta after we got married."

Mark didn't know where Constanta was. "Why did he do that?" he asked nonetheless.

"He thought we'd be safer there. He kept a small apartment in Bucharest where he tended to his business."

Mark was certain that Ahmet conducted more than just business in that apartment. He kept the thought to himself. "Have you considered moving to Turkey? Latif would be delighted to be closer to his grandchildren."

Miruna put her glasses back on and pondered the question. "No, but that's a thought. I'll keep it in mind." She looked at him, her hazel eyes once again bright behind the spectacles.

Loud footsteps on the staircase interrupted them. Miruna looked behind her toward a swarthy figure approaching in cumbersome steps. "My ride is here."

"Iancu," she said, "this is Mark, Nicolae's old friend from Turkey."

Iancu gave Mark a suspicious look under thick, dark eyebrows.

Mark recognized the name from Ahmet's iPhone screen, the two incoming calls in the Royal Suite before he discovered Ahmet's body. He was older, in his sixties maybe, dark complexioned, his face deeply creased, charcoal eyes sunken behind a bulbous nose. He wore a well-fitting business suit that lessened his girth, with a white, well starched shirt open at the collar. Thick dark chest hair protruded from the opening. He extended a stout hand to Mark, with short stubby fingers, ornate cufflinks on his wrist. He wore a prominent gold ring with an inlaid diamond on his pinky.

"Iancu is Nicolae's executive administrator," said Miruna, still in Turkish, as Mark exchanged a firm handshake with him.

"*Enchanté*. I am Iancu Negrescu." He was ceremonious in his French.

He looked at his watch and picked up Miruna's Hermès bag, handing it to her. "We'd better get going." His Turkish was better than Miruna's, with only a slight accent.

Miruna sat down and took out a hand mirror from her bag. She examined herself coquettishly, licking a finger and rubbing an invisible smudge off the edge of her lip.

Mark tapped Zeynep, who was tending to the two college students nearby, and asked her for the bill.

"We have some time still, don't we?" Miruna asked Iancu, facing him through her mirror.

"Not if you're checking this." Iancu had a deep baritone voice; he sounded impatient.

Miruna put her mirror away and closed the purse. She turned to Iancu and nodded her head toward Mark. "Mark is the one who discovered Nicolae's body." She stood up and straightened her skirt.

Iancu stared intently at Mark, surprised by Miruna's announcement. "Would you like to come with us?" he asked Mark. "We have room in the car."

"Yes," Miruna agreed. "Come and see me off at the airport."

"Why not?" said Mark. "I have nothing else to do."

"Iancu can bring you back downtown afterwards. He is staying here for a few days," she said.

Mark threw a few bills onto the table, hoping that he had tipped adequately. He scrambled down the stairs to catch up with Iancu, who was carrying the suitcase with Miruna in tow.

At the curb was a dark Mercedes, engine humming. Iancu opened the back door for Miruna and Mark. He then settled into the front passenger seat and gave orders to the chauffeur in Romanian.

Chapter 26

* * *

The hazy, overcast Thursday morning had turned into steady rain. The wipers of the Mercedes beat a steady rhythm as Iancu returned from the airport terminal and took Miruna's spot on the back seat. He didn't have any overcoat and the shoulders of his suit were damp. He combed his thick, dark hair with stubby fingers, shaking rainwater off. He asked Mark where he wanted to go, in Turkish.

"Gresham," Iancu ordered the driver, tapping him on the shoulder with his damp right hand. A drop of water glistened his gold pinky ring. The drop highlighted sparkles from a diamond set atop, at the widest part of the ring. It covered almost half of his chunky finger. The driver, a young man with a flat-top crew cut, nodded.

"If you'd rather, we can speak English," Iancu said ceremoniously, his accent distinctly British with a touch of what Mark suspected was Romanian.

"That would be better, thanks," replied Mark.

"So," said Iancu, "you and Nicolae were old friends?"

Mark's phone chimed. It was Mustafa. *Finally*, thought Mark with a sense of relief.

"Where are you?" Mustafa texted. "I came by the hotel and you weren't there."

"Can't talk, will be back at hotel soon," tapped Mark into his phone. He then looked at Iancu. "Yes. Back in Istanbul, many years ago."

The car was taking a convoluted way to downtown that Mark, having traversed Üllői út twice, did not recognize. It made one turn after another, through narrow side streets.

His phone chimed again with a text from Mustafa. "Look me up when you get there."

"And you," Mark asked Iancu. "What did you do for him?"

Iancu sat erect, his expression flinty, his fingers clasped in his lap, partially concealed under the girth protruding from his open jacket. The pinky ring peeked out, shining.

"I managed his various businesses," he said, looking straight ahead. He then turned to his window, examining raindrops that raced back in speeding lines.

Mark was dying to know what those businesses were. But he had a more urgent question. "Do you know what he wanted from me? Why he summoned me here?"

"He wanted you to get him into America," said Iancu. His deep-set eyes were almost invisible beneath his bushy eyebrows. He had broad furrows on his forehead. "He needed to get away from here."

"Here?" Mark was stupefied.

"I mean Romania, Turkey, you know..."

"Eastern Europe?"

"Yes."

Mark was confounded that Ahmet might expect him to somehow smuggle him into the U.S. Once again, there were too many questions popping into his mind all at once.

"Why?" asked Mark.

"We received a threat. He did not feel safe here. He wanted to escape first, then relocate his family."

"What kind of threat?"

"A vague one; we weren't sure. But it was real. I can't go into the details."

"It was real all right!" Mark thought he may have sounded mocking. He checked Iancu for a reaction. Iancu nodded in agreement, his expression somber. Mark wondered whether the man had any sense of humor. "I saw your name on Ahmet's iPhone the night I found him dead. You called him twice."

Iancu's stoic demeanor betrayed a fleeting glance of surprise before he recovered himself and said, "Tell me what happened."

Mark had assumed this was why Iancu had invited him to his car. There had been a distinct change in his attitude when Miruna told him that Mark had discovered Nicolae's body.

Mark recounted the events of his arrival to Budapest and his discovery of Ahmet in the Royal Suite. He left Mustafa out of it. Iancu listened attentively.

"I think we're being followed." The chauffeur interrupted them in English. He had made himself invisible but was obviously listening to their conversation.

They were on a wide boulevard, three lanes each way, separated by a wide green median in which yellow trams ran along rails set into concrete. Iancu calmly turned and looked behind.

"Where are we?" he asked.

"Károly körút, on our way to Erzsébet Square."

"Which car?"

"The silver BMW."

Mark turned back, too, and spotted the car several car lengths behind.

"It's appeared, disappeared and reappeared since we left the café," said the chauffeur.

"Pull to the side," ordered Iancu. "Let's see what it will do."

"I think they may be following *me*," said Mark. "Do you have any reason why anyone would follow you?"

Iancu hastily turned to Mark, eyeing him dubiously. "I don't know," he said firmly. "Anything is possible."

The chauffeur pulled to the curb and turned off the engine. The BMW sped by, two shadowy silhouettes in the front seats, impossible to make out.

"Let's stay here and see what happens," said Iancu.

They sat quietly, listening to the patter of the rain on the car roof, the windshield misting. The driver lowered his window a bit and observed the passing traffic.

"Why do you think you're being followed?" asked Iancu.

"Have you heard of an Olga Kaminesky?"

Iancu mulled over the name.

"Sexy blonde, late thirties, tall, big boobs," offered Mark helpfully. "Masseuse."

"Sounds like an Olga I knew years ago," Iancu replied. "What about her?"

"She was at the same hotel, at Gresham Palace. She gave Ahmet a massage before he died."

Iancu leaned to check the passing traffic from the driver's open window while pondering what he had just heard.

"How do you know all that?" he asked.

"Long story," said Mark. "Let's just say that I was curious about her, and last night I set out to look for her. Two guys pursued me there and shot at me. I think they might still be looking for me."

Iancu looked Mark over, up and down, as if he were seeing him for the first time, his forehead more furrowed, thick eyebrows converging to conceal his eyes.

"Aren't you," Iancu asked, baffled, "a doctor?"

"Yes." Mark betrayed a slight smile, pleased with the impression he was making.

"There they go," said the driver. The silver BMW slowed down as it came aside the Mercedes, then sped off.

"I bet they won't do that again," said the driver.

"Pull out now!" Iancu ordered. "And go slow."

The chauffeur did as ordered and soon plunged into more side streets.

"Did you meet this Olga?" asked Iancu.

"Yes," said Mark, and countered with his own question. "What do *you* know about her?"

Iancu shook his head side-to-side. "Nicolae," he said, "was into too many women. Olga was one he should have screwed once and left alone."

"How can you?" Mark quipped. "Have you seen her?"

Iancu's meaty lips parted, a hint of a smile, acknowledging Mark's point. "I haven't seen her in years," Iancu said. "I didn't know she was in Budapest."

"How did Ahmet hook up with her?"

"She was a two-bit prostitute, a very good one, very attractive," said Iancu. "Nicolae," he paused and shook his head again, "he liked prostitutes."

"Yes, I know," said Mark. "He was that way in Istanbul too, when I knew him."

Mark recalled Varol. He had never returned there, but Ahmet had. Ahmet became a regular with Yıldız, who in turn developed into a legend at the school as the best Varol girl, thanks to Ahmet's incessant remarks. Sometime later Ahmet told him that the working women at Varol began jokingly referring to Yıldız as Ahmet's wife.

"They saw each other on and off for a while. Then Olga disappeared." Iancu turned to the back window as he recounted his story. "I don't know what happened to her. They said she had found a rich guy who married her."

Iancu scrutinized the back window again. He clasped his hands and in a formal tone said, "I am fortunate that I do not have the same inclinations as Nicolae. I am happily married. Just one wife."

He paused and let his message sink in.

"There was no way to keep track of all the women Nicolae bedded," added Iancu.

"Did Miruna know all this?"

"How could she not!" said Iancu, turning forward again. He addressed the driver in English. "I think you lost them."

"I think so too," he replied.

"Well done, Dumitru." Iancu patted the chauffeur's shoulder.

He then turned to Mark. "Miruna had no choice but put up with it."

"So did Ahmet's mother, with Latif Bey."

"Latif," said Iancu. His somber expression broke. "That's another story," he chuckled. He had a coarse, throaty laugh.

"How is he?" asked Mark. "I have fond memories of him. A very charismatic guy."

"He finally settled down," said Iancu. "He lives with a young woman, Romanian, from Brasov. She has been good to him." He chuckled again. It sounded like a snort. "She may be the only woman Latif has not cheated on."

Mark pondered this news. Father and son, both with Romanian women. Could Latif also have been in business with Ahmet?

The Mercedes emerged from a small side street and circled Erzsébet Square. Mark realized they were close to the hotel.

"Listen," he said to Iancu. "There is someone else here, a Turkish guy who is also embroiled in this mess. He might be helpful to you."

"Who?"

When Mark uttered Mustafa's name, it clearly did not register with Iancu. Mark told him Mustafa was a former policeman, now a private agent. Iancu nodded.

"He was looking for Ahmet for another reason," Mark said. "Hired by Meltem, Ahmet's Istanbul wife."

"Oh, yes. That woman!" Iancu was vexed.

"Anyhow. Mustafa's mission was derailed by Ahmet's death, but he is still here and he might also get targeted by these guys who pursued me, or the police. He is stuck in this whether he likes it or not."

"What was his mission?"

Mark briefly summarized Mustafa's account, without getting into how he had tracked Ahmet down. "I think we need to meet, the three of us."

The rain had become heavier, loudly pelting the window and roof. Mark watched a blurry silhouette of the Chain Bridge slowly pass by his window.

"Tell me again," said Iancu, "what did Nicolae look like when you found him?"

Mark described the scene in the bathroom, Ahmet in the tub. Iancu listened attentively.

"How do you think they killed him?" asked Iancu.

"I don't know," said Mark. "But there will be a preliminary forensics report available today. I might be able to get some information from the police."

The driver pulled up in front of Gresham Palace. The rain had eased up and was no longer pounding the car. A doorman formally opened Mark's side of the car door.

"Just a minute," Mark said to the doorman and closed the door. He turned to Iancu. "Let's exchange phone numbers. I'll let you know if I find out anything."

As they quietly tapped into their phones, Mark said, "One more thing."

Iancu did not look up.

"About Olga."

Iancu finished tapping and examined his phone screen.

"This rich person she married. Could that be a guy named Cesar? Cesar Kaminesky?"

Iancu looked up from his phone, eyebrows elevated, eyes wide. He had small, beady eyes, like those of a bear. For a moment he was speechless.

"How do you know about *him*?"

"Ahmet contacted me with a message hidden in a radiology report from Romania. His name was on it as the patient. I put two and two together. You know, Kaminesky..." Mark savored the stunned expression on Iancu's face.

"I asked Olga about it," he continued. "She said they were related, but wouldn't tell me how."

Mark opened the door. Iancu extended his hand to him, his pinky winged wide with the gold ring. "You are a clever man," he said. "No wonder you are a doctor."

Mark shook his hand firmly. *Yeah, right*, he thought, recalling Mustafa's opposite remark after he had rescued him.

The doorman appeared, ready with an open umbrella.

"Who is he?" asked Mark. "Cesar."

Iancu was staring beyond Mark, thoughtful, trying to make sense of what he'd just heard. "A go-between," he said. "Another one I have not seen in years."

As Mark exited, Iancu added. "Let me look into it. I can tell you more later, when we meet again."

Mark nodded to the doorman and together they walked a few paces to the entry steps, the umbrella protecting them both. It was a luxury he didn't need, but enjoyed anyway. As he stepped up to the magnificent entrance, he noticed a familiar car parked up ahead, toward the end of the driveway. It was a white subcompact Audi with red diagonal stripes on its trunk door, a thin, barely perceptible light bar across the roof and a blue stripe at the top of the trunk with the word *Rendőrség* inscribed in it.

Could it be the same one that had taken him to the District V police station the morning before?

Chapter 27

* * *

Metin sat across from Mustafa Bey in the Turkish headmaster's small second-floor office overlooking the front yard. School was in session and the building was eerily quiet. Metin had been summoned just after a break, when class began. He'd never been to the headmaster's office and surveyed his surroundings with apprehension, avoiding eye contact with the fearsome principal.

Mustafa Bey stared at him through thick eyeglasses under bushy eyebrows. He was short and stocky, well groomed, his tie perfectly knotted, his collar stiff and white. He held his hairy hands folded atop his desk.

"We have reason to believe," he said with measured gravitas, "that you might be involved with a group of misfits...." He stopped, sizing up Metin's reaction thus far.

Metin knew what this was about. He tried suppressing butterflies in his stomach as he shifted in his chair. He searched for a plausible answer. He felt his cheeks burn and cursed himself for being so easily prone to flushing. It always gave him away.

Mustafa Bey continued. "I hope to God it isn't so."

The year before, in Lise I, Mustafa Bey had taken notice of Metin after he successfully recited a lengthy poem in Turkish Literature that had flummoxed the rest of the class. Now Metin's lofty standing was about to plummet.

"I am sorry," Metin mumbled. "They needed help."

Mustafa Bey closed his eyes and raised his head up in a pained expression. Metin could not bear to watch him. Worried as he was about his punishment, he was more concerned with how his parents would react to the news. He had never been involved in even minor infractions. Now this?

This was big. And he had just confessed.

* * *

It was Ahmet who had gotten him into it, soon after their Lise II year began. Ahmet called him late one afternoon, after school ended, and asked that they meet in a sandwich shop in Osmanbey. Metin hastily left his apartment, inventing an excuse for his mother, who was preparing dinner.

"You won't believe this," said Ahmet, his mouth full of grilled cheese panini. They sat on high stools by the picture windows of the shop. "There's a group of kids who have figured out how to break into Mr. Burritt's office."

The Welsh chemistry teacher, a bald, stocky man with a bombastic disposition, was apparently unaware of the caper. Ahmet continued breathlessly, flecks of food flying out of his mouth, "They stole the upcoming exam questions, the ones we have next week."

Metin was not surprised with the news. Cheating was common, the methods used ever so inventive. He had heard through the grapevine that some math questions had been similarly stolen from Mr. Surry's office, but had not been able to confirm the rumors.

"This *tost* is good," said Ahmet, holding his half-eaten panini up to his mate. "You want a bite?"

"No," said Metin, "Mom's making dinner." He put his Coke bottle down. "So who are they?"

"Yusuf and Hagop."

It figured. Starting from their *Hazırlık* years, those two had received countless beatings and reprimands. How they survived without expulsion was a mystery.

"How did they manage to do this?" he asked.

"Some upperclassmen did it last year and got away with it. They passed on the know-how to our class."

"What upperclassmen?"

"It's better that you not know."

"So why are you telling me this?"

Ahmet swallowed his food and took a big gulp of *ayran*, a yogurt drink, his expression getting serious. "You see," he said, wiping wet yogurt from his upper lip with his hand, "they managed to get in and out of Burritt's office undetected."

Metin realized what was coming and he said it first. "But they don't know the answers to the chemistry questions, right?"

"You got it." Ahmet became bubbly. "You are so smart."

"Wait a minute." Metin held his hand up.

Ahmet nodded and smiled.

"No, way!" Metin was emphatic. "I am not doing it."

"But you're the only one we can think of who can solve this problem."

"Are you in on this too?"

"Nooo...." Ahmet denied theatrically. "There is no way I am breaking into any office, like a thief."

"Who exactly did these mysterious upperclassmen first approach with this information?"

Ahmet shook an index finger at his mate. "I am telling you, buddy. You're the smartest." He threw Metin a charming, toothy grin.

Metin could not help but smile back. Ahmet relaxed. "Yes," he said. "Those upperclassmen came to *me*. I put Yusuf up to the job."

Metin shook his head in disapproval.

"Call me a go-between, a facilitator," shrugged Ahmet.

"*Simsar*?" asked Metin. The word meant broker in Turkish.

"Yeah," said Ahmet out loud, as if the word were an epiphany to him. "Once you're on board, the team will be complete."

They took sips from their drinks.

"Chemistry is really rough," said Ahmet. It was a compulsory class for all students. "I am barely pulling a fifty in the class." They were graded on a numerical scale, from zero to one hundred. Fifty was the minimum passing grade. "You're pulling what, seventy?"

"Eighty-five," corrected Metin. With a future interest in medicine, Metin had plunged himself into this challenging subject with greater enthusiasm than his mates.

"See? You're the only one who gets it."

"There *are* others."

"What, the girls?"

Metin understood Ahmet's problem. There were plenty of girls who excelled academically, Günsu foremost among them. But none would ever participate in such a scheme.

"Look, all you have to do is give us—give *me*—the answers." He shot another toothy smile. "Me, your good buddy."

Metin was silent, hesitant.

"You don't have to have anything to do with those hoodlums, Yusuf and Hagop," Ahmet added solemnly.

* * *

"Name all the noble gases in the Periodic Table and their atomic numbers."

Metin shook his head in disbelief. This was an incredibly easy question. They were all in column eighteen of the Periodic Table, the rightmost one. Metin had practically memorized all the elements of the table. Helium 2; Neon 10; Argon 18; Krypton, Xenon and Radon, 36, 54, 86.

The question didn't even ask why they were called *noble*, a subject that intrigued him more. These elements were all highly unreactive, except under certain extreme conditions, reluctant to enter relationships, so to speak, with other elements. Whoever coined the term *noble* must have thought that these elements were reminiscent of European aristocracy with similar proclivities. To Metin, the inert nature of the eighteenth-column elements was more akin to the girls in his school who were impossible to date.

Metin glanced away from the stolen exam questions and thought about Günsu for a moment. She was a noble gas, all right. The only element she seemed keen to relate to was Ahmet. Would the two of them as a pair constitute an "extreme condition"? He chuckled and shook his head again, this time in resignation.

Metin would forever remain an ordinary element, lost in the multitude that populated the Periodic Table. There was no chance for him to interact with, say, argon, number eighteen. Argon fascinated him. Even though it was the third most abundant gas in the Earth's atmosphere, more common than water vapor, very few knew about it, and they were mostly science geeks like himself.

Metin cleared his thoughts and plunged back to the test. It consisted mostly of questions that required rote memorization, like the one on noble gases. But there were a few exceptional ones that required math equations, and these he found more challenging. He managed to solve them with some effort. He figured he would have gotten seventy-five without the advance questions; now he could get a hundred.

* * *

Metin had warned Ahmet that none of them should turn in a perfect exam. It would invite suspicion, especially if those two fuck-ups who stole the test, and who were so far failing the class, did so.

It all went according to plan. Mr. Burritt did not seem to suspect anything, and as the school year progressed, Metin regularly received upcoming tests in advance. Ahmet raised his grade to sixty-five, Yusuf and Hagop to slightly over fifty. Several other boys who were in trouble also received the stolen secrets, causing chemistry scores among boys to approach closer to those of the girls. Mr. Burritt complimented the boys and told them to keep up the good work.

After about three months, Ahmet told Metin that their mates could no longer break into Burritt's office. The lock had been changed. Metin wondered if the gig had been discovered, but to his relief, in the weeks that followed nothing happened.

Soon Yusuf and Hagop were again flunking, and Ahmet had settled back down to fifty. While Ahmet's grade fluctuation was not that noticeable, those of the other boys were. Rumors arose that something was up, that the teaching staff was suspicious of a major cheating scheme.

Metin approached Ahmet with this. Ahmet was calm. "Don't worry," he said. "After all, you and I did not break into that office, did we?"

He put an arm around Metin's shoulder and whispered in his ear. "We're in the clear."

* * *

Mustafa Bey took a fountain pen from his desk and examined it silently.

"Sait discovered Mr. Burritt's open office door," he said, still looking at his pen. Sait was one of the custodians. "At six in the morning when he came to work."

Metin silently cursed Yusuf and Hagop. He could not believe that those two misfits had forgotten to close Burritt's door.

The headmaster continued. "We changed the locks and began keeping an overnight custodian, as a watchman."

Metin wondered why Mustafa Bey had not announced the discovery sooner.

"We didn't know who the culprits were," continued Mustafa Bey, "but Mr. Burritt is no fool."

Metin listened with a sinking stomach.

"By observing grade trends in his classes, he narrowed down the suspects to two in particular." The headmaster rolled the fountain pen between his fingers. "Both are weak students. They would have needed help."

He fixed his gaze on Metin. "I am very dismayed that it was you." He cleared his throat. "Very disappointed."

"Why did you focus on me?" asked Metin, hesitantly.

"We canvassed students that Mr. Burritt identified as capable of providing correct answers to the tests. I've been interviewing each."

"The girls too?"

"Yes, every name he gave us. Now it was your turn."

Metin realized that he should not have confessed so quickly until he knew more. Had he played it cool and lied in the beginning, he might have wiggled out of the situation. Now it was too late.

* * *

That afternoon Ahmet accompanied him on his walk back home. Metin was quiet and dejected as they left the school building, while Ahmet kept a bounce in his step, upbeat as ever.

"Don't worry," he said. "They won't harm you. It's those two idiots Yusuf and Hagop who'll be in real trouble."

Metin stopped and gave Ahmet a cold stare.

"You did not tell him about me, did you?" Ahmet's grin disappeared.

"He didn't ask. He had a list of students whose grades were suspicious. You were not on the list."

Ahmet did not respond. He merely walked on with a smug smile on his face. They stopped by a record store and admired European LPs on display, as they always did on the way home.

"See, you told the truth," said Ahmet. "The honest boy that you are."

They stared at a catchy new album cover of a man strangely attired in tight white pants and brown platform shoes. He was stepping into a green and gold landscape that was actually a wall mural.

"Mustafa Bey likes you," Ahmet continued. "He will appreciate your candor. He won't get you in trouble."

Metin stared at the strange man on the album cover. He wore a blue patterned white jacket with the name *Elton John* inscribed on the back in bold letters.

"This guy," said Ahmet, pointing to the man in the photo, "he is real good."

The name of the album was *Goodbye Yellow Brick Road*. Metin did not know what it meant. Years later, after he moved to America, he would recall the moment and realize how close he had come to his own goodbye to his yellow brick road.

Chapter 28

* * *

The Gresham lobby was bustling with activity, incoming guests closing wet umbrellas and removing their coats, outgoing ones apprehensively observing the rain, bellmen everywhere, busy like ants. Kollázs was well lit and full with a late lunch crowd. A group of smartly dressed businessmen waited to be seated at the entrance. Mark stopped and momentarily observed the reception desk, also lively. He realized that his daily routine was in a jumble. He had had lunch with Miruna at the Csiga Café when it should have been breakfast. Now it was past two p.m. and he was not hungry. Instead, he felt the irresistible tug of jet lag drawing him to bed. He rubbed his forehead and eyes, determined to resist.

A tap on his shoulder jolted him.

"Sorry, I didn't mean to startle you."

Mark turned around and was surprised with the fresh face of Jasmin, dusky hair neatly combed down to her shoulders, dark-rimmed spectacles highlighting keen auburn eyes. She wore a crisp, navy blue jumpsuit with a black duty belt and sidearm, her blue cap slightly tilted on her head.

"I didn't know I was being summoned to the police station again," said Mark, surprised.

"Oh, no. That's not it."

Mark gently grabbed her arm and led her away from the crowd by the entrance. They sat at an empty table in the piano bar. After scanning her surroundings, Jasmin reached for a side pocket on the pants of her jumpsuit.

"I am merely returning your passport," she said, pulling out the document.

Mark felt a sense of relief as he reached for it. "Thank you." He flicked through the pages, then looked up at her. "You didn't need to give me this personally. You could have left it at the reception desk."

Jasmin avoided his gaze for an instant, looking around the bar. There was no pianist. An idle bartender was polishing wine glasses with a towel, ignoring customers seated on barstools. A group of tourists sat at a distant table, peering over maps and guidebooks.

"Actually," she replied, a bit embarrassed, "I did want to give it to you in person." She then looked down at her lap.

"How long have you been waiting for me?"

"Oh, about fifteen minutes or so."

Puzzled, Mark surveyed the young officer up and down. "Why?"

"Do you know that you caused quite a buzz in our unit today?" She seemed impressed by his feat.

"What unit?"

"The investigation unit." Jasmin looked at him with admiration.

"What do you mean?"

"Your little adventure last night…at Erzsébetváros." Jasmin paused and awaited affirmation.

Mark shook his head in dismay as he recalled Kárpáty's creepy visit to his room.

"Yes," she confirmed. "The word is that you got yourself into some serious danger." She had misinterpreted his gesture.

"Is this why you came here?" Mark was still baffled. "To tell me that?"

"No, not really."

Mark waited.

She changed the subject again. "Did you do any sightseeing after we parted yesterday?"

"Yes, Andrássy út. Very nice."

Jasmin smiled appreciatively.

"I went to the Lotz Terem Café. What an impressive place. The architecture, the decor "

Jasmin nodded, eyes wide. She wasn't a police officer now, but rather a schoolgirl pleased to receive recognition from a teacher. "I am so glad." Still smiling.

Mark halted and wiped his own smile off, gazing at Jasmin with curiosity.

"Actually," she said, hesitating, "I was wondering if you would like to have dinner with me."

Mark leaned back in his chair so astonished that he looked somber. He pondered the question.

"I have some friends who have an unusual restaurant," she continued, "quite unassuming."

She paused and waited for Mark's expression to clear. He leaned forward and listened more intently.

"But the food is very good. Authentic, homemade Hungarian."

"Well, thank you very much for your hospitality."

"You're welcome." She looked at her lap again. "But I do have an ulterior motive."

It could not be, thought Mark. That sort of thing only happened to Ahmet.

"You see," she continued, still haltingly, "you're the first person I've met who lives in San Francisco." She locked her gaze with his, now more determined. "I wanted to know...for you to tell me...what it is like." There was a hint of pleading in her tone that surprised Mark.

"Well, sure! Of course." Mark was relieved. "Yes, thank you very much. I accept your invitation."

The tension in the air dissipated. They smiled at each other.

"Good. I can pick you up here at eight p.m. How's that? I'm off duty tonight."

It occurred to Mark that, given Olga's ominous admonition, it would be good to be escorted by a police officer when he went out tonight. "That's perfect," he said. "I seem to still have my sleep cycle altered. That'll be about my wake-up time."

They got up and headed toward the nearby lobby. "Why do you want to know about San Francisco?" asked Mark.

"I'll tell you tonight."

Mark escorted her through the lobby hallway toward the entrance. It was still lively and noisy, multiple conversations echoing from the high ceilings, highlighted by occasional laughter here and there.

Jasmin leaned into him. "I heard a rumor that they are assigning a case officer to you, one that's working on your side of the investigation. You've suddenly become very important."

"Who's that?" This could not be good news.

"I don't know." Jasmin looked at him with pride. "Kárpáty is too busy to keep an eye on you personally."

Wonderful, thought Mark glumly.

They passed through the door, Mark nodding to the doorman who gave him a formal bow. The rain had lost its earlier fervor, now a mere drizzle. The air smelled fresh, grassy. They walked to her patrol car, disregarding the drops.

"Do you know if a preliminary forensics report has been issued yet on the Radu murder?"

"No, but I can easily find out," Jasmin said. She explained that as a rookie cop, one of her numerous gofer duties—aside from providing chauffeur service to witnesses—included sorting and distributing newly issued documents.

"Would you like to know what it contains?"

Surprised by the offer, Mark tried not to sound overly eager. "That would be nice," he said.

"Certainly," she said. "If it comes across my desk."

Mark opened her car door and they shook hands. She offered him another card with her name and number. He refused. He still had the one from yesterday. He asked her if she knew his number. Of course she did.

Mark watched the Audi drive away with a twinge of excitement. Jasmin was an unanticipated gift. What it would deliver, he did not know. But he looked forward to it.

Chapter 29

* * *

Mark returned to his hotel room with a bounce in his step. Tired as he was, he felt elated with the revelations of Iancu and unexpected surprise of Jasmin. He could not wait to see both again. The room had been impeccably cleaned, the clothes he had thrown about neatly hung in the closet, the sweaty items from last night's chase laundered and neatly folded at the edge of his bed. He took the laundered shirt and was smelling its floral bouquet, when a flashing message light on the house phone caught his attention.

It was a female voice, in Hungarian-tinted English, requesting that Mark notify Commissaire Gérard's office at the first possible opportunity. He wished to pay Mark a visit at his hotel. Mark realized that he had forgotten about delivering the Romanian radiology report to the Interpol officer. He called the number and a secretary, the same voice as in the message, told him Gérard would be on his way. It would be no more than half an hour, she said, thanking him for his prompt response.

There was no sense in lying down quite yet. Mark searched his shoulder bag for the report and re-examined it, focusing on the name Cezar Kaminesky again. *A go-between*, Iancu had said. For what? Why would Ahmet send him this man's abdominal and pelvic CT findings? Why was he in possession of the report in the first place? Were Ahmet and Cezar such close friends that Cezar was comfortable sharing his medical problems with Ahmet, especially if Olga was Cezar's wife and Ahmet was having an affair with her? But then who knew? Sometimes spouses are oblivious to affairs with close friends. The whole thing made no sense. He would have to bring up the subject with Iancu again when they met.

His cellphone interrupted his thoughts.

"Metin?" It was Günsu.

Mark realized in dismay that he had forgotten to call her. "Günsu, I am so sorry, I didn't call."

"I've been waiting, worried." She did not sound reproachful, just concerned.

"Events here took over. Too much going on, too fast."

"What events?"

Mark paused. How could he summarize all that had happened?

"Police," he said. "And others."

"Did they find out what happened?"

"You mean who killed him? No."

"You know, I've been worried for years that something like this might happen to him." She sounded more in control of her emotions, not in shock as she had been during their last conversation.

"Günsu," Mark asked, "had you been seeing Ahmet for long?"

"Yes."

"Where?"

"Here, in Istanbul." She sounded surprised at his question.

Not as surprised as Mark was upon hearing her answer. Ahmet was taking regular trips to Turkey, and yet remained incognito.

"How did he travel there?"

"What do you mean?" Günsu sounded genuinely puzzled.

"Just that. Did he fly to Istanbul? Where did you see him?"

"He came to my apartment and stayed with me," she said. "He usually had someone drive him here."

"From Romania?"

"Oh." Günsu finally seemed to comprehend Mark's point. "That, I don't know. He never told me."

Mark recognized that exploring Ahmet and Günsu's relationship, if he cared to do so, would take a face-to-face meeting with her, maybe over several days. Asking her such questions shortly before Commissaire Gérard's arrival was pointless. He decided to change the subject.

"I met his wife," he said, knowing well that this might be risky. But he felt she needed to know.

"Meltem is in Budapest?" Günsu was confounded.

Mark had to think for a moment, to recall who Meltem was. He sighed.

"What? What's the matter?"

Mark hesitated, contemplating what words to use.

"No," he finally said. "I have never met Meltem. Her name is Miruna. She is Romanian."

No response. Mark heard muffled sobs.

"I am sorry," he said, rubbing his forehead. "I did not know that you..."

"Tarık warned me. Over and over." She was quietly crying. "I refused to believe him."

"Who's Tarık?"

"My son."

Mark wondered when the surprises would end. He recalled the last time he had seen her, during their high school reunion. She had mentioned she was divorced but had not told him about any children.

"How old is he?"

"Twenty-five," she said.

That would make him a small boy at that time.

"Do you have any other children?"

"No, just him."

Mark looked at his watch. "Listen, Günsu," he said, determined now. "I will come to Istanbul and visit you. Then I can tell you all that's happened here and you can fill me in on your life. Deal?"

"Yes, wonderful." Her voice brightened. "You're welcome to stay at my apartment. It's spacious. You can stay in Tarık's room."

Mark was not sure he was ready for that. "Thanks for the offer," he said. "I might take you up on it but I'm not sure. Let me make some arrangements first."

"It's so good to hear from you," said Günsu. She sounded relieved.

"I won't give you a specific time for another call. I'm sorry I made you wait. I'll call you when I can."

"All right."

"Okay then. Goodbye," said Mark, as he prepared to hang up.

"Metin!"

Mark took his finger off the screen and brought the phone back to his ear.

"What is she like?" asked Günsu.

"Who?"

"The Romanian wife." A slightly exasperated tone.

Do you really want to know, he wanted to say.

"Upset," he said. "Bereaved." He paused to let that register. "As you are."

Chapter 30

* * *

Mark waded through a noisy crowd spilling onto the stairs of the third-floor apartment. It was mostly young men, fellow college students he hardly knew, standing around in small groups, each holding a beer can or plastic cup, conversing, mostly about classes. Their noise was nearly drowned by the disco beat emanating from the apartment, Donna Summer singing *Hot Stuff.* He wondered how neighbors on other floors put up with this.

Inside, the crowd was thicker, the music louder. A cramped living room was a makeshift dance floor with two couples gyrating clumsily, the girls being the first females Mark encountered. It was a typical University of Chicago party, almost all men. Mark had quickly tired of these in his first year, where he lived in Pierce Hall, a dorm at the northeast edge of the campus, overlooking desolate Garfield Avenue. Parties there were not this big, but equally wearisome. Now in his sophomore year, this was the first party that Mark had reluctantly agreed to attend, mainly because Megan, who lived in this apartment with four other flat mates and who was his partner in a photography class, had invited him.

There was a concentration of revelers in a narrow hallway, spilling out of a room. Mark hesitantly headed in that direction, passing a group of upperclassmen sharing a joint. He had never gotten used to the pungent, skunky smell of marijuana. A serious-looking black guy with a comb sticking out of a large

Afro offered him a nearly spent stub. Mark politely declined and moved on. The small room was noisy. It seemed to be the heartbeat of the party. To his surprise, Mark discovered it was a laundry room.

Several young men were passing a large soup ladle around that had been dipped into a washing machine, from which they poured an orange liquid into plastic drinking cups. Mark took one and retreated back to the living room. He spotted Megan in a far corner, by the stereo, surrounded by men. Mark stood, cup in hand, and awkwardly looked around, unsure what to do next. He watched the dancing couples without interest.

A hand grabbed him by the arm. "Hi," said Megan, shouting over the music. "I'm so glad you came." She was a tall brunette with pretty blue eyes and a toothy smile. "Do you like the drink?"

Mark took a sip and coughed. It was harsh, orange-flavored poison.

Megan laughed. "Pretty bad, huh?"

"What is it?"

"One of my roommates, Gary, is a research assistant at Searle." Searle was the chemistry building in the quadrangle. "He brought over some lab alcohol. They mixed it with water and Tang."

Mark had heard of washing machine parties but had never attended one until tonight. "This is a big apartment," he observed.

They were in an old building off Kenwood Avenue, north of the campus. Once upon a time it had been a magnificent mansion. Now it was cut up into multiple rental units for students who no longer wished to live in the dorms. Rents were high despite dilapidated conditions.

"Come," she said, pulling Mark by the arm. "Let me show you my room."

There were several boys in her room, smoking dope. She politely shooed them off and closed the door. Mark was relieved when she promptly opened a window to air out the smoke. It was cold outside but he did not mind.

The room was spacious, larger than Mark's in the dorm. There were several posters tacked onto the walls, Bee Gees, Bob Dylan, the musical *Tommy*. The largest was over her bedpost, the movie *Love Story* with Ali MacGraw and Ryan O'Neal standing back to back, Ali's head tucked into Ryan's nape. Ali stared into the room with a contented smile.

"I hate disco music," Megan said as she plopped onto her bed. She patted a spot next to her, inviting Mark to sit. "I'll show you some photos I took in high school."

It was a folder of black and whites, mostly landscapes, misty rivers, gnarly trees in silhouette, a full moon rising over low-lying hills. Mark examined the photos keenly. They seemed mature to him compared with those he had taken back in Istanbul. He studied the moonrise shot more closely.

"I took that with a Hasselblad 500 EL," she said quietly. She was pleased that he had chosen this one. "And a tripod, of course."

"Whew. Expensive."

"It was my father's. He owns a whole bunch of cameras. We went out on a night shoot together. He was really impressed with that shot."

Mark looked at her curiously. "Are you and your father close?"

Despite wearing no makeup, she was pretty up close, with a clear, light complexion, thin, long lips and alluring blue eyes. She stared back at the photo. "Yes," she said, and chuckled. "You might say I'm daddy's little girl. The youngest of the family. The rest are all boys."

"Did he teach you photography?"

"Yes, but he doesn't take shots like this. He is more technical, more into cameras as gadgets."

"So how did you come up with these?" Mark pointed to the portfolio, intrigued.

"A teacher I had in high school," she said, shuffling through the photos and showing him one of a deer lying low in tall grass, its antlers blending into the scene and yet striking. "He said that I had an instinctive talent for it."

Mark examined the photo and fell into contemplative silence, ignoring the loud beat reverberating in the apartment.

"Homesick?" she asked, breaking his silence.

"Yeah, a bit!"

She squeezed his wrist. "You've traveled a long way." Her voice was consoling.

He was pleased that she preferred private time with him amid the multitude of young men in her apartment. He looked at her hand on his wrist. "You too." She was from upstate New York.

"Geographically, maybe," she said, squeezing again. "Culturally, not as far as you."

She leaned in toward him. Mark felt the electricity of the moment. As Megan slowly closed her eyes, he knew what he needed to do. Instead, he suddenly jerked himself loose and stood up, heading toward the open window. He took deep breaths of cold air, thinking of a similar moment in the galley of a sailboat in Tarabya, nearly three years earlier, yet it seemed like a lifetime ago. He still had not gotten over his embarrassment of that moment.

"What do you think we should take up for our photo shoot assignment?" he asked loudly, rubbing his cold hands together.

Megan eyed him with curiosity. "The Chicago River," she said.

"You mean like Marina City, Wrigley Building, the Michigan Avenue Bridge?"

"Not really. I was thinking more of the gritty side of the river, west of downtown. The industrial side."

"Have you been there?" Mark asked with surprise. The students lived in an insular South Side campus, surrounded by a sea of bad neighborhoods, and rarely ventured out.

"Sure," she said, confidently. "Several times."

She closed the photo folder and put it away. She then came to him, took his hand in hers. "But I won't show you the photos I took. You'll have to come up with your own ideas."

Still holding his hand, she led him toward the door. "Come on, let's go back to the party."

* * *

They snapped clothespins on wet prints and hung them in the red safelight of the dim darkroom. Megan pointed to the emerging image of a black cantilever bridge in the foreground, its roadway elevated, amid the gray backdrop of a ruined warehouse building.

"This one is going to be good," she said. It was Mark's photo.

"You hardly took any," he commented, standing close to her by the workbench.

She didn't answer. After fiddling with a photo still submerged in a tub, she asked, "Did you have a good time?"

Apprehensive at first, Mark had indeed found the experience exhilarating. They had set out from Hyde Park early Sunday morning, the weekend after her party, in her compact Datsun. The weather was bitingly cold and they were bundled up as they walked deserted streets on the west side of the river, the neighborhood eerily redolent of a war zone despite slick downtown skyscrapers hulking nearby to the east. Mark's hands nearly froze handling his camera with his gloves off, but he did not mind. Megan didn't speak much, just led the way with determined steps, as if she were a tour guide. Mark shot scenes that he never before thought would be photo worthy.

"I loved it," said Mark. "It was an eye-opening experience."

Afterwards they huddled in a warm delicatessen near Rush Street and downed bagels and cream cheese with piping hot coffee as Mark's hands returned to life. She asked him about his life back in Turkey and listened with keen interest. Now they were back in her apartment to process the film, in a makeshift darkroom she had created in her bathroom.

"Good," Megan said, as she hung the last print. "I had already shot what I needed. The outing was for you." Mark stared at her, fazed. "Come on. Let's get out of here," she said.

They sat side by side on the edge of her bed while waiting for the photos to dry. Mark stared at Ali MacGraw, who seemed to be looking directly at him.

Mark reached for his wallet. "I want to show you a shot I took back in Turkey." He pulled out a small black and white and handed it to Megan.

Megan studied the photo with interest. "Very pretty," she said. "Was she your girlfriend?"

"No, but she was a friend, a classmate."

Megan looked at the photo again.

"I snuck up on her while she was sunbathing on an island near Istanbul."

"It doesn't look like that," said Megan. "It looks more intimate, more one-on-one."

"Yeah, I know. That's the way it came out."

She handed the photo back to him. "You were in love with her, weren't you?"

Mark put the picture away. "Once upon a time," he said. "But she was not into me."

Megan took his hand in hers. "It's a great shot," she said. "You managed to capture your own feelings in it."

They looked at each other.

"You're a natural photographer," she continued. "Your work shows your feelings, like an open book."

Mark felt the same electricity as he had the night of the washing machine party.

"You know," he said. "You are the first girl I have felt comfortable around... on this campus."

She leaned in toward him, and this time she didn't wait. Mark accepted her first kiss with relief. The others followed with abandon.

Chapter 31

* * *

Mark zipped up his coat and slung his bag across his opposite shoulder. The elevator was slow as usual and stopped on every floor, the guests going down quietly minding their business. As he waited for the doors to close on the second floor, his text message chimed.

"I am in the lobby." It was Mustafa.

But Mustafa wasn't there. Mark peeked into the lobby area from the elevator alcove and spotted the tall figure of Gérard sitting stiffly by one of the chairs near Kollázs where Mark himself had sat. A tap on his shoulder startled him.

"*Merhaba, Metin Bey.*" Mustafa greeted him in Turkish. *Hello, Mr. Metin*. Mark looked at him, eyes wide with surprise, and broke into a laugh.

Mustafa was fully geared as a hockey player, wearing an oversized jersey with bulky sleeves that hung low, down to his black shorts. A prominent *Budapest Stars* logo was printed on the chest next to a large five-edged star. His legs were completely covered with thick, long socks. He held a long stick, curved at the bottom, brushing the ground near his Adidas sneakers. He lifted off his black, visorless helmet to reveal a military haircut, his formerly unruly mop of hair gone. He smiled broadly at Mark, his moustache also gone, his nose more pointy and protuberant than ever.

"Didn't you recognize me?" he asked teasingly.

Mark could not stop laughing as he gazed at Mustafa's taut scalp. He had even trimmed out his unibrow, his eyebrows thin and well separated.

"Hockey?" said Mark, incredulous.

"There is a major game, international," said Mustafa. He looked younger with his new disguise. He'd been standing by the elevator door all along. Little wonder Mark had not spotted him.

"I didn't know that Turkey had a national hockey team," said Mark. Turkey did not have a hockey tradition.

"Hungary," corrected Mustafa, still grinning. "They're playing Russia."

"Since when have you been a hockey fan?" Mark asked in disbelief.

Mustafa stopped grinning. "Since you sucked me into all that trouble last night," he said, "with those fucking gypsy thugs."

Mark wrinkled his forehead in curiosity.

"I am not sure if that *pezevenk* spotted my face when he was shooting at my car." He called the shooter a pimp. "Best to change my looks. Come." He took Mark by the arm and led him toward the lobby.

"No, wait a minute." Mark told him about Gérard, who was still sitting at the same spot.

"I have much to tell you but don't have time to talk right now," Mark added, and peeked around the alcove again. "Quick—what have you been up to?"

"Long night," said Mustafa. "Stayed up getting the car fixed."

"Did you look into that bar?"

"Yes, I'll tell you about it later."

"And Meltem?"

"She told me to disengage and return to Istanbul."

"When are you leaving?" Mark felt a twinge of disappointment about losing Mustafa.

"Don't know," said Mustafa. "It's up to you."

Mark looked at him quizzically.

"Go meet your police officer," Mustafa ordered him. "We'll talk later."

* * *

Gérard quietly examined the three-page document Mark handed him, focusing in particular on Ahmet's handwritten message in capital letters. He sat stiffly upright, his legs crossed, and removed his glasses as he looked up at Mark, who stood over him. His eyes were dull gray, squinty. A group of noisy customers left Kollázs laughing, obviously tipsy.

"*Merci*," said Gérard. He stood up and tucked the document into a well-worn, brown leather attaché case with a single slide-lock in the front. "Let's take a walk, shall we?" He gently placed his palm against Mark's back.

They walked silently toward the entrance, Gérard covering his wispy white hair with a gray fedora and buttoning his raincoat. He was taller than Mark and walked awkwardly, with long, stork-like legs, his old-fashioned attaché case gently swaying by his side.

"You've made quite an impression on Hungarian police, Doctor." He uttered the last word in French, *docteur*, rolling his "r."

The rain had stopped. The air was crisp and clean. They walked along the hotel driveway and turned right into Zrinyi út. It was a quiet, narrow street onto which the windows of Kollázs opened. Down at a distance, the silhouette of a grand church interrupted the street.

"What have you heard?" asked Mark.

"That you've been prying into matters you should not." Gérard looked straight ahead, not making any eye contact.

"Did Kárpáty tell you that?"

"No," said Gérard. "He does not communicate much with us."

"I gathered that," mumbled Mark, inviting a quizzical look from Gérard.

Zrinyi út was a neatly cobblestoned pedestrian mall, thinly populated at this end. The streets that crossed it were all narrow and carried brisk one-way traffic. Mark wondered where they were going.

"You and he seem to be following different agendas," Mark went on. "He seems to have no interest in the black-market kidney business."

"You are very perceptive, monsieur." Gérard's voice was monotonous.

Mark enjoyed the compliment. "So how come you're intimately involved in this affair?"

"What affair do you mean?" Gérard walked on.

"This murder...Radu," said Mark. He paused. "I looked up that Turkish doctor you asked me about, Gazioğlu. He performs black-market kidney transplants." He looked for a reaction in the Commissaire's face. There was none. "What is the connection between Radu and this doctor?"

As they approached the big church, Zrinyi became more crowded with evening promenaders. They passed a few sidewalk cafés and came upon a strange statue in the middle of the road at another cross street, Őctőber 6. út. It was of a short, stocky army general wearing a World War I uniform, facing the majestic church up ahead, with his hands folded behind his back. The statue could have been mistaken for a live person in the crowded street.

Gérard pointed to a café directly across Őctőber 6. út, with several sidewalk tables along Zrinyi. "Would you like to sit down and have something, an espresso?"

Mark did not need coffee. His jet lag was tugging at him and he was anxious to get some sleep before his dinner with Jasmin.

"Yes, sure," he answered, nonetheless.

The café was called Nonloso. After waiting for a break in the cross traffic, they took seats on one of the outdoor tables, facing the basilica on one side, and Őctőber 6. út on the other. The basilica was a neoclassical structure with an imposing central dome flanked by two tall bell towers. It dominated the Parisian-style buildings leading up to it. The café had six outdoor tables. Red blankets were folded over the seats, for use by chilly customers. Two tall blackboards flanked its door, announcing the food and drink menu in chalk. They clashed with the formal brickwork of the arched door, topped by a carved statue of a bearded male face.

Zrinyi was more crowded here as it approached the church. A group of young men passed by, all wearing hockey uniforms with Russian insignia on their chests. They carried half-consumed beer mugs instead of hockey sticks and spoke loudly in Russian, laughing boisterously.

"I hope it's not too chilly for you," said Gérard, offering his blanket to Mark. "We can go indoors, but I love the sight of this church in late afternoon, as the sun sets."

Mark had his own blanket that he draped around his shoulders. He reached into his bag to pull out his Budapest guidebook.

"*Szent István*," said Gérard, guessing Mark's quest. "The basilica is one of the tallest buildings in the city, besides the Parliament."

Mark recalled his drive to Kárpáty's office and, for a brief moment, shivered in the cold.

"It means St. Stephen's, named after the first king of Hungary." Gérard waved for a waiter. "Are you sure you don't want to sit inside?"

Mark bundled himself tighter and put the guidebook down. "Yes. I'm okay."

Gérard pointed to the basilica. "They have very good concerts there. You might want to catch one before you leave."

"I am afraid another time," Mark answered. "I'll be leaving soon."

"For San Francisco?"

"No. Istanbul, I think."

Gérard's eyes widened, betraying surprise. The waiter arrived before either could say anything else. Mark realized he was hungry, his meal routines having turned topsy-turvy. He ordered a *palacsinta*, Hungarian crêpe, a chimney cake, and a *Coca-Light*. Gérard asked for a double espresso.

"Homesick?" remarked Gérard, after the waiter left.

"You might say so. I'd like to visit an old friend who is distraught over the news of Radu's death."

"Beautiful city, Istanbul," Gérard mused. "I love their seaside fish restaurants on the Bosporus. So pretty." He shifted in his seat, opened his coat buttons and crossed his legs. "Although, unfortunately, I can no longer partake in your national drink. What was it called?"

"*Rakı*," said Mark.

"Yes, *rakı*." Gérard pronounced it like *wraque* in a heavy French accent. It made Mark chuckle. "My stomach can no longer handle it."

"So," said Mark, encouraged by the Commissaire's banter. "The Turkish doctor and Radu?"

"Dr. Kent," Gérard looked toward the basilica, then turned to face Mark. "We've been pursuing your old friend for many years, for various reasons." He paused.

"Lately he has been of interest in the black-market kidney trade. We have reason to believe that he may be a broker." He stopped and corrected himself. "Well, he may have been...now that he is gone." His voice trailed off.

A broker! Mark recalled Ahmet's first venture as a broker, back in Istanbul, when he connected Mr. Burritt's stolen chemistry exams with Mark. Mark himself had pointed this out to him. Mark was not exactly sure what a kidney broker did, whom exactly he brought together. He would have to research that.

"Why is he of interest to French police?" Mark asked.

Gérard pondered the question. "Let's just say that French citizens have been victimized."

Two more young men passed by them, fully geared like Mustafa had been, in Budapest Stars hockey outfits. Gérard didn't seem to notice them.

"And this doctor, Gazioğlu," said Mark. "Was he an associate of Radu?"

"Gazioğlu has associated himself with many. If you looked him up on the internet, you may have gathered as much."

"Yes, I did."

The waiter brought their drinks. Gérard took a cautious first sip of his coffee.

"What do you think all this has to do with Radu's murder?" Mark was being too direct with the evasive Frenchman. He did not expect a useful answer, but it wouldn't hurt to try.

"We don't know," said Gérard with surprising candor. "We are as surprised by this assassination as everyone else."

Mark was taken by the word *assassination*. He pushed on with more courage. "So how is it that you're getting information from Hungarian police? Surely it is not Kárpáty that's cooperating with you."

"Our connection with them is at higher ranks than the investigator." Gérard took a larger sip with a slight slurp.

Mark realized that he would not penetrate beyond that answer. So, Kárpáty was presumably being ordered to work with French Interpol whether he liked it or not. Ahmet must have been quite important. Why else would Hungarian higher-ups call Gérard into the case so fast?

The waiter brought him a plate of double crêpes, which he quickly dug into while Gérard gazed at the street. There were more people strolling by as the late afternoon light began dimming. Mark no longer paid attention to hockey outfits as more passed by at regular intervals. Mustafa had obviously chosen a good disguise. The crêpes were sweet, filled with chocolate pudding, and they boosted his sagging energy.

Gérard waited for him to take a break and then asked, "I understand that you sought to meet a certain Olga Kaminesky, a masseuse at the Gresham Palace hotel."

Mark was no longer surprised that law enforcement knew about his secret. He nodded and took another large mouthful of crêpe, washing it down with Coke.

"How did you know her?"

Mark wiped chocolate off his lips, contemplating how to answer that. He had tampered with a piece of crime scene evidence and this could get him in trouble. But Gérard seemed to have a different agenda. Could he take a chance with him?

"She had given Radu her business card with her personal number written on it. I figured she gave him a massage before he was assassinated."

It felt strange for Mark to use that same word, *assassinated*. It was as if suffering this fate were a distinction reserved for the elite, people that Mark never imagined he would encounter in his own life.

"And how did you come to see this card?"

"It was on the coffee table of Radu's suite at the Gresham. Right where you sat when you first questioned me."

Gérard shifted in his seat, turning his chair around to face away from the basilica and toward Mark.

"Doctor," said Gérard in a serious tone, "I am sure you are aware that you just admitted to a crime."

"How so?"

"Oh, come now, Doctor." Gérard bore a sardonic smile. "You are more intelligent than you let on. Don't tell me you don't realize that removing that card from the scene is a major indiscretion."

Mark eyed the chimney cake that the waiter had slipped by without him noticing. The Commissaire's little lecture made him feel bold and reckless. He had never been good about breaking rules or covering up his tracks, as Ahmet had been. Mark recalled his quick confession to Mustafa Bey, his headmaster, when the wretched cheating affair had been discovered in high school. His punishment had been light compared with the two who broke into Mr. Burritt's office. Yusuf and Hagop had failed the year and were forced to repeat it, whereas he was given only a written reprimand. No one was expelled because the school needed their tuitions. Nonetheless, the disappointment of his parents had been punishment enough for Metin.

Now, sitting across from this French officer, he was in more serious trouble, and it somehow didn't bother him.

"Monsieur le Commissaire," Mark said with an air of formality and as much of a French accent as he could muster. "What is it that you want from me? You could have accepted that radiology document in a number of impersonal ways, without ever seeing me again. Instead you are taking me on this walk as though you're my tour guide. Why?"

Gérard did not seem moved by Mark's brash statement.

"For reasons that are unclear, sir," he said as he lifted his espresso cup, "you have inserted yourself into the middle of a complex crime investigation. You are in over your head. You have stirred up people, dangerous people, whom I doubt you know how to deal with. But that's beside the point. I am not here to judge or criticize you. Nor am I interested in what aspects of local law you may have broken. I merely want to know what you know. What you've uncovered." He took his last sip of coffee.

"Fair enough."

Gérard's soliloquy boosted him. So Interpol needed his assistance, his knowledge. *Wow,* he thought to himself. In less than forty-eight hours he had turned from a dull American radiologist to a European sleuth. *How cool is that*! Mark prepared to reveal his findings to the Commissaire, from one investigator to another.

Just then he was taken by yet another hockey outfit, a solitary figure promenading on Zrinyi. He slowed down by Nonloso and, as he passed behind Gérard, lifted off his helmet to reveal a pointy nose and closely cropped scalp, smiling.

Mustafa! What was he doing here?

Mustafa put his helmet back on and swung his hockey stick along the pavement, connecting with an invisible puck. Mark was momentarily nonplussed. As Mustafa slowly moved on toward the basilica square, Mark followed him with his eyes. Mustafa's prominent jersey remained distinct for quite a while before it disappeared.

Chapter 32

* * *

Mark looked at his watch and realized, with dismay, that there was little likelihood of catching any meaningful sleep. The sun had nearly set and lights were coming on in the businesses that lined Zrinyi. The basilica's white façade was already bathed in floodlights. They reflected onto a large square around it where people meandered, taking photos with their phones.

Gérard had noticed Mark's startled look and turned back to the street in search of its cause. By then Mustafa, still visible, was but another hockey fan at some distance.

"Olga Kaminesky and Nicolae Radu had a relationship," said Mark, drawing the Commissaire's attention back to him. It was time for Mark to reveal his cards.

Gérard, stony-faced, waited for more.

Mark sipped his Coke and continued. "Not just a one-time massage at the Gresham. It goes back years. They had an on-and-off affair. In Romania."

"Did she tell you that?" asked the Frenchman. He brought his chair closer to the table and placed one hand on his attaché case that lay next to his empty espresso cup.

"Yes." Mark answered with assurance.

"How did you come to speak with her?"

"We met," said Mark, "last night." He chuckled. "It ended in all that commotion that's got the police riled up." Mark summarized the events at the Mercy club and his meeting with Olga in a back office.

Having offered Gérard a juicy morsel, he now sought something in return. "I have learned that this masseuse is a suspected accomplice in Radu's assassination. Am I correct?"

Gérard smiled, his lips taut, highlighting delicate creases on his thin cheeks. "Bravo, Doctor," he said. "So far you've been more helpful than local police." He played with his empty espresso cup, looking deeply into it as if it held an important clue. Then he looked up at Mark. "And may I reiterate," he said, his face serious, "that you have embroiled yourself in a situation, *très risqué*."

Mark pushed on. "Do you have any idea how she may have assisted the assassination?"

"No," said Gérard. "Local police have not been forthcoming with any information yet."

Mark looked at his chimney cake. It was a hollow brown cylinder with multiple rings etched on, coated with sugar. As he cut into it, several rings broke off. He picked one up with his fingers and took a bite. He was no longer tired. His conversation with Gérard was giving him an unexpected boost. The cake was sweet, doughy, and yet had a slightly burned flavor as if it had been barbecued. He curiously examined the remaining piece between his fingers.

"It is said to be the oldest pastry of this country," said the Commissaire, his eyes on Mark's plate. "They call it *kürtőskalács*."

Mark ate the rest of the piece. "Strange flavor," he said, with a full mouth.

"They cook the rolled dough over charcoal." The Frenchman reached over to Mark's plate. "May I?"

Mark handed him a ring that had broken off. Gérard took a small bite and delicately chewed it.

"A savory treat," he said. "They usually sell it in street corner booths. For me, forbidden, *malheureusement*." The Frenchman leaned back. "Diabetes." He wiped his mouth. "*Merci*."

Mark nodded with a sympathetic smile and released his next bombshell. "Have you come across a Cezar Kaminesky during the course of your investigation?"

"How did you come across that name?" asked Gérard, his voice slightly louder, betraying surprise.

"Cezar?" Mark nodded toward the old attaché case atop the table. "It's in the document I handed to you."

Gérard quickly slid the lock, as Mark looked on, amused.

Gérard hastily leafed through the radiology report. Mark observed him quietly, curious whether the officer would notice it. Gérard put the papers down and looked at Mark.

"First page," said Mark. "The name of the patient whose abdomen and pelvis was CT'ed."

Gérard adjusted his spectacles and examined the name, slowly rubbing his goatee as he pondered.

"Who is he?" asked Mark. "Is he part of the black-market kidney ring?"

"He is a bad character, a gangster," said Gérard, still staring at the document. He then looked up. "Operates mainly in Romania."

"Well, it seems to me that he and Olga have some sort of relationship." Mark had the upper hand and spoke with confidence. "Same last name. As far as I could gather from Olga, they might be married."

Gérard returned the report to his attaché case. "Interesting," he said. "We will look into this."

"Can you tell me any more about Cezar?" Mark aimed to capitalize on his coup.

"He has been into various rackets, drugs, prostitution, protection."

"Same ones as Radu, maybe?"

"Maybe," said Gérard.

"Has your organization uncovered any connection between the two of them?"

"These criminals are all interconnected," said Gérard.

"Here's something I don't understand," Mark continued. "My friend Ahmet, Nicolae, was having an on-and-off affair with Olga, who might be this Cezar's wife. If so, how could the two men cooperate with each other?"

"It's possible," said Gérard. "Especially in my country." His thin lips parted into a sly smile. "Who knows," he added, "when it comes to love triangles, anything is possible."

"But suppose that Cezar discovered the affair," said Mark. "Wouldn't he have a motive to kill Ahmet?" He paused to let that sink in. "That would make him a likely a suspect."

Gérard nodded but did not answer.

"But if so, what is his name doing on this radiology report that Ahmet used as a ruse to contact me?"

Gérard waved for the bill. "*Docteur,*" he said as he reached for his billfold, ignoring Mark's question, "you have been most forthcoming." He placed a few forints on the small pewter plate with the bill and stood up, buttoning his coat. "Come," he beckoned. "Let's walk."

They walked toward the wide plaza in front of St. István, crossing yet another small one-way street where they dodged speeding traffic. The cobblestoned plaza was lined by hefty apartment buildings that were dwarfed by the imposing church. It was sparsely lit, people milling about mere silhouettes. St. István's two bell towers, supported by Greek columns, glowed high above.

"Do you have any idea why Radu contacted you?" asked Gérard.

Mark looked around his surroundings searching for Mustafa. It was impossible to recognize anyone unless they came up close. He zipped his coat higher to cover his neck. He recalled Olga's admonition about watching his back when out of the hotel and felt a passing sense of dread.

"Apparently he was seeking my help in fleeing to the United States," said Mark, "to escape some threat he perceived in Romania. How I was supposed to help him, I don't know."

"Did Olga tell you that?"

"No, I found that out from Iancu." Mark pulled out his phone and searched his contacts list. "Iancu Negrescu," he said. "Have you heard of him?"

The Commissaire chuckled. "Doctor," he said, "you seem to have discovered some fairly important criminals in your short stay here."

"Well," replied Mark, his dread replaced by pride, "I did not actually meet Cezar Kaminesky in person. But Iancu, I did." He hoped he was being humble.

"Where?" asked Gérard.

Mark briefly summarized his meeting with Miruna and subsequently Iancu. They walked farther into the plaza and stood by iron railings near the steps to the church.

"So," said Mark, "is Negrescu dangerous, like Cezar?" In anticipation of their upcoming meeting, it seemed prudent for Mark to know what police thought of Iancu.

"No, he is not," said Gérard. "He is very smooth, a legitimate businessman by all appearances. He has successfully shielded Radu from prosecution by Romanian authorities."

Mark debated whether to tell the Commissaire that he was planning another meeting with Iancu. He decided against it, especially since he wanted to keep Mustafa off the police radar, if possible.

"Is that so special? I figure Romanian authorities can be easily bought." Mark was pleased that he sounded like a man of the world. Never mind that until the day before, and his Lotz Terem encounter with Mustafa, the thought would not have crossed his mind.

"Very perceptive," Gérard replied. "But even in Romania, corruption has its limits. Negrescu has steered clear of such trouble and kept his *patron* safe." He used the French word for *boss*.

Mark was not convinced of Gérard's conclusion. After all, Ahmet had been successfully terminated. Iancu, loyal as he may have been, had obviously failed in his mission. Or was Iancu a traitor? Could he have intentionally sacrificed his boss? If so, Mark was in for more trouble.

Mark looked at his watch and decided to keep his thoughts to himself. "I must be returning to my hotel," he said. "I have a dinner engagement."

"Very well," said Gérard. He offered his hand. "*Merci beaucoup.* For the document, and the information."

They shook hands firmly. Mark had been intimidated by the cold formality of the Frenchman when they first met, more so than Kárpáty and his bluster. But Gérard had turned out friendlier, more trustworthy.

"I will request our FBI liaison in San Francisco to fetch the original from your office, if you don't mind." Gérard reiterated his request from their first encounter.

"Sure," said Mark.

Gérard then reached into his attaché case and removed a business card, handing it to Mark.

"If you do visit Istanbul," he said, "we would much appreciate if you can convey to us any new information you might have."

Mark could not read the card in the dark. Gérard touched the card with the tip of his index finger. "This is a knowledgeable officer that you can contact. I believe you may know him."

Mark turned the card in the direction of the church steps and placed it under the reflecting floodlight. "Leon Adler," it read. He pondered the name. It sounded familiar.

"He studied in an English high school in Istanbul, the same one that you might have attended."

Mark now remembered. A Jewish boy, an upperclassman. Mark recalled an easygoing, affable sort, a good runner who won the annual cross-country race at the field in Okmeydanı two years in a row. He had a vague impression that Leon had emigrated to Israel with his family before graduating from high school.

A policeman! Was this possible? His old school did not aim to produce lawmen as alumni.

"Yes," he said quietly, still staring at the card. "I didn't know him well. He was two years ahead of me."

"He is stationed in Istanbul as a liaison from Israel." Gérard was back to his formal self. "Keeping an eye on the black-market kidney trade is one of his missions. He can be helpful to you."

Mark was stupefied by the array of former schoolmates who had popped up after his attempt to reconnect with Ahmet. He pocketed Leon's card.

"How?" he asked the Frenchman. "How can he help?"

"*Docteur*," said Gérard somberly, "if I may be blunt."

Mark gave Gérard an accepting nod with a smile. *As if you haven't been blunt so far*, he thought.

"In your foolhardy quest to remain embroiled in this Radu matter, you are likely to run into more trouble." He paused to let that sink in. "Worse trouble than what happened to you yesterday."

Gérard gently patted Mark's back. "Having a law enforcement contact in Istanbul might offer a measure of safety. *N'est-ce pas?*" He lifted his fedora in an elegant salute and began walking away. "*Adieu.*"

Mark watched the Commissaire meld into the silhouettes of the dim plaza, contemplating his comment. He tightened the collar of his jacket around his neck to ward off another wave of chill that passed through his body.

Chapter 33

* * *

Mark surveyed the crowd at Szent István tér and contemplated his walk back to the hotel. The spacious plaza around the basilica had various crowded outdoor cafés. One in particular, on the north side of the church, behind an obelisk, was several times larger than Café Nonloso, where Mark and Gérard had sat, with outdoor tables in front of tall, arched windows flanked by intricate stone work. Mark could only make out silhouettes sitting at these tables. He was about to embark on his first solo outing since the attack of the night before. Remembering Olga's admonition, he wondered who, if anyone, might be lurking in menace.

Mark was pleased with his meeting with Gérard. It somehow mattered to him that he had left a favorable impression with the old policeman. The Commissaire had been sly, stingy with information. Yet he still had revealed that Ahmet was a broker in the kidney trade and that his murder was an assassination. Olga and Cezar Kaminesky were clearly important figures, albeit hazy.

Mark began cautiously walking across the plaza, his eyes darting in every direction. Gérard's last words rang in his ears. *You are likely to run into more trouble,* he had said. *Worse trouble than what happened to you yesterday.*

Up ahead was a steady stream of cars and mopeds on Sas út, a one-way street that separated Szent István tér from Zrinyi. Mark checked his watch. It was approaching seven p.m. Jasmin would be picking him up in about an hour.

He barely had enough time to get to his hotel, freshen up, and change clothes. As he waited for a break in traffic, Mark surveyed his surroundings. No one seemed to be following him.

Mark crossed Sas into Zrinyi and walked with a thicker crowd of Thursday evening promenaders who strolled languorously, couples arm-in-arm, some staring at storefronts, others conversing with people sitting at the outdoor café tables. Mark wondered where Mustafa was. A young couple, walking briskly, brushed by him. Startled, he jumped and stared after them. He scanned his surroundings again. No one took notice of him. He texted Mustafa. *Where are you?*

He walked on toward the corner of Őctőber 6. út, approaching Café Nonloso. The statue of the short, chubby World War I general stared at him across Őctőber 6. Mark checked his phone, willing Mustafa to answer. As usual, Mustafa was ignoring the missive. Mark recalled Mustafa's disguise and chuckled. The idea of Turks playing hockey was ludicrous.

Suddenly he felt a hard object pressed against his right rib cage. He turned and was surprised to see a short man with a raincoat folded over his right forearm, standing very close to him. He was dark-complexioned, his black hair slicked back. He had a lean, athletic build.

"Don't say anything," the man whispered, pressing his gun barrel harder into Mark.

Mark carefully slipped his phone into his pocket and looked into the man's dark eyes, flooding with dread as an image flashed in his mind. It was of this same man intently focused on Mark while he raised his gun and aimed. The night before, that moment had passed in a flash as Mustafa sped off, but the image was indelible.

"Continue walking," said the man. "Slowly."

Mark shuddered and took a hesitant step. He wasn't sure he could maintain his balance. He was nearly paralyzed with terror. A hand grabbed his left arm, squeezed and steadied him, pushing him on. This second man was taller, with unruly hair covering his ears, all except the tips of his earlobes, from which a pair of prominent gold earrings protruded. He did not make eye contact with Mark, looking straight ahead toward Őctőber 6. út, firmly holding on to him. Mark recognized the bouncer who had stood by the stage of the Mercy nightclub.

"Come on, walk!" The short man ordered.

They took a few herky-jerky steps toward Őctőber 6. út. "Act normal. We're friends out for a stroll," said the guy holding the gun.

Mark nodded. They had gotten him. There was no way to escape this time. Mark wondered what they intended to do with him. Hopefully, not much in this crowded street.

The outdoor tables at Nonloso were full, the same waiter who had served Mark and Gérard meandering among the customers. Traffic flowed steadily one way at Őctőber 6. út, cutting across Zrinyi. The two men aimed Mark toward the right, nearly brushing the tables of Nonloso. Mark shuffled on, eyeing the customers helplessly, hoping for someone to come to his aid.

They were headed toward a stationary car at the curb, a silver BMW. Mark recognized the car as the one that had followed him and Iancu. As the trio approached the car, its engine came to life. The short guy lightened the pressure of his gun barrel now that Mark was obediently taking steadier steps.

It felt strange to be alone in such a big, lively crowd, more frightening to Mark than the dark, solitary Almássy tér the night before. Just as they reached the BMW, Mark noticed a small white van drive by on Őctőber 6. út. It had a large painting of the suspension bridge across the Bosporus at Ortaköy with a compact Baroque mosque at one end, its two minarets rising parallel to the European pillar of the bridge. It was an iconic photo of Istanbul. The words *Bosporus Autojavítás* were painted below the photo. As the van whizzed out of sight, Mark was filled with regret that he would not be visiting Istanbul after all.

The bouncer with the gold earrings let go of Mark and went around to the opposite side of the BMW, opening the back door on the driver's side, while the short gunman opened the one on the right and gave Mark an inward shove. Mark ducked to enter while his abductor held a firm grip on his coat, pushing him in.

Before he could turn and sit, Mark felt a sudden pull backward, out of the car and toward the curb. He lost his balance and hit his head on the door frame before tumbling to the sidewalk. The legs of his abductor were splayed next to him. There was a swishing sound and a loud crunch. The man grunted. Mark turned to look at him. An object had just slammed into the short man's face at the bridge of his nose. Blood was splattered all over his face, making him unrecognizable. His gun fell out of his hand, thudding to the ground. Another swish and slam, this time to his chest. The man whistled as air rushed out of his lungs. The curved tip of a hockey stick rested on his chest. Adidas sneakers kicked away the gun.

"Get up, quick!"

A hand extended toward Mark, who was still sat on the sidewalk, dazed. He looked up and saw Mustafa in his Budapest Stars hockey outfit. Mark felt a trickle of blood running down his own face. He had cut his left forehead when he hit the car. He rubbed his face.

"Never mind that! Come on. We have no time."

Mustafa firmly grabbed him with one arm and lifted him off the ground. As Mark regained his balance, he saw a rapidly moving shadow, the earringed bouncer, rushing toward him and Mustafa. The hockey stick swished again, slamming onto the man's neck, instantly dropping him to the ground. A second blow followed, this time to his head, the stick sliding along the ground as if the man's head, now lying on the cobblestones, were a puck. Mark heard a sickening crunch as the blow landed.

The promenading crowd nearby stopped and formed a semicircle around the brawl, a safe distance away. It all happened fast, but to Mark it was in slow motion.

"Let's go!" ordered Mustafa, pulling Mark toward the café tables closest to the curb, the customers looking on in amazement. The BMW took off in a roar, disappearing into Őctőber 6. út, leaving the two wounded abductors bloodied, on the ground.

Mustafa and Mark ran down the sidewalk beyond Café Nonloso. Halfway down Őctőber 6., Mustafa abruptly stopped and pointed toward vehicles that were parallel parked across the street.

"Quick, let's cross." Mustafa momentarily eyed the traffic and jutted into the flow, abruptly stopping an oncoming car with an upturned palm. He gestured to Mark, tilting his head toward a van parked across the street. As the two dashed, the van's back doors opened and Mustafa ducked in, hockey stick first. Mark hesitated and looked the van over.

"Come on, get in! We have no time."

Mustafa's hand stuck out of the back of the van, waving Mark in. Mark's left eye was blurred by the blow he had received. He was nonetheless struck by the logo on the side of the van. It was the Bosporus Bridge coupled with the Ortaköy mosque. Mark dove into safety, as if it were home.

* * *

"Give me your phone," said Mustafa, extending his hand.

They sat across from each other, on side benches in the windowless back of the van, swaying this way and that as it sped away on Őctőber 6.

"What for?"

The van had a grimy smell, a mixture of gasoline and commercial grease. It was dim inside, the only light coming from the cab up front.

"I think we are clear, *Mustafa Abi*," came a voice from the cab in Turkish.

Mark handed Mustafa his iPhone. Mustafa quickly turned it off.

"Why did you do that?"

The van took a sharp turn and they both swayed in their respective seats, Mark nearly falling off his bench.

"How do you think those two found you?" Mustafa was disdainful.

Mark wiped his face and looked at his bloodstained finger. "I don't know," he said. "I was careful to look around. I didn't think I was being followed."

Mustafa handed him a towel from his bench. "That's right."

The towel was supposed to be white but it was riddled with black stains. Mark looked for a clear spot and wiped his face.

"They were sitting at the big café across from St. István, the one by the obelisk."

Mark found another clear spot on the dirty towel and pressed it against the cut at the edge of his left eyebrow. "How did they know I was there? It was too dark to make anyone out."

"My guess is they were tracking your cellphone signal."

Mark released the pressure of the towel. He was sure he would get a shiner. "Can they do that? How does the phone company give them access to that?"

A passenger jumped over the back of the front seat and joined them, a younger man with a cheerful smile. He sat next to Mustafa, moving deftly within the rolling cab.

"Did you get them, *Abi*?"

Mustafa lifted his hockey stick. Despite the dim light, blood stains were visible at its tip.

"I sure did," he said proudly.

"Why were you following me?" asked Mark, irritated that Mustafa kept this up.

"For your own good." Mustafa was indignant. "I spotted that *pezevenk*, the one who shot my headlight, soon after you and that old man sat at Café Nonloso. I figured it could not be a coincidence that he was loitering around you, and with a partner."

Mark realized he should be grateful to Mustafa. He again dabbed the towel on his cut.

"It's no longer bleeding," said the new guy sitting next to Mustafa.

"They went past Nonloso without looking at you," Mustafa continued. "They strolled up to the church plaza and sat at that big café on outdoor tables. All the while that little *pezevenk* was checking his mobile phone. I'll bet you anything he was receiving your location from his phone company contact. After your Interpol guy split and you began walking away from the church, they sped into Zrinyi ahead of you. They must have figured you'd go back to your hotel the way you came."

"That's great detective work, *Mustafa Abi*," said the younger man.

"Yeah," Mustafa said. "Thanks for making it there on time. I didn't want to wait for you at that corner any longer than I had to." He pointed to the cab up front. "I called these guys as soon as those two scrambled out of their café. I wasn't sure where they'd get you. As it turned out, I gave them a good spot to wait for us."

"I'm sorry." Mark was contrite. "Thank you for rescuing me, again. Olga had warned me that if I left the hotel I'd be in danger."

"Sound advice," said Mustafa. "I suppose now that she is no longer at the hotel, they can't get past the security system to get to you."

Mustafa's comment startled Mark. He had not thought about Olga's admonishment as a tacit admission of her complicity. He opened his mouth to express his surprise but then thought better of it. It would provoke more mockery from Mustafa.

"I know the other one, too," Mark said instead. "He was a bouncer at that strip joint, Mercy. You gave him quite a head injury with that stick." Mark recalled the crunch on the vertex of the man's head. At the very least, it had to have caused a depressed skull fracture, maybe more. He had read countless CT scans over the years of brain contusions and subdural bleeds with such trauma to the head.

"You were at the Mercy strip club?" The new man was impressed. "How was it?"

"Meet Ergün," said Mustafa, pointing to him. "Ergün, this is Doctor Mark, from America. He used to be Metin, but he is no longer Turkish."

"*Memnun oldum.*" Ergün bowed his head politely. He was probably in his early thirties, short and slim, with closely cropped dark hair and a clean-shaven face. His *I am glad* had a slight Anatolian accent. Mark exchanged a wobbly handshake with him across benches as the van sped on.

"I wouldn't recommend that club," said Mark. "The women were too young. Mere teenagers."

"M'mmm. Sounds good." Ergün turned to Mustafa for approval.

"It was also way too expensive. Three hundred dollars just to enter."

Mustafa laughed. He pointed to Mark. "He is a sucker," he said to Ergün. "Don't ask him about strip joints. He knows nothing about them."

Mark felt a pang of shame as he did back in high school, when his more testosterone-fueled mates made fun of him. He wished he could be more like them, but it didn't seem possible. He let the comment slide.

"How do you two know each other?" he asked Mustafa.

"Family. Turgut, our driver, is my cousin. Ergün here is his nephew." He turned toward the front of the cab and shouted, "Turgut, say hello to our esteemed guest."

"*Merhaba doktor bey*," they all heard a gravelly voice, the invisible driver saying *hello* in Turkish.

"You need to keep that phone turned off." Mustafa addressed Mark. "And stop walking around the city by yourself."

"What do they want from me?" asked Mark.

"They work for Tibor Bognár," said Mustafa. "A Slovakian crime boss. He runs a number of rackets here, including several nightclubs."

"You just hit Bognár's men?" Ergün asked Mustafa, fascinated.

"You bet." Mustafa nodded.

"Wow, *Abi*. That guy's trouble. We keep clear of his cars."

Mark wondered what Ergün meant by that, but chose to keep quiet.

"It's not me they want," said Mustafa. "They don't even know me. They're after *Doktor Bey*." He nodded in Mark's direction.

"I am not sure why they were so stirred up when I contacted Olga," said Mark, this time in Turkish.

Ergün interjected. "Your Turkish is good," he said. "And you're locking horns with Bognár." He was impressed. "Exactly what kind of doctor are you?"

"Never mind," said Mustafa, cutting off Ergün with an upturned gesture of his arm.

"Were they the ones who killed Ahmet?" Mark asked.

"I doubt it." Mustafa was firm. "They are just sloppy thugs," he added. "Did you see how their driver sped away and left his mates bloody, on the sidewalk?"

"Yeah, I wondered about that."

"Bognár's men are not sophisticated," said Mustafa. "Look how easily I botched their abduction." He was pensive for a moment. "Whoever killed Ahmet did a clean job. Slick. In and out. No clues, no waves. Not Slovakian."

"How do you know about Bognár?"

"What do you think I've been doing today?" Mustafa spoke Turkish. "Pulling thirty-one?" This was Turkish slang for jerking off.

Ergün chuckled.

"I've been nosing around your beloved Mercy nightclub. It didn't take much to discover who owned it. Bognár does not keep his operations terribly secret. He needs everyone to know and fear him."

The van came to a stop.

"We're here," said Turgut.

They heard a garage door open with a steady squeak. The van drove in.

Mark looked at his watch. "Damn," he said. "I have a dinner date in half an hour. She's picking me up at the hotel."

Chapter 34

* * *

"*Hoşgeldiniz*," said Turgut, effusively shaking Mark's hand. *Welcome.* He was tall and stocky, with a hirsute face that was in pronounced contrast with his bare, wrinkled scalp. He swung his arm around. "Our humble home."

"Metin Bey, meet Turgut." Mustafa introduced the driver. They all stood by the van they had just exited, a small white Skóda Roomster. Mark examined the words *Bosporus Autojavítás* painted in large black letters on its backside, under the iconic picture of the suspension bridge and Ortaköy mosque, this time up close. "What does that mean?" he asked, pointing to *Autojavítás*.

"Car repair," said Turgut.

Mark looked around. The Skóda barely fit into the only open space in what appeared to be a small autobody shop. A nearby car was missing its front end and windshield, its make unclear. Farther up, an Opel Astra had no doors, seats or steering wheel. Over on the other side was a fully intact Renault Megane that did not seem in need of any body work. The garage floor was greasy and cluttered with small tools, buckets, gas canisters, torches and other objects that Mark did not recognize. He looked for signs that this was a residence, since Turgut had called the place home. There were none.

"Turgut fixed my rental car last night," said Mustafa, putting one arm over his shoulder and giving him a tight squeeze.

At the far end of the garage Mark spotted what looked like an office with two figures huddled behind a spacious window. One of them was Ergün, who had quickly disappeared after exiting the van. The garage continued beyond the office, into an unlit space.

Ergün emerged from the office. "*Amca*," he said to Turgut, *uncle*, "tea is ready."

"*Buyrun*." Turgut extended his arm toward the office as if he were a maître d'.

The office was as messy as the garage. It had a large desk by the window facing the garage, a table and chairs in the middle, and a couch at the other end. A young man, no more than twenty, poured tea out of a small brass samovar atop a desk, amid paperwork and tools. He ceremoniously handed Mark the first glass, a traditional tulip shape, with two cubes of sugar on the saucer. It was a classic gesture of Turkish hospitality.

"*Teşekkürler*." Mark thanked the young man in Turkish.

"You're welcome," he responded, in English with a Turkish accent.

He served Turgut next. Turgut pushed aside several unwashed plates of leftover food on the table to make room for his tea. He put a broad arm around the young man's shoulders. "Murat," he said in Turkish, looking at the young man with pride, "is my other nephew." He disengaged. "See how well he speaks English? He is a bright boy, with a good future."

Ergün pulled up a chair next to his uncle and blew on his tea glass. Turgut gave him a gentle slap on the back of the head. "Unlike this one here, this *kazık*."

Ergün chuckled. His uncle had just called him a dummy.

"Do you all live here?" asked Mark, looking around the cluttered office, bewildered.

Murat hastily cleared the dirty plates and pulled up more chairs for Mark and Mustafa. The large couch at the other end, torn in several spots, was the only evidence of possible sleeping quarters.

"Practically," said Ergün. "We work day and night."

Mark looked at Mustafa quizzically.

"Turgut came here from Germany. Munich," said Mustafa. "He used to work for an autobody shop there."

"Actually," Turgut interjected, "I started at the BMW plant in north Munich, near the Olympic Stadium. My family came to Germany from Balıkesir in the 1960s, when I was a kid. My father worked in car plants. I followed in his footsteps."

"His father is my *amca*," said Mustafa, *my father's brother*. "My family also comes from Balıkesir." It was a western Anatolian town close to the Sea of Marmara.

"Yes." Turgut took a sip of tea. "Anyway, eventually I moved on to an auto-body shop that a German acquaintance owned. Then this opportunity came up in Budapest, you know...my own business. I moved here ten years ago and it has been very good."

"They do a brisk business here," said Mustafa.

"Yes," Turgut agreed. "I taught the business to this *salak*." Another slap on Ergün's head, another *idiot*. Ergün laughed harder.

"My *amca* has been good to me." Ergün deferentially nodded to his uncle. "He brought me here from Balıkesir four years ago and made me his *çırak*." *Apprentice*.

Murat stood behind his uncle and listened with amusement. Turgut squeezed Murat's arm. "This one," he said, "will not waste his life in our dirty business." Turgut paused and lit a cigarette. He took a deep puff and continued, "I promised my sister in Istanbul, his mother, that I would get Murat educated. Make him a gentleman."

"But first, I too have to learn how to cut up cars," said Murat. Now it was his turn to receive a slap on the back of the head.

"My date," said Mark to Mustafa, looking at his watch. "We need to call her."

He produced Jasmin's *Rendőrség* card and handed it to Mustafa. Turgut and Ergün leaned in curiously, took a peek, and snapped back, gazing at Mark, perplexed.

"You're dating a policewoman?" Mustafa lifted the card quizzically.

"She asked me out," said Mark sheepishly.

"Hungarian? From Budapest?" Turgut was dumbfounded.

"Yes," said Mark. "She might give me some inside information about the investigation into Ahmet's death."

"Surely she doesn't want to date you for that reason," said Mustafa.

"Look!" Mark was getting irritated. "Will you stop asking questions and call her? You wanted my phone off. We'll have to use yours. I don't want to stand her up."

Mustafa produced a cellphone from his pocket and offered it to Mark. Turgut, acting faster, reached for his office phone at the nearby desk and dialed. They all watched intently as Mark spoke with Jasmin, explaining that he would be late. Mark stopped in the middle of the call and asked the garage gang, "Where and when do you think you can drop me off to meet her?"

"At *Nyugati,*" said Turgut. "We're not far from there."

"Half an hour?"

"Sure," said Turgut.

Mark hung up. "It's a deal," he said. He returned to the table. "What's *Nyugati*?"

"Railway station," answered Mustafa. He motioned Mark to sit down.

Mark nervously looked at his watch.

"Relax," said Mustafa. "We're only five minutes away. We have time to talk."

He handed the cellphone, still in his hand, to Mark. "Here," he said, "I bought this for you. It's a Cello Mobile." Mark examined the small, basic, no-frills phone. "It's a rental," said Mustafa. You can call out with it and I can call you. I know the number."

"What about mine?" Mark pulled out his iPhone.

"If you keep it on, they can track you through the phone's GPS signal. I suggest that if you have to use it, do it in short spurts."

Mark placed both phones into his shoulder bag. His tea had gotten cold. He finished it in three fast gulps, no sugar, drawing surprised glances from the garage gang. His approach to tea was about as strange as his plan to socialize with police.

"There is a police officer named Kárpáty," Mark said to Mustafa. "Budapest police. He is in charge of investigating Ahmet's murder. He might be looking for you. He knew the license plate of your rental. He was going to track you through that. I sent you a warning text early this morning. Did you get it?"

"Yes." Mustafa seemed unfazed. "I'm not worried about the police," he said.

"This Kárpáty," said Mark, "is not an ordinary officer. He has some strange work habits." He recounted the investigator's visit to his hotel room, emphasizing that Kárpáty knew too much, too soon, about their clash at Almássy ter.

"H'mmm." Mustafa gave the account some thought. "He may be in with Bognár."

Turgut interjected. "The police, if they're corrupt, they don't take sides with anyone," he said. "They go with whoever pays them best."

"Yes," Ergün underscored his uncle's point, "we know that all too well."

Mark turned to them. "How?"

Murat interjected. "*Doktor Bey*, would you like more *çay*?"

Mark accepted the offer. Turgut ordered a second round for everyone.

"In this garage," Ergün said to Mark, "we mostly dismantle cars. My *amca* and I can take a car apart in one day."

"In bigger operations with more mechanics," said Turgut, "it can be done in two hours."

"But here," Ergün completed his uncle's point, "it's just the two of us."

"We have our own police contacts," said Turgut, "who we pay to look the other way."

"Weren't you busted a while back?" asked Mustafa.

"Yes," said Turgut. "One of our trusted police contacts turned on us. He was getting a better deal from a guy named Bartoš, a competing shop. Slovakian."

"It was a bad time," Ergün added. "They shut us down for several weeks. It took a lot to get us out of that bind."

Murat served more tea. He intently followed the conversation.

"But that fucker got his due," said Turgut. "He tried to do the same to Bognár's car operation. It didn't work out well."

"Yeah," Ergün chuckled. "Didn't that asshole Bartoš have his legs broken?"

"No, not his legs," explained Turgut. "His right arm."

They all sipped tea as they contemplated the fate of Bartoš. Mark tried to conceal the chill he experienced while listening to the story. He had apparently also run afoul of Bognár and now had more than his right arm at risk.

Murat inserted himself into the silence. "*Doktor Bey*, I understand you are from California?"

"Yes."

"Have you ever been to Seattle?"

"Sure. Many times. It's a short plane ride from San Francisco. I go to conferences there. Why do you ask?"

"That's where I want to live," said Murat.

Murat had a doe-eyed sincerity that Mark found refreshing. It reminded him of the world he had left behind when he flew to Budapest. He was amazed at how rapidly his life had changed.

"Why Seattle?"

"Because that's where Bill Gates lives." Murat's face brightened as he expressed his dream. "Microsoft."

Funny, thought Mark. When he was a kid, growing up in Istanbul, he had wanted to live in Texas and become a cowboy. He chuckled at the thought. What a filthy job real cowboy work was. Youthful dreams!

Murat noticed his chuckle and his face darkened.

"I'm sorry," said Mark. "I was not laughing at you. Thinking of something else."

Turgut gave the young man a slap on the back. "See, *Doktor Bey*, my nephew here, he has his head on right. He wants to *be* somebody. Not like us."

"But I still want to learn how to cut up cars as fast as you," said Murat.

"We'd better take our esteemed guest to his date," said Mustafa, placing his empty glass on the table.

Mark asked for a restroom. Murat lit the back side of the garage and directed him to a door at its far corner. Mark was surprised by how neat and clean this area was, stocked with various car parts organized in different piles, windshields here, fenders there, bumpers elsewhere. Turgut and Ergün obviously cared about the fruits of their labor.

The toilet was in as much disarray as the rest of the garage. Mark washed his hands and face and looked at his reflection in a cracked, faded mirror above the sink. He was haggard, his hair a mess, his face in need of a good shave, his eyes tired. The cut near his eyebrow was already swollen and bruised. He realized he had missed his jet lag sleep. He was hungry too. Traditional Hungarian food, Jasmin's promise, sounded good. He hoped the delay in connecting with her had not spoiled it all. He sprinkled water on his hair and combed it with his fingers.

They all assembled by the Skóda van, Mustafa entering the back first. Mark shook Murat's hand. "If you come and visit me in America, I'll take you to Seattle."

Murat gave him a firm handshake and toothy smile.

"I can't promise you Bill Gates, though," Mark added as he jumped into the back as well. "I don't know him personally."

Turgut and Ergün took the front seats, Turgut driving again. As they left the garage, Mark asked, "So what do you do with those car parts?"

"We sell them in Turkey," said Turgut. "It's very lucrative."

"They have a good business going here," Mustafa explained. "They have local *suppliers*," he gave the word a mocking emphasis, "here in Hungary, who provide them with cars. As they said, they avoid stepping on the toes of bigger fish. In Turkey they have a network, all from Balıkesir, who distribute the parts. It's all a sort of extended family business. Safer that way."

"Every few months we make regular trips to Turkey." Turgut spoke from his invisible driver's spot. "The paperwork that legitimizes our load costs us more than our police contacts."

Knowing they would arrive at the train station soon, Mark directed his attention to Mustafa. The two were dim silhouettes facing each other in side benches at the back of the van.

"What did you mean when you said that your stay in Budapest would depend on me?" he asked, referring to Mustafa's comment by the elevator at Gresham.

Mustafa laughed. "Look at all the trouble you've gotten yourself into," he said. "If it weren't for me, you'd be dead now, twice over."

"So?"

"So, I need to stay here until you decide to leave. *Someone* needs to protect you."

"Thanks a lot," said Mark, skeptically. "Don't you have a family back home?"

"Yes, my wife Hülya and two youngsters, a boy and a girl, eight and ten. Hülya is a teacher in a private school in Üsküdar."

"Don't they miss you?"

"They're used to me being away on different jobs. Besides," Mustafa added, "you've become a pretty good investigator yourself. I am waiting to see what else you'll uncover."

"Thanks," said Mark. That was the more plausible reason for Mustafa to stick around.

Mark realized that he was being used, but he didn't mind. After Gérard's earlier compliment, Mustafa's similar remark boosted his sagging energy. Radiology was suddenly a far distant memory. He was getting addicted to the new, perilous world into which he had plunged.

What would his father think if he saw Metin this way, he wondered. He would surely disapprove. Sadık Bey had passed away years ago, but not before he attended his son's graduation. He was proud of Metin, happy that his son had carried on with the life Sadık had charted for him. Now an American Mark had replaced the Turkish Metin, and he had veered off the path, into a hazardous, adventurous one. Mark hoped that he would not suffer the fate of his ancestor Nurettin, whom he had secretly envied.

The van stopped and began slowly backing up. "We're here," Turgut said. Mark edged closer to the door and prepared to get up. It's good that Sadık Bey was no longer around, Mark thought, to see him this way.

They heard the front doors open. "You two stay put," said Turgut, sticking his head toward the back compartment. "We're parked across from the station. Ergün and I will check out the area first."

"Good idea," said Mustafa. "We don't want our esteemed doctor to get assaulted again."

For a moment everything was silent, the back of the van darker. They could hardly see each other.

"I met Ahmet's Romanian wife and his business manager," said Mark. "His name is Iancu Negrescu. Have you heard of him?"

"No."

"Iancu knows a great deal. He seems pretty loyal to Ahmet and his family." Mark paused to contemplate what he had just said. "Ahmet's Romanian family. I think you and Iancu need to meet. I might be able to arrange that. Iancu is also interested in what I uncover, especially from the police. He in turn might give us more information about Ahmet's business dealings in Romania."

"See what I mean?" said Mustafa with mock pride. "I have good reason to stay in Budapest, with you."

Mark was getting accustomed to Mustafa's ridicule. He ignored the remark. "Gérard, the Interpol officer, confirmed that Ahmet was a broker in a black-market kidney scheme. This is why he was drawing international police attention."

"I heard some rumors about that in Istanbul during my search," said Mustafa. "Nothing I could confirm."

"Have you heard about a surgeon named Gazioğlu? Interpol is very interested in him."

"The name rings a bell. He was in the news, I think, back in Turkey. Something about the Turkish government shutting down a clinic of his."

"I found it very interesting that his name was brought up by police immediately upon Ahmet's death." Mark was assured in his assessment. "I have a gut feeling that the two are somehow connected."

The back door of the van opened and suddenly they were lit again. Mustafa was still wearing the oversized Budapest Stars jersey and black shorts.

"The coast is clear," said Turgut. "I think she is waiting for you across the street, by the McDonald's booth at the other end of the station."

For a moment Mark and Mustafa ignored Turgut.

"You know what else I discovered from this French officer?" Mark didn't wait for Mustafa to answer. "That in Istanbul they have an officer who works as an Interpol liaison, and this guy is another English High School graduate, from around my time. Can you believe that?"

Mustafa shook his head in disbelief. "Exactly how big was this school?"

Mark laughed. "Not that big. Our graduating class was only around sixty."

He crouched forward and exited the van. Mustafa followed. The cool air, devoid of grease and oil odors, felt good. Mark zipped up his coat, put on his shoulder bag and took a deep breath. They were parked in a side street that curved out of Teréz Körút, the main boulevard by the station. A small plaza with a subway entrance at its center separated them from Teréz. Yellow streetcars crisscrossed the middle of the busy boulevard, stopping at a long station between the plaza and the *Nyugati* train station across.

"I think I want to go Istanbul," said Mark.

"Don't we all," Ergün interjected. "I crave grilled fish and *rakı* by the seaside." He was standing next to the *Bosporus Autojavítás* sign on the van.

"This schoolmate, Leon, he was an upperclassman. I haven't seen him since then, but he would remember me. He was an easygoing sort. Nice guy. I think he could help us. Besides, there's someone else who invited me there, a woman whom I'd also like to see."

They walked through the plaza and waited by a crosswalk at Teréz. The yellow streetcars had cleared away, leaving that station empty. Mark gazed across at *Nyugati,* two graceful, neoclassical red buildings, each with twin towers, separated by a wide, glass-lined entrance with a giant triangular glass dome. At the far end, next to the station building, was a strange McDonald's, a stand rather than a shop, green in color rather than the usual red and yellow. Among the scant crowd on the sidewalk by the booth, Mark spotted the slender figure of Jasmin, leaning against her car at the curb.

"You seem to have no shortage of women you'd like to see," said Turgut.

"*Darısı başımıza*," added Ergün hopefully, *same fate for us*. The two laughed.

They crossed Teréz to *Nyugati*. As they walked toward the McDonald's, Mark said to Mustafa, "Your mission with Meltem Hanım may not have died with Ahmet after all."

Jasmin had noticed Mark and his entourage and began walking toward them. Mustafa held Mark's arm and stopped him for a second.

"You've been a godsend," he said to Mark seriously, devoid of his usual mocking expression. "Be careful."

They exchanged quiet glances, Mark nodding in appreciation. "Don't worry," he responded. "I'll have personal police protection."

Jasmin looked radiant in civilian clothes, a simple outfit of tight-fitting blue jeans, white shirt showing through a black leather jacket, her stride confident and feminine on high-heeled boots. Without epaulettes, her shoulders were narrower, her hips wider. *She looks sexy*, Mark thought. Her hair, combed down simply, was held back by a dark band, her eyes lustrous in contact lenses. She smiled at the group and said hello to Mark.

Embarrassed by his disheveled appearance, Mark instinctively brushed his hair with his fingers. He wished he looked better than he did.

Turgut and Ergün looked at Jasmin in disbelief. Mustafa stood back, trying to remain inconspicuous.

"Wow," said Ergün, in Turkish. "I wish I was a doctor like you." He turned to his uncle. "Only rich doctors can attract women like that."

Turgut nodded in agreement. "The rest of us," he said, "we get scraps."

Chapter 35

* * *

"Let's toast!" Perry Laughton held up a flute of champagne. "To the success of our youngsters."

He was jovial, his beefy cheeks crimson from two whiskey sours he had downed. As he took a large gulp, some spilled onto his brightly colored necktie, elegantly tied in a precise knot.

"Ooops!" He patted himself with a cloth napkin and looked at his guests. "My apologies," he said loudly. "We Americans! We're sometimes brutes when it comes to manners." He laughed out loud, his belly quivering at the edge of the table.

Sadık Bey and Füsun Hanım stared at Mr. Laughton in stony silence, politely refraining from agreement.

An impeccably dressed waiter delicately handed out menus in smart blue folders with a Pump Room insignia. Mark stared at a multitude of beige, balloon-like lights that crowded the ceiling of the elegant dining room. It was like being beneath a galaxy of brightly lit planets. He had arrived early with his parents and they had waited for Megan's family at the entrance of the restaurant, in front of a wall filled with framed photos of famous customers. He recognized David Bowie and Richard Nixon.

Mark had not experienced this sort of glitz in the south side of Chicago, nor Istanbul, except for an outing with Ahmet and his father to a nightclub called Maksim. As Mr. Laughton droned on, Mark eyed his parents sitting next to him. They seemed ill at ease.

Perry Laughton threw his large arm around his daughter, slathering her cheek with a theatrical kiss. "I am so proud of this young lady," he bellowed.

Megan smiled and stared at the elaborate place setting in front of her.

"As you must be of your son." He addressed Sadık.

"A lovely graduation ceremony, wasn't it?" Abigail Laughton interrupted her husband. "And that Rockefeller Chapel! So impressive."

Megan's mother was slim and delicate, and looked nothing like her daughter. Her red hair was well coiffed, curls cascading onto her shoulders. She wore a slender, strapless dress that betrayed a bony physique, with almost no cleavage despite the low cut. Friendly as she was, her words came out with an air of haughty chic.

"As impressive as any European cathedral."

"Indeed," said Sadık. "I did not expect to find such a classic piece of architecture in Chicago. I thought it was all skyscrapers here."

He took a sip of champagne. Mark eyed his father curiously. Sadık was not a drinker, and he had nearly put away a whole glass. His English, already cumbersome, was getting muddled.

The Laughtons did not notice anything astray. "There is a bit of everything in a big city like this," said Perry, more subdued. "I must say, when Megan chose Chicago over other colleges, I was concerned." He was articulate despite all he had imbibed. "Not about the education, mind you." He paused. "But about the neighborhood where she would live."

"It's a lovely campus," Füsun chimed in, speaking for the first time. It was their first visit to Chicago and all they had seen of the south side was Lake Shore Drive and the leafy, Neo-Gothic quadrangles of the University campus. She did not get what Perry was referring to.

Laughton stared at Füsun for a moment, the trial lawyer in him sizing up whether he should argue with her. "Yes, indeed," he tooted instead. He eyed his daughter fondly.

A waiter poured more champagne. They all stared at the bubbles.

Sadık changed the subject. "We thank you, Mr. Perry," addressing Laughton formally, as would be customary in Turkish, "for your generosity and hospitality." He raised his champagne flute. Füsun gently pressed his arm down and took the glass away from him.

"Our pleasure," Abigail responded. "We're so pleased that your son has come into Megan's life."

Mark and Megan exchanged glances, uneasy with the awkward love-fest between their parents.

"I have an announcement," shouted Perry, after shooing off a waiter checking in for menu orders. "I will be buying a house for our young couple in Palo Alto. My graduation gift."

Megan looked at her father, stunned.

"Sir, you don't have to do that," Mark said.

"No, son. I do." Laughton was firm. "I saw the crappy conditions in which you survived through college. Now that you're engaged, you need to be in better digs. It is near the train station, so you can commute easily."

Megan was headed to a Ph. D. program in English at Stanford, while Mark had been accepted for a master's program in biochemistry at U. C. San Francisco, fifty miles north of the Stanford campus in Palo Alto. It was a one-hour commute by car in decent traffic. Mark wasn't sure how long it would be by train.

"Mr. Laughton—" Sadık began.

Laughton interrupted him. "Perry. Please call me Perry, my dear Sadık." He pronounced the name *sadduck*, as most English speakers did.

"Perry." Sadık started again. "Your generosity is overwhelming. I don't know how to thank you. I hope that someday, soon maybe, you and your lovely wife can visit us in Turkey and we can counter with our Turkish hospitality."

"Oh, we'd love to," gushed Abigail. She looked at her husband. "Wouldn't that be wonderful, dear?"

"Indeed," Perry affirmed. "I've been to your charming country once, on business. But Abby here has not. We accept your invitation. Let's toast!"

Sadık raised his champagne glass again. This time Füsun did not stop him.

* * *

Sadık lowered a lighter into his pipe with a shaky hand, staring at the lights of Grant Park and scant traffic on Lake Shore Drive beyond.

"I shouldn't have had all that champagne," he said. "I won't sleep well tonight." He already looked worn down, jet lag tugging on him, exhausted from nonstop activity since he had arrived from Istanbul.

"Tomorrow I was going to take you up the Sears and John Hancock Towers," said Mark. "Maybe we should delay that and let you rest."

Sadık did not answer. He puffed his pipe and stared at the dark expanse of Lake Michigan beyond the park and Lake Shore Drive. "Go check on your mother, will you? See if she's asleep."

They were in a luxurious suite at the Hilton on South Michigan Avenue, compliments of Perry Laughton. It had a breathtaking view of the lakefront. Füsun was already fast asleep.

Father and son sat on opposite armchairs facing the windows, a coffee table between them. "I like this girl you chose," said Sadık, referring to Megan, "but her father…." He took a long puff from his pipe.

"I know," said Mark, with a laugh. "He means well, but he can't help being who he is. They'll be in New York State and we'll be in California. A safe distance, wouldn't you say?"

Sadık set his pipe down on the table, took off his spectacles and rubbed his eyes. He stared at the bust of Barbaros, hero admiral of Sultan Süleyman's navy, at the head of the pipe.

"Metin," he said wearily, "your mother insisted that I have a word with you." He put his glasses back on, halting them halfway up his nose.

Mark waited expectantly, but his father went into another one of his silent spells. "About what?" Mark finally prodded him.

"It's something I figured you would have discovered by yourself," said Sadık awkwardly. "But your mother and I want to make sure."

Mark guessed what his father was referring to and realized how difficult it was for Sadık to air this openly. "Why?" he asked.

"Well." Sadık was hesitant. He played with his pipe as though he could not decide if he should light it. "You are about to marry this young woman. We want to make sure that you know how to…" His voice trailed off again.

"What makes you think I don't?" Unable to conceal his vexation, Mark's voice rose.

Sadık sensed his son's aggravation. "We heard rumors," he said wearily. "Back in Istanbul."

Mark gazed at his father with astonishment. "Rumors? What rumors?" His father was not one to be taken into rumors.

"Okay." Sadık paused to gather some courage. "It was actually Latif Bey."

"Ahmet's father?" Mark's voice rose further, this time with surprise.

"Yes, him." Sadık finally decided to light his pipe again. Mark waited impatiently, as the lighter hovered above the grand admiral's head, tottering.

"He took me out to lunch at the Hilton in Harbiye." Sadık exhaled his words with a cloud of smoke.

"When? Why?" Mark was incredulous.

Sadık thought for a moment. "A few weeks before you two graduated from high school."

That was four years ago, thought Mark. He had never heard of this.

"A very charming man," said Sadık. "A gentleman."

Mark could not imagine his father chummy with Latif.

"He wanted to meet me," Sadık continued, "and express his pleasure about you being a good friend to his son. He said that you helped Ahmet a great deal. Kept him on the right path. Otherwise, Latif Bey was afraid Ahmet might have strayed into who knows what."

Mark had never seen himself that way and had nothing to retort with. He listened in disbelief.

"Anyway, Latif Bey mentioned something about a place called Varol." Sadık looked out the window, eyes away from his son.

Mark sank in his armchair, his surprise turning to dismay. He could no longer see his father's face. He didn't want to.

Sadık droned on. "You probably don't think that I know about such places." He paused, longer than usual. Mark leaned forward and peeked at him, pipe in hand, staring blankly at the window.

"I have never frequented them, for sure. But I *have* heard of them. Who hasn't?"

"So, what did Latif Bey say about it?" Mark asked softly, embarrassed after all these years.

"That his boy, and other boys, had visited there. And that they were spreading rumors about you having been there too."

Sadık lumbered out of his chair, stood up, and faced his son as he leaned against a window. "Look, I wasn't surprised to hear this." He paused, waiting for his son to lock eyes with him. "I wasn't upset, either." Mark finally managed to look into his father's eyes. "You know—boys will be boys."

"But," Sadık continued, "Latif said that the rumors were about you being...." He paused and shook his head. "Unable to perform."

Mark knew this was coming. At the time, despite Ahmet's assurances, the word had gotten out in school, and he had caught a good deal of grief from his school mates. His shame flooded back as though it were yesterday.

"So you see," Sadık said gently. "On the eve of your marriage...." He stopped again as he detected Mark's dread. "Your mother made me do it," he said defensively. "We just wanted to make sure that you were okay. That...you know...."

"Dad, I *am* okay," said Mark, annoyed. "Megan and I have been together for over two years and you have nothing to worry about."

He did not tell his father how awkward it had been at first, and how patiently Megan had guided him through. That's when he realized that Istanbul was past history and that he was in love with Megan.

"Good!" Sadık was relieved. He walked over to a nearby trash can and dumped the ashes of his pipe. "I am going to bed then," he said quietly. "Your father-in-law gave me a headache."

Mark wondered if Latif had also mentioned another secret outing of his with Ahmet, to the glamorous Maksim nightclub, where Mark had met a famous gangster. But Sadık was finished, waddling toward the bedroom.

"Dad," said Mark, his voice now firm. Sadık stopped and faced his son. "Thanks for everything."

"Everything what?" Sadık asked curiously. "Laughton paid for it all."

"No, I don't mean that." Mark paused and repeated more emphatically. "I mean, *everything*."

Sadık gave his son a dismissive shake with his right hand and shuffled on.

Chapter 36

* * *

"What happened to you?" Jasmin seemed stunned by Mark's appearance. Mark turned around and watched the Turkish gang jaywalk across Teréz Körút, narrowly missing a yellow streetcar that started out of the station. "Don't ask," he said wearily. He could just imagine how awful he must look.

Jasmin hooked her arm into his and they began walking. Out of her police uniform she had a different aura than when he first met her. She was more like a Girl Scout then. Now she was a woman. Mark savored the feel of her on his arm.

She continued to stare at Mark's haggard face. "You look like you've been through a fight and lost."

"Long story," said Mark as they walked toward a blue and white Smart car parked across from the McDonald's booth. "I'll tell you later."

"I see you made some Turkish friends here." Jasmin steered her Smart car away from Nyugati and into streets that Mark did not recognize. "So quickly."

"Yeah, well," he answered, "I didn't really look for them. They all found *me*."

Jasmin threw a quick glance at Mark and smiled. "You're more attractive than you think." She chuckled. Her Hungarian accent made it impossible for Mark to make out whether she was mocking or making a pass at him. "You've certainly caught the attention of many in Budapest."

"More than I care to."

At a stop light in a brightly lit intersection, she extended a finger toward the swollen spot on his forehead. It was already getting purple. She gently touched it. "Do you want to tell me now?"

Mark did not flinch, even though the spot was tender. Her touch felt good. "More commotion," said Mark. "I am sure you'll hear about it tomorrow at the police station."

"I'm off tomorrow."

Mark briefly recounted his abduction and rescue, leaving out the chop shop. "Those two guys were seriously injured," he added.

"H'mmm," Jasmin said thoughtfully. "Messy." She drove into what looked like a former industrial area, now gentrifying with a forest of modern ten-story apartment buildings, all with small balconies, all alike.

"Zrinyi is usually busy with pedestrians," she said. "I bet there will be confusion among witnesses about who did what to whom."

The thought had not occurred to Mark. "You mean they might think that *I* beat those guys up?"

"The police will figure it out," she said. "You said that the second guy might have a crushed skull from a hockey stick, right?"

"Yes."

"That will be obvious to forensics. Also, there are surveillance cameras at every corner on Zrinyi. Once they examine their footage they will know that you weren't carrying a hockey stick."

She drove down a street where the apartment buildings were more densely clustered. She stopped and backed the Smart car into a tiny spot. Mark looked around. The street was quiet and residential. Jasmin had parked in front of two identical buildings that were connected to each other on the ground floor with a grocery store. It was the only commercial entity around.

"Are we having dinner?" he asked, perplexed.

"Yes," she said. They sat in the dark car for a moment. "Your Turkish friend, what was his name?"

"Mustafa."

"Was he wearing a helmet?"

"Yes."

"Then he might be difficult to identify."

They got out of the car. "But who knows what whoever sent those goons will think." She spoke as though talking to herself while she locked the car.

Standing by the passenger door, Mark stared at Jasmin and for a moment he froze. She was correct. The only account Bognár would receive of what happened at Zrinyi and Őctőber 6. would be from the driver of the BMW who sped off and probably did not see much. The two injured guys were unlikely to remember that it was Mustafa who hit them. The first was assaulted from behind and soon blinded by his own blood. The second guy would surely have retrograde amnesia from his head injury. It was not difficult to imagine their boss concluding that Mark caused all the damage.

Jasmin rapidly surveyed an array of bells at the door of the building and rang one. The door buzzed and she opened it.

"Do you know Tibor Bognár?" asked Mark, as they entered a small foyer with an elevator ahead.

"No." She pressed the elevator button.

"Where are we going?" Mark stood behind her.

"Restaurant."

Mark hesitated and took a step back toward the door, looking out into the street.

"It's an apartment restaurant," she said. "Come on."

* * *

A modern, spacious elevator swiftly took them up to the sixth floor where Jasmin rang a bell next to a door sign that read *Étterem Ferenc.* A short, chubby, white-haired woman wearing an apron, her hair netted, hugged Jasmin and they kissed on the cheeks. She eyed Mark's bruised face nervously. Jasmin smiled and said a few words in Hungarian to calm the woman down.

An inviting smell of herbs and frying chicken infused the place. They passed a small foyer and went through a formal living room into a narrow open kitchen, next to what appeared to be a family room with couches and a TV stand. In the middle of it, near the kitchen, was a table, obviously placed there temporarily, for it blocked traffic, on which were laid cutlery, serving plates, and some appetizers, already prepared.

Ferenc was at the oven, next to a boiling pot, wearing a white chef's coat with an upturned collar, stirring up some sauce on a skillet. He appeared to be in his thirties, tall and square-jawed, dark hair shortly cropped, with long, lanky arms. He looked at his guests and smiled.

"*Üdvözöljük*," he said to Jasmin, who waved back. Jasmin introduced Mark. "Welcome," said Ferenc, in English. He momentarily stopped stirring and stared at Mark before returning to his sauce.

Jasmin led Mark into a bathroom off the kitchen. "We need to clean you up," she said. "You're scaring people."

She seemed to know her way around the apartment. Mark examined his face in the clear, brightly lit mirror while Jasmin searched for a bottle of alcohol and cotton swabs. There was blood caked in spots over his face. His left eyelid was purple and swollen. Jasmin gently cleaned him, her face close to his, her eyes concentrating on her task. Her youthful beauty reminded Mark of his early days with Megan. As Jasmin's alcohol wipe seared into his cut, Mark felt the pain of losing Megan all over again.

"There," she whispered, "much better," as she applied a Band-Aid to the cut. Jasmin smiled, her face still close to his. Mark breathed in her floral scent. He was attracted to this young woman, her lips within kissing distance, and it disturbed him. He took a step back toward the mirror and examined his face.

"You could be a good nurse," he said, looking at her reflection in the mirror. He brushed back his hair with his fingers. "If you ever want to leave police work."

The old woman was waiting for them in the kitchen. She led them out to a balcony. Jasmin introduced her to Mark. "This is Edit," she said, "Ferenc's mother-in-law." The woman examined Mark with a more friendly expression and bowed her head gracefully. She had rosy cheeks, her white hair short and curly beneath the net. She did not speak English.

"I guess we're eating outdoors," said Jasmin. "I hope you don't mind the cold."

A small table had been laid out for two at the narrow balcony. Edit busied herself turning on a gas-powered space heater that towered over the table. The balcony overlooked the Danube, affording a different panorama than the architectural splendor around the Chain Bridge. The river was glassy calm. The opposite shore appeared to be uninhabited land, just silhouettes of trees and low-lying hills. Mark went to the railing and looked out. It was as though they had left the city for the country, even though they hadn't come that far. He inhaled the fresh breeze. Tired as he was, the chilly, clear air enlivened him.

Jasmin sidled next to Mark. "*Hagógyáry* Island," she said, pointing to the shore across. "The word means shipyard. That's what it was once. Now it is mostly a nature preserve. They hold a big music festival there in the summer."

A young woman interrupted them, hugging and kissing Jasmin, the two animatedly exchanging Hungarian words with each other. The woman was wearing an overcoat and holding a small bag of groceries.

"Meet Bianca," said Jasmin, "Ferenc's wife."

Bianca was tall and pretty, with long, straight black hair in a ponytail and blue eyes. She seemed to complement Ferenc well, Mark thought.

Edit returned with four elegantly tall aperitif glasses filled with a clear drink. Just then Ferenc appeared, his chef's coat fittingly stained.

"Ah," he said, "just in time for the *pálinka*." He kissed Jasmin on the cheeks and warmly shook hands with Mark. "I'm sorry I could not greet you properly earlier." He was cheerful. "The *paprikash* sauce needed attention." He picked a glass and raised it; Jasmin and Bianca followed. Mark looked at the remaining glass on the tray with hesitation.

"It's *pálinka,*" said Jasmin. "Homemade brandy. Traditional Hungarian."

"*Egészségedre*," said Ferenc, *To your health*, and without waiting for the others, took a gulp.

"Careful," advised Jasmin. "It's pretty strong."

The apricot-flavored drink barreled down Mark's throat like a fireball.

"Looks like you've had an accident," Ferenc said to Mark. "I hope it wasn't too bad."

Jasmin said a few words to Ferenc and Bianca in Hungarian. They both stopped and eyed Mark curiously. Jasmin whispered into Mark's ear, "I told them that you've been assisting us in an investigation and you got embroiled in a brawl."

Edit brought appetizer plates, cold cuts, sausages, vegetables, and a bright orange dip with a side of crostini.

"What exactly is an apartment restaurant?" asked Mark, hoping to change the subject.

"Just what it means," said Ferenc. "Instead of conducting business in a shop, we do it at home. More personal that way, intimate."

"We usually have ten or twelve guests," added Bianca. "But Jasmin here is special."

"We've been best friends since childhood," said Jasmin, standing up and embracing Bianca.

Mark wondered how they fit a dozen people into this small apartment. It would have to be in the family room they had passed earlier. Intimate indeed.

"When Jasmin said that she was bringing a special guest from San Francisco, an American doctor, Ferenc and I were happy to open our restaurant just for you two." Bianca bowed slightly as she uttered these words, in the manner of a polished waitress.

"We didn't know that he was also Mr. James Bond," quipped Ferenc. "Now you enjoy the appetizers, and I'll go back to the kitchen."

"This drink is like poison," Mark commented to Jasmin, after the rest left.

Jasmin chuckled. "Quiet, they might hear you." She took another sip of hers. "It is our national drink. Homemade, fermented fruit juice. Everyone makes some and everyone has their own recipe. They tried to ban the practice during communist times but were unsuccessful."

"Hungarian moonshine?"

Jasmin looked up at the sky. It was a moonless night. She turned back to Mark quizzically. Now it was Mark's turn to chuckle. "American slang," he said. "Never mind."

He popped a radish in his mouth. "M'mmm," he said. "Unusual. Sweet almost."

"Butter radishes," Jasmin said. "Special to Hungary." She dug in her bag and removed an envelope while Mark took another radish. She put the envelope on the table and pushed it toward Mark. "I have a surprise for you."

Mark removed the contents of the envelope and stared at a four-page document entirely in Hungarian. It was titled *Elsölenges Jelentés*. He looked up at Jasmin quizzically.

"Preliminary forensics report," said Jasmin. "On the Radu murder."

Mark handed it back. "What does it say?"

She gave it a quick glance. "I reviewed it earlier," she said. "Basically that they think the cause of death was asphyxiation."

Mark remembered the small dots of blood in Ahmet's eyes, petechiae. He had already come to the same conclusion. "Do they know how?"

Jasmin shuffled through the pages. "Some sort of gas, probably." She read intently from a page.

"Why do they think that?"

She ran her index finger through a line in the report. "The bruise marks on his cheeks." She looked up at him.

Mark recalled the thin diagonal bruises extending from Ahmet's nostrils toward his lips. "A mask!"

Jasmin nodded.

Mark had seen countless patients with oxygen masks on their faces. None got bruises from them. Ahmet had to have struggled against his. The scene in the Royal Suite *was* violent, after all. "Any idea what sort of gas?"

"No." Jasmin picked up a radish and examined it between her fingertips. She had obviously already read this part. "They mention the need for airtight removal of his lungs and trachea during his autopsy and withdrawing air samples from it for gas chromatography." She bit half of the radish. "It will take many weeks before we know."

The killer—or killers—had been well trained, sneaking in and out of the Royal Suite as they did with no disturbance, Mark thought. How in the world had they accomplished this while carrying a container of gas? It had to have been small, like those oxygen tanks that people with lung disease carried.

"They placed the time of death around shortly before you found him," Jasmin continued, reading from the document. "They mention you here, that there was no rigor mortis based on your testimony. The body was stiff by the time the evidence team got there."

Mark recalled taking Ahmet's wrist pulse and how easily his arm had moved, as though Ahmet was simply asleep.

"Do they mention a massage he had at the spa?"

"Yes. The spa log is another item that helps pinpoint the time of death."

The *pálinka*, combined with the heating lamp, was warming Mark up. He unzipped his coat and took it off.

"No fingerprints," continued Jasmin, reading from the second page. "Except for yours, on his passports and phone. You already told the police you had touched those."

Mark nodded.

"They did a thorough search for other items that may have been used to asphyxiate him. In particular they focused on pillows—there were lots of pillows—for body fluids such as saliva or blood. Nothing turned up."

"There was a wet spot on the carpet and on the bed," said Mark.

Jasmin shuffled the pages silently. "There!" She read for a moment. "Yes. They think it was urine. His gown was also wet with urine."

"I had gathered that." Mark recalled the smell on his fingers after touching the spot on the carpet where he had picked up Ahmet's broken spectacles. "Do they draw any conclusions from the location of the wet spot?"

Jasmin read through the entire document. "No," she said. "They just mention the spot. That's all. What do you think?"

"I don't know," Mark said pensively. "His glasses were on that wet spot in the carpet, broken. He may have involuntarily urinated there. Maybe that's where he was killed."

"Interesting."

For a moment, they both fell silent. Mark hesitantly eyed the glass of *pálinka*. He decided to take another, tiny sip. Jasmin laughed as he grimaced afterwards.

"He had bruises around his wrists," Mark continued. "Was he handcuffed?"

"Yes, they think he was."

"What about those lines around his torso and thighs?"

"They describe that in some detail. Parallel lines at regular intervals." She leafed through the document and read out loud. "Four-and-a-half centimeter intervals."

She looked up at Mark and took a generous sip of *pálinka*. "They don't say more. No guesses. No conclusions."

"Those marks were very peculiar," said Mark. "I wonder if they have no conclusions because they don't know what the marks are."

"Possibly."

"Any comments on who did this?"

"Nothing at all," said Jasmin.

"How about whether there was more than one person?"

"As I said," Jasmin did not look at the document, "nothing."

"Anything about the security system of the hotel and how it was bypassed?"

Jasmin looked at Mark curiously. "Why do you ask?"

"Mustafa, the Turkish private eye," said Mark. "He heard rumors from hotel employees that this was an inside job. Olga, the masseuse, may have assisted the killer."

Bianca appeared with a carafe of white wine and began pouring some for both. Mark pushed away his half-empty glass of *pálinka* and took a sip. Better.

Jasmin folded the forensics report and placed it in its envelope. She looked at Bianca and spoke briefly in Hungarian.

"I'm sorry to interrupt." Bianca hurried away.

Jasmin handed the report to Mark. As Mark placed the envelope in his shoulder bag, Bianca returned, wine bottle in hand. "This wine is very nice," he said, taking another sip. "What is it?"

"A dry Furmint, from Kiralyudvar." Bianca stood over Mark as he took another sip. It was a rich, aromatic wine with scents of herbs and a hint of smoke. It tasted like dry white Bordeaux.

"What's the varietal?" asked Mark.

"As I said. Furmint. It's the same grape that is blended for the famous Tokaji wine." Bianca smiled and poured him some more.

"I thought Hungarian wines were all sweet, like Tokaji."

"This dry style of Furmint is becoming more popular." Bianca left the bottle on the table and retreated to the kitchen.

"Thank you," Mark said to Jasmin, "for the forensics information." He took a slice of what turned out to be smoked tongue. "I hope you won't get in trouble for it."

"No," said Jasmin. "I copy documents like these for different departments frequently. No one will notice."

"Still," said Mark, "leaking it to someone like me could cause problems."

"Yes." She smiled and leaned back in her seat confidently. "I checked with a senior advisor before I did it. He thought I'd be okay."

Mark was surprised by this revelation. How could a higher-ranking officer condone a leak? But he let it go. He was more curious about something else.

"So what is it that you wanted to know about San Francisco?" he asked.

"How long have you lived there?" she asked.

"Let's see." Mark ran through the years for a moment. "Over twenty years."

"What is it like?"

"Very beautiful," said Mark. "Hills, lots of hills, all with views of water. Two peninsulas that jut out at each other, just like Istanbul, where I grew up. Bridges. Suspension bridges. Same as in Istanbul."

"What about the people?"

"Friendly. Casual. Friendlier than in the Midwest, where I spent time before."

"Are there flower children there?"

Mark placed some orange dip on a crostini and eyed Jasmin with curiosity. "Why do you ask?"

The dip was strange. It had a creamy flavor but spicy too, paprika obviously, but it also had a curious salty, fishy flavor. Jasmin noticed his puzzlement.

"It's *körözött*," she explained. "Another Hungarian tradition. I promised you a classic homemade Hungarian meal. Remember?"

Mark took another helping while Jasmin licked some off the tip of her knife. "It's a cheese spread, based on Philadelphia cheese, with paprika of course, but not too much. Everyone has a different recipe for it. Ferenc puts anchovy paste in it. So it's sort of fishy."

"It goes well with this wine." Mark took another sip of the Furmint. After the *pálinka*, small as his sips had been, the wine was giving him a buzz that enhanced his fatigue.

"My mother," said Jasmin, "dreamed of being a flower child, of living free in San Francisco."

"A hippy!" Mark was surprised. "When I was growing up in Istanbul, in the nineteen-sixties and seventies, it was a mecca for hippies. We didn't like them at all."

"There weren't any in Hungary," said Jasmin. "My parents grew up in communist times, under the Russian boot."

"Let me tell you a story." Mark took yet another helping of the *körözött*. The dip was addictive. "When I was a teenager, I once rode a public bus with my uncle. The bus was going to Sultanahmet, the district where all foreign hippies congregated. We stood by several hippies in the back of the bus. They looked shabby and smelled bad."

Mark smiled as the memory replayed in his mind. "My uncle turned to me and said that he hoped I would not turn into one of them. He gave them a disgusted look. If you do, he said, I'll kill you. They had no idea we were talking about them. I told my uncle that he need not worry. There was no way I would do that."

"I had an uncle," said Jasmin, "a great-uncle actually, who died in the Russian invasion in nineteen fifty-six." She took a sip of wine. "I never knew him. Only a photo of a handsome young man that hung in our living room. He was a legend in our family."

The story reminded Mark of Nurettin, his legendary Ottoman ancestor. He wished he had a photo of him.

"San Francisco is no longer a big hippy hangout," said Mark. "But if you go to Golden Gate Park, at one end of it, next to Haight-Ashbury, you can still find a few left over from that era."

"When I was little," said Jasmin, "my mother and father used to listen to rock-and-roll music on the radio from a pirate station, and there was this song...." She hummed the tune.

Mark chuckled. "San Francisco," he said. "'Be sure to wear some flowers in your hair,' right?" He briefly joined her, humming. "Yes, I liked it too. Scott McKenzie."

"Who?"

"That's who sang it. But that song came out in the late sixties."

Jasmin leaned forward, looking more intently into Mark's eyes. "It was a sort of anthem for my mom and dad. They grew up dreaming of freedom and to them, San Francisco was the ultimate symbol of it."

There was a refreshing sincerity about Jasmin, a youthful enthusiasm that Mark remembered he too once possessed. Jasmin looked at Mark with a glitter in her eyes. "I've always dreamed of San Francisco. Wondered what it was like."

She leaned into the table, toward Mark. "Then you came along, and you were so different."

Mark leaned in, too. "How?"

"Sophisticated," she said. "Exotic." Their hands touched. Mark pulled his back. "Then you turned out adventurous, too. So daring."

It was quiet on the balcony, peaceful. Jasmin kept her gaze on Mark. She was so attractive, thought Mark, so enticing, yet so young. Ahmet crossed his mind. If he were sitting here, in Mark's chair, there would be no doubt about what he would do.

Mark leaned back and abruptly poured wine for both of them, accidentally spilling some. "I'm just old and clumsy," he said. "I've been in a rut back home. My job is routine. My marriage is a mess. Then I come here and after the shock of finding my friend dead, I plunge into a…" he hesitated and then recalled Ferenc's comment. "A James Bond fantasy." He took a larger sip of wine. "I am not daring," he said. "I am just foolish."

"I think you're exhausted," said Jasmin tenderly. "You've been through a lot. When was the last time you slept?"

Mark smiled sardonically. "I no longer remember."

They stared out into the darkness of the river for a while, wine glasses in hand, and said no more.

Bianca and Edit appeared with large bowls. "And now, our main course," said Bianca ceremoniously. Mark and Jasmin stared at the food while Bianca placed a new carafe on the table, this time of red wine.

"Chicken *paprikash*," said Jasmin. "Ferenc's special recipe." Pieces of chicken floated, barely visible, in an orange-brown sauce. Mark stared at another bowl of what looked like Israeli couscous.

"*Tarhonya*," Bianca chimed in. "Our own variation on the traditional accompaniment to chicken *paprikash*."

Edit brought a plate of pickles that she laid next to the bowls.

Jasmin pointed to the *tarhonya* bowl. "Chicken *paprikash* is usually served with *spaetzle*, a different kind of egg noodle, German. *Tarhonya* is more Hungarian." She assembled a plate for him with serving spoons. "You put your chicken on top of it."

"Put more sauce on it, dear," said Bianca. She turned to Mark and smiled. "We want to make sure our guest remembers this dinner."

"Oh, I certainly will," said Mark, eyeing Jasmin, who smiled back. He leaned in and inhaled the spicy aroma of his plate as Jasmin placed pickles on the side.

"You have to have it with the pickles," she ordered him. "Tradition."

Mark took a sip of the ruby-red wine. It had hearty fruit and strong tannins. He raised the glass and looked at Bianca.

"Kekfrankos," she answered him. "From Sopron, near the Austrian border."

They tucked into their plates. The food was good and hearty, wiping out the tannins of the wine that turned out to go well with it. Mark realized how famished he'd been, the crêpes and chimney cake at Nonloso a distant memory. His adventures of the day settled in on him, along with the food and wine, bringing on a languorous torpor. Ferenc and Bianca joined them, also partaking in wine and food, carrying on an animated conversation with Jasmin in Hungarian and English. He viewed them through a haze, while his chicken *paprikash* disappeared fast.

He awoke to a jolt on his shoulder. Ferenc was pleasantly smiling, close to his face. "Tired, eh?"

Jasmin was a blur across the table. "You have to have a bite of the dessert before we leave," she said.

Mark stared at a slice of yellow cake, thin and high, standing next to a glazed apricot sliced in half, apricot juice dripping off its sides. He took a bite.

The bold flavors, sweet yet tart, momentarily awakened him. "Sorry," he said to Ferenc and Bianca, who sat near the table at the edge of the balcony. "It's been a very long day."

Bianca lifted a small glass of golden liquid. "Have sip of our famous *Tokaji Aszu* before you call it a day."

It was pleasantly sweet and high in alcohol. He shouldn't be drinking much of it, he thought. He wasn't sure he could make it out of the apartment upright. But he finished the glass anyway. The last thing he remembered was Jasmin, looking at him intently, her lips parted in an alluring smile, extending her hand across the table and squeezing his.

Chapter 37

* * *

Mark awoke to the loud ring of his iPhone. It was in a fold of the couch on which he was lying, still fully clothed. He groped for the phone and answered it, eyes closed. The voice of Ben Allen, chief of radiology at Kaiser, San Francisco, was at the other end.

"Ben?" Mark opened his eyes and looked around. Where was he? The small room was dimly illuminated by city lights. There were silhouettes of a nearby coffee table, an armchair by the window, and a flat-screen TV at the other end.

"Mark, what are you up to out there?"

He sat up, trying to figure if he was in San Francisco. "Where?"

"In Europe," screamed Ben, "wherever you are."

"Budapest?"

"Mark, are you all right?"

Mark ran his free hand over his hair and rubbed his forehead, trying to reorient himself. A sharp pain zinged him into more arousal as his fingers brushed against his bruised eyelid. He almost screamed but held back.

"Yes," he murmured, as the ache receded. "It's nighttime here." He pressed the home button of his phone. Three forty-five. His mind was foggy. He remembered *pálinka*, and wine—white, red, dessert.

"Mark, two FBI agents came to our office today." Ben was clearly disturbed. "They wanted some documents from your files."

Mark tried to clear the cobwebs in his head. Damn, he thought; he shouldn't have drunk so much. "FBI," he said, thoughtfully. Then it all came to him. "Oh, yes." More animated. "They're just looking for a radiology report from Romania. Did Nancy give it to them?"

"No," said Ben. "We didn't know what to give them. Romania? What radiology report?"

"Never mind," said Mark. "It's a long story. I'll explain it when I come back home."

"Mark, we're concerned about you. These FBI agents made us feel like you've gotten yourself in some trouble."

"What did they say?"

"Not much. It's what they did not say, their attitude. They said that an Interpol liaison in Hungary was seeking this report. Why the hell would Interpol be interested in our medical records?"

Mark stood and walked to the window. He didn't know how to answer the question. He stared down at a narrow street outside from what he took to be a second- or third-story window. It was well lit and deserted, the apartments across all dark. "Look, I'm okay. The report they're looking for is not ours. It's something personal. I need more time here, in Europe. Another week maybe. Can you rearrange the schedule?"

"I don't know," said Ben skeptically. "You know we're short-handed. We need you back. Soon."

Mark heard a shuffle and turned around, back into the room. A slender silhouette lithely approached him. As the streetlight illuminated her, Mark recognized Jasmin in a slim T-shirt that was too short, revealing the tip of her panties and long, shapely legs, feet bare. He took a step toward her. Jasmin's hair was disheveled, eyes dreamy. For a moment Mark wondered if he were hallucinating.

She came closer and grabbed his free arm. He could smell a familiar floral odor on her, mixed with a faint hint of alcohol. Her body nearly touched his. He noticed erect nipples beneath barely noticeable mounds under her T-shirt.

"Ben," he said. "I have to go."

* * *

Her kiss was resolute and tender, her naked body smooth and warm. They lay sideways in darkness, in her small bed, their legs intertwined. Her skin felt good, rubbing against his. How long had it been since he'd had such contact?

She kissed him again. Her hand slid down the side of his body and in along his groin. She spread her legs a bit. He let her sidle him, now aroused, toward her as she let him feel her wetness. She was gentle and methodical. He wanted to push on but he hesitated. He was more awake now, her actions having cleared his cobwebs. An image came to his mind of the first time he saw her in her blue uniform, a Girl Scout. He withdrew.

She leaned in, trying for another kiss. He untangled his legs and turned around, trying to put some distance between his body and hers, but the bed was too small. His feet jutted out of the end. She turned and lay on top of him, her erect nipples pressing against his chest. He saw the whites of her eyes, peering into his, a fleeting glimpse before she closed them and their lips touched. She straddled him at his mid-body, gently rocking herself back and forth, painting him with her wet spot.

"Jasmin," he murmured. She continued slowly, smoothly, determined. "Jasmin, please stop."

She sat up on him, her weight pressing further against him, arousing him yet more. "What's the matter?" she asked quietly, releasing the pressure a bit. "Don't you want it?"

He drew her back toward him, their breaths mixing inches apart. "Oh, I do.... You can't imagine how much I do."

She reached down and gently grabbed him, adjusting herself, ready to take him in.

"Wait a minute."

He gently tilted her off him, their bodies again facing each other sideways. "Jasmin," he said firmly. "I am very flattered and very...very attracted. But I can't."

He instantly regretted saying it. He was glad Ahmet was not around to witness what he had done. *Crazy*, he would have said, *to turn away a gift like this. Look at her, so young and beautiful!*

She lay on her back and stared at the ceiling. He lay by her and caressed her flat, smooth stomach.

"I'm sorry," he whispered. "You could be my daughter. I just don't think it's right."

She gave him a quick look, eyes wide, then turned away, pulling the bedsheet over both of them. They lay quietly for a while. Mark eventually broke the silence.

"How did I get here?" he asked.

"You passed out at Ferenc's several times. He helped me get you down to my car. You were in no shape to go to your hotel."

He heard his phone chime. Email. "Shit," he said, and bolted out of the bed, almost tripping as his feet got entangled on his clothes, lying on the floor. He retrieved the phone from the living room couch.

"What's the matter?" she asked as he hastily drew the blanket over his torso.

"The phone!" He fiddled with it, scrolling through useless email. "How did it turn on?"

"I did that," she said. "I was looking for your friend Mustafa. I thought maybe he'd come and fetch you."

"Did you find him? He's on my list."

"You had two phones in there. The Cello Mobile was on and had no information. I found his number in the iPhone but he didn't answer."

Damn him, thought Mark.

"How come you have two phones?"

"Mustafa told me that they're tracking my whereabouts through the iPhone. I am supposed to keep it off. He gave me the Cello Mobile, a rental, as a spare."

"Who is tracking you?"

"Bognár's men. The ones who attacked me on Zrinyi."

Her teeth glittered in the light of the phone screen as she smiled broadly, facing him. "Don't worry about them," she said, turning in toward him again. She kissed him lightly on his cheek. "You're with me now. Under police protection. Let them come, if they dare."

She was a grown woman again, an unflinching professional. He had the urge to resume what she had started.

"Keep your iPhone on."

She turned her back to him and pulled the covers over her shoulders. "Let's go back to sleep," she said.

He embraced her from behind, his arm around her midriff, his face nuzzled into her neck.

"Thanks," he whispered, "for a wonderful evening."

She took deep, regular breaths, faintly snoring. Mark lay awake, eyes on the dark ceiling, wistful about what could have been.

* * *

He awoke to the ring of the iPhone again. Bright daylight was streaming through a crack in the curtains. He was still naked, in Jasmin's bed.

"Mark, how are you?" It was Joel, his divorce lawyer, his voice a bit hoarse.

"Good," said Mark. He looked at a bedside clock nearby. Eight fifteen a.m. "What time is it where you're at?"

"Past ten p.m.," said Joel. "I tried you earlier, soon after I came out of court, but your phone did not answer."

Mark pulled the covers off and sat up in bed. "Sorry," he said. "Someone turned my phone off." He looked for his pile of clothes by the bed. They were gone except for his shoes. "What's up?"

"Bad news," said Joel.

He was going through a divorce, his boss back home was cross with him, a gang of thugs were in pursuit, intent on killing him, he'd spurned a beautiful young woman, and then slept naked next to her. How much worse could it get?

"Your house on Telegraph Hill..." Joel hesitated.

For a moment Mark thought maybe a fire, or earthquake. He waited.

"The judge gave it to Angie."

"How can that happen?"

"Well, in a manner of speaking. He ruled that Angie has community property rights over half the value of the house."

"But I thought we would split between the Carmel place and San Francisco. She would get Carmel and I would keep my place."

"The numbers didn't work out that way. The judge essentially accepted her accountant's analysis of your assets. It was different, as you know, from ours."

"So, what now?"

"You have to sell the house and split the proceeds with Angie, unless you can come up with enough cash to pay her half the value."

"I don't have that kind of cash."

"I figured."

Mark took the phone off his ear and rubbed his face with his hand. He surveyed Jasmin's bedroom. It was small and spartan, her bed occupying almost all of it, nightstands on each side, a sliding closet door with a full-length mirror next to the bathroom entrance, hardly any decorations. "So where am I going to live?"

Jasmin walked in with a small cup in hand, smiling. It looked like Turkish coffee. She wore the same plain T-shirt he had seen her in earlier, but her legs were covered in long, baggy, colorful pajama pants. She placed the coffee next to Mark and went to her closet.

"You can crash at my place, buddy," said Joel. He then chuckled. "But no more than a week. You know my wife."

"Thanks," said Mark. *No thanks,* he thought.

"Have you found any hot Hungarian chicks yet?" Joel asked effusively. He must have just returned from a bar, thought Mark. Joel did that often.

Jasmin dropped a large wool gown on the bed next to him. Mark looked up at her. She wore her eyeglasses and her hair was neatly tucked behind her ears. She was a policewoman again, but without her uniform.

"As a matter of fact, yes." Mark smiled at Jasmin.

* * *

"How did you know I took my Turkish coffee without sugar?"

Jasmin sat cross-legged on the sofa where Mark had been sleeping earlier. "After last night, I figured you're not a sugar loving type."

Mark laughed. The coffee was strong. He tightened the cloth belt around his gown and pulled the collars in closer. The room was chilly. The gown was too big for Jasmin's slender frame. "Whose gown is this?" he asked.

"Dáni," she said. "He's a flight attendant for Wizz Air. He no longer uses it."

"Why?"

"It turns out he prefers Russian women. That's where he usually flies."

"Sorry," said Mark.

"No," Jasmin got up and took Mark's empty cup. "It's better this way. I only wasted two years with him. Just think. It could have been a lifetime." She walked to her open kitchen aside the living room and rinsed the used Turkish coffeepot. "Would you like another?"

"Yes, I would."

As she stirred water and coffee over a fire, she told him that while he was still asleep, she had placed his clothes in her washing machine. They reeked of automotive grease and sweat, she said.

"How long till they are ready?" asked Mark.

"Soon," she said, her back turned to him.

He walked over and nudged close, observing her hands. The floral scent she had emanated the night before was replaced by fresh soap and shampoo. She turned and smiled at him, then turned back to the coffee. The small pot was near a boil, the coffee inside building a dark brown head. Just before it erupted over the rim, she deftly removed it from the fire and poured the steaming coffee into a small Turkish cup.

"Where did you learn how to make Turkish coffee so well?" asked Mark, as he held the cup up and blew off the steam.

"My father," she said. "He has Turkish friends. He has visited Turkey many times." They returned to the living room, she to the couch and he to the armchair by the window. "He is a retired policeman."

"Funny," said Mark. "You and Mustafa have something in common. Mustafa was a policeman too at one time, and so was his father." He took a sip. "I bet yours is proud of you."

She crossed her legs again. "So far I haven't accomplished much. Merely finished the academy." She thought for a second. "Yes, I suppose he *is* proud. At least I haven't screwed up."

"Showing me that forensics report may be your first screwup," said Mark.

"Don't worry about that." Jasmin shifted in her seat. "Remember last night, when I said that a senior advisor thought I'd be okay?"

Mark recalled her remark. "Yeah, that puzzled me."

"Well, that was my father."

"Why would he do that?"

"I can't tell you too much. Let's just say that he does not trust the lead investigator on the Radu case."

"Kárpáty?" Mark's voice rose in surprise.

"Yes," she said and stood up. "Are you done with that coffee?" She took his cup to the kitchen sink.

Mark was left pondering what she had just said. He was pleased by this validation of his instincts about the eccentric inspector.

Jasmin returned, plopped down on the couch and removed her glasses. She loosened her hair with her fingers, then let it fly free as she briskly shook her head around. She stopped and smiled at Mark. Suddenly she was a sexy woman again.

He got up and sat next to her. "Last night," he said, edging closer, "I was very flattered by what you did."

She cast her eyes down, embarrassed.

"Do you know how long it's been since I had any kind of intimacy with a woman?"

The question surprised her. She looked at him, eyes wide, and shook her head no.

"I am going through a divorce. That phone call this morning, the one you heard when you brought me coffee in bed, was from my lawyer in the U.S." He looked away from her, toward the windows. "When a marriage is on the rocks, sex is the first casualty."

"What about others?"

"For her, yes. That's what prompted the divorce. For me, no."

She reached out and caressed his cheek. "How long were you married?"

"About ten years," he said, squeezing her hand by his cheek. "She is my second wife. My first died in a scuba diving accident."

"I am sorry," said Jasmin.

"You sort of reminded me of her—Megan—that was my first wife's name."

Jasmin brushed her hair back. "Do I look like her?"

"No," Mark said. "Last night." He hesitated. He wasn't quite sure how to put it to words. "When you took charge…you know what I mean?"

Jasmin nodded slightly and waited.

"That reminded me of Megan." He fell into deep thought for a second. Jasmin did not speak. "She was young then too, younger than you, when she did the same." Mark rubbed his forehead, embarrassed. He brushed up against his bruise again. "Ouch!" He yelled this time.

Jasmin caressed his temple just to the side of the bruise, looking deep into his eyes. "Sounds like you were in love with her."

"Yes," he said, his face downcast. "It was a big loss for me. I should not have turned around and married again so soon."

"Why did you?"

"I was lonely. I grieved a long time. Angie, the second one—she was a cute X-ray tech, young, flirtatious. She took my mind off of it. At the time, she lifted my spirits."

"Like I am doing now?"

Mark smiled and caressed Jasmin's cheek. "Not quite the same," he said. He stood and walked toward the window. Looking out, he spoke with his back to Jasmin. "Anyhow," he said, "Angie wanted children and I didn't."

He turned back and faced her. "Megan and I had had none. I felt I was too old to have children with Angie." He went back to the armchair and settled down. "So, she is pregnant now. About to have the child she so wanted."

"Not yours?"

"No."

Jasmin stood up. "I'll go check on your clothes." There was a slight catch in her voice. "They should be done by now."

She took a step toward him. Mark stood and stopped her. "About last night," he said, gently squeezing her arms. "I am glad you did what you did." He gave her a hug. "It was a great night, last night," he whispered in her ear. "The dinner, your friends, your bed. I'll never forget it."

Chapter 38

* * *

"So what's next?" Jasmin took a sip of cappuccino, her croissant half eaten. Mark stared at framed black-and-white photos of Hungarian artists populating the wooden panel behind Jasmin's padded bench seat. They all seemed from a bygone era, as did Central Kávéház, the Art Nouveau café near Jasmin's apartment on Karolyi út. Mark sat across from her on a chair at a small white marble tabletop. On a nearby corner, a large black and white figure was etched into a mirrored wall, a stocky middle-aged man lounging in a three-piece suit, cigarette in an uplifted hand, staring blankly at the tables of the café, a famous poet from the 1930s.

"I am leaving tomorrow," said Mark. He took another bite of his *rétes,* a strudel-like pastry, chewy and rich with poppy seed flavor.

"Back home to San Francisco?"

Jasmin watched Mark as he examined the interior of the café, taking in the opulent bar near the entrance, a nearby round table for six, surrounded by deep armchairs, and a smartly uniformed, white-aproned waitress eyeing their table attentively. Mark leafed through a leather-encased menu that had the feel of a small book.

"I don't think so." He looked at his watch. The *rétes* would be his lunch. They had lingered at Jasmin's a while. "To Istanbul. As soon as I get back to Gresham, I'll make arrangements."

Jasmin raised her eyebrows. "You mean you didn't plan on visiting Turkey before coming here?"

"That's right."

Mark took a sip of pomegranate juice and stared at the brief history of the café in the first page of the menu, open to business since 1887. He looked up at Jasmin, so young and lively in this elegant mausoleum of departed artists. Mark had been like her once upon a time, in Istanbul.

"My original plan was just Budapest, a brief three-day visit, a reunion with Ahmet. I can't believe how it has turned out."

"Why Istanbul?"

"I need to see old friends. One in particular." Mark waved the waitress for the check. "She's quite distraught over Ahmet's death. I need to console her."

Jasmin wore the same plain shirt and jeans as the night before, her slim body well outlined. She adjusted her eyeglasses. "She couldn't be your daughter, I suppose?"

"No," said Mark, with a gentle smile. "My age." He reached out and took a sip of Jasmin's cappuccino. "Someone I should have reached out to years ago."

* * *

Mark placed a credit card next to the bill while Jasmin went to the restroom. He looked into his shoulder bag and examined the contents within, his wallet, his Budapest guidebook, the envelope containing the preliminary forensics report, and two cellphones. He took the phones out. The iPhone was still on. After scanning through useless email, Mark turned it off.

"Still fussing with your phone?" Jasmin was back, her jacket on, ready to leave. She stood over him.

"I'm waiting for my credit card," said Mark as he opened the small Cello Mobile flip phone Mustafa had given him. "You'd better take this number down," he told her, "in case you need to reach me and the iPhone is off."

Jasmin tapped the number into her own phone. "Let's walk," she said. "We can take the streetcar to your hotel. It's not far from here."

They walked out of the café and Jasmin led him through Ferenciek tere, a one-way street lined with more sidewalk cafés. Mark nervously eyed his surroundings, memories of Zrinyi still fresh in his mind. At the corner of Kossuth Lajos út, a busy boulevard where people poured in and out of subway entrances, the station also named Ferenciek tere, Jasmin pointed left. Across the boulevard was a busy bus stop with another large crowd getting in and out of several buses lined up by the curb. Mark stopped and eyed the crowd.

Sensing Mark's concern, Jasmin tugged at his arm. "Come on," she said confidently, "quit worrying about being followed."

"Do you have your gun with you?"

"No," she said. "I don't need a gun to protect myself." She looked in his eyes. "Or you."

"Let's go this way." She led him on Kossuth Lajos toward the white suspension bridge he had seen from his taxi when he arrived in Budapest.

The bridge was reminiscent of the Golden Gate but lower to the ground and shorter. Still, as they approached closer, Mark found it as striking as the Golden Gate within its own context of a narrower waterway beneath, looming over old buildings nearby. They took steps that descended to Jane Haining rakpart, the riverside boulevard. To their right *Kossuth Lajos* rose up toward the bridge. They stopped at a rail station in the middle of Jane Haining, the bridge a behemoth towering over them. A number 2 yellow streetcar soon arrived. It was old-fashioned and nearly empty. They boarded and stood near the rear door, holding on to railings as Mark intently observed the riverside vista.

"Erszébet Bridge," said Jasmin, pointing to the white suspension bridge, majestic from this viewpoint. "It means Elizabeth. English speakers call it the Elizabeth Bridge."

Across the river at the end of the bridge was a single building to the left that sprawled along the opposite riverside drive, with an impressive hillside at its back.

"Rudas, right?" said Mark, pointing to the building as he recalled the taxi driver who had identified this along with the Erszébet Bridge when he arrived.

"Yes," said Jasmin. "Rudas baths started out as a Turkish *hamam* in the fifteen-hundreds. It has been enlarged with successive additions over the years."

The streetcar started. Mark noticed a strange mixture of architectural styles on the various connected façades of the bath house before the building disappeared behind the massive roadway of the bridge.

"It is a favorite of Kárpáty's," said Jasmin, pointing in the direction of Rudas.

The streetcar rattled along, now offering a grand vista of the Buda Palace on a low-lying hill across the river.

"The bath house?" asked Mark with surprise.

"Yes," said Jasmin. "He likes to conduct business there, in the saunas and hot tubs."

"He's a strange man, creepy," Mark remarked. "I'm not surprised your father doesn't like him, but why?"

Jasmin looked out the window. "My father doesn't think Kárpáty is an honest cop, but there are many who disagree with him. He is considered a capable investigator, but eccentric."

"How so?" Mark took his eyes off the river view and concentrated on Jasmin.

"Well, for beginners, Kárpáty is a loner. No family. They say he was married once, long ago, but no children."

The car stopped at the next station and its old doors noisily opened, revealing a plaza dominated by an elegant building with tall arched windows. Medieval battlements topped the columns on its façade. Several tourists entered the car, cameras in hand, carrying on in German.

"There are rumors that he might be a homosexual," Jasmin continued. "You know, hanging out in baths like that."

As the streetcar started, the tourists looked out of their window and laughed. They were passing a realistic bronze statue of an elf-like girl sitting on the railings along the streetcar line. A young woman was posing for a photo aside it, her arm around its shoulder.

"Vigadó tér," said Jasmin. "That building is the *Vigadó,* a concert hall. They recently put up that statue here."

She returned to her subject. "His proclivity for bath houses sparks gossip," she said, smiling at Mark. "This is not San Francisco. Homosexual activity is not well accepted in our police world."

Up ahead the Chain Bridge, intricately ornamented as compared with the simple but elegant lines of the Elizabeth, was enlarging in view.

"I think he has a drinking problem, too," said Mark.

Jasmin let out a laugh. "If we weeded out drinkers from our police force, this city would be totally unprotected."

The streetcar stopped at the plaza in front of the Gresham Palace, the hotel hidden behind trees. *Home*, thought Mark, with relief. He looked forward to a leisurely bath and shave.

"I think there is more to it," said Mark, as they exited the streetcar. "Let me tell you."

As they crossed the plaza, he recounted Kárpáty's three a.m. visit to his hotel room the night before last, and how he knew too much, too soon, about what had happened between him and Bognár's thugs.

Jasmin listened with interest and did not interrupt. They stopped in the middle of the plaza as Mark looked back at the view across the Chain Bridge. On the opposite side of the Danube a funicular line cut across the leafy hillside, Buda Castle to its left.

"Sounds like Kárpáty might be in with these gangsters," remarked Jasmin.

"I don't know how else to explain it," said Mark. "Here's something else. Have you seen any news of Radu's murder in the papers or on TV?"

Jasmin thought for a moment. "No."

They began walking toward the hotel entrance and waited for a break in traffic along the elliptical roadway around the plaza.

"Doesn't that seem strange to you? Such a high-profile event in a luxury hotel."

"What are you getting at?"

A brief lull in traffic. They ran across. An attentive doorman keenly eyed them, ready to serve. They stopped short of the door, a few paces away from him.

"I asked Kárpáty about it and he gave me some bullshit answer about Hungary not being the U.S." He looked around and said, in a hushed voice, "I think he suppressed the news."

"Why would he do that?"

"Maybe whoever did this doesn't want it to be out."

Jasmin stared toward a bronze statue rising out of the lawn at the left of the plaza. It was of a male figure standing erect, wearing a Roman military uniform with a cape, atop a tall, red pedestal with four guards at its base. She thought for a moment.

"I'll have to run all this by my father," she said. "The degree of corruption you're suggesting is a pretty serious charge."

"So what?" Mark chuckled. "I am a nobody. Who would believe me?" He looked at the statue. "Who is that?"

"Ferenc Deác," said Jasmin. "A statesman from the eighteen hundreds."

Mark turned toward the door. An attentive doorman had already opened it for them. "Do you want to see me in?"

As they walked through the door with its intricate ironwork, Jasmin commented, "If we can make it stick, we can send Kárpáty away for good."

They stood by the concierge desk. "I'd be careful if I were you," Jasmin warned Mark. "There may be others in cahoots with Kárpáty."

Chapter 39

* * *

The belly dancer sidled up to Latif Bey, bending her body back into a graceful curve, shaking her chest side to side. Her arms were raised wide, golden finger-cymbals briskly beating to the *Çiftetelli* rhythm of the music. Oblivious to the personal show, Latif took a drag from his cigarette and surveyed his guests, two men and two boys, his son Ahmet and his classmate Metin. They were in Lise II now, friends for years, one more year left in high school. The dancer leaned back farther, her long raven hair flowing down like a silk curtain, brushing lightly against Latif's bare scalp. Latif turned and looked up at her with a slight smirk. Latif's adult guests were also inattentive to the dancer. Metin, however, was captivated, observing her every move.

She straightened and gracefully rotated to the beat of the music. She wore a sky-blue bra, each cup shaped like a star, her ample breasts almost bursting out of the edges as she jiggled them. Her bright red lips parted into a wide smile as Latif shifted his chair closer to her. She nimbly wiggled her hips for him, standing up straight, her arms graciously executing invisible arcs in the air. Latif reached into his jacket and pulled out his wallet. She briskly turned and arched back again, this time bringing her left breast close to his face, her torso stationary while she kicked her legs to the rhythm of the music. She was barefoot, her slender ankles highlighted with gold anklets, her toenails painted bright red. Latif stuffed a bill into the edge of the bra. As she rose up and began stylishly executing pirouettes, Metin's eyes almost burst out of his sockets. Imagining what was wiggling within the pair of blue stars was alluring enough. But what astonished Metin was the bill that stuck out of her bra, coming around and around. It was 100 liras, an unimaginably generous tip.

Earlier, a chauffeur-driven Mercedes had dropped off Latif and the boys at the entrance of *Maksim*, Istanbul's most glitzy *gazino*, cabaret, at Sıraselviler street just off Taksim square. A four-story neon marquee to the left of the building, above the starlit canopy of the grand entrance, announced the headliner as Güneş Yumlu, the most glamorous of all singers.

Metin had told his parents that he and Ahmet had to study tough math problems for an upcoming test the following week. The session would last well into the evening. Pleased with their son's advanced preparation for such an important test, his parents had readily approved. On the verge of entering a forbidden world that Meliha Hanım, his aunt's neighbor, had so disapprovingly mentioned years ago, Metin burst with anticipation. He had been intensely curious since that card game so long ago.

As the dancer prepared to leave Latif's table for another, her leg brushed by Metin's outstretched knee. Her thighs were pale, fleshy and smooth. She wore a dainty V-shaped belt that held a transparent skirt, all blue, with slits down the sides that allowed unimpeded views of her upper thighs, pelvis and buttocks. Her slight touch sent electric shocks into Metin's body. She momentarily locked her dark eyes with his. Metin gazed back, embarrassed. She smiled. He looked away, unable to bear it.

A long catwalk jutted from the main stage into the spacious hall, an elevated platform that ended in a T-shaped forward stage. Countless tables were filled with well-dressed socialites, many of them regulars at *Maksim*. A thick haze of cigarette smoke hovered over them. The tables lined the catwalk that extended deep into the cavernous room. Latif and his guests sat at a premium table near the forward stage. The dancer had begun her show on the main stage and advanced down the catwalk to the forward one. She had then descended into the audience and picked Latif's table for a one-on-one. Latif gestured for a waiter and whispered some *meze* orders into his ear.

The dancer spotted a group several tables away beckoning her and turned to move in their direction. She was suddenly halted by Ahmet, who flew out of his chair and rapidly shed his navy blue sports jacket, tossing it at the table. He stood in front of her, arms spread wide, hips and chest quivering. She observed him for a split second and spread her arms out to match his pose. She began a new rhythm with her finger cymbals and jiggled her breasts while producing slow waves on her midriff with sensual pelvic thrusts. Ahmet opened his shirt collar, loosened his tie, and danced deftly, the two momentarily a smooth couple. The audience erupted into applause. Metin observed his mate's well-practiced moves with pride and jealousy.

Ahmet gave his father a brief look and stretched one arm toward him. Latif, laughing, handed him another bill that Ahmet slipped into the edge of her other breast. She continued dancing, her hair swaying this way and that, her bare feet kicking, then sidled her breast closer to Ahmet. He leaned down and kissed her bare flesh on the inside of the cup, near the bill. The audience erupted into more applause.

Latif Bey's guests, who so far had been stony-faced, gave Ahmet a private applause as he plopped back into his chair, sweaty and grinning.

"Your son is becoming quite the ladies' man," said the older of the two, a slim, balding man, dark complexioned, with thick black eyebrows and moustache. He wore a beige shirt, the top three buttons open wide, and a maroon silk scarf stylishly wrapped around his neck that disappeared under the shirt. His suit jacket was draped over his shoulders, his arms free of the sleeves. He spoke slowly and with much gravitas, in a deep, Anatolian-accented voice. The younger man next to him, also balding and with a wider, more downturned moustache, was dressed simply in an old checkerboard patterned jacket and white shirt open at the collar. He remained silent and deferential.

Latif Bey nodded in appreciation. Before he could answer, the waiter came with a tray of cold *meze* plates and began spreading them on the table. There was a bowl of roasted hazelnuts to go with Latif's whiskey on the rocks, and plates of feta cheese, melon, and black olives in olive oil with slices of fresh bread, for the *rakı* that the two guests were sipping.

Latif threw a couple of hazelnuts into his mouth. He was impeccably dressed in a blue business suit, with a broad red and yellow striped tie, his well-starched shirt collar tightly buttoned. He sat upright but relaxed and extended his arm toward the *meze* plates, revealing an ornate gold cufflink. "*Buyrun,* Ibrahim Bey," he offered his guest of honor.

Ibrahim extended an arm out of the jacket tenting over his shoulders and picked an olive with his bare fingers. He coarsely spat the seed onto a small plate in front of him and licked the olive oil smeared on his fingertips. Latif then extended a fork and deftly speared another olive, the seed disappearing into his palm and graciously deposited to his plate.

"What do you think?" Ahmet said to Metin. "Do you like it?"

"Amazing," Metin answered. "I've never been to *Maksim* before."

"Wait until Güneş Yumlu starts her show. She knows my father, you know."

"Yes, I do. I met her in Tarabya, on your yacht, remember?" Metin wished he had a cool father like Latif.

"Who is this man?" he asked Ahmet, nodding toward the obviously more esteemed guest.

"You don't recognize him?" Ahmet seemed surprised. "That's Kara Ibrahim. I don't know his last name. That's what everyone calls him. He's been in the newspapers quite a lot."

Metin took a second, closer look at the man with amazement. *Kara* meant dark. He may have acquired the moniker by virtue of his Kurdish complexion, but nowadays it carried another meaning. Ibrahim was a famous gangster based in the southeastern Turkish town of Urfa, on the Syrian border. His exploits were the stuff of legend, splashed all over tabloid news in breathless articles. There was steady speculation in the press about his illegal activities, mostly as a smuggler, but also about ruthless attacks against his rivals, accounts full of beatings and assassinations. His love life was regularly on display in black-and-white photos of the older man with very young, well made-up women. The police, despite years of trying, seemed unable to make any charges stick against him, another subject that fascinated the media.

Ibrahim quietly sipped his milk-white *rakı*, a quintessentially Turkish anise-flavored brandy, from a tall glass with two ice cubes, while Latif leaned closer to him, discussing business. Ibrahim's companion listened with interest. Ibrahim nodded, cut a piece of cheese, placed it on his plate, and whispered back. The belly dancer had completed her routine and a traditional Turkish band, seated at the main stage, played instrumental *fasıl* music from Ottoman times. The headliner was soon to start her show. Metin could not make out the conversation amid the background din.

"Who's the other guy?" he asked Ahmet quietly.

"I don't know. Kara Ibrahim always shows up with someone, each time a different one."

"You mean you've seen him before?" Metin asked in amazement.

"Sure," said Ahmet, reaching for the bowl of hazelnuts. "My dad has been doing business with him for years." He plopped several into his mouth and offered some to Metin.

A tall, slender man approached the table and leaned toward Latif Bey. "*Merhaba*," he said. *Hello.* "*Hoşgeldiniz.*" *Welcome.*

He was well dressed in an expensive suit, with a handkerchief in his chest pocket that matched his tie. He shook hands first with Latif, then Ibrahim. He was in his forties and had a receding hairline above a long pointy nose. His long sideburns were newly in fashion, his black hair well trimmed. He spoke with an impeccably articulate, proper Turkish accent.

"Fahrettin Aslan," said Ahmet to Metin, pointing to the man.

He need not have done so. Metin knew about the owner of *Maksim*, a famous impresario who had nurtured many stage singing careers including the gorgeous Güneş Yumlu. Fahrettin Bey also commanded a regular presence in tabloid papers and magazines. He enjoyed a favorable reputation. Latif introduced him to Ibrahim's sidekick and Metin. He politely shook hands with the sidekick, giving a mere knowing salute to Ahmet. Metin, who had never before seen the man in person, was much impressed. This glamorous night definitely beat math homework.

Latif pulled out a pack of fine American Kent cigarettes from his inner coat pocket and offered one to Fahrettin Bey, who accepted graciously. Kara Ibrahim refused. He was smoking a coarse, unfiltered *Bafra* brand. Latif extended a fancy lighter to Fahrettin, then lit another for himself, casually tossing the lighter and pack of Kents on the table. It was a deluxe cardboard box, white with a blue stripe atop bearing a golden European chateau at its front end. A banner-like inscription announced a *famous micronite filter* beneath the blue *Kent* sign.

Metin stared at the expensive cigarette package and thought of America, a land he dreamed of moving to. If he ever got to live in America, he thought, he would change his last name to Kent, an elegant name, easier for Americans to pronounce than his Turkish one, Özgür. He would change his first name, too. *Mark* maybe. *Mark Kent*, he thought, and he smiled. It sounded like James Bond. How cool!

Loud Western pop music interrupted his reverie. An off-stage announcer feverishly introduced the much-anticipated star of the night. House lights dimmed, and a spotlight caught the dazzling Güneş Yumlu in a long, silver, sequined gown with ample décolletage, microphone in hand, gracefully advancing on stage. Her well-chiseled baby-doll face was radiant in the spotlight. She was slender, with long, delicate arms bejeweled with golden bracelets, a prominent diamond ring glittering on the hand that held the microphone. Her well-coiffed platinum blonde hair had bangs that covered her forehead and flowed to her shoulders. As the audience gave a rousing applause, she smiled wide, revealing once again that sexy gap between her two front teeth. Metin was instantly captivated, unable to take his eyes off her.

She stood on the main stage in front of her band and sang *Dönemezki Bana*, a Turkish version of a sugary Italian song, her backup music entirely European in its instrumentation. It meant *He Can't Return to Me*, the lyrics dripping with melodramatic angst about a broken love affair. No one really paid attention to the song. It was merely another ornament, like her dress and accessories, to her sparkling stage presence. Latif and Ibrahim intently followed her, also enchanted. Fahrettin Bey stood amid the smoky haze, proudly smiling. Ahmet was the only one oblivious to the star. He reached over and took several sips of whiskey from his father's glass.

After a rousing applause, Güneş Yumlu followed with *Sensiz Bensiz*, *Without You Without Me*. Then she slowly walked off the main stage, graciously acknowledging guests sitting at the best tables along the catwalk. By the end of the song she was at the forward stage, bowing gracefully to applause by Latif's table.

Latif threw her a hand kiss, leaving his arm extended toward the star. Metin, beguiled by Yumlu, so close now that he could smell her enthralling perfume, noticed Latif's gesture and momentarily took his eyes off the singer, observing Latif with admiration. When he turned back, the singer had taken a deeper bow to the persistent applause, her face leaning off the stage, closer to their table. She locked eyes with Latif and gave him a playful wink. Latif acknowledged her with multiple double-hand kisses.

She stood up and turned back to the main stage, revealing a deep cut in her gown that exposed her smooth, sexy backside. She gestured her band and it began an up-tempo, silly European song, *Çapkın Kız, Lewd Girl.* Halfway back, she turned around. Dancing lithely to a Polka beat, she sang *My Name is Lewd Girl,* her eyes locked on Latif. Kara Ibrahim gave Latif an approving nod. Metin just looked back and forth between Güneş and Latif, his eyes wide, his jaw slack.

* * *

They waited under the starlit awning as Ibrahim's car departed first. Two burly Kurdish bodyguards vigilantly eyed the crowd, forming a small phalanx by their boss. Ibrahim thanked Latif and after shaking hands with him, ruffled Ahmet's hair. Tipsy from his father's whiskey, Ahmet stood a bit unsteady and giggled. Ibrahim then offered his hand to Metin.

"Well-behaved boy," he said to Latif as he shook Metin's hand. "Your son is keeping good friends."

Metin could not believe that he was actually touching a real-life gangster. Strange as it was, the experience was more enthralling than meeting Fahrettin Aslan or a brush with Güneş Yumlu. Surely this was the first and last time he would ever come so close to an infamous criminal.

"Come, boys," said Latif, gently patting his son's head and then motioning them toward his Mercedes. The boys settled into the back seat while Latif sat up front during the brief ride to their apartment in Şişli.

Latif lit a new cigarette and exhaled through a crack in his window. He then turned to examine the back seat. Ahmet had dozed off. Metin sat upright, wide awake.

"That was fun, wasn't it?" he said to Metin.

"Yes. Thank you for inviting me."

"No problem." Latif took another puff and turned forward. They were passing through the Osmanbey quarter, close to home. "Ibrahim is correct," he said, still looking ahead. "You've been a good friend to Ahmet."

He then turned around and looked at his son, who stirred but did not awaken. He grinned at Metin. "You two," he said, "have a great future ahead of you."

Chapter 40

* * *

The Gresham lobby was abuzz with activity. Mark and Jasmin stopped short of the registration desk to bid goodbye under the gilded glass dome and pointy chandelier. They were about to embrace when a fully uniformed *Rendőrség* officer in a dark blue jumpsuit approached them. He was about Jasmin's age, tall and brawny, with deep-set blue eyes, his blond hair shortly cropped. He smiled amiably at Jasmin as they exchanged a few animated words in Hungarian.

"This is Oszkar," said Jasmin, introducing him to Mark. "We work together."

Oszkar stared at Mark curiously, his smile erased. He was focused on Mark's left eye. "We've been waiting for you, Doctor," he said seriously, in decent English.

Mark expected *what happened to your eye,* in follow-up. None came.

"Why?"

Jasmin interjected. "They want to question you about what happened at Zrinyi and Őctőber 6. yesterday."

"All right." Mark tried to appear friendly. "Let's do it." He gestured Oszkar toward the piano bar.

"Not me," Oszkar said casually.

Jasmin explained. "Oszkar is on sentry duty. They couldn't locate you anywhere. So they assigned officers to the hotel, in shifts."

Mark was secretly pleased with the attention he had attracted. "Who wants to talk to me? Kárpáty?"

"I don't know." Oszkar pulled out his cellphone and began tapping it. "My orders are to report to the station if I locate you."

As Oszkar spoke, Jasmin whispered to Mark. "As I told you yesterday, Kárpáty assigned someone else to keep an eye on you. I bet he won't be happy about you disappearing last night."

"Do you know who it is?"

"No."

Oszkar interrupted his conversation and looked up at Mark. "They are asking that you come with me to the station for an interview."

Mark's heart sank. "Can't they come here?"

"I am afraid not." Oszkar was firm and formal. "That's not standard procedure."

It was for Kárpáty a couple nights ago, Mark thought to himself. He looked at Jasmin. "Can I at least freshen up before I go?"

Jasmin spoke Hungarian to her colleague. They seemed agreeable with each other. She turned to Mark. "That's okay, as long as you don't take too long."

"I'll wait right here," said Oszkar.

Mark and Jasmin walked toward the elevators.

"I don't like this," said Mark, with consternation.

She squeezed his arm. "Look, it's a formality. I told you last night that it is unlikely for them to consider you a suspect. You're just a witness. Answer their questions and it'll be over before you know it."

Mark wasn't convinced. "I wish it were you driving me back and forth again."

They were out of Oszkar's line of sight. Jasmin put her arm around his. "I am flattered but I'm off duty. Oszkar won't be much of a conversationalist. And don't expect any dates with him."

"He didn't seem curious about you and me," Mark said.

"It's not his job to ask questions. He's merely on sentry duty."

An elevator opened. Jasmin led him toward it.

"But I bet I'll get a lot of ribbing at the station tomorrow, after Oszkar tells everyone that he saw me here with you."

She kissed him on the cheek. "You can also bet that the investigator, whoever he is, will ask you where you were all night," she whispered into his ear.

Mark hugged her. "What shall I tell him?"

Jasmin caught the elevator door that was about to close and held it for Mark. Two hotel guests, young Americans, ran in breathlessly ahead of Mark. They laughed and thanked Jasmin for holding the door.

Jasmin let go of the door. "Tell him anything you want," she said. "Tell him the truth."

* * *

Mark looked at himself in the bathroom mirror. He was gaunt and worn. His raccoon eye and two-day-old beard made him look worse. The scar on his forehead throbbed. No wonder Oszkar had gazed at him the way he did.

He examined his naked torso. He had lost weight and his skin seemed to be sagging. By now, if everything had gone according to plan, he would have been well rested, well fed, and full of stories about Ahmet and his escapades of years past. Instead he had plunged into an unexpected adventure in an unfamiliar world that was tossing him around like a rudderless boat.

He drew a hot bath and began applying shaving cream on his face. *It didn't have to turn out this way*, he thought. After the tragedy of Ahmet's death, he could have given the police a full and honest statement and returned home, or as Kárpáty had suggested, become a tourist in Budapest for a few days. He felt like Alice, who plunged into a rabbit hole and found herself in Wonderland. Olga's business card had been Mark's rabbit hole. If only he had left it alone. Mark ran a razor down his cheek. He was trapped all right, like Alice, but not in Wonderland.

The hot bath relaxed him, his clean-shaven face giving him a boost. He thought about Jasmin, her youthful beauty, so innocent yet so self-assured. He recalled her naked silhouette and felt her allure all over again. He switched to Olga and relived her beguiling magnetism. Mark was sure that last night, had it been Olga instead of Jasmin, he would have gladly, enthusiastically gone through with it. He closed his eyes and slid down, dipping his head in the hot water. Maybe he *was* in Wonderland.

As he emerged and opened his eyes, the image of gypsy thugs chasing after him erased Mark's daydream. Their boss was lusting after Mark's blood. He had yet another police interrogation and he did not look forward to it. Mark wondered how he was going to extricate himself from all this.

He massaged his arms and legs with a lathered loofa sponge, enjoying the sensation. He had felt intoxicating adrenaline rushes at Almássy and Zrinyi. He craved more. He knew this meant further trouble, but he couldn't help it. He had an inkling that his intended journey to Istanbul might sink him deeper into this new and dark Wonderland. Still, he needed closure with Günsu, it would be interesting to catch up with Leon, and if he somehow got to see old Latif Bey one last time before he passed away, he would be very pleased. Mark closed his eyes and let Wonderland vanish from his mind.

* * *

Mark sat in a sterile interrogation room at the same District V police station where Kárpáty had interrogated him the morning after he found Ahmet's dead body. The surroundings were drab and claustrophobic, bare gray walls, not even a two-way mirror that he so often saw in police shows. Just a metal table and two uncomfortable metal chairs. Jasmin had been right about Oszkar. He had driven Mark without uttering a word.

Mark shifted uneasily on his chair. Sitting across from him was Sergeant Gusztáv Zoltán. "Thank you, Doctor, for your cooperation," he said politely. He pulled out a notebook and placed it on the table.

The man was nothing like Kárpáty. Zoltán was in his forties, tall and very slim, with a long, high cheek-boned face, deep-set gray eyes, and luxuriant dark hair, combed and greased in a 1950s style. He was dressed neatly in a dark suit and tie. His posture was stiff, his manner businesslike.

"No problem," said Mark.

"I am here to take your statement about an altercation that occurred on or about seven p.m. last night at Zrinyi út, not far from Szent István Basilica." Zoltán poised a pen on his notebook in a ready gesture.

"How are those two men doing?"

The sergeant tilted his pen and looked up at Mark, surprised that *he* was the recipient of the first question.

"One is in intensive care with a serious head injury. The other had more minor injuries, a broken nose, some rib fractures. He was released from the hospital to our custody."

"He was the gunman," said Mark.

Zoltán dropped his pen and pushed his notepad away. "Who are you referring to?"

"That little, short guy, the one with the broken nose. He held a gun to me."

"Doctor," said the officer, "there are surveillance cameras on Zrinyi, and there was a security camera at the café in front of which the altercation occurred."

Mark was not surprised with the first bit of news. Jasmin had told him that. He wondered if the Nonloso camera had caught enough of Mustafa to identify him.

"The footage we reviewed, sir, shows you walking on Zrinyi, in a direction away from the Basilica, with those two injured men. It appears like you three were out for a stroll and were then suddenly attacked by a man bearing a hockey uniform."

Zoltán spoke slowly, his words carefully enunciated as though he were self-conscious of his Hungarian accent. He continued. "It appears, Doctor, that you three were perhaps friends, or acquaintances."

"Hardly," said Mark, leaning back in his chair and crossing his legs. "Those two men were kidnapping me at gunpoint. The short guy had a concealed gun and told me to *pretend* we were friends out for a stroll."

Zoltán hurriedly took some notes and did not look up from his pad. "Why would they do that, Doctor?"

"You tell me! I have no idea."

Zoltán gave Mark a quiet stare. Mark took his momentary silence as a sign of disbelief.

"It all began when I contacted a certain masseuse who works at Gresham Palace, a woman named Olga Kaminesky." The name did not seem to have an impact on the sergeant. "They've been after me since."

"Do you know who they are?"

Was this a trick question? The investigator obviously had to know who they were. Mark did not want to reveal that he knew about Bognár.

"No." Mark tried to appear relaxed. Here he was again, evasive with the police, falling yet deeper down the rabbit hole.

"This Olga Kaminesky." Zoltán paused and studied her name on his notepad. "How do you know her?"

"I don't."

"So, then, why were you contacting her?"

Mark studied Zoltán's expression. It was flat and formal. Kárpáty, his boss, had blurted out Olga's name without asking Mark anything else about her. He had acted as if he already knew everything about Olga. If so, why was this man, whom he presumed to be Kárpáty's envoy, asking such a question?

"I had heard that she gave good massages…you know…ones with a happy ending." Mark smiled and winked. "So I went to that strip club, Mercy, and looked for her."

Zoltán jotted down what Mark said. "And did you get your massage?"

Mark had started it, now he couldn't turn back. He continued spinning his yarn. "Yes and no. They took me to some back room there, in that building where the Mercy club is. She gave me, let's say, an unsatisfactory massage, and charged me way too much. So we got into a dispute."

Mark could not believe the words coming out of his mouth. Zoltán, listening and nodding, showed no signs of disbelief. Pleased that he was getting away with it, he continued. "Before you know it, they had called a couple of thugs to shake me down and I was running away from them in that neighborhood. What was it? District VII?"

Zoltán didn't answer. He patiently waited for more.

"I was fortunate. I managed to get away from them."

"So do you think that they came after you again yesterday?"

"Maybe. I don't know." Deeper down the rabbit hole he went. "If I may are you involved in the Radu murder investigation you know with Inspector Kárpáty?" It was a bold, impertinent question, and Mark did not expect an answer.

"No, sir."

Zoltán's ready answer surprised Mark. "Then, why are you here?"

"As I said, I am here to take your statement about what happened last night and issue a report."

So he was merely an emissary. Mark found it odd that a detective sent to interview him would know little about the case. But then with Kárpáty at the helm, Mark figured one could expect anything.

Zoltán continued. "This man in the hockey outfit who assaulted your abductors. Do you know who he is?"

"No." The lies were coming more easily now, more naturally. "There were a whole bunch of hockey fans on Zrinyi that evening, all partying. What for, I don't know. When those guys took me toward a waiting car and I realized that I was being abducted, I cried for help. This man came out of nowhere and helped me. I am so grateful to him."

"Did you speak with each other? Did he identify himself?"

"No, sir." Mark paused for a moment, closed his eyes and rubbed them with his thumb and forefinger, as if reliving the event were painful. Actually, he needed time to think up a plausible extension to his tale. "We ran away from there, on that small cross street. What was it? October 8?"

"Őctőber 6.," corrected Zoltán. "It is the date of the Russian invasion in 1956."

"Sorry, October 6." Mark opened his eyes and stared at the policeman's writing pad. "That little guy's gun had dropped onto the sidewalk. He could have reached for it and shot at us. We ran as fast as we could."

Mark hoped that they had not been surveyed down Őctőber 6. If so, what he was about to say would expose his lie. He tried to hide his apprehension and took the risk. "When we were out of sight, we stopped and caught our breath. Then I shook the man's hand and thanked him. I had the impression that he was a bit, you know...tipsy."

Mark scanned the sergeant's face for a reaction. Nothing. "He accepted my thanks and said that he had to go. Friends waiting at a bar, or something like that. He had a foreign accent."

At least the last bit was true. Mustafa did speak with a Turkish accent.

"What sort of accent?" asked Zoltán.

"Russian."

Mark felt his pulse quicken while the officer quietly jotted down more notes. He had never before uttered such an outrageous series of lies, and to a policeman, of all people. He thought about his high school days when he was caught aiding those misfits who stole chemistry exams and needed solutions. Had he lied to his Turkish headmaster then as easily as he was doing now, he would not have been in any trouble. Mark realized how much, in just a few days, Wonderland had changed him.

Nonetheless, he was nervous. He stood up and shook his legs, pretending that they had fallen asleep.

"Doctor," said Zoltán, "where were you during the rest of the night?"

Here it comes, thought Mark. He leaned on the table with both arms. "I was on a dinner date."

"May I ask where?"

"A wonderful restaurant, in someone's private apartment by the river. What was the name?" He paused and searched his mind, his gesture genuine this time. "Something *Ferenc*. The first word means restaurant in Hungarian."

"*Étterem?*"

"That's right. That's it. *Étterem Ferenc*."

"I know the place." Zoltán was more interested now. "Who took you there?"

"One of your own. A police officer from your station. Her name is Jasmin." He recalled her last words before the elevator door closed. *Tell them the truth*, she had said.

"Jasmin Virág?" The sergeant was puzzled. "Lázló Virág's daughter?"

Mark realized that he did not know Jasmin's last name. It was on the card she had given him but he had paid no attention. "Is he a retired police officer? Her daughter is a new cop in your station?"

Zoltán nodded.

"That's her." He sat down again.

The sergeant stopped writing and stared at his notepad, trying to comprehend the surprise news.

"I met her the day before yesterday. She drove me to this station for fingerprints and a DNA sample. Afterwards, she offered to show me around town." Mark felt more at ease with this subject. At least he was telling the truth. Furthermore, his interrogator's clearly puzzled expression amused him.

"Doctor, we've been looking for you since the altercation and you never came to your hotel."

"That's right. I was with Jasmin."

Zoltán stared at him silently, his disbelief breaking down his professional façade. He focused on Mark's left eye as if seeing it for the first time.

"And how did you acquire that bruise?"

"At Zrinyi, when they tried to kidnap me. I hit the edge of the door opening, you know, of that car they were shoving me into."

"Did you receive any first aid for it?"

Mark figured the cameras had to have captured his bleeding face. The officer obviously had not seen the footage. "Jasmin," he said. "She cleaned it up and dressed it at Ferenc's place."

Zoltán put his pen down and closed his notepad. "If I may say sir, you seem to have diverse taste in women." He shook his head in disbelief. "From Olga Kaminesky one night to Jasmin Virág the next."

Ahmet would have been proud of me, thought Mark. "Will that cause any trouble for Jasmin?"

Zoltán thought for a few seconds. "I doubt it," he said. "She is not assigned to the Radu murder investigation."

"She is very talented," said Mark. "I am very impressed with her."

Zoltán's lips stretched into a sarcastic smile. He stood up. "Thank you for your prompt response and cooperation, Doctor." He pocketed his notepad. "I will report your statement to Inspector Kárpáty. He may want to speak with you himself. If so, we may have to summon you again."

Wonderful, thought Mark. Lying to Zoltán had been easy. Kárpáty would be something else. Mark did not look forward to it.

The sergeant asked for his phone number and Mark gave him the one of the Cello Mobile.

The interrogation was over. Zoltán offered to take him downstairs, where Oszkar waited to drive him back to his hotel. They walked quietly through an empty hallway toward a drab elevator.

"Officer Zoltán," Mark said in the elevator. "Earlier you said that you had the man in custody. The gunman."

"Yes."

"Why?"

"He was wanted on an outstanding warrant," answered the sergeant. "Now, with your testimony, we can add to the charges."

"Warrant for what, sir?"

"Assault with a deadly weapon."

The elevator door opened and they exited into a narrow lobby.

"But first," Zoltán continued, "we'll have to identify and locate that man in the hockey outfit."

"If you do," said Mark, "please express my gratitude to him."

He shook Zoltán's hand.

"Thank you for your cooperation, Doctor."

As Mark exited the building with Oszkar, he decided his fears about this interrogation were unfounded. It had not been that bad after all.

Chapter 41

* * *

Mark entered Iancu's dark Mercedes, this time as a sole passenger. The driver, the same one as before, held the back door open for him. The afternoon was clear and sunny. The car, newly washed, gleamed luxuriously. They set out from the Gresham driveway, circled around the plaza past the Chain Bridge and took the riverside drive south.

"I'm sorry," Mark said. "I did not catch your name last time."

"Dumitru," said the driver, his eyes on the road.

"Do we have far to go, Dumitru?"

"No, sir. Just down by the Szabadság híd. We'll be there in ten minutes."

"The what?"

"Bridge, sir. Liberty Bridge."

They were already approaching the Elizabeth Bridge. Dumitru pointed beyond, to the old-fashioned wrought-iron bridge with pillars that looked like minarets. It was the first Danube bridge Mark had seen on his way in from the airport.

"Is that where Iancu is staying?"

"No. It's sort of…" the driver thought for a minute, "an office."

The scenery was familiar. They were backtracking along the same route Jasmin had taken him to his hotel earlier that day.

"Where are you from, Dumitru?"

"Brasov," he said.

"Romania?" Mark tried to recall where he had heard that name.

"Yes."

Mark remembered. The radiology report with which Ahmet contacted Mark had originated in Brasov.

They passed under the elevated road leading to the Elizabeth Bridge and stopped at a light facing the station where Mark and Jasmin had picked up a tram.

"Do you know a Regina Maria clinic in Brasov?"

"Yes, sir. A hospital." Dumitru looked at Mark through his rearview mirror. "I had an appendectomy there when I was in middle school. How do you know about it?"

"Oh, I'm a doctor," Mark said offhandedly. "Radiologist. I recently received a CAT scan report from Regina Maria." He looked out the window at the Danube River flowing lazily, with hardly any watercraft floating on it. "Where exactly is Brasov?"

"In Transylvania," said Dumitru. "About two hours west of Bucharest by car. Beautiful countryside. Good skiing nearby. You should visit."

"Transylvania, huh?" Mark thought for a minute. "Dracula," he said.

Dumitru laughed. "Yes, that's all we hear from foreigners. Dracula's castle is only a half an hour from Brasov, in Bran."

"I should come for a visit sometime," said Mark thoughtfully.

The Mercedes was moving slowly. Mark observed the Rudas baths across the river, still puzzled by the hodge-podge of architectural styles in its various adjoining buildings. Its southern tip was the most modern, with a curving glass façade and a peculiar, dome-shaped structure on its flat roof.

"How long have you been working for Iancu?" Mark was enjoying his chat with the driver.

"Two years. Since I was discharged from the army."

"Is that all you do for him, drive?"

"No, sir," said Dumitru. "I am part of the protection team."

Mark was not surprised. "I was impressed by how well you drove the other day."

"Thank you."

They passed an old yellow tram going in the other direction. "That silver BMW that you spotted," said Mark, "that was following us. Do you remember it?"

"Of course."

"Have you seen it again?"

"No, sir."

Mark admired Gellért Hill across the river, behind Rudas baths, a patch of undeveloped, raw nature amid a crowded metropolis, with the tall statue of the Hungarian Lady Liberty at its peak, her arms soaring toward the sky.

"I saw that BMW yesterday."

Dumitru drove on and did not answer.

"They tried to kidnap me into that car."

Dumitru turned back and threw a split-second glance at Mark, surprised.

"I could have used an army man like you," said Mark. "Protection."

"So, what happened?"

"I managed to escape with some unexpected help."

"Is that why you have a bruised eye?"

"Yes."

The Liberty Bridge was bulky and industrial compared with the sleek Elizabeth Bridge, or the sumptuous Chain Bridge. Yet, despite its heavy iron girders, its lines were as graceful as the other two. The Mercedes stopped at a long light in front of it before turning left into Fővám tér.

"Did you know Nicolae?" asked Mark.

"Radu? Yes."

They were on another large boulevard lined by colossal nineteenth-century buildings and the ubiquitous yellow trams in the middle, these more modern and sleek.

"I drove Radu on several occasions in Romania. And twice to Turkey."

The news startled Mark. "Where in Turkey?"

The Mercedes slowed down near a large building that looked like a train station.

"Istanbul," said Dumitru. He stopped the car. "We're here."

A tall, well dressed, lean young man rushed the Mercedes from the curb and opened Mark's door.

"Wait a minute." Mark was disappointed that the drive was so short.

The man stood at attention by the open door while Mark reached forward toward the driver's seat and placed his hand on Dumitru's shoulder.

"Thanks for the interesting ride," he said out loud. Then, more quietly. "When you drove Radu to Turkey, how did you cross the border?"

Dumitru turned back to face Mark and scrutinized him. Sensing the driver's hesitation, Mark said, "Radu and I were childhood friends."

"You found him dead at that hotel, didn't you?" Dumitru had obviously listened in on Mark's conversation with Iancu during their last ride.

"Yes," said Mark.

Dumitru exited the Mercedes, came around to the curb and exchanged a few words with the new man at the back door. He then gestured for Mark to exit the car.

Disappointed, Mark rose out of his seat, nodded hello to the new man and began walking away from the car. Dumitru called him back. He was leaning in, toward where Mark had been sitting. He emerged, straightened up and pointed inside. "Here," he said.

Mark looked in. The back seat of the Mercedes had been folded to reveal a compartment between the back rest and the trunk. It was large enough to fit a good-sized person.

"Custom made," said Dumitru. "Even has air conditioning and fresh oxygen supply."

He then came around and opened the trunk of the Mercedes, with Mark in tow. It was empty. There was no indication there that a secret compartment existed within.

"We crossed the Turkish border with Radu in there," said Dumitru as he returned the back seat to its upright position.

"Is that how Radu came to Budapest, too?"

"No." Dumitru closed the trunk. "I didn't drive him." He returned to the back door and righted the back seat. "There is no need for it," he said. "Romania and Hungary are both EU. No border check."

"Ah, of course." Mark felt stupid.

"He probably took the train," Dumitru added. "Radu never flew. Too many identity checks in airports. He did not like to drive, either, unless he had a chauffeur. He liked trains. He felt safer in them."

"Did he come to Budapest without bodyguards?"

"I don't know."

Dumitru exchanged a few words with the other man who had stood by silently. He was taller than Dumitru and more muscular, his physique obvious in a tightly fitting gray suit and tie. He had shortly cropped dark hair and thick Slavic lips above a protruding chin.

"Iosif says Radu came by himself."

Iosif closed the back door of the Mercedes, buttoned up his suit jacket, and beckoned Mark toward the grand building behind them.

Mark shook Dumitru's hand. "I hope to see you again."

Dumitru nodded, as he had done at the Gresham driveway.

Chapter 42

* * *

The building looked like a giant airplane hangar inside, but was from an era before flight. A soaring ceiling in the center, supported by a series of arched iron beams, gave the impression of a post-industrial cathedral. Huge windows fell upon flanking roofs on each side, letting in abundant light. Iosif led Mark through a central passageway full of people, lined by stalls that sold multicolored vegetables, meats of every kind, and dry goods. There was salami everywhere, long, thick cylinders hanging like awnings from the tops of stands. Sprinkled in between them were paprika kiosks, selling a rich variety of spices.

Mark stopped at various stalls while Iosif patiently waited. Upstairs was a second story of merchants selling mostly clothing and souvenirs, their stalls supported by slim iron beams interconnected by wrought iron aerial walkways. Far in one corner people sat at counters near a cluster of restaurant kiosks, eating. From his vantage point Mark could not identify what the food was. Above it all was a vast empty space that rose toward the soaring cathedral roof.

What an amazing waste of space, thought Mark. This place could only have been built in a bygone era, when space was cheap.

Iosif led him through maze-like inner passageways lined by more salami vendors, butchers, several stalls of bakery products, and a coffee shop or two. Mark stopped in front of a bakery to admire an array of colorful pastries behind a curving glass display.

"We'll have snacks and drinks later," said Iosif, at attention a few steps back. He had a thick, baritone voice.

Mark turned and looked at him. "Where?"

Iosif pointed to a staircase up ahead, with iron banisters. "Downstairs."

Mark followed him. "I was expecting an office building, not this," he said. "Where are we, anyway?"

"*Vásárcsarnok*," said Iosif. "It's Budapest's central market."

"Iancu has an office here?"

Iosif began descending the stairs that led to the basement with Mark in tow. "Not quite," he said.

* * *

The basement of the giant indoor market featured more butcher shops and an array of pickle vendors. Iosif had taken him into one in a far corner, nodding hello to a bald, pudgy old man behind the counter. The kiosk was small, with a refrigerated glass display of pickled cucumbers, carrots, broccoli, onions, garlic, and peppers, all in identical open blue tubs. There was a small area behind it for the vendor to move about, and a back shelf full of more pickles in tall glass jars, submerged in their juices. A narrow doorway opened into a back room that was twice the size of the kiosk. Iosif and Mark had to duck to enter through the opening, constructed for shorter men. Mark found Iancu in the storage room, standing by a small table in one corner.

Iancu was dressed casually in a dark warm-up suit that revealed his sizeable girth. "Good to see you again," he said warmly. He then fixed his gaze on Mark's bruised eyelids. "What happened?"

"Those guys who were following us yesterday, in that silver BMW, do you remember?"

Iancu nodded.

"Well, they found me." Mark smiled sheepishly. "Later, in the evening."

Iancu stared at Mark's blemish, squinting behind his bulbous nose.

"Fortunately Mustafa came to my rescue and we gave them the slip. But not before this small bump."

Iancu somberly shook his head sideways several times. "You are," he said in his low, baritone voice, "the most unusual doctor I've ever met."

Mark smiled and held back a *thank you*, even though he recognized that Iancu had not meant this as a compliment. He turned around and examined his surroundings in bewilderment.

"We own this shop," said Iancu, sensing Mark's surprise.

"You and Nicolae?" Mark wondered why they would desire a pickle business in a foreign country.

Iancu sat down at the table. "We also own coffee shops in Brasov and Constanta, a bakery in Chisinau, a travel agency in Skopje, and a barber shop in Bratislava."

"These are Nicolae's businesses that you manage?" Mark was incredulous.

"Technically, yes." Iancu crossed his legs. Dark chest hairs protruded above his zippered top. "But they are not our main businesses. Let's just say that they are convenient offices. Safer that way. Discreet." He extended his arm and swept it around, his short, stubby fingers open wide. "Those guys looking for you—they won't disturb you here."

Mark decided not to tell Iancu that the pair had been neutralized. Instead, he asked, "What about Bucharest? Do you operate out of a real office there?"

"No. No offices," Iancu responded firmly. "Our cars and cellphones are sufficient. Bucharest is our home base."

Iancu called out for Iosif, who was chatting with the vendor behind the pickle counter. "Would you like tea or coffee?" he asked Mark.

Mark realized that he had again missed a meal, his lunch time having melted away between Jasmin and Sergeant Zoltán, then with various phone calls in his room before being summoned by Iancu. He was thankful for the *retés* brunch at Central Kávéház, but that was many hours ago. As Iosif dutifully departed to fetch drinks, Mark hoped he would bring some promised snacks, hopefully something other than pickles.

"Did you notify your friend, the Turkish private eye?"

"Yes," answered Mark. "He should be here soon."

Iancu had given him the address of what turned out to be the Central Market and had left instructions for Mustafa to call a certain phone number when he arrived.

"So when are you going back home?" Mark asked Iancu after sitting down at his table.

"Tomorrow morning. I am done with what I came here for."

"And what was that?"

"To collect Nicolae's body and make funeral arrangements."

Mark examined a shelf of plastic jars that contained mixed pickles. They were randomly stacked, with large beige beans in some, red and white radishes in others. Interspersed among them were mixed assortments with large, round, yellow onions, tiny black olives pasted on them as eyes and small curved pieces of red pepper as mouths. Smiley faces. In one corner was a Tower of Babel of smiley faces, a rickety stack.

Iancu noticed Mark's gaze. "Would you like to try some pickles?"

"Oh, no. Thanks." Pickled vegetables on his empty, stressed-out stomach seemed more perilous to Mark than Bognár and his thugs. "When is the funeral?"

"Next week," said Iancu. "Will you be able to attend?"

"Why so long? Muslims bury their dead within twenty-four hours."

Iancu chuckled. It sounded like a coarse cough. "I thought you said you knew Ahmet intimately."

Mark noticed that he had referred to him by his Turkish name, probably intentionally.

Iancu continued. "You should know that he was not religious."

"Yes," mumbled Mark. "That was our upbringing in Istanbul. Secular. I'm the same way."

"He wouldn't have given a damn when his funeral occurred. Besides, Budapest police released his body only today. The autopsy was late yesterday. We also have the logistics of getting him to Bucharest, obituaries, invitations, you name it."

"I would like to attend," said Mark, "but I don't know if I can stay in Europe that long. My boss in San Francisco was unhappy about giving me a few days off to come to Budapest to begin with. He is pushing me to return as soon as possible."

"When are you going back?"

"I'm not," said Mark. "I just made arrangements to fly to Istanbul tomorrow afternoon. Turkish Airlines."

The last-minute ticket had been a stiff fare. With the flight nearly full, all they had available was a business-class seat. Mark had no choice.

"How did you break *that* news to your boss in America?"

"I haven't, yet." Mark did not look forward to the inevitable conversation with Ben Allen.

Iosif and the old man behind the counter entered with cups of Turkish coffee and tulip glasses of tea. Mark took coffee, Iancu tea. *Where are the snacks?* Mark wondered.

"Why Turkey?" asked Iancu.

"I need to meet some old friends," said Mark, after blowing steam off his coffee. "You might know them." He took a sip. "One of them is Günsu. It seems that Ahmet was having some sort of an affair with her."

Iancu put a cube of sugar in his tea glass and stirred, his thick, dark eyebrows bunched together in a frown. "As I told you yesterday, it was hard to keep up with Nicolae's liaisons. I knew he had a regular in Istanbul but I didn't know her name."

"She is an old friend of mine, too, and she is very upset. I need to comfort her."

"Who knows how many women there are out there who will need to be comforted," Iancu murmured.

Mark thought about Olga. She seemed in need of consolation too, when they last met. He kept the thought to himself.

The old pickle vendor crouched through the door with a tray of food. "*Lángos*," he announced in a croaky voice. "From upstairs."

He placed four plates on the table of what looked like small pizzas but with strange crusts.

"Aaah!" Iancu acted as though he just rose from a slumber. He examined each plate with interest. "This is a treat," he said to Mark enthusiastically. "The *lángos* stands on the second floor of this market are famous." He reached over and stuck his globular nose into one of the plates. "M'mmm. And for good reason."

Mark was pleased to see some food, but at the same time annoyed by the interruption. Iancu had not revealed anything yet. As he examined the strange offerings on the table, Mark remembered what Commissaire Gérard had said about Iancu. He had called Iancu *a fairly important criminal* but *very smooth, a legitimate businessman by all appearances.*

"So what is this?" Mark leaned in and inspected the plates.

"Hungarian fried dough," said Iancu. He pointed to one with sour cream and shredded cheese on top. "This is traditional." Another one was plain, an irregularly round, lightly browned piece of dough, slightly puffy. "This plain one is also traditional. It's actually not plain. It has garlic."

Iosif approached the table and cut himself a slice of another that had shredded cheese and pepperoni. "Now, that is *not* traditional," he said, pointing to Iosif's choice. "They're just imitating pizza."

As Mark began cutting off a piece from the traditional sour cream and cheese *lángos,* there was a commotion at the door and Dumitru entered, announcing something in Romanian. Iancu and Mark turned toward the door. A lanky figure crouched awkwardly though the small opening and straightened himself up. He wore brown lederhosen with a casual white shirt, white knee-high socks, and bulky hiking boots. He leaned on a walking stick that resembled a ski pole and raised the brim of his red plumed Tyrolean hat. He grinned broadly from beneath a long, pointed nose.

"*Guten nachmittag,*" he exclaimed, in a fairly authentic German accent.

Iancu looked at the new visitor suspiciously. Mark broke into a laugh. It was Mustafa.

Chapter 43

* * *

The *langós* was crunchy, salty and filling. Mark hurriedly shoveled it in while Iancu and Mustafa went through mutual introductions.

"I knew Ahmet well," said Mustafa. "I provided security for him before he left Istanbul."

He sat slightly away from the table, his knees spread apart, his Tyrolean hat nearby, resting atop a jar of pickles.

"Mark told me that you work for Meltem nowadays." Iancu had become more stiff and formal since Mustafa's arrival.

"She hired me to track her husband down. We have not known his whereabouts for years."

Mark wondered how much of his mission Mustafa would reveal.

"And you found him." Iancu eyed him under bushy eyebrows. "When?"

"Just before he got killed."

"Unfortunate coincidence." There was a hint of sarcasm in Iancu's tone.

Mark stopped eating and watched the two men, his gaze switching back and forth between them. He wondered if Iancu suspected Mustafa as the culprit in Ahmet's murder.

Mustafa was unfazed. He stood up and examined the stack of pickle jars with smiley faces. He picked one up and held it to Iancu. "Do you mind?"

"Be my guest."

Mark interjected. "What's with the get-up?"

Mustafa looked down at himself. "Do you like it?" He picked up his Tyrolean hat and placed it on Mark's head, swaying side-to-side to see how well it looked on him.

"I don't know what's more bizarre," said Mark. He took the hat off and patted the red plume at its side. "Turks in hockey outfits, or this?" Then he said seriously, "They're looking for you."

"Who?" asked Iancu.

"Budapest police."

While Mustafa sifted through the assortment of pickles he had opened, Mark elaborated.

"The episode outside the Mercy club when I was chased, the gunshots, they invited police attention. He," Mark pointed to Mustafa, "rescued me in a rented car and they have its license plate."

"They won't track that down," said Mustafa, his index finger sifting through pickles. "I used a fake name to rent that."

"Then yesterday," Mark continued, "when they tried to abduct me on Zrinyi Street and you beat up those two guys—one of them is seriously injured, by the way, in the hospital—police have video footage of it."

"Good luck identifying me," said Mustafa. "They have nothing here that they can match my face with." He picked a small cucumber and threw it in his mouth.

"I don't know how you can be so glib about all this." Mark pushed away his empty *langós* plate.

"I checked out of my hotel and ditched the car after your first escapade." Mustafa answered seriously. "I am staying at Turgut's, where they can't find me. I will be out of this city tomorrow when you leave. You *are* leaving, right?"

Mark did not know if Turgut's van with its distinctive Bosporus logo had been spotted by cameras or witnesses. Sergeant Zoltán had not mentioned this in their encounter, but the officer was still early in his investigation and new evidence could come forth any time. He felt that Mustafa's sense of security was foolhardy. This was not a good time to argue with Mustafa, however, not in front of Iancu. Mark curtly confirmed that he planned to fly to Istanbul the next day.

"I am quite sure I can last another day in Budapest under the police radar," said Mustafa with self-assurance. He carefully removed a smiley-face onion from the pickle jar and examined its eyes and mouth. "That is," he locked his gaze on Mark, "if you don't get into any more trouble." He took a bite of the onion and made an unsmiley face. "Ugh! This is pretty sour."

Mustafa turned to Iancu. "I doubt that this guy will stay out of trouble, though," he said, pointing to Mark. "He seems to attract it like a magnet." He chuckled. "Meltem Hanım is unknowingly paying for his protection."

"What do you mean by that?" Iancu was puzzled.

"I have no more business here now that Ahmet is gone," explained Mustafa. "The only reason I'm staying here is to protect this *budala*." He used a Turkish word for fool.

Mark shook his head. "Don't believe that," he said to Iancu. "He is actually here because he waits for what I uncover. I somehow seem to have easier access to information."

"How do you know that the police are looking for him?" Iancu asked Mark.

"I have been interrogated numerous times by them since I've arrived." Mark turned to Mustafa. "Including this afternoon, by yet another one. Not Kárpáty. He wanted to know all about the fight at Zrinyi."

"What did you tell him?" asked Mustafa.

"Nothing. I lied."

Mustafa raised his eyebrows.

"I told him I had no idea who you were."

"Can you believe that this guy is a doctor?" Mustafa asked Iancu, with a familiar mocking tone.

They both surveyed Mark, Iancu seriously, Mustafa grinning.

"I've been wondering that ever since I met him," said Iancu.

Mark was pleased with the impression he was making. There was one more glass of tea left on the table, untouched. He reached for it and took a sip without putting any sugar in. It was cold. Iancu noticed and ordered his bodyguards to fetch more tea. Mark dug into his shoulder bag and pulled out an envelope.

"I received the preliminary forensics report on the Radu murder from Budapest police," he announced, proudly waving the envelope, then handing it to Iancu.

Iancu removed the document and glanced through it. He motioned to Dumitru, who had remained by the door while Iosif left to fetch drinks, and asked him to take a look. Mark gathered that Dumitru could read Hungarian. While the bodyguard leafed through the report, Iancu turned to Mark. "How did you get this?"

"Our able investigator here had to prostitute himself," Mustafa interjected. He brought the jar of pickles to his mouth and took a gulp of pickle juice. Mark winced.

"He had to endure a fancy dinner and an all-night date with a pretty policewoman to get this report."

Mark felt himself blush as Iancu gazed at him in surprise.

Dumitru returned the report to his boss and said a few words in Romanian. Iancu nodded approvingly. It appeared that the document had been authenticated.

"I can summarize the findings," said Mark.

Iancu and Mustafa both leaned toward him, Mustafa straightening his posture and abandoning his quest for pickles.

"Ahmet was handcuffed and asphyxiated in his hotel room shortly before I found him."

"Do you read Hungarian?" asked Iancu, pointing to the report.

"No," said Mark, "my police contact translated it for me." He spoke as if having a police contact in Budapest was as natural as a tour guide.

Iancu interjected. "This policewoman," he said, "how did you establish an inside contact with local police so fast?"

"Pure luck," said Mark.

"How can any woman resist this glamorous American?" interjected Mustafa, laughing.

Mark gave him an annoyed look. "My contact is not investigating Ahmet's murder," he explained to Iancu. "She is a rookie cop on patrol duty who is also assigned mundane errands. She drove me to the police station. That's how we met. Don't ask me how we ended up having dinner. It's a long story and it has nothing to do with Ahmet."

Mark looked at Mustafa sternly. Mustafa got the message and remained silent.

"How do they think he was asphyxiated?" Iancu asked.

"Some sort of gas, maybe." Mark paused to let his comment sink in. "The scene was very clean. No blood, no fingerprints. There's no evidence on his neck of strangulation, nor any evidence that he might have been smothered with a pillow or other such object. The only evidence of asphyxiation was petechiae in his sclerae and bruises on his cheeks—that may indicate a mask was forced on his face."

Iancu gave Mark a quizzical look. "Petechiae?"

"Sorry. Tiny blood spots in the whites of the eyes. Common in asphyxiation."

"And the mask? What sort of mask?"

"The lines on his face went from his nostrils to the edges of his cheeks." Mark drew simultaneous lines on his own face with his two index fingers. "It would have been something akin to a medical mask, like what anesthesiologists use."

"What kind of gas?"

"They don't know. They should be taking air samples from his lungs and analyzing them to find out. It might take weeks to get the results."

Mustafa turned to Iancu. "Do you know of anyone who might have this sort of modus operandi?"

"It was all very clean and neat," added Mark. "Almost clinical."

Iancu thought for a moment. "No. Most of the people we deal with, around Romania, Moldova, and nearby – those who might kill, they are violent people. Messy murderers."

Iosif entered with a new tray of piping hot tea for everyone, including the bodyguards. The conversation halted as they all took first sips.

Mark continued. "There were other strange findings in Ahmet's hotel room."

Iancu and Mustafa leaned forward. The bodyguards retreated to the entrance, tea glasses in hand.

"To begin with, there were these strange lines all over Ahmet's body."

"What kind of lines?" asked Mustafa.

"Just regular, parallel lines. On his torso, arms and legs. The report describes them but draws no conclusions. I don't think they have any idea what these are."

"What else?" Mustafa asked.

"There was a prominent stain on the bedroom carpet, near the door, and his eyeglasses lay in the same spot, broken. I saw all that before I found Ahmet's body. Those broken glasses made me realize something was seriously wrong."

"He was nearly blind without his glasses," said Iancu.

"I know that." Mark took a sip of tea. "When I was there, the stain was still wet. It was urine."

"What was Ahmet wearing?" asked Mustafa.

"A bathrobe. One from the hotel. Why do you ask?"

"Well," said Mustafa, "either Ahmet pissed on the carpet or the killer did. But why would the killer do that? So it's reasonable to assume it was Ahmet. Did he have any underwear on?"

"No," said Mark. "But remember, his body was in the bathroom, in the tub."

"I get that." Mustafa was serious and thoughtful, his usual irreverence having vanished. "Seems to me," he said, "that the spot where you found the pee stain and his glasses is where he was killed."

"Yeah," said Mark. "I had already reached the same conclusion. He may have involuntarily urinated as he was dying and his glasses fell amid the struggle."

Iancu listened but did not offer any opinions.

"That means that the killer moved the body," Mark continued. "I wonder why they did not clean up the pee stain."

"They may not have had the time or the means to do so. How would they do that? Use the towels in the bathroom to dab the urine and leave evidence?"

"You said there were no fingerprints, right?" Iancu asked.

"That's right." Mark turned toward him. "I think Mustafa is correct. Whoever the killer was, or maybe there was more than one, they were fast and efficient. The main investigator on the case, Kárpáty, he told me that this was a professional hit, an assassination. These people would have carefully avoided leaving evidence."

"Did Ahmet have any engagements that evening?" asked Mustafa.

"Me," answered Mark. "We were to meet down at the lobby and spend the evening together. For whatever reason, he changed his mind and invited me up."

"Whoever killed him probably did not know that he was to meet with you." Mustafa was alert, his mind racing.

"Yes," answered Mark. "Most likely."

"Here's what I think," said Mustafa. "I think the killers—for this sort of job I bet there was more than one—they figured that the body would not be found until the next day, probably by the hotel's cleaning staff. They would have no reason to clean up a pee stain. It would dry up by then."

"Why would they move the body to the bathroom?" Mark asked.

"How did the body look? Did he look like he had suffered a violent death?"

"No, not at all." Mark was following Mustafa's logic. "The first impression the body gave was that of a possible heart attack. That's what I thought. That's what a hotel cleaner would have concluded."

"Right," said Mustafa. "It was designed to raise the least amount of alarm. They probably moved the body to the bathtub because it would be less conspicuous than him lying on the carpet, less alarming."

"It sure did look less alarming at first glance. Nothing gruesome," Mark confirmed. He took a sip of tea and thought for a second. "They could not have expected Ahmet's body to be discovered so fast. As it is, the early discovery did not help catch who did it."

Iancu had been mostly quiet through this part of the conversation. He rubbed his forehead with the tips of his stubby fingers, looking deep in thought. He turned to Mark.

"You said that Olga, the masseuse, may have helped the killers. Have you heard anything from the police about how she may have done this?"

"No," said Mark. "As far as I know she has not been interrogated and I am quite sure she has left Hungary by now."

"How do you know that?"

"During our last conversation two nights ago, she told me that she was leaving soon."

"How many times did you talk to her?" Iancu seemed surprised that Mark had had multiple contacts with Olga.

"Three," said Mark. "But the first one doesn't count. I went to book a massage with her and she pretended to be someone else."

"Why?"

"Because I showed her a business card she had given Ahmet. It spooked her."

"Where did you get that?"

"I swiped it from Ahmet's room."

Mustafa stood up and walked over to Mark's chair. His movement attracted attention from Dumitru and Iosif. He squeezed Mark's shoulders and proclaimed, "He was born to be an investigator but he didn't know it."

The bodyguards followed Mustafa like vigilant guard dogs with their ears up. Mustafa moved away from the table and leaned against a pickle rack. "Olga admitted to aiding the killers," he said, "in a roundabout way."

"Correct." Mark turned to Iancu. "After my meeting with Olga at the Mercy nightclub, I called her that same night. That's when she told me she was leaving. She also told me that I wouldn't be safe anywhere in Budapest except inside my hotel. So far her prediction has been accurate."

"Now that she is not at the hotel, there's no one to help attackers get past the security system," Mustafa added, recalling the point he had made after rescuing Mark at Zrinyi.

"What is the security system?" asked Iancu.

"The elevators are activated by the key card that opens the hotel room door. They are programmed to open only at the floor where the room is located. There is a camera monitor system but, as far as I can tell, it is aimed only at the elevator doors. I don't believe the police caught any perpetrators in the camera monitor system."

"Did they tell you that?" Iancu no longer appeared surprised by the depth of inside information Mark seemed to possess.

"No," Mark answered. "But in my first interview with them, they led me to believe that they had reviewed the camera footage quickly, soon after they were called in. Since they have no leads on who did it, I assume they did not identify anyone suspicious on the footage."

"So," said Mustafa. "The killers needed a route other than the elevator, most likely stairs. Do you know if the stairs are key-carded too?"

"I don't know," said Mark. "I never took any stairs. But I bet they are. They could not possibly have tight security on elevators and leave the stairs unattended."

"Right." Mustafa thought for a moment. "That means that the killers had to know ahead of time not to take the elevators, and they would have to have key card access to the stairs and to Ahmet's suite. A master card would do that."

"Yes, like one that hotel employees might have," said Mark. "Olga didn't have to do much to aid the killers. Just give them the layout and a master key."

Iancu had been playing with the ring on his pinky while listening to Mark's exchange with Mustafa. "If this Olga is the same one I recall from years ago," he said thoughtfully, "Nicolae had a special relationship with her, a long-term one, like a mistress. I don't know why she would have turned on him and helped in his assassination."

"Good point." Mark was excited by Iancu's comment. "Let me tell you something. At the Mercy nightclub, when I met with Olga, I got the distinct impression that she was distraught about what happened and that she didn't know what she did would lead to Ahmet's murder. I think she was an unwitting participant in this."

"If that is so," Mustafa interjected, "who put her up to it?"

"Could it have been Cesar?" asked Mark. He addressed Iancu. "Did you look into Cesar and his relationship with Olga?"

"Cesar Kaminesky," Iancu spoke slowly and deliberately, "has disappeared."

Chapter 44

* * *

The old man tending to the pickle shop entered the back room and exchanged a few words with the bodyguards. He waved at Iancu.

"He is closing," said Iancu.

Mark briefly exited the room and stood behind the front counter of the pickle kiosk. The lights of the basement floor were down, as were various signs lighting the neighboring stores. There were no more visitors in the aisles. He stepped out of the kiosk and stretched his limbs. The chair inside the back room had been uncomfortable. He thought about the conversation with Iancu and Mustafa. So far it had been largely one-sided, Mark delivering most of the useful information. It was time for Iancu to step up.

Back inside, he found Iancu and Mustafa quietly conversing, their interaction less tense than it had been in the beginning. The room had a stale, vinegary smell of pickles, more distinct now that Mark had breathed fresh air outside.

"We did business with Latif Bey for many years," Iancu was saying, "before his son arrived."

"What sort of business?" asked Mustafa.

"Textiles," said Iancu. "We imported Latif's textiles from Turkey. In those days, communist times, the business was clandestine. Latif's goods were in high demand, especially the lingerie. Very valuable."

"What about other goods?"

Iancu pondered the question stony-faced. "From time to time," he answered, "there were others, yes."

Mustafa did not push the point. He let Iancu continue.

"Ahmet had gotten himself in some trouble in Istanbul and needed a new life, a new identity. He was bright and full of youthful ideas. Latif promised us that he would open a new trade connection for us through eastern Turkey to the Middle East, Syria especially. He had sent his son there as an apprentice."

"Would that be with someone named Ibrahim?" Mark interjected. He stood by the table, reluctant to sit yet. "I don't know his last name but he was called Kara Ibrahim, a Kurdish man from Urfa."

Iancu looked at him, bushy eyebrows creased, betraying surprise. "Yes," he said. "How did you know?"

"I met the man once, in Istanbul, many years ago. Latif Bey took Ahmet and me to a nightclub and Ibrahim was there. He was hard to forget." Mark turned to Mustafa. "Do you remember the name? He was frequently in the newspapers in those days."

"No, that was before my time," said Mustafa. "I was too young then."

"I had the distinct impression that Kara Ibrahim was a smuggler." Mark was deliberately blunt, trying to provoke Iancu into revealing the true nature of their business.

"As I said," Iancu ignored Mark and addressed Mustafa. "Ahmet brought us some new and lucrative lines of business. And in return we gave him a new identity: Nicolae Radu."

"Who is us?" Mark interjected again. "Were you associated with others?"

Iancu turned to Mark and nodded. Apparently this was an acceptable question. "Yes," he said, looking up at him. "We were several partners, all Romanian, all related to each other. I was the youngest and the only one who saw potential in Ahmet. The others were suspicious of him. They thought him a rotten, wealthy kid who would bring trouble."

"He did, didn't he?"

"Not really." Iancu didn't get Mark's point. "Business is what it is. We had ups and downs. He and I handled the rough stretches all right." Iancu reached for the open pickle jar that Mustafa had sifted through and removed a red radish, shaking off the juice. "My associates became very jittery after Ibrahim was assassinated in Hatay."

"I didn't know that," said Mark. He recalled Kara Ibrahim's security arrangements at Maksim. They had ultimately failed. "I suppose that was inevitable."

"It happened a few years after Nicolae's arrival." Iancu rolled the radish between his fingers in a manner similar to how he rolled his pinky ring. "That's when I broke off with the family and devoted my business interests solely to Nicolae. By then we had branched off to other endeavors. The loss of Ibrahim did not hurt us too much." He popped the radish in his mouth. "Those were opportunistic times, with communism and Ceausescu gone, and a free-for-all economy. Nicolae built a chain of retail stores where we sold textiles, and also maintained a brisk import-export business. We also created a construction company that turned out to be quite lucrative."

"So when did he get into the organ trade?" Mark asked nonchalantly as he sat down.

Iancu abruptly turned to Mark, his left arm swinging involuntarily. It knocked the half-empty jar of pickles off the table, the remaining pickles rolling across the floor. Iosif and Dumitru rushed over to collect the mess.

Sensing that Iancu would be evasive, Mark added, "Interpol is investigating Ahmet, here in Budapest." He was emphatic. "I met with a French officer who is an Interpol liaison to the local police. He seemed to be mainly interested in Ahmet's activities in the organ trade. He told me Ahmet was a broker."

There was a brief silence as Iancu watched his guards clean up the pickles, pondering an answer. Then he turned to Mustafa and Mark, letting out a sigh. "It was another line of business proposed to us by Latif Bey," he began. "He made the preliminary introductions."

Mark and Mustafa looked at each other, eyebrows raised. This revelation about Latif's involvement was a bombshell for both. Staring at his ring, Iancu did not notice their reaction.

"It began about a decade ago," he continued quietly. "And it was lucrative." He looked at Mark with a somber expression. "It swiftly became our largest line of business."

"What were Latif's introductions?" asked Mustafa.

"It began as a simple proposal." Iancu seemed resigned to discussing the subject freely. "Latif had a young doctor and two Israeli brokers who were looking for live kidney donors. The clients were mostly Israeli citizens with failed kidneys. Latif asked us if we could find them donors in Romania and Moldova. The Israelis offered hefty commissions in return."

A glum smile broke out on Iancu's lips. "This was the sort of thing Nicolae was very good at." He looked at Mark. "He had a special knack for bringing people together. He was very charming, even though he was not totally fluent in Romanian."

"I know what you mean," said Mark.

"Soon we had developed a pretty elaborate network of recruiters and a steady supply of donors. The Israelis were happy and so were we, with the profits, even though these did not quite match what we brought in from construction and textiles."

"Who were the donors?" asked Mustafa.

"Poor villagers, mostly men. For some reason, many clients seemed reluctant to receive kidneys from women. They came from all over Romania and Moldova. Moldovans were cheaper. We didn't care how much each cost. At the time we were receiving our commissions based on the number of live donors we contributed."

"Where did the transplants take place?"

"In Turkey. Various clinics, mostly near Istanbul and Ankara. We did not know the details and, at the time, it wasn't of much interest to us."

"Did you run into any trouble with law enforcement?" asked Mustafa.

Iancu chuckled. "That's the thing," he said. "It was so much easier than our other businesses where we were regularly harassed by customs and police. We had to reserve large outlays to bribe them, and this added to our overhead. But with kidneys we had minimal police interference. The business cost us very little."

Mark wondered why businesses like textiles and construction would attract police and customs attention. They were obviously fronts for other, more illicit activities. He refrained from posing questions on the subject, fearing that they might derail Iancu's account, by far his most forthcoming thus far.

"Then," Iancu continued, "Nicolae went on a couple of back-to-back trips to Turkey. His father was sick, heart trouble. When he returned he was all fired up about setting up a full organ trade operation in Romania and taking the entire business over from the Israelis. In his usual way, he put a network together rapidly."

"So what happened in Turkey that changed things?" Mustafa was captivated by the story.

"He met the doctor," explained Iancu.

"What doctor?" asked Mark. "The transplant guy or whoever was treating his father?"

"Actually," Iancu smiled, "they were the same. The transplant guy mediated Latif's illness, finding him appropriate specialists. He acted like a family doctor. Latif's heart trouble turned out not too bad, a small heart attack. He received..." Iancu hesitated, putting his right hand to his chest. "Something in the veins of his heart."

"Stents?"

"Yes, that's it."

"Those go into arteries, the coronaries."

"Whatever," said Iancu. "While Latif was going through all this, Nicolae met the doctor and they hatched up a plan to create a Romanian organ network. It was brilliant. The doctor offered to come over and train local doctors on how to do transplants, supervising them until they were proficient. Nicolae already had a recruitment apparatus in place for donors. All they needed to do was add a medical infrastructure — which was simply a matter of recruiting people — and this proved to be easy."

"What about recipients?" asked Mark. "Were they hard to pry from the Israeli brokers?"

"As it turned out, we actually didn't have to." Iancu was savoring his tale. "The doctor connected us with various brokers in different countries. There was a big backlog of recipients all willing to pay one hundred fifty to two hundred thousand dollars for a kidney."

"You mean there was more business than anyone could handle?" remarked Mark.

"Correct. So the business exploded. It became very big. Nicolae handled most of the high-level recruitment and connections. I dealt with lower-level providers, you know, the army of field workers we had to organize, recruiters of donors, medical labs, surgical teams, secretarial workers who scheduled procedures, you name it."

Mark brought the question back to Cesar. "Was Cesar Kaminesky part of this network?"

"Yes," said Iancu. "He headed our Transylvanian connection, based in Brasov. He was not a direct employee, more an independent contractor. I did not know him well. Nicolae handled him. Cesar was good. He delivered us a great deal of business, both in donors and in procedures."

"Where were the procedures done?" asked Mark.

"Which ones?"

"The ones Cesar mediated."

"In a hospital in Brasov, associated with Regina Maria."

The name startled Mark. It was the same one as in Ahmet's radiology report.

"Regina Maria is a national network," added Iancu. "The Brasov hospital is part of it, along with some outpatient clinics, also located there."

"The doctor," Mark said, "Latif's Turkish connection." He paused to ensure Iancu was paying attention to what he was about to ask. "Would that be a man named Gazioğlu?"

Iancu sank back in his chair and nodded. He seemed no longer surprised by Mark's knowledge.

* * *

"Our man here could be an honorary police detective," Mustafa mockingly proclaimed as he stood behind Mark and patted him on the back. He sat back down and observed Mark with a smirk. "Tell us: how did you charm so many police officers in such a short time, to get so much information?"

Annoying as Mustafa was, Mark realized that he had indeed pried a good deal from police. He ignored Mustafa and addressed Iancu.

"Gérard, the French officer, told me that there is an Interpol red alert out for Gazioğlu. He's on a most-wanted list."

"We haven't seen him in a while," answered Iancu. "He fulfilled his promise to us and trained local doctors in our service areas. We have two good surgeons in Brasov who perform the transplants smoothly and with minimal complications. We no longer need him unless we want to open a new service region."

"Does that mean you don't know where he is?"

"Yes," said Iancu. "I suspect he is still in Turkey. It's easier for him to hide there."

He rolled his pinky ring again, thoughtfully. "I am no longer interested in him," he said in a determined voice. "I have decided that I will divest myself of that line of business."

Mark and Mustafa raised their eyebrows, and almost simultaneously asked why.

"Nicolae was the executive. I would have to step up and assume his role, cultivate his contacts. It's a challenge."

"Seems to me to be a challenge well within your capabilities," said Mark.

"True." Iancu nodded appreciatively at the compliment. "But the business is getting too hot." He paused, looking for the right choice of words. "This threat that we received, the one that caused Nicolae to panic and contact you…." He paused again. "I believe it came from our kidney business."

He cleared his throat. "I have a son—he is twenty-six—who is apprenticing with me. He will eventually take over my businesses. I don't want any harm to come to him. We do well enough with our other operations. We don't need the aggravation."

"So what was the threat?" asked Mark.

"A death threat," answered Iancu. "Vague one."

"From whom?"

"We don't know. The information came from one of our more reliable operatives in Brasov. His name is Enver Muratovich, a Bosnian refugee who came to Romania as a child many years ago. He is one of our best recruiters. Enver spends a good deal of time in Moldova. He recently came to us with news of a serious plot to assassinate Nicolae. He had heard the buzz through the grapevine in Chisinau, but was not sure of the precise source."

"Are death threats common in your line of business?" asked Mustafa.

"Yes, we got some from time to time." Iancu was frank. "And Nicolae usually brushed them off. He was cavalier about such threats. But this one really spooked him. I don't know why. He knew something—something he didn't share with me—that made Enver's warning particularly serious."

"Why do you think he didn't share it with you?" asked Mark. "Sounds like you two were pretty close."

"We were," said Iancu. "In many ways he was like my little brother." He chuckled. "Albeit an ill-behaved one."

"But charismatic." Mark shared Iancu's sentiments.

Iancu became grim. "I think Nicolae might not have wanted me to know in order to protect me and my family. He did that occasionally over the years, when he took risks he knew I would disapprove of."

"What about his own family?" asked Mark.

"He had Miruna and his children well segregated. They lived in Constanta, by the Black Sea, while Nicolae kept a separate apartment in Bucharest where he tended to business. When he was with his family in Constanta—they lived in a well-guarded compound—he never conducted business in their presence."

"You weren't that way?"

"No. I live in Bucharest. My wife and children are fully aware of all my business activities. I have a daughter, she is thirty-two, married and with two children, who is my full-time accountant. And I have my son, who I am grooming as an heir."

"How," asked Mark, "did Ahmet expect me to help him in America?"

"He had a plan to abscond to the U.S. We ship goods across the Atlantic on a regular basis. He planned to use one of our cargo ships to secretly travel there. He did not like to fly."

Mark already knew this from Dumitru.

Iancu continued. "He considered you his most trustworthy contact in the U.S. He had a plan to have you extract him from a West Coast port, like Los Angeles or Seattle, and keep him in hiding until he could establish a new identity and gain a foothold in your country. We had other contacts in America, but they were all business counterparts, unreliable."

"What about Miruna?"

"Nicolae thought they would be safe in Constanta until he set himself up in the U.S. Then he would bring them over."

"How did he expect to set himself up?"

"As I said, Nicolae was very resourceful when it came to establishing new contacts. He had plenty of money to spread around."

"The U.S. is not Romania," said Mark. "It's not as corrupt. I still am not sure how he expected to get a work permit, I.D., citizenship."

"Believe me," said Iancu, "he would have done it."

"If he was planning to uproot his whole life and family, this threat must have been very serious indeed," said Mark, more to himself than to Iancu. But he knew that Iancu was on a roll. This was the most opportune time to extract as much out of him as he could.

"Tell me something else," said Mark. "Why did Ahmet choose Budapest for a meeting place?"

"We considered Budapest a safe city. We did not have any direct business interests here. No rivals. Nicolae used Budapest often for brief trips to meet people. I suppose he figured it would be safe for you as well."

Mark could think of several sarcastic retorts to this remark. Ahmet had gotten himself killed and plunged Mark into more trouble than he had ever lived through.

"In my opinion," said Iancu with conviction, "Nicolae's assassination was not a plot that originated in Budapest. It came from abroad, most likely Moldova, as Enver suggested. If it wasn't Budapest, the hit would have occurred somewhere else."

"Do you think that Cesar had something to do with it too?" asked Mark.

"Maybe, I don't know." Iancu shrugged his shoulders. "As I said, he has disappeared. Since you brought up his name the other day, I had my people run inquiries around Brasov, where he lives. No one can find any trace of him."

"What about his business?"

"It's a well-organized operation," said Iancu. "He can oversee it from hiding."

"You know," said Mustafa, "we've been thinking of this Cesar Kaminesky as a sinister character. But if he disappeared, isn't it possible that he, too, is afraid, like Nicolae? Or even maybe assassinated?"

"Possible," murmured Iancu. "I don't know enough to venture a guess. Not yet. Anyhow," he continued, "I received an unexpected message from a local Budapest businessman earlier today, who is acting as an intermediary. The message was that Nicolae's death was a result of a misunderstanding. Whoever is behind it wants to clear the air. They don't wish to start a war back in Romania and Moldova. I'll be meeting him later tonight."

"Who is it?" asked Mark.

"Someone named Tibor Bognár."

Chapter 45

* * *

"Why didn't you let me tell Iancu I knew Bognár?" demanded Mark, as he stood with Mustafa on the sidewalk at Fővam ter. The Central Market hulked as a dark silhouette behind them, lifeless at this late hour. Up ahead the Liberty Bridge was brilliantly lit, its heavy ironwork glowing like jewels, its pointed pillars topped with radiant flying eagles. A lonely streetcar traversed the bridge approaching them along the otherwise deserted boulevard.

"He is a big boy," said Mustafa. "He can take care of himself."

A pair of bright headlights swiftly grew as a dark Mercedes came to a stop nearby. Mark cocked his head toward it with alarm. He relaxed when the driver emerged from the idling car and waved at him.

"Are you sure you don't want me to take you back to your hotel?" It was Dumitru.

"Certain." Mustafa answered for Mark. "I'll accompany him. He'll be fine." He beckoned Mark to move on. They began walking in the direction of the luminous bridge, its lights reflected in intricate wavy patterns along the lazy surface of the Danube.

Mark apprehensively made a circular sweep of his surroundings, concerned about another ambush. This area seemed more conducive to it than the lively pedestrian mall at Zrinyi. Twice bitten, he didn't carry the same sense of safety that Mustafa displayed with bravado.

Mark waved goodbye to Dumitru. “Are we going to walk to the hotel?”

“No,” said Mustafa. “We’ll take the streetcar.” It was the same line Mark had taken with Jasmin earlier in the day.

Mustafa adjusted the brim of his Tyrolean hat. “I wanted you to come with me so we can have a private conversation.”

They descended toward the riverside drive. “Can you believe that crock of shit about Bognár?” remarked Mark.

“I don’t know,” said Mustafa. “Maybe he is indeed an intermediary.”

“You still think Bognár’s men did not commit Ahmet’s murder?”

“As I said before,” said Mustafa, “it seems too neat for his thugs, too precise. Your description of the forensics convinces me even more.”

They waited in a dimly lit streetcar stop. A young couple were kissing nearby, oblivious to their presence.

“I still think this meeting between Iancu and Bognár is ill advised,” Mark muttered in a hushed tone.

After their initial surprise at Iancu’s announcement, Mark had attempted to respond but Mustafa, rising quickly out of his seat, had grabbed his arm and given him a stern gaze. Iancu did not seem to notice. Their meeting ended soon after and they walked out to the empty expanse of the massive indoor market, Iosif letting them out of a side door with a key.

When they were alone, Mustafa had told Mark that he did not want their knowledge of Bognár revealed to Iancu. He wasn’t sure what either was up to. It was prudent to steer clear of both. “It’s no longer any of our business,” pronounced Mustafa. “We’ll be out of Budapest soon.”

The single streetcar was another clunky, old-fashioned one, with two elderly people up front and the enamored lovers from the station nuzzling by the back windows. Mark and Mustafa preferred to stand, holding on to leather straps hanging from the ceiling in the middle of the car.

“I am surprised that Latif Bey is still active,” said Mustafa. “I thought he had retired.”

“Me, too.” Mark observed the lit statue atop Gellért Hill across the river, the Rudas baths a silhouette beneath the hulking rock along the riverside. The

Elizabeth Bridge, also opulently lit, soon overpowered the scene as the streetcar approached it.

Mark continued. "I'm also surprised that Ahmet apprenticed with Kara Ibrahim in southeastern Turkey. Did you know anything about that?"

"No. I just provided security for Latif's properties. I had no information about his business activities."

"He was a notorious smuggler," said Mark. "Ruthless."

"Ahmet turned out different, didn't he?" Mustafa chuckled. "Smoother, slicker."

The streetcar stopped at the station by the Elizabeth Bridge and opened its doors. No one got on or off.

"That textile business is probably just a front for smuggling," continued Mustafa. "Women? Drugs? Weapons? God knows what." He paused for a moment. "And their construction business is ideal for money laundering."

"How so?"

"They can engage in large cash disbursements without attracting government attention, such as payroll or land purchases. With false documentation, illegal money can be made to appear legitimately used in such transactions."

Mark thought about Mustafa's explanation for a second. He did not fully comprehend the concept, but he did agree that Ahmet's legitimate businesses were probably fronts for other illegal ones.

"Do you realize," said Mark thoughtfully, "that Latif sowed the seeds of his son's destruction by sending him to Romania, while he actually thought he was rescuing him?"

"Latif did that much earlier," answered Mustafa grimly, "the way he brought up that boy."

Mark had an image of Meliha Hanım playing cards with Mark's mother and aunt in Nişantaşı, all those years ago. She had accurately foreseen Ahmet's fate.

They exited the streetcar by the Chain Bridge, its lights no longer as alluring as they had been when Mark first arrived in Budapest. They stood by the entrance to Gresham Palace. The doorman was missing from his usual spot.

"When are you checking out of the hotel tomorrow?" asked Mustafa.

"Around eleven in the morning, I suppose."

Mustafa straightened Mark's askew collar. "Where will you stay in Istanbul?"

"At the Hyatt, in Harbiye, near Taksim."

"Whew! Expensive."

Mark looked behind him at the floodlit walls of the Gresham. "Not as bad as this one." He smiled.

"I'll be back the day after," said Mustafa.

"How are you traveling?"

"Turgut has a shipment of car parts leaving tomorrow. I'll be in the truck, part of the cargo."

Mark shook his head in disapproval.

"If you want you can stay at my place after I arrive," said Mustafa. "We have an extra room. Hülya wouldn't mind."

The comment evoked memories of Joel's invitation in San Francisco, making Mark realize that he was soon to be homeless in his hometown. "Where do you live?"

"Bostancı." It was on the Asian side, away from the city center.

"A bit far from the action."

"Might be safer," said Mustafa, his mocking tone returning. "Knowing you, I bet you'll create trouble in Istanbul."

"I have an invitation to stay with this woman named Günsu in Nişantaşı," said Mark. "She is," he corrected himself, "*was*, Ahmet's mistress."

"H'mmm," remarked Mustafa. "She seeks a quick replacement."

"No, it's not like that. We're old friends."

"I bet," said Mustafa, his mockery in full swing. He reached for Mark's shoulder bag. "Show me your phones."

He examined Mark's iPhone and nodded approvingly. It was turned off. He then opened and closed the Cello Mobile, the small flip phone he had rented for Mark.

"What shall I do with it?" asked Mark.

"Leave it at the reception desk when you check out. I'll pick it up later."

Mark tucked the phones in his bag and turned toward the door. Mustafa squeezed his arm and stopped him. "One more thing."

Mark gave him a *what now* look.

"Remember what Olga told you," said Mustafa sternly. "You are not to leave this hotel again until you catch a taxi to the airport."

"Yes, sir!" Mark gave him a mock salute, like a soldier.

"Go soak in those luxurious baths of your hotel. Get a good night's sleep." Mustafa looked him over. "You look like shit," he said. "Like you haven't slept in days."

He was right, Mark realized. He felt like shit, too.

"And put an ice pack on that black eye. You don't want your Turkish mistress to see you this way. Do you think that she'll take in a *serseri* like you?" The word meant a tramp or a punk. "Now have a good flight and we'll see each other in Istanbul."

The doorman appeared, and Mark nodded hello to him as Mustafa distanced himself and crossed the street to the elliptical park in the square. Soon he was a strange silhouette with his Tyrolean hat, backlit by the Chain Bridge—a German maybe, or perhaps an Austrian, heading briskly away with his walking stick.

Chapter 46

* * *

Metin was on a beach, camera in hand, a strange camera with an unusually wide, long lens that he had trouble carrying. As he snuck up on her he had trouble balancing the lens, and for a moment, he was filled with a terrific fear that it would fall over onto her face. She lay prone, eyes closed, enjoying the sun, oblivious to him. "Günsu," he called out to her, while still looking through the viewfinder. Her lovely lips stretched thin into a smile and she opened her eyes, two dark pearls, wide and radiant, ready to swallow his camera.

Suddenly she was on top of him and he was helplessly pinned down, her outstretched arms pressing his shoulders, her powerful hips thrusting down on his. He felt an insatiable desire as she lowered her head towards his. "Do you want me?" she whispered hoarsely into his ear.

For a moment he was fretful about his camera that seemed to have disappeared. He looked left and right, avoiding her fiery gaze. She noticed his distraction and pressed down on him harder. "Never mind that," she ordered.

"Yes, Jasmin," he said, "I want you." He looked at her closely, surprised with her metamorphosis. "Badly," he added.

She clasped his penis. He prepared himself for the bliss to come. She squeezed hard. Then harder. She squeezed as if it were a fruit from which juice was to be extracted.

"Stop," he said. "You're hurting me."

She ignored him. The pain became more intense. He felt as if his entire mid-body were being crushed. He struggled to get out from under her but she had him helplessly restrained. He closed his eyes and forced his shoulders up and down in a futile attempt to break the lock of her body, his head wildly waving from side to side in panic.

All of a sudden the pressure let up, but the pain lingered. He opened his eyes, ready to reproach her. He was seated in a lounge chair on a vast sandy beach, waves crashing in at a far distance. He looked down at himself, to where it still hurt. He was fully dressed in the same outfit he wore while exploring Budapest. A silhouette crowded his face.

"Why did you do this to me?" groaned the shadowy figure woefully, a male voice.

Confused, Mark examined the new face eye-to-eye with him, backlit by a bright sun. He had a turban, like a Sikh Indian, and large gold rings that hung low from each ear lobe.

"Why?" repeated the man.

Chapter 47

* * *

He had purple blotches around his swollen eyes. It was not a turban he was wearing on his head, Mark realized. It was a craniotomy dressing. As Mark recognized the bouncer from the Mercy nightclub who had been clubbed at Zrinyi, he was filled with terror.

"I didn't," protested Mark.

Somewhere in the distance a phone rang. He looked around at the sand. There was no one else on the beach. The ringing persisted.

"You'll pay for this," growled the bouncer, a large butcher knife in his right hand glistening in the sun.

The phone kept ringing, louder.

"No!" screamed Mark, and he opened his eyes.

The phone was still ringing, at his bedside table. The room was dark and calm. He picked up the receiver.

"Mr. Kent?"

"Yes," he rasped, while instinctively rubbing his groin. No pain. He scanned the dark expanse of his room. No Günsu, Jasmin, or that hideous man.

"Mr. Kent, my name is Horváth. I am calling from the District V police station. I hope I didn't disturb you at this hour." Horváth's voice was deep. He spoke slowly and off rhythm, as if he had difficulty selecting English words.

"What time is it?"

"Eleven fifteen."

"Night or morning?" Mark brushed his hair back and waited for an answer, unaware that his question might seem odd.

"Near midnight, sir."

Mark glanced at the lit clock on his bedside table that confirmed Horváth's claim. He turned on a light and stood up, phone receiver in hand, fully reoriented from nightmare to real world.

"I'm sorry," he said. "You woke me up from a deep sleep."

"My apologies."

"So what do you need?" Surely they would not want another interview at District V at this hour.

"Sir, I have a message from Inspector Kárpáty. He would like to have a meeting with you."

"When?"

"Now," said Horváth. "As soon as you can be available."

Another meeting in the dead of night? Kárpáty was up to his old tricks.

"Do you know where Rudas baths is located?"

"He wants to meet with me in a bath house?" Mark was startled.

"Yes, if you don't mind. It is not far from your hotel."

"Is it open at this hour?"

"Yes, sir. On Fridays and Saturdays, Rudas is open until two a.m."

Mark was not sure whether to accept or decline the invitation. "Why does the inspector want to see me?"

"We are aware, sir, that there was a leak of confidential material from our files," said Horváth, his voice formal and businesslike, "regarding an ongoing murder investigation."

Shit, thought Mark. His thoughts immediately turned to Jasmin, hoping she was all right.

"The inspector knows that you are in possession of documents that should not have been made available to you."

How had they discovered? Mark wondered.

"We know that you are preparing to leave Budapest tomorrow on the Turkish Air direct, to Istanbul."

Damn it! They had been checking up on him.

"The Inspector does not wish to cause any trouble for you. He requests that you return the documents. He is willing to discuss the case with you and summarize his findings before you depart. We understand that you were a close friend of the deceased. We feel that you are entitled to the information." He was offering an olive branch.

Mark wondered what else Kárpáty had uncovered. "Okay. What do you want me to do?"

"Take a taxi to the bath house and check in at the ticket booth. You'll receive further instructions there."

"Uhm," said Mark awkwardly. "Is this a fully naked place?" He remembered the Turkish baths of his childhood in Istanbul, authentic ones that did not cater to tourists. He doubted this one in Budapest would be that way. "I didn't plan on visiting any bath house when I flew out here. I don't have any attire."

"No problem," said Horváth. "You will be provided with a towel and a swimming suit when you arrive. Tell the attendant you are there to meet the Inspector."

"Give me a few minutes to get dressed."

"Thank you for your cooperation." Horváth hung up.

Mark sank back onto his bed and pondered this unconventional invitation. He had less than twenty-four hours left in Budapest. As Mustafa had so emphatically put it, he needed to stay out of trouble for this brief time. Staying in the safety of the hotel would keep him out of trouble. But what if he disobeyed Kárpáty? Would Budapest police create a problem for him at the airport?

Mark was aware that he was flying to a non-EU country and that he would go through passport control at the airport before boarding his plane. He could easily be detained there, still have an encounter with Kárpáty—he expected that it would be unpleasant, as all had been—and miss his flight. It seemed safer to go to Rudas now and get it over with.

As Mark began dressing, he recalled Jasmin's account of Kárpáty's reputation among his colleagues, how he liked to hold meetings in bath houses. An off-hour, late-night invitation to a bath house for official police business was bizarre, but quite possibly routine for Kárpáty. He then wondered about the other rumor Jasmin had mentioned. Could the inspector have some sort of homosexual intent? Mark peered at himself as he combed his hair in front of the bathroom mirror. He had never been the type to whom gay men were attracted, and no such invitation had ever come his way.

Mark left the bathroom and checked the contents of his shoulder bag lying on the entryway table. It was highly unlikely that Kárpáty had carnal intentions, but if so, he would tactfully refuse. He decided that dealing with a homosexual proposal would be easier than explaining his possession of the forensics report. He removed the Budapest guidebook from his bag, but left his two cellphones, wallet, and passport inside. He then took out the envelope containing the forensics report and shuffled through its pages, neatly folding and reinserting them, as if the document needed to be returned tidily. He called the hotel front desk for a taxi while he dropped the report into his bag.

* * *

It was a clear, moonless night, the floodlit buildings and monuments of Budapest casting a radiant glow on the landscape. As Mark's taxi traversed the Elizabeth Bridge toward Buda, he realized that this was his first crossing of the Danube. The river was devoid of any watercraft, its choppy waters altering the lights they reflected into disquieting, cubist reflections. Up ahead, the Rudas bath complex stood alone at the foot of the bridge to the left, deserted it seemed, under the monolithic Gellért Hill, its sheer rock surface eerily floodlit behind the bath house.

The taxi took a one hundred eighty-degree curve exiting off the bridge and turned south onto the riverside drive. Mark became more apprehensive as it slowed by the Rudas complex. He wondered if he should have warned Mustafa, or maybe Jasmin, that he was headed to Rudas and to Kárpáty. What good would that do? The inspector had summoned him and Mark felt that he was the only one who could resolve the situation. A single northbound yellow tram passed by in the median. It was completely empty, as were the dark sidewalks of the riverside drive. The Buda side of the river was obviously not as popular in this sector as its counterpart in Pest, where tourists and revelers promenaded at all hours of the night.

The taxi stopped at an indistinct door between a two-story plain white building to the right, and a taller, nineteenth-century yellow one with arched windows to the left. A sign in black block letters announced *Rudas Gyógyfürdő* above the entrance. Mark entered a small foyer with ticket booths by the door and a small bar directly ahead, lit with a red neon sign announcing *Rudas Café,* atop a modest display of liquor bottles. The young bartender stood behind his counter, chatting with a blue uniformed older woman wearing a white scarf over her head.

The ticket booth was a long, bar-like counter with three pay stations. A single attendant sat at the middle one, a stocky young man who was busy eating a large piece of pie. He looked up at Mark with an apologetic face, cheeks full, lips smeared with whipped cream. Mark explained why he was there.

"Oh, yes," said the man, as he wiped his mouth with a paper napkin. He reached out for an envelope, then stood up and looked around. The foyer was empty. He walked out of his station, called out to the woman at the bar, then returned.

"Please give this to the lady," he said, "and she'll show you upstairs to the changing area." He sat back down and cut another piece of pie with his fork. "We usually take a security deposit for the towel and swimming suit you'll receive, but this has been waived. Make sure you return them on your way out. Otherwise your host will be charged a penalty for the missing items."

"Where's Inspector Kárpáty?" asked Mark.

"He left a message asking that you wait for him at the main swimming pool. The locker room attendant upstairs will show you the way."

The uniformed woman quietly led Mark up a flight of stairs between the bar and ticket booth. She handed him to a young man wearing a white T-shirt and shorts, who sat at a counter with towels behind it. He was short and slim, with a well-trimmed beard. He examined Mark's paperwork.

"Another special guest," he said with a hint of surprise in his voice. His English was good.

"Did Kárpáty invite others?"

"No," he mumbled, still examining the papers. He walked back and pulled out a plain white towel. "Never mind," he said, laying the towel on the counter.

"It was a different party." He eyed Mark up and down. "Now, what size swimming suit do you wear?"

It took some effort to translate American measurements to European ones. The young man, whose name was György, was friendly and helpful. He brought out several suits and ushered Mark to a nearby locker area where he instructed him to try each and select the best fit. He also handed Mark a red plastic wrist band with a faceless watch-like center. This was to be his electronic access to his locker and to the different parts of the bath complex, each segregated with a turnstile the device opened.

Mark asked him if he could keep his shoulder bag, explaining that he had his wallet and mobile phone in it. György ran a cursory outside inspection and told him that regulations did not allow this. It had to be tucked away in a locker. But since this was not a busy evening and Mark was a special guest, he would allow it. Mark thanked him and offered him a tip, which György politely refused.

They walked across a smartly decorated skyway adjoining the two buildings above the main entrance, György leading. Mark followed, with his towel over his forearm, shoulder bag slung diagonally across, flip-flops slapping against the marble floor.

In the middle of the walkway an arresting view caused Mark to halt and look out the window. It was the Elizabeth Bridge again, its Pest half framed by the dark silhouettes of the two Rudas buildings, glowing gloriously over the glistening river. Mark felt as if he had left a familiar, secure world in Pest for an uncertain one far away, even though Rudas was not that far from his hotel.

György stood nearby and waited patiently, accustomed to the pause the view provoked. He led Mark downstairs to the older building, past a wrist band-activated turnstile, into a vast indoor swimming pool. It was an imposing space with a soaring ceiling and two stories of colonnaded arches. The enormous rectangular pool was flanked by spacious side aisles with tall arched windows that looked out at the river on one side and Gellért Hill on the other. Each side had a wide boulevard traversing the outside of the building. Along the short edges of the pool were the entrance and exit. Mark and György stood near the entrance, by a small waterfall that poured water into the pool through a thin slit.

The side aisles had wicker chairs for customers to rest. Mark noticed a young man sitting under one of the middle arches, near the pool. He wore the same outfit as György and languidly observed a solitary swimmer in the pool. Mark guessed he was a lifeguard. A young couple waded beneath the waterfall, bodies immersed in the pool to their necks, carrying on a cheerful conversation. György approached the guard and exchanged a few words with him. He then returned to Mark and told him his host had not yet arrived. Mark was welcome to swim, if he so wished.

As György disappeared, Mark exchanged a nod with the guard and walked toward one of the arched windows to take in the view. Across the shimmering Danube, a lineup of cruise boats were docked on the Pest side. The Elizabeth Bridge dominated the skyline on the left with its gracefully lit suspension cables, competing for attention with the more massive and elaborately lit Liberty Bridge on the right. While the view was breathtaking, Mark nevertheless observed it with the unease of a soul contemplating the Styx. He was, he realized, a long way from home, not just San Francisco but also from the Gresham, which, for better or worse, had become his home away from home.

Mark turned back to the pool area, randomly choosing a chair. The pool was lit from within, casting a bright blue hue onto the vast space above. He looked at his watch. It was a few minutes past midnight. There was no sign of Kárpáty or, for that matter, anyone. The solitary swimmer, an old man with a sallow face and saggy skin, came out of the pool and gave Mark a polite nod as he headed toward the locker area. The couple immersed by the waterfall were kissing, oblivious to anything around them.

Mark suddenly realized how tired he was. He sighed and slumped in his chair, fighting the urge to close his eyes. Absent-mindedly and out of habit, he removed his iPhone from his shoulder bag and turned it on. He scrolled through worthless emails that had accumulated while the phone was off, methodically erasing them with eyes half mast. He cast occasional glances at the two ends of the pool for any sign of the elusive inspector.

As he turned off his iPhone, a motion in his peripheral vision attracted his attention away from it. An object glistened on one of the railings along the second floor, at the opposite side of the pool. It was a large diamond ring reflecting the pool light in rainbow colors. Mark recognized the hand that grasped the railing, the ring on the pinky finger. He suddenly became alert, his eyes focused on the upstairs railing. A shadowy figure leaned over and looked down at the pool. There was no doubt about who it was.

Chapter 48

* * *

Mark wiped the sweat off his forehead as he stood in the warm and humid pool house and contemplated what he just saw. It had been a ghost-like apparition, Iancu's square, stocky face cast in pale blue, as if he were dead. He wore a white towel over his shoulders. The apparition disappeared in a split second, the diamond-ringed pinky pulling off the railing. The lifeguard, no longer bored, keenly observed Mark.

"What's up there?" Mark asked him, urgently pointing to the second story.

"Rest area," he answered, puzzled by Mark's inexplicable alarm. "For the saunas."

"How can I get there?"

The lifeguard pointed to where Mark had entered with György from the locker area. "You have to go back out to the lockers and across the walkway to the sauna area. There's an attendant there who can show you the way."

The kissing couple had stopped. They, too, were observing Mark curiously.

Mark glanced at the colonnaded upstairs terrace, once again empty. It would take too long, he figured. In the meanwhile he might miss Kárpáty. Where was he, anyway?

Mark tried to regain his composure, thanked the guard and returned to his seat. He was unsure whether what he had seen was real or a dream. He thought he might have dozed off. After briefly pondering what to do next, he removed his Cello Mobile rental phone from his bag and dialed.

To Mark's surprise, he answered on the first ring.

"Mustafa," Mark breathlessly whispered into the phone, "I think I just saw Iancu."

"At the Gresham Palace?" Mustafa was incredulous.

"No, at the Rudas baths."

A three-second pause.

"Don't tell me that you are at the Rudas baths!" Mustafa was obviously annoyed.

"I am," said Mark. "I had no choice. I was called here by the police you know that inspector. Kárpáty. The one on Ahmet's case."

"Why would the police call you to a bath house at this hour of the night?" said Mustafa, still irritated. "I can't believe the place is even open."

"It is," Mark confirmed. "Not too many customers, though."

"Didn't I tell you not to leave your hotel?" Mustafa sounded like a reproachful teacher. "You can't stay put, even for a moment. I had a bad feeling you might do something like this."

"Look," said Mark, firmly cutting him off. "There is something seriously wrong, and I am not quite sure what it is." He heard a deep sigh on the other end. "I was summoned here by Budapest police. They threatened to block my departure tomorrow if I did not come."

Mark looked around the pool area. The young couple had gotten out and were toweling themselves at the edge, by the waterfall. The guard was still keenly eyeing Mark.

Mark turned away from the guard and faced one of the tall picture windows displaying the lights of Pest. "So I came here. I've been waiting for Kárpáty for half an hour and he hasn't shown up. In the meanwhile, who do I see here, but Iancu!"

"Did you talk to him?"

"No," said Mark, casting a quick glance back at the pool. "He was upstairs, at a spot I can't easily reach. I just caught a brief glimpse of him."

"What about his bodyguards? Were they with him?"

"I don't know."

"Wasn't he to meet with Bognár tonight?" Mustafa had finally calmed down. He was apparently thinking the situation through.

"Maybe he already did," said Mark. "Maybe he decided to catch a last bath before returning home to Romania."

"It doesn't sound right."

"Well," said Mark, "I'm tired of sitting here, waiting. I'll go look around and see if I can find him."

"Okay, be careful."

Mark was about to hang up when Mustafa interjected. "Until what time is this place open?"

"Two a.m."

"I'm on my way," Mustafa said. "Keep your Cello Mobile on."

* * *

Upstairs, the locker area appeared abandoned. Mark went in and out of toilets and showers, searched two locker rooms, and came back to the towel counter. He stopped and leaned on the counter, thinking of what to do next.

György appeared, carrying a tall stack of freshly laundered, folded towels, surprised to see Mark there. "Finished already?"

"Have you actually seen Inspector Kárpáty?"

The urgency in Mark's voice startled the young man. "No," he said, laying the towels on the counter.

"Do you know what he looks like?"

"Yes, he is a regular customer." György faced Mark. "Is there a problem?"

"You mentioned other special guests that came here tonight." Mark tried to sound calmer, but his words came out insistent. "Would one of them be someone named Negrescu? Iancu Negrescu. A Romanian."

György's eyes widened with surprise. He hesitated for a moment. "Are you a policeman?"

The question took Mark aback. "No," he said. Then he realized what he had to do to get the attendant's attention. "I'm FBI. Do you know what that is?"

György stiffened, as if coming to attention, his eyes nearly popping out of his sockets as he silently nodded yes.

"San Francisco office, California. I am here on a joint investigation of an international crime ring " Mark hoped he wasn't coming across as a fake TV character. "With Budapest police. Kárpáty. I am concerned about the inspector's safety. He should have been here by now."

"I'll let you know as soon as he arrives," said György, his voice lower, and with newfound respect.

"What about Negrescu?"

"Yes," said György. "You're correct."

"Did he come here alone?"

"No. With two other men."

"Let me guess," said Mark. "Their first names are Dumitru and Iosif, correct?"

"Yes, sir!" György was clearly impressed.

"Where are they?"

"I haven't seen them since they arrived. They were going to use the thermal bath and saunas."

"Thermal bath?"

"It is the oldest part of the complex, built by the Turks." György pointed down to the staircase that led back to the entrance and ticket booths. "It's on the ground floor, on the other side of these stairs." He looked at his watch. "There's no attendant there any longer."

Mark raised his wrist band. "Will this get me in?"

"Yes," said György. "You have full access to everything."

Mark turned and rushed toward the stairs.

"Do you want me to lead you there?" György yelled after him.

Mark was already near the base of the stairs, taking the steps two and three at a time.

Chapter 49

* * *

Mark panted as he took his first view of the thermal bath. He had just run down a long hallway. The beauty of the place stopped him dead in his tracks.

It was an old Turkish *hamam*, authentic and ancient, with a large octagonal immersion pool in the middle encircled by eight colossal stone columns. A dome high above emitted shafts of night light through round openings covered with colored glass, red, green, gold and blue, a technicolor Milky Way. The colors expanded into a hazy rainbow in the steam above the pool. The shallow water, crystal clear, reflected the dome lights in a tight, round cluster of incandescence.

The *hamam* seemed deserted. Mark stepped closer to the pool, into the area within the columns, and shouted, "Iancu!"

All he received in response was his own voice, eerily reverberating in the empty space. Sweat once again erupted from his pores.

He looked back to where he had entered, a pair of arched entryways, well lit, with a small fountain in between. The sound of its running water mixed in with other fountains in each corner of the *hamam*. Above the fountain was a white, tombstone-like plaque that announced *Rudasfürdö Kupola Csarnokát Szoloki Musztafa Budai Pasa 1566-1578*. Mark gathered that this was in honor of Sokollu

Mustafa Paşa, a now obscure Ottoman governor of Buda, who had built the original bath house.

He took a few more steps along the perimeter of the bath. The imposing circular colonnade was enclosed in a simple square building of four stone walls. At each corner were small, triangular side pools with their own running fountains. He walked out of the colonnade and examined the one nearest him. This area was less hazy, but dimly lit. A brass sign announced the temperature of the water, thirty-three degrees Celsius.

Mark walked over to another corner pool along the plain stone wall. It was identical to the previous one except for its temperature, thirty-six degrees Celsius. When he turned to look at the next corner, he froze. There was a body there, sprawled at the edge of the pool, supine and stationary. Mark broke into goosebumps and shuddered with fear.

He looked back at the entrance, then scanned the tranquil *hamam.* He was alone.

He took a step toward the body and looked closer. It was a man, thirtyish, skinny and of medium height. He wore a white shirt that clung to him, wet with sweat, gray slacks and black dress shoes, obviously not a bather. A large pool of blood beneath him flowed along the moist stone floor into the nearby immersion pool, turning the water crimson. His throat had been slit deep and wide. His head hung slightly sideways by the edge of the pool, revealing a perfectly round trachea amid the red, butcher-block meat of his exposed neck muscles.

His ashen face was curiously tranquil, eyes closed, his thin, well-groomed beard surprisingly devoid of blood that had flowed down farther below. His long black hair hung into the pool, gently floating. Mark did not recognize the man.

He took a couple steps back and pulled his shoulder bag open, searching for his phone. He needed to call Mustafa and let him know. He could not feel his Cello Mobile. He quickly walked to the better lit, arched entryway and visually inspected the contents of his bag.

Shit! The little phone was not there. In his hurry, he must have left it on the table at the swimming pool.

He looked around again, apprehensive, for signs of anyone. All was quiet. He still had his iPhone. He thought about turning it back on, but it would need a few seconds to boot up. It occurred to him that maybe he should first inform the bath house staff at the nearby ticket area and have them call the police. He threw the phone back in the bag and hurried out to the foyer.

* * *

The ticket booths and nearby bar were abandoned and no longer lit. Mark stood for a second, puzzled. He looked at his watch: ten minutes to one. The place should be open for another hour, but it seemed closed. He crossed a turnstile and walked upstairs to the lockers. The area was lit but abandoned. György was nowhere to be found. He stopped and collected his thoughts.

Iancu and his guards had been in the bath complex; they most likely still were. The dead body he had just encountered was clearly not one of them. Was it possible that Iancu's crew had killed him?

There was no sign of Kárpáty or any other Budapest police in the bath house. Instead, Iancu, who was to meet with Bognár, was there. And now, a dead body.

Was it possible that Iancu had been lured into a trap and his guards were defending him? If so, had Mark himself also been lured into the same trap?

He put his hand inside his shoulder bag and felt his iPhone. Should he call? He remembered Zrinyi and decided not to. If he could find Iancu or one of his guards he would be safe. He had last seen Iancu in the upstairs area that, according to the pool guard, connected to the saunas. They were in the opposite direction to the aerial walkway that led to the big swimming pool. Mark rushed in that direction.

The entrance to the saunas was marked by a large, yellow tiled, glass-enclosed communal shower. He activated the turnstile at the entrance with his plastic wrist band. There was an attendant's desk next to it, empty. He turned right and entered a complex of Finnish saunas, some small, others large. No sign of Iancu.

He came out and tried the entry turnstile in reverse, to go back to the locker area. It did not allow him. He saw another small hallway that he presumed would lead to the rest areas on the second floor. He was soon where Iancu had stood when Mark had spotted him, Mark's own hand on the dark iron railing, his head peeking downstairs. The pool was still lit but there were no swimmers, nor was the guard any longer there. He spotted his Cello Mobile on the table down below, where he had sat.

The rest area featured an array of recliners and nearby tables, all empty. At the far end was a set of stairs that led down. He took them to the first floor, where another turnstile did admit in reverse, toward the locker area. But now, Mark wondered what was up ahead, in the more modern, southern part of the complex. Iancu and his guards clearly were not in the older area that he had already searched. Mark pushed on ahead.

He entered a swank, brightly colored set of modern immersion baths and Jacuzzis, and walked past a wet, blue tiled transitional area into the narrow southern tip of the complex. Here the building came to a curving tip of picture windows that gave a breathtaking view of the river, the Liberty Bridge, Pest, all floodlit. Mark hardly noticed. Instead, he concentrated on the riverside drive and sidewalk, also on display. There was no sign of anyone outside.

The southernmost tip of the complex featured yet more immersion pools, each with modern Art Deco fountains emitting waterfalls. At the far end was a staircase that curved around the tip of the building. Suddenly he heard a commotion on the stairs, multiple hurried steps with screams and shouts. He cautiously approached the staircase and took a few steps. The noise got louder.

Soon he was overtaken by a stampede of scantily clad, wet youths, no towels, running down in a panic. There were three young women, two topless, and five men, one completely nude. They brushed past Mark, sopping wet, the women shrieking. They did not seem to notice him.

"Hey!" shouted Mark, as they were about to disappear around the curve. "What's going on?"

One of the young women stopped and looked at him, surprised, as if seeing him for the first time. Her face was partially covered with stringy blond hair. She had small bare breasts with erect nipples and goosebumps all over.

"They're killing each other up there!" she screamed to him in accented English.

"Up where?"

"On the roof."

She turned back and ran to catch up with her group.

Mark looked up. He recalled reading in his guidebook that Rudas featured a large rooftop Jacuzzi, famous for its view of the city. It occurred to him that the bath complex may have been evacuated, all except for the rooftop, where the group he just encountered had been partying, until whatever fight was raging within reached them.

Mark hesitated about what to do next. He could run along with the youths and try to exit the bath complex, but he wasn't sure if whoever evacuated the place had left sentries downstairs. He could easily fall into their arms. By the looks of it, Iancu and his guards may be on the roof, and if they were winning the fight, he would be safe with them.

He heard a door open upstairs. Loud grunts emanated until the door abruptly shut. Mark could no longer think logically. He had only two choices, go up or go down.

His curiosity got the better of him. He quietly inched up the semicircular staircase onto a second-floor restaurant lobby that was dimly lit, and up the next flight of stairs to a clearing. Double glass doors led out to the rooftop. They displayed no activity, just the glittering surface of the Danube and the lit buildings of Pest, with the ever-present floodlit bridges, Elizabeth and Liberty, framing the view on each side.

Mark stopped and caught his breath. His heart was beating fast. He quietly approached the glass door and opened it.

* * *

The night air was crisp and dry, and quickly worked into Mark's bones. He was wearing nothing but a swimming suit, his shoulder bag still improbably slung diagonally across his torso. He felt an immediate chill as he stood on the modern roof deck at the southern tip of Rudas. Transparent glass railings afforded a view of the river. The deck tapered toward its southern tip as if it were a ship, with empty recliners all over. Eight concrete curving ribs that created a dome-like effect topped the hulking, semicircular structure that dominated the tip. The pool was elevated from the deck with a set of steps leading into it.

Mark spotted a dark silhouette wiggling at the very top step. He walked toward it.

The city lights provided enough illumination for Mark to distinguish figures. The silhouette lifted itself up with an effort into a partial sitting position. Mark recognized the familiar face of Iosif, still dressed in the suit he had worn at the Central Market. Iosif emitted an unmistakable groan.

As Mark came closer to the set of stairs with Iosif atop, a strange object caught his attention at the first step. He leaned to have a closer look and quickly jerked back. Atop, Iosif extended an arm toward him. "Dumitru," he moaned. Mark did not hear him as he stood, petrified, looking at the bottom step.

Iancu's prominent pinky ring glowed in the night, reflecting the city lights falling upon it. The ring was still on Iancu's hand. But the hand lay by itself atop the step, a tiny pool of blood next to it. The rest of Iancu was nowhere to be seen.

Iosif groaned loudly again. Mark wrenched his eyes away from the grisly sight and quickly climbed the steps. He knelt by Iosif, who fell back, his body sprawled partly on the top step, partly on the edge of the large Jacuzzi. Loud sloshes of the whirlpool overwhelmed Iosif's own gurgling breaths.

Iosif's smart suit jacket was torn in various places and his white shirt was fully red. Mark spread the jacket and tore open Iosif's shirt. He had multiple stab wounds on his chest and belly, one near his left nipple spewing small swells of blood at regular intervals. A large gash on the left side of his neck was briskly oozing blood.

With no way to offer first aid, Mark felt helpless. Iosif's breaths were irregular and bubbling. He was bleeding to death.

"Dumitru," Iosif groaned again, eyes closed.

Mark shook him gently. "Iosif! Where is Iancu?"

Iosif groaned in pain and lifted his head slightly. With great difficulty, he turned and pointed in the direction of the Jacuzzi. The water was bubbling a pinkish red. Suddenly Mark smelled the unmistakable metallic odor of blood mixed with the sharp stab of chlorine.

Iancu was floating at the opposite end, face and torso up, his handless right arm spread out, his head bobbing at a terrifyingly unnatural angle off his body. He had been nearly decapitated, his head attached to his body by only a flimsy strip of skin and muscle on one side of his neck.

Mark felt Iosif's hand on his bare back. Still dazed by the sight of Iancu, Mark stood as if frozen.

"Dumitru," Iosif moaned once more, and he pointed north, in the direction of the old buildings comprising the rest of Rudas. Mark looked that way and saw no one, but now he noticed bloody footprints on the deck, leading away from the Jacuzzi toward the next building, the one that housed the giant swimming pool.

"Is he alive?" asked Mark loudly. "Did he escape?"

Iosif nodded and collapsed, his head slumping to one side.

* * *

"Call the police immediately," Mark shouted into his iPhone. He stood by the glass railing overlooking the Danube, away from the horror of the Jacuzzi. "They killed Iancu and maybe one of his bodyguards." Mustafa had not answered. Mark was leaving a message. "Call for ambulances, too."

He threw his phone into his bag and looked at the deck more carefully, taking a brisk walk around it. There was no way out but the way he came, through the glass door that led back into the building. Dumitru might have escaped through the rooftops of the complex, but there was no way Mark would try that. There was nothing to do but trek back to the lockers and try to exit the building as fast as possible.

All was quiet as Mark took the stairs down to the second floor, where he had previously passed a restaurant without paying attention. Now he stopped and looked. He was at a foyer near the tip of the building with a bar and bistro tables, for clients to enjoy the view in the direction of the Liberty Bridge. It was empty and dimly illuminated by outside light from its spacious windows. On the opposite side was a formal restaurant, tables and chairs neatly arrayed, with yet another bar deep within.

As Mark made a move toward the next set of steps leading to the ground floor, two dark figures emerged from the restaurant. With his back turned to the restaurant, Mark did not see them. They grabbed him, one at each arm. Startled, Mark tried to shake loose.

"Let me go!" he shouted, as they dragged him into the restaurant.

Mark's feet, still in flip-flops, were no longer firmly on the ground. He kicked to no avail as he was carried away like a puppet doll.

Chapter 50

* * *

"So, you're the one who wasted two of my best!"

Mark looked up. The man was fortyish, lean and wiry, with thinly cropped blond hair, blue eyes deeply set within a stern, Slavic face. His thin eyebrows seemed frozen in a perpetual frown. He wore a simple white tank-top shirt that revealed well developed pecs, and an elaborate tattoo of a lion's mouth on his left shoulder, its sharp teeth ready to bite. As he eyed Mark up and down, his lips curled in a smirk.

"Mr. Bognár, I presume," said Mark, surprised with his self-assured voice, considering the bind he was in.

Mark was sitting at a table in the empty restaurant, dimly illuminated by outside lights, with one of Bognár's men standing behind, his pistol aimed at Mark's neck. Another one, stocky and middle-aged, sat across the table from him, profusely sweating as he examined the contents of Mark's shoulder bag.

Bognár turned to the older man and said something in a Slavic-sounding language, different from Hungarian. They both laughed, Bognár louder and longer, as he scraped a chair and sat down facing Mark.

"I told Matej here," said Bognár, pointing to the man who was methodically emptying Mark's belongings onto the table, "that it's hard to believe a skinny old man like you could inflict enough damage to hospitalize two of my men."

Mark realized that Jasmin's prediction about the fight in Zrinyi had come true. He thought about protesting his innocence but stopped himself. Bognár, who was leaning back on his chair, his legs spread apart, seemed impressed with Mark's feat. He was eyeing Mark with what might have been respect.

Matej handed his boss Mark's passport, which Bognár examined carefully.

"Listen," he said, leaning closer to Mark. "First let me warn you not to attempt anything like what you did at Zrinyi yesterday." He looked up at his man holding the gun. "Andrej is easy with the trigger."

Mark turned and looked at Andrej. He was young, skinny, and dark complexioned, with long dark hair in a ponytail. Andrej gave him a yellow-toothed smile and cocked the safety of the gun.

"We refrained from using our guns earlier so as not to cause panic in the bath house," continued Bognár. "But now that our mission is complete and we're about to depart, a single shot wouldn't be of much harm."

That's why everyone was cut up, Mark realized. He looked at the two goons who worked for Bognár. *Matej and Andrej*, Mark thought, *how silly*. If it were in a movie he would have laughed at this Laurel and Hardy couple with their comically rhyming names.

"Doctor Kent." Bognár looked up from the passport. "I am told that you're a doctor. Is that correct?"

Mark nodded. Bognár shook his head left and right in disbelief. "Doctor," he continued, "I owe you a debt of gratitude."

Mark looked at the gangster wide-eyed, puzzled. Matej now passed along Mark's iPhone. Bognár held it in his hand, pressing its home button and tapping here and there as he mumbled, "You're making us a lot of money."

He looked at Mark and smiled wide. Two gold teeth glistened on each side of his upper jaw. "You see," he said, tapping Mark's lap in a friendly gesture, "at first we were contracted simply to provide protection to the masseuse." He loudly kissed the tips of his left fingers in a gesture of admiration. "A nice piece of ass, wouldn't you say?"

Mark nodded. All three gangsters broke into a loud laugh, Matej pumping his right wrist back and forth in an obscene gesture.

"You'd like to shag her too, hah?" Bognár slapped Mark's thigh. "You're my kind of doctor!" He waited for the laughter to subside. "Anyhow, then you came along and we received a new mission, and more money." He paused and waited for Mark's reaction.

"You mean, killing me?" said Mark. His voice was relaxed. Menacing as these goons looked, Mark sensed that they had no intention to harm him.

"Yes, good guess." Bognár continued toying with the iPhone as he elaborated. "You gave us the slip, but then led us to Negrescu."

Mark's heart sank as he realized that his ride in Iancu's Mercedes had led to the Romanian's demise. "How did you identify him?"

"We had heard of him but never met him. One of our men, the one whose head you cracked open, knew Negrescu from a prior job he had in Romania. He is the one who identified him."

The image of Iancu's severed hand with its flashy pinky ring turned Mark's stomach. He winced. Bognár didn't seem to notice.

"Do you know how valuable Negrescu turned out to be?" Bognár wiped his right thumb and forefinger together. "*Beaucoup d'argent*," he said, with a decent French accent. *Lots of money.*

"Who is paying you?" Mark asked with disgust.

"You will meet them soon." Bognár turned to Matej and spoke in what Mark guessed was Slovak. Matej extended him a cigarette and a lighter.

"You, Dr. Kent, are now worth more alive than dead," Bognár said, with irony in his voice. He took a deep drag and blew the smoke away from Mark. Then he turned his attention to Mark's iPhone screen. "Mustafa," he mumbled.

Mark's heart sank again as he realized Bognár must have been scrolling through his recent calls. Bognár handed the phone back to Matej, issuing instructions in Slovak. Mark heard *Mustafa* several times. *I should not have made that rooftop call by the Jacuzzi*, he thought ruefully.

"Our client in Chisinau changed his mind. He now wants you alive."

"Chisinau, in Moldova?"

"Yes, Dr. Kent, in Moldova."

Mark paused a moment, contemplating what Bognár just said. A few days ago he'd had no idea where Chisinau was. Now he was wanted by criminals from this obscure city, thugs presumably more dangerous than the Slovaks he presently faced. How had he come that far this fast?

"Who?" he asked.

Bognár took another drag from his cigarette and exhaled a name along with the smoke. "Vadim Rusu and his men."

Mark stared at him blankly.

Bognár continued. "You've gotten them quite curious. We in Budapest don't give a damn about you. In fact, if I may say so, I kind of like you. If circumstances were different, I wouldn't mind sharing some of my homemade *pálinka* with you. I make good *pálinka.* Strong. Apricot flavor. Did you get to taste some *pálinka* while you were here?"

"Yes," said Mark, recalling the poison-like drink he had swallowed at Ferenc's apartment restaurant. "It was very good," he lied.

Bognár turned back to Matej and the two acknowledged Mark with appreciative nods.

Emboldened by the reaction, Mark asked casually, "Who is Vadim Rusu?"

"A big shot," said Bognár. "Used to be police chief in Tiraspol." Moldova again. "Former KGB," he added, taking a final puff on his cigarette.

Mark interrupted. "He's Russian?"

"Doctor, you're a clever man. Yes, 'Rusu' means Russian. But he is Transnistrian. Their secret service is still called KGB."

Mark had no idea where Transnistria was but did not want to interrupt the gangster further.

"He's now a civilian, based in Chisianu. Has widespread business interests."

"So why do his men want me?"

"I suspect you took them by surprise," Bognár said thoughtfully. "They don't know who you are and what business you have here with Nicolae Radu and Iancu Negrescu. They were very, shall we say intrigued, when we told them that you met a French policeman from Interpol."

A younger man, tall and dark, entered the restaurant, exchanged a few words with Matej, and headed to the bar behind the dining room. He pulled out a bottle of Scotch and several glasses. Bognár offered Mark a glass of Scotch, straight up.

"No, thanks."

Bognár drank the Scotch in one gulp and extinguished his cigarette in the empty glass. "So, Dr. Mark Kent, they offered us more than Negrescu if we delivered you alive and unharmed." He turned to the man at the bar. "Another."

Mark's mind swirled. This Rusu character sounded like the sort of person Iancu and Ahmet might have done business with—shady business, no doubt. He wondered if Commissaire Gérard knew him. Mark suddenly wished the avuncular Frenchman were there to shield him from these Slovakian thugs. He figured that if he was going to meet Rusu soon, there was no use in asking further questions about him. Besides, he had another, more pressing question.

"Did you kill Nicolae Radu?"

Bognár looked at Matej, then Andrej. He shook his head, as if he were insulted. "No. It's a messy affair. We did not want any part of it."

So Mustafa was correct about Bognár's gang.

"Rusu sent two special operatives to do the job," continued Bognár. "Former army men, Transnistrian KGB. Rusu still has a lot of power in the organization."

Mark imagined well-trained, disciplined, seasoned killers. No wonder the scene at Ahmet's Royal Suite was so clean. "Why did they kill him?"

"Something to do with the black-market kidney trade." The gangster boss was surprisingly forthcoming. "Don't ask me what," he added dismissively. "We don't engage in that business."

Mark wondered what Ahmet may have done to raise Rusu's ire. Iancu had described Ahmet as a smooth businessman. Whatever it was, Mark suspected Ahmet had not done it intentionally.

Matej interrupted the exchange to hand Bognár the forensics report he had finally discovered in Mark's bag. Bognár examined the papers with interest and, after another sip of Scotch, waved them at Mark's face.

"How did you come to possess these?"

Mark answered him with a question. "Where is Inspector Kárpáty? He summoned me here for this very same question."

"The Inspector is not here." A menacing smile broke out on Bognár's face.

Mark understood. He wondered how far he could provoke the gangster. "You made quite a mess here." He nodded upstairs toward the roof deck with his head. "The police will have a field day with all the evidence you left."

Bognár raised his Scotch glass, and before taking a sip, gave Matej a *can you believe this guy* look. Matej stopped sifting through Mark's belongings and shook his head in disbelief. *No.*

"There will be no police investigation, Doctor," Bognár said confidently. "And the witnesses," he pointed toward a banquet room in an annex at the back of the restaurant, "will not talk."

The entrance to the annex was curtained off. Mark realized that was where the Rudas staff was being held.

"Inspector Kárpáty *will* arrive here," Bognár continued in the same assured tone. "But by then you'll be gone. He'll see to it that loose ends are tied."

He handed the forensics report back to Matej. "An American tourist," said Matej sarcastically, in heavily accented English that surprised Mark, "who possesses police documents and has connections in Budapest with French police and a Turk." He stuffed the report back in its envelope.

"And who beat my men to a pulp!" added Bognár.

"I say he's police," said Matej. "Or maybe FBI, or CIA."

Mark wished that he had accepted Bognár's Scotch after all.

Chapter 51

* * *

Mark had been amused by how easily he had convinced the naïve youngster tending to the towels that he was FBI. Now these Slovakian thugs had arrived at the same conclusion, and they were about to hand him over to efficient Moldovan killers. A chill went down Mark's spine.

"I bet Rusu's men will have a tougher time with you than they did with Nicolae Radu." Bognár smiled, revealing his two golden teeth.

Mark did not get a chance to answer. The gangster's attention turned to two new men who entered the restaurant wearing large bath towels around their waists and blue plastic sandals, their hair dripping wet. They were younger than their boss but lean and muscular, like him. They deposited a large machete and a hunting knife, also dripping wet, onto a table and spoke, with some urgency, in Slovak. The sight of the knives caused Mark's own hands to tingle and sweat as he recalled Iancu's severed right hand on the steps of the Jacuzzi.

A lively discussion ensued between the newcomers and Bognár's other men, at times rising to an argument. Something was amiss.

Matej laid open a Rudas brochure and they all peered at a map, Matej and Bognár pointing to various spots.

With the gangsters distracted, Mark thought about making a run for it, but it would have been to no avail. There were six of them and maybe more elsewhere. The two new guys were obviously the ones who had executed the deadly work upstairs, and the gang had waited for them to clean up. Bognár had said that they were finished and about to leave. Yet they seemed to be stalled. It occurred to Mark that maybe they were missing the dead guy in the Turkish *hamam*.

"There is a dead body in the thermal baths," he offered helpfully, his voice loud.

The argument stopped and all eyes turned to Mark.

"Throat slit." Despite his precarious situation, Mark enjoyed the moment. It deluded him into thinking he was in control. "He's not one of Negrescu's men. Is he who you're looking for?"

Bognár was momentarily speechless. Then he rapidly shouted instructions to his men. The two with bath towels peeled out of the restaurant, knives in hand.

"Thank you, Doctor," Bognár said. He had stood up and was towering over Mark, whose fantasy of being in control vanished. "That must be Lukas. He was assigned to guard the entrance. It seems he lost his way."

He's lost more than that, Mark thought. "One of Negrescu's men did it," he said aloud. "The one that got away."

Bognár nodded with an admiring smile. "It's been a pleasure to know a true professional of your caliber," he said, extending his hand to Mark. "Fortunately for us, all *we* deal with is sloppy Hungarian inspectors who can be easily bought."

Bognár's handshake felt surreal. Decades ago a teenage Metin had shaken the hand of Kara Ibrahim in front of an Istanbul nightclub, thinking that this man would be the first and last gangster he would ever encounter. Little did he know that at middle age, there would be another, and in such precarious circumstances.

"What happens now?" asked Mark.

"We'll hold you here briefly, until we clean up and collect Lukas." Bognár disengaged his hand from Mark's and took a step back. He barked some orders at Andrej, who squeezed Mark's arm, motioning him to get up. "Then, you'll be driven to a rendezvous with our Moldovan friends. They're on their way."

Bognár motioned his other men with his head and they all walked toward the stairs. "*Bon voyage*," he said to Mark, tipping an imaginary hat, before he descended.

* * *

The banquet room was compact, a small alcove for private diners. There were no tables, just chairs. Mark recognized several Rudas staff sitting inside, including the bartender, the older woman in blue uniform, and the stocky young man who had been eating cake at the ticket booth. They sat glumly, unperturbed by Mark's arrival.

Andrej exchanged a few words with a tall, broad-shouldered man sitting by the curtains, his buffed muscles bursting out of his white tank top, his crew cut a closely trimmed blond bush. He smiled as he spoke to Andrej, relaxing the semi-automatic rifle he held stiffly on his lap.

There was only one window in the room. György and the lifeguard from the pool stood by it, observing the view outside. György's face brightened into a wide smile when he spotted Mark, and he motioned toward him.

Alarmed, Mark cut him off with a stern look and an abrupt upraised palm by his waist. Having this young man gush over him was the last thing he needed. He sat down quietly in a solitary chair away from the others and, covering his face with his hands, took stock of his predicament.

Horrific images of Iancu, handless and dead, floating in the Jacuzzi, and Iosif, all bloody, his voice gurgling, interrupted his thoughts. Mark fought off a wave of nausea. He stood up and took a few deep breaths, looking out at the darkness of the riverside boulevard.

György sidled up to him. "What's going on?" he whispered.

"Gang war," Mark whispered back. "They're killing each other."

György gasped loudly.

"Shhh!" Mark admonished him. He threw a quick glance at the burly guard, who fortunately was preoccupied with his cellphone. He turned back to György. "Where are the customers?"

"Gone," György whispered back. "They ordered the staff to evacuate the customers and close down. I wasn't there. I was in the laundry. They found me later, soon after you left me for the thermal baths."

"They missed a group in the rooftop Jacuzzi," said Mark grimly.

"Was that all the screaming and commotion we heard?"

Mark nodded. He wondered where that group had stampeded to. Most likely the lockers, he thought. It occurred to him that his own clothes were in those lockers and wondered if the gangsters would allow him to retrieve them before he left for Moldova.

"Listen," he whispered to György, in a determined voice. "I called for help. Hopefully they'll arrive soon." He wasn't as sure as he sounded, but he needed to boost the young man's morale. He hesitated for a moment, then continued.

"They will be taking me away."

"Who?" asked György.

"These thugs."

György's eyes widened with fear.

"It's okay," Mark reassured him, even though he felt less than okay. "I think they will release all of you unharmed."

György nodded.

"I want you to do me a favor," Mark continued.

"Yes, anything!"

"I left a mobile phone near the large swimming pool, on the Danube side. It's on a table close to where I sat." Mark eyed the lifeguard who stood nearby, quietly sulking at the window. He seemed oblivious to their discussion. "It's a small flip phone."

Mark thought for a moment while György stood at attention like a loyal dog. "I want you to retrieve the phone and if you have a chance, sneak it back to me. Don't let them see it."

"I shall!"

* * *

They released the Rudas staff soon after but told Mark to wait. He and György did not speak again, György throwing Mark an anxious backward glance as he exited through the open curtain into the restaurant. Mark looked away, into the distant lights of the river.

Andrej arrived a few minutes later and exchanged words with the guard. He motioned for Mark to get up and they left the restaurant, one guard on each side, Andrej gently holding onto Mark's arm.

"What about my bag and possessions?" Mark asked him anxiously, searching the tabletops of the restaurant with his eyes. "My passport and wallet." He had given up on the iPhone.

Andrej gently pushed him on and did not answer. The burly bodyguard engaged Andrej in a brief Slovak conversation.

"He does not speak English," the guard explained to Mark. "He says they have your bag and possessions in the car. They'll hold them until you're delivered to your destination."

There was nothing to do but continue walking.

Chapter 52

* * *

Commotion raged in the lobby. Bognár's men had discovered the rooftop Jacuzzi partyers. They were now all dressed and huddled by the stairs near the ticket booths. Two women were loudly sobbing. Mark, still in his swimming suit, with a towel over his shoulders, wondered how Bognár and Kárpáty would suppress them as witnesses. He felt another chill go down his spine.

Outside, Mark saw that the familiar silver BMW was parked at the curb. Matej stood in front of it, anxiously looking inside. He spotted Mark and Andrej, and waved his partner on.

Several Bognár men appeared, carrying body bags. The burly blond guard who had helped Andrej accompany Mark dashed off to help. The sight of the body bags caused the young partyers to wail more loudly. Bognár's men shouted at them to keep quiet, with little success.

Mark looked at a large clock that hung opposite the ticket booths. It was two a.m., closing time. Matej made yet more urgent gestures, pointing down-river in the direction of the Liberty Bridge. Someone opened the door, stepped out, and hastily got back in the car. "Police!" he yelled.

There was an upheaval deep in the bar area where, among dim shadows, Mark recognized Bognár, drinking with his men. Several rose in alarm. Bognár calmly ordered them back down. Mark guessed that he was expecting Kárpáty. Maybe Bognár's men did not know his deal with the corrupt inspector.

Andrej urged Mark on and they began walking toward the door. A rustling, followed by urgent footsteps behind, caught Andrej's attention.

"Wait a minute!" It was György. He held Mark's clothes in a disorganized bundle by his chest.

Avoiding Mark's eyes, György hurriedly addressed Andrej in Hungarian. Andrej nodded and György extended the clothes toward Mark, took his towel, and asked him to return the orange electronic wristwatch, as if he were just another patron leaving after a refreshing swim. As Mark fiddled with the watch strap, his pants slipped off the bundle in György's arms. György knelt and retrieved them, brushing up against Mark as he stood up. Mark felt a hard object slip into the side pocket of his swimming suit, concealed by the bundle of clothes György handed him. It all happened in a split second.

Mark did not get a chance to put his clothes on. Andrej pushed him toward the curb, where Matej held the back door of the BMW open. Standing in the night air with just a swimming suit, Mark felt a strong chill before he clumsily entered the car, the bundle of clothes spilling from his arms into the back seat. The door slammed shut and the two gangsters rushed to the front. Mark looked out his window. He locked eyes with György, who was standing inside the entrance. Mark gave the young man a nod. György placed his right palm against the glass door in a gesture of farewell.

* * *

The BMW peeled away from the curb, tires screeching as the driver made a U-turn north in the direction of the Elizabeth Bridge. Mark spotted numerous flashing lights on the riverside drive as he buttoned his shirt. Police cars were spilling out of the Liberty Bridge, headed toward Rudas. Andrej, sitting in the front passenger seat, craned his neck, anxiously observing the scene.

Kárpáty could not be arriving so conspicuously with so many police cruisers. Mark felt a glimmer of hope. Maybe his plea to Mustafa had gone through. But as the BMW ascended the ramp to the Elizabeth Bridge, he fell into despair. Police might be arriving in time to intercept Bognár and his gang, but it was too late for him.

A column of black Mercedes buses, each bearing the word *Rendőrség* (police) in bold white capital letters above their front bumpers, passed them on the bridge, strips of red and blue lights flashing atop. They were also aiming for Rudas. Mark spotted paramilitary silhouettes at the windows, eyes shielded with helmet-visors, rifle muzzles pointed up.

Andrej made an alarmed call on his mobile, his voice loud and hurried as the BMW exited the Elizabeth Bridge and plunged into the deserted boulevards of Pest.

Chapter 53

* * *

"Where are you?" demanded Mustafa. "Police have full control of Rudas and have not found you anywhere."

Mark was in a filthy bathroom, standing against the closed door. He'd managed to get away from his captors for a minute and had called Mustafa on his flip phone.

"Somewhere near the airport," he said. "They have kidnapped me. I am being held in a warehouse. They're waiting for a team of Moldovans to take me to Chisinau."

Mark slipped his pants on, trying to balance the small phone between his head and shoulder. "Their boss is someone named Vadim Rusu. He is the one who ordered Ahmet's murder. Did you get that name? Rusu!"

The phone slipped off his shoulder and clunked onto the concrete floor. "Shit!" he whispered. He zipped up his pants and picked up the phone.

"Did you hear what I said?" Mustafa asked.

"No, the phone fell."

"I got the name. Rusu. Now, can you be more precise about your whereabouts?"

Mark hastily tucked his shirt into his pants. "I know we took Üllői út toward the airport. I recognized it. Just before the final approach to the airport, we turned right and crossed some railroad tracks. There are a bunch of airport hotels here and some businesses. "

"Okay, got it."

"Where are *you*?" asked Mark.

"At Rudas. What a mess!"

"Did they get Bognár?"

"Yes, the whole gang is in custody."

"Did you see the body bags?"

"Yes," said Mustafa. "I identified Iancu and Iosif for the police."

Mark wanted to ask more but worried that Andrej and Matej would be suspicious of how long he was taking. He had asked them for permission to remove his swimming suit and put the rest of his clothes on in the bathroom. They had acquiesced without protest.

"How did you manage to keep the rental phone with you?"

"Long story," said Mark. "Just a stroke of good luck."

"Okay," said Mustafa. "No matter what happens, don't let on that you have that phone."

As if you need to remind me, Mark thought.

"And make sure it is not off."

"Okay. Listen, I've got to go."

Mark hung up and looked around the dank, stark bathroom. There was no decent spot to conceal the phone. He settled on a garbage basket, half full of used toilet paper and paper towels. He turned on the silencer and made sure that the phone was well beneath the litter. Then he flushed the unused toilet.

* * *

The Moldovan lifted an iPad and told Mark to stand still. Mark turned to his right and stared at an opened passport Andrej was holding up, nearly touching Mark's cheek. Its identity page faced the iPad. It was Mark's own passport.

"Look at me, please." The man had a thick black moustache and an equally thick accent.

Mark did as he was told and a flash went off. Suddenly Mark recalled Ahmet's murder scene at the Royal Suite of the Gresham Palace. The passports by the bathtub, one of them open. Ahmet's head had been very close to it. *They must have done the same thing,* Mark thought. They most likely had no time to have Ahmet pose for an identifying photo, as Mark had just done, so they shot the picture after they killed him.

Mark now realized that Ahmet's fate was also in store for him. Strangely, he was no longer terrified, as he had been at Zrinyi when he was kidnapped. He was too weary and resigned to his fate.

The man examined the photo and showed it to his partner, who stood behind him. The pair had arrived two hours after Mark emerged from the bathroom. Mark had been dozing in a makeshift cot Bognár's men had rigged when Andrej shook him awake. The newcomers looked alike, both of medium height and lean, both with curly, thick black hair and bushy dark moustaches. They wore black uniforms with no insignia, heavy army boots, tight slacks, zippered windbreakers and dark baseball-style caps. They each carried a sidearm and shouldered a submachine gun.

The one who told Mark to look at him clearly seemed to be the leader. He had unzipped his windbreaker, revealing a muscular physique beneath a tight black turtleneck. He briefly barked orders to Bognár's men in Hungarian. Matej obediently headed toward the door and exited the warehouse. Mark presumed he was assigned sentry duty.

The Moldovan ordered Mark to sit down by the metal table. He sat across from Mark while his partner and Andrej stood back, his partner keenly surveying the perimeter of the warehouse.

"You are a doctor?" asked the man.

"Yes."

"Are you involved with organ transplants?" The man was polite but curt.

Mark eyed his wallet and iPhone, which Andrej had tossed, along with Mark's passport, onto the table between the two men. His interrogator seemed uninterested in them.

"No."

"You are Turkish. Correct?"

"Yes." Mark wondered what this man wanted. Bognár had given him the impression that he would be interrogated in Chisinau, by their boss Rusu.

"Do you know a Turkish surgeon named Mahmut Erkan Gazioğlu?" The man's Turkish pronunciation was better than his English.

Surprised by the question, which Commissaire Gérard had first posed to him, Mark nevertheless answered calmly. "I've heard the name."

"Do you know his whereabouts?"

So Gazioğlu was wanted by the Moldovans, too, not just Interpol. Mark wondered why. "No," he answered. "I just know the name. I don't know this doctor in person."

The man sat erect and did not shift his position. He had a neutral but stern expression. He abruptly changed the subject. "Are you associated with the FBI?"

Here we go again, thought Mark. The mistaken impression, partly his fault, was no longer amusing. "No."

The man's expression did not change, nor did he challenge Mark. He changed the subject yet again. "This Turkish man you've been with, Mustafa. Is he MIT?"

This was one of the first questions Mark had asked Mustafa when they first met at the Lotz Terem Café. Was he an agent of the Turkish secret service?

"No," he answered candidly. "He is a private citizen."

"What business does he have with Nicolae Radu?"

The interrogator's partner took a step toward the table, his interest piqued by the question.

Mark contemplated how to answer. This man seemed to be screening him with preliminaries. He presumed they would be conveyed to Chisinau in preparation for more in-depth questioning later. He decided to tell the truth.

"He represents Radu's Turkish ex-wife, in a divorce-related matter. He is a sort of private detective."

"Do you know Mustafa's whereabouts?"

"He is in Budapest. I don't know where."

The man said a few words to Andrej in Hungarian. Andrej pulled out his mobile phone and withdrew out of earshot.

Mark took advantage of the break to ask a question. "Are you taking me to Chisinau?"

"Yes."

"Are we driving?"

"No," said the man, firmly. "Flying."

So that's how they had arrived so fast, thought Mark. He presumed it was a private plane. The fact that he'd been brought to this warehouse so near Ferihegy Airport now also made sense.

The man continued. "We expect you to cooperate," he said authoritatively. "We will not restrain you, because we don't have to. If you make any unexpected moves, the consequences will be severe."

Mark nodded. These two Moldovans were a different breed from Bognár's slovenly gang of Slovakians. They were paramilitary and business-like. Mark figured they may well be the ones who killed Ahmet. He had no intention of trying any escape.

The interrogator made a brief phone call on his mobile, then made an announcement in Hungarian. His partner began moving toward the door of the vast, empty warehouse.

"The plane will be ready in one half hour," the Moldovan said to Mark.

"My passport and belongings," Mark pleaded.

The man eyed the items on the table. "We'll bring them along."

Mark sank in his chair and tried to appear calm. He was about to be transported to an unfamiliar place with no support from the likes of Mustafa, Jasmin, or Gérard. He wondered how they would eliminate him once they got the information they needed.

So much for intrepid adventures in foreign lands, he thought. When he set out overseas from San Francisco five days ago—had it really been just five days?—he had not expected any of this. After stumbling on his old mate's dead body, he had made a series of audacious moves, thrilled by the opportunity to be like his Ottoman ancestor. Now he was facing the same fate as Nurettin.

A sudden explosion jolted Mark out of his thoughts. He looked up to see the door of the warehouse on fire. The Moldovan interrogator flew out of his chair and rushed toward the door, submachine gun poised in his arm. His partner, seemingly unfazed, was knelt in position near the burning door, his gun aimed toward it. Andrej stood by Mark and exchanged a fearful glance with him.

Within seconds Mark heard several pop-pops, like firecrackers. The room filled with a thick, smoky cloud. Mark's eyes instantly began burning and he instinctively shut them. The Moldovans began firing, the repetitive clatter of their guns deafening as it reverberated off the warehouse walls. Mark heard return fire from outside.

Mark's hands and feet, still bare, were burning. As he breathed more smoke, his throat went into spasm and he began coughing uncontrollably. The sound of a gunshot to his right forced him to open his eyes and look. Amid the blur of the smoke, his tear-filled eyes spotted several simultaneous muzzle flashes from within the door. Andrej fell with a thud as the cracking of semi-automatic weapons continued inside the warehouse.

Mark saw dark, shadowy figures enter through the still-smoldering doorway. He rubbed his burning eyes and they burned worse. His nose emanated mucus in a way he had never before experienced. He struggled out of his chair and fell back onto the cold concrete floor, eyes closed, certain that he would die soon.

"Mark Kent! Are you Mark Kent?" Someone shook him violently.

There was no more gunfire. In the eerie silence, the words *Mark Kent* echoed loudly, giving Mark the impression of a dream amid the thick smoke.

"Yes," he uttered in a barely audible, hoarse voice.

He was suddenly jolted to a sitting position by forceful hands and a breathing mask was slapped onto his face, its fastener roughly tightened, pressing painfully against his ears.

Instantly the image of mask bruises on Ahmet's cheeks flashed through Mark's mind. So this is how it was all going to end. He wondered what sort of gas they had used to kill his mate. Would it be the same for him? How much would he suffer as he suffocated?

"Breathe," the voice ordered. He had a Hungarian accent. "Breathe deep."

Mark held his breath and tried to shake the mask off, but it was firmly fastened. His mouth and nose felt on fire. A large gloved hand pushed the mask harder onto his face. "Breathe," ordered the voice again, as the edges of the mask pressed painfully against Mark's cheeks. Mark was too enfeebled to fight back. Hopefully it would end quickly. He inhaled.

The relief of fresh air surprised him as Mark took two deep breaths. His eyes still burned and snot poured down his cheeks as if it were a waterfall. But this no longer mattered. He was alive. They were not asphyxiating him, after all. How else were they going to do away with him, Mark wondered.

Two pairs of arms grabbed him by the armpits and lifted him up off the cot. His arms and legs limp, he became airborne. For the second time in this nightmarish night, he was carried away, against his will, like a puppet doll.

Chapter 54

* * *

It was still dark outside, the lights of Ferihegy Airport a backdrop on the horizon. Mark was aware of red and blue flashing lights around him. In between deep breaths from a green plastic oxygen mask, he blew his nose and cleaned the snot off his face, using the entire box of tissues someone handed him. He could feel his dizziness subsiding. He looked around and saw that he was sitting at the foot of a gurney inside an ambulance, its back doors open. The chilly air felt good on his bare feet, which were still burning.

"*Hol van?*" *Where is he?*

The voice addressing the paramedic sounded vaguely familiar.

Mark took off his mask and leaned out for a look. The flashing lights were coming from small *Rendőrség* cruisers, a large black Mercedes bus similar to those he had seen earlier at the Elizabeth Bridge, an armored SWAT vehicle, and three ambulances. Two paramedics were hurriedly carrying an intubated figure on a gurney, one rhythmically pumping an Ambu bag. As they slid the gurney into an ambulance, Andrej was illuminated by the light within. Mark felt bad for his captor. He had been gentle with him, and had unwittingly allowed György to slip him the Cello Mobile phone.

"My apologies for the tear gas." Mark was startled by the same voice that had spoken with the paramedic.

Sergeant Gusztáv Zoltán was standing outside the ambulance door, his well-pressed suit jacket buttoned, his tie perfectly knotted, his luxuriant greased hair well combed, not a strand out of place. "Feeling better?"

Mark nodded and discarded his oxygen mask.

"There was no way to get you out of there safely without surprising your kidnappers." Zoltán did not look like he had actively participated in the rescue.

"How did you find me?" Mark's voice was still hoarse.

"We traced your mobile signal. The information you gave the Turkish private eye about your general whereabouts helped tremendously."

Mark nodded and wanted to respond but was overcome with yet another fit of cough. Zoltán waited. "Can you walk yet?" he asked, when Mark had finished.

Mark made an attempt to get up but was unsteady on his feet. A paramedic appeared and supported his arm, helping him exit the ambulance.

Mark took a few cautious steps and was relieved to find he was still standing. Surveying the scene around him, Mark spotted two more stretchers, each cradling a body, near a police van that SWAT officers were guarding. The bodies were uncovered, dark silhouettes in dark uniforms, immobile. They looked dead. Mark wondered if they were the pair of Moldovans.

"Come with me," ordered Zoltán.

Mark hesitated. Still slightly disoriented, he nonetheless had enough sense to wonder if he should trust Zoltán. As if reading his mind, the sergeant said matter-of-factly, "Kárpáty is under arrest."

Mark held on to Zoltán as they slowly walked away from the thicket of police vehicles. "But it was you guys, from District V, who summoned me to the Rudas baths."

Zoltán walked on, without looking at Mark. "No, we didn't."

"A guy named Horváth."

A tall, lanky figure emerged from the dark, approaching them with an awkward walk, his legs long and stork-like. He wore a fedora and raincoat.

"Horváth is another renegade officer, Kárpáty's accomplice." Zoltán waved at the approaching figure. "He is under arrest, too."

The man took off his hat and shook hands with Zoltán. He then turned to Mark and smiled broadly beneath thick brown-rimmed spectacles, his white goatee spreading wide.

"I believe you two know each other," said Zoltán.

Mark had never seen a smile like this before on the Frenchman's face. He had an urge to throw himself at Gérard and give him a bear hug, but he held back.

"*Félicitations*!" said the Commissaire. *Congratulations!* He gave Mark a firm handshake.

* * *

It was still dark. The effects of the tear gas had now completely worn off, and Mark shivered in the chilly air. An unmarked Volkswagen van pulled up to the curb, its interior lights on.

"Come," said Gérard. It was his van. "Let's get you out of the cold."

The van was cool inside. Mark sat in the back, wrapped in a blanket the driver provided. "Are they both dead?" he asked Gérard, who sat next to him.

The interior lights of the van went out. Mark and Gérard became two dark silhouettes in conversation.

"The Moldovans? Yes."

"Were they the ones who killed Ahmet—Radu?"

"Our preliminary assessment is yes, they were."

Gérard was no longer reticent, as he had been during their meeting in Zrinyi. Mark was pleased that he was being treated like a colleague. "How so?" he asked.

"Budapest police have already matched them to camera footage from the Gresham lobby the day Radu— Ahmet — was killed. They entered the hotel on the afternoon of his death."

Mark wondered why the pair had made no attempt to conceal themselves. They could have used a service door or some other, more hidden, entrance.

"They have no criminal record in Hungary," Gérard continued. "We have initiated a search of our databases for any international information on criminal activity. I doubt we will find any."

No wonder they didn't care about being caught on general hotel footage, thought Mark. In Hungary, they were just a pair of visitors.

"They did not look like Bognár's gangsters," said Mark. "They looked paramilitary."

The Frenchman acknowledged Mark's comment with a nod. "Your tip about Vadim Rusu was quite interesting. He has not been on our radar screen."

"He's not in the transplant business?"

"No," said Gérard. "He is a legitimate businessman. He may have some corrupt practices, but he is not a criminal."

Mark paused. The idling van was warming up. He slid the blanket off his shoulders. "I don't get it," he said. "If Rusu ordered Ahmet and Iancu's assassination, I figured that maybe they had some business rivalry."

"It does not appear so," said the Frenchman. He then continued. "Since receiving your tip, we've found a different Rusu in our transplant-related databases, a Dima Rusu."

Mark listened expectantly.

"His name is on a list of victims that includes the French citizen who drew me into the case."

"Victims of what?"

"Kidneys, illegally stolen. They died of medical complications afterwards."

"You mean they were unwitting donors?"

"Correct. The French victim I am referring to was an arms salesman who disappeared from a hotel in Tiraspol. He reappeared several days later in a Braşov hostel, ill and with a scar on his flank. He died afterwards of widespread infection."

"They stole his kidney?"

"It appears so," said Gérard.

"Tiraspol," Mark murmured. "That's in Transnistria, correct?"

The Frenchman smiled. "Your knowledge of geography is admirable."

Mark chuckled. "I just heard that name recently. I don't really know where it is."

"Between Moldova and Ukraine. It is struggling for independence from Moldova."

Mark nodded. "Rusu and his men were from there?"

"Correct." The Frenchman was matter-of-fact. "They're well trained and disciplined. Former Russian army and secret service."

"So who's this other Rusu?"

"He appears to be Vadim's son."

An eerie silence descended on the pair as Mark processed the news. Gérard watched him keenly.

"Oh...my...god," said Mark quietly.

"I knew you would figure it out," said Gérard, with an almost paternal pride.

"You mean this is all some sort of revenge?"

Gérard nodded. "Dima Rusu was discovered dead, also in Braşov, under similar circumstances, about two weeks before you received your first contact from your old high school friend."

Mark exhaled loudly. "So the threat Ahmet received was from Vadim Rusu." He paused to think, still needing time to process the information. "That means Ahmet knew about Rusu's son. The way he panicked, he must have known Rusu meant business."

"Correct," said Gérard. "We figure his organization was involved with this sort of organ procurement. Pretty risky."

"I can't believe it," Mark answered. "Iancu led me to think that they ran a clean operation, free of these kinds of risks."

"By and large, they did," said Gérard. "We suspect that it was Cesar Kaminesky who contaminated their donor pool with such acts."

There it was again. The mysterious Cesar. "Have you found him?"

"He has disappeared." Gérard echoed what Iancu had said the day before.

"What about Olga, the masseuse. Was she married to Cesar?"

"Yes. We received confirmation on that from our agent in Bucharest."

Mark wondered where Olga was now, and how she was dealing with the unfolding events. Her voluptuous image flashed through his mind. He wished he'd had more time with her.

Gérard interrupted his thoughts. "Your tip on Kaminesky was most interesting. We still haven't figured out why his name was on that radiology report."

Mark no longer cared. He changed the subject. "You know those two Moldovans, Rusu's men: they asked me about the surgeon, Gazioğlu. The one you were interested in."

"He is probably a target, too. Rusu's men seem to be aiming to eliminate your friend's entire transplant operation."

"Do you know where Gazioğlu is?"

"We have not located him yet. We believe he is hiding in Turkey."

"I'm headed there this afternoon," said Mark. "To Istanbul."

Gérard shook his head in disapproval. "Haven't you had enough in Budapest?" He spoke in a fatherly tone. "You should be returning home to San Francisco."

Headlights approaching from behind illuminated the interior of their van. The car behind them stopped.

"Looks like your ride is here," said Gérard. Earlier, Zoltán had informed them that a car would be arriving to take Mark back to his hotel.

The driver opened the electronic sliding door of the van. Mark wrapped himself back up in the blanket again as frigid morning air quickly filled the Volkswagen's interior.

"I can't go back home yet," he said. "I promised a friend in Istanbul that I would visit her."

"I knew you would say that," said Gérard with resignation. "I don't need to emphasize that the danger from Rusu is not over. He will assume that you killed his two operatives. You will remain in his crosshairs."

Mark shook his head in disbelief. "Bognár mistakenly thought that I had beaten up his two men in Zrinyi. Now Rusu."

"Bognár may have been wrong," said the Commissaire as they exited the van. "But Rusu will not be. You did, in a manner of speaking, kill his men."

Mark shook his legs in a futile attempt to warm them, but his bare feet did not take to the cold pavement. He did not answer the Frenchman, but knew he was probably right.

"We owe you a debt of gratitude," Gérard said formally. "Without you, I don't believe we could have made as much headway with this case."

"Especially with Kárpáty at the helm," Mark added.

"Indeed," confirmed Gérard. "With him out of the way, we can now proceed with more ease."

A stocky man exited the car behind them. Gérard extended his right hand to Mark. "We would like to hear from you in Turkey," he said, "through our man Leon Adler, whom I spoke to you about—your old mate from school."

Mark nodded. They shook hands.

"Best of luck in Istanbul."

Mark could no longer hold back. He embraced a flustered Commissaire in a tight hug.

Chapter 55

* * *

The driver looked to be in his seventies, with white hair and a prominent gut that left little room between his body and the steering wheel. The car drove slowly on a road with various darkened businesses. They came to a stop at a railroad crossing and waited for a long, slow freight train to pass.

The driver pulled a CB radio microphone to his face and began talking into it in Hungarian. Mark, sitting in the front passenger seat, traced the cord to a radio unit beneath the dash. Higher up, a digital clock on the dash announced the time: ten past five.

A voice crackled in the static, answering the driver. Despite the distortion, Mark recognized it. "Jasmin!" he shouted in surprise.

The train had passed. The driver threw the car in gear and engaged the railroad crossing. Afterwards he gave Mark a smiling side glance and extended his right hand. "Lászlo Virág."

Exhausted as he was, all the adrenaline having left his body some time ago, Mark was suddenly alert. "Jasmin's father?"

The man nodded while he watched a red light at a wide intersection ahead of them. Ferihegy Airport was to the right. Mark realized that he had to get back to his hotel, gather his belongings, freshen up (was that even possible at this point?), and return to Ferihegy later this afternoon for his flight to Istanbul.

Virág turned left.

"What did she say?" asked Mark.

"That she is still at Rudas. She'll be there a while."

They were on Üllői út, driving toward the heart of the city. Mark figured Virág was taking him back to Gresham.

"You should be proud of your daughter," said Mark. "A wonderful young woman."

"I am," answered Virág. "She helped organize the attack on the bath house. For a young officer new in the force, this is a big deal."

Mark wasn't quite sure how Jasmin received such a crucial assignment. He was impressed.

Üllői út was empty. Virág drove fast, running red lights at every intersection, as if he were driving a police cruiser.

"I thought you were retired," Mark said after the third such red light.

"I am," said Virág, with a hoarse chuckle. Sensing why Mark had made the remark, he added, "I miss my old cruiser. Old habits..." he paused to scrutinize another red light before running it, "they don't die easily."

"So this is not an official police car?"

"Correct," answered Virág. "My private car."

"I don't understand," said Mark. "Shouldn't I be with police, I mean...real police?" He regretted his choice of words the moment he said them. "Sorry. I meant active police."

Virág smiled at Mark's discomfiture. "This is what Jasmin wanted."

They were already off Üllői út, in the city center. Mark soon recognized some of the buildings of District VIII.

"I'm impressed that Jasmin gets to have so much say," Mark said. "How does she do it?" He hoped it sounded more tactful than his last statement.

"Ask your Turkish friend, the private investigator."

"You mean Mustafa?" Mark was vexed.

Virág nodded.

"How do you know about him?"

Virág gave him a sideways glance with a smile. He slowed down and began obeying traffic lights as early-morning commuters started to fill the streets.

They passed by the Boscolo Hotel with the New York Café and continued on Erszébet körút.

"Quite a night, huh?" Virág checked an address on a piece of paper while he waited at a traffic light, then looked up. He clearly was not going to answer Mark's question about Mustafa. "Romanian and Slovakian gangsters, all in one place. Explosive combination."

"It was," Mark agreed. "No explosions, though. Knives and machetes."

They sped past the Nyugati railway station. This was not the way back to Gresham Palace.

"I'm glad Kárpáty was finally exposed. We've been trying to nail that son-of-a-bitch for years, but he's been slippery. He's had his own band of loyals within the department who have shielded him."

"I know," said Mark. "Jasmin told me."

Virág continued. "And we got Bognár, too. I'm telling you! What a night!" He nodded proudly. "My Jasmin was the only connection between you and the police. Via your Turkish friend, of course."

Mark realized that his phone calls from Rudas had sparked a decisive police response. At the time, he had felt alone and helpless. He silently thanked György for being brave enough to drop the phone into his swimming trunks.

Virág slowed and began examining passing street signs. "My little girl will get a commendation for this," he said with delight. "And maybe an early promotion."

"Good! She deserves it."

There was still one issue troubling Mark. "Her station house, District V, is aware that Jasmin leaked a confidential document to me, a forensics report. What about that?"

"Yes, they've talked to me about that," said Virág. "No problem. They figured she was onto something big when she befriended you. They are impressed with her initiative and the results it produced."

Mark wondered how impressed they would be if they knew the true extent of Jasmin's initiative.

"Ah, there!" Virág stopped the car in front of *Bosporus Autojavítás*.

Chapter 56

* * *

Turgut and Ergün stared at Mark, speechless, as Mark examined the contents of his shoulder bag. Virág had retrieved it from his back seat as he said goodbye to Mark; Zoltán's men had delivered the bag to him while Mark was with Gérard. Mark's wallet, passport, and iPhone were in there. The forensics report was gone. He didn't care. He had no use for it anymore.

"What happened to you?" demanded Turgut.

They were standing inside the garage, which was as messy as when Mark had first seen it. As the two Turks looked him up and down, Mark, too, examined himself. He was still barefoot, his pants and shirt stained and in disarray. His face and hair were probably equally disheveled. He fit in well with the grime of the garage.

"Why am I here?" asked Mark.

"That's what Mustafa wanted," Ergün answered. He was in coveralls, as was his uncle, his hands and face streaked with oil. They looked like they had been working through the night.

"Where is he?"

The two mechanics led him into the office where, in the darkened room, they pointed to a figure curled up sideways on the old couch, snoring loudly.

"He arrived less than an hour ago," whispered Turgut. "Very tired."

As his eyes adjusted to the darkness, Mark noticed that there was some room on the couch beyond Mustafa's bent legs. He collapsed onto it. The couch was hard, its surface rough. At that moment it seemed like the most luxurious piece of furniture Mark had ever encountered.

"I think I'll rest a bit, too," he said to the two bewildered Turks, and he closed his eyes.

He felt a sense of peace that he had not experienced since his arrival in Budapest. He felt at home amid these Turks whom he had not even known five days ago. This grimy garage was a better safe-house than the luxurious Gresham Palace. He fell asleep instantly.

* * *

"You look like shit," said Mustafa.

Mark smelled bread toasting somewhere. He stretched and rubbed his back, stiff from the couch. He extended his arm to Mustafa and asked him for help to get up. Mustafa looked no better. No longer dressed in disguise, he had bags under his eyes, his collarless Turkish shirt was crumpled and dirty, and his body smelled of sweat.

"Breakfast," Murat announced, holding a platter of freshly toasted bread. He bowed to Mark in a gesture of respect.

The table in the middle of the office had been set up with plates of feta cheese, black olives, butter, jam, tomatoes, and cucumbers. A small TV set blared. Murat passed around the tulip-shaped glasses of tea. Turgut and Ergün joined in, Turgut flinging a wrench onto the sofa before he sat down at the table.

Mark and Mustafa were famished. They ate silently and fast, filling up on large *boluses* while the mechanics sipped tea and mindlessly eyed the TV. Murat hovered around the table like an attentive waiter.

"What time is it?" asked Mark with a full mouth.

"Ten to eight," said Ergün.

"Shit!" Mark was alarmed. "I need to get back to my hotel and pack up. I have a plane to catch."

"No, you don't," said Mustafa. He spat an olive seed onto his plate.

Mark stopped eating. "What do you mean?"

"I mean, my friend, you are not flying out of Budapest, or taking a train or a bus."

"Why?"

"Not safe after what happened last night. Bognár and Kárpáty may have a long reach."

"But they're in custody," Mark protested.

"Even so." Mustafa was emphatic.

"So how am I supposed to leave Budapest?" Mark realized how much he had anticipated a visit to Istanbul, the prospect of seeing his city of birth, of reconnecting with Günsu, Leon, even Latif Bey if possible.

As Mustafa prepared to answer, Murat interjected. "Look! You're on TV."

All eyes turned toward the small TV set that projected a still photo of the Rudas baths from across the river in Pest. The scene changed to nighttime, with countless flashing lights and people being escorted out of the main entrance. The announcer spoke Hungarian in a voiceover.

"What are they saying?" asked Mark.

"They arrested the infamous Slovakian gangster Tibor Bognár after a gang war in Rudas that left three dead," Murat translated.

A still photo of Bognár in black and white appeared, younger and leaner than the one who confronted Mark earlier that morning. He wore his trademark white tank top. It was shot from his left side, with a clear view of the lion's mouth on his shoulder. The announcer seemed to be summarizing Bognár's career as various images of the man flashed rapidly on the screen, younger and older, including a mug shot from a prior arrest.

The footage then cut to a middle-aged reporter, his heavy coat buttoned up, as he approached people exiting the bath. He pointed the microphone at a young man in a white T-shirt and slacks.

"Hey," said Mark. "I know that guy. That's György." György spoke animatedly, the camera zooming in on his tired face. "What's he saying?"

Ergün gestured to Mark to stay quiet. As the camera returned to the reporter, who seemed to be summing up the news, Murat turned to Mark.

"He said that there was an American secret agent in the bath house who helped apprehend the criminals and saved everybody's life. He said he thought the American was FBI."

Now all eyes were on Mark. He smiled sheepishly. "I had to make that up to get him to cooperate with me."

"You mean that American agent was you!" Murat exclaimed, much impressed.

An elegant female studio anchor continued the story, a still photo of Rudas behind her. It shifted to footage of a stocky, older man with jowly cheeks and thick lips who spoke with an air of authority.

"Who's that?" Mark asked.

"Chief of Budapest police," remarked Turgut.

Murat translated in real time. "'The operation undertaken by combined forces from several Budapest jurisdictions was the result of undercover investigations that came to a successful conclusion with the arrest of Bognár and his men. We believe that there is sufficient evidence in the premises to convict them all.'"

An unknown voice asked the chief a question, which he answered. Murat continued to translate.

"In this operation, we were not aided by any branch of American law enforcement."

"He is technically correct," said Mark.

The news went into a commercial and Turgut turned off the TV. "You are a most unusual doctor."

"More like James Bond," said Ergün admiringly.

"FBI," murmured Mustafa, shaking his head in disbelief.

"Don't say anything," Mark warned him, his index finger pointing to Mustafa's face. Turgut and Ergün laughed.

Mark spread some butter on a piece of bread. "I have a lot to tell you," he told Mustafa. "But first tell me, what happened last night?"

"After your first call, when you spotted Iancu, I smelled a rat. I called Jasmin. I still had her card you had given me. She started the police response. At first it was going to be something small, a couple of squad cars checking things out at Rudas. Then when I got your second message, with news of dead bodies, I called her immediately and the police response became massive."

"So, how come I'm not with the police? Don't they want my testimony?"

"You heard the police chief, didn't you?" Mustafa said. "You don't exist." A sly smile broke out on his face. "That was a deal I made on your behalf with the cops." He paused, still smiling, and examined Mark's disbelieving face. "Via Jasmin."

"What deal?"

Mustafa became more serious. "Look," he said, "the main thing is to get you out of Budapest as soon as possible, and safely."

Mark nodded in agreement.

"If you stay here and assist the police, you'll be hung up in Budapest for many more days and most likely will have to revisit several times to testify in trials."

The prospect was definitely not appetizing.

"The deal was that in return for keeping you anonymous, and getting you out of the country today, the police would claim full credit for collaring Bognár and keep the lid on Kárpáty. They want to silently prosecute him without any splashy scandal. It's good P.R. for them."

As unbelievable as it all sounded, Mark was somehow not surprised that Mustafa had pulled this off. "But you told me I couldn't leave Budapest," he protested.

"Not by plane, train, or bus," Mustafa corrected him. "You're going in Turgut's truck."

Chapter 57

* * *

"You have a visitor," shouted Murat, knocking loudly on the bathroom door.

Mark had just taken a shower in the auto shop's grimy bathroom. He zipped up the gray jumpsuit he had been given and slipped on a pair of undersized flip-flops. He looked at himself in the mirror before answering. The suit was supposedly clean but had permanent stains all over. It was Turgut's, too loose for Mark's slender frame and too short, its legs rising up to mid calf. Mark finger-brushed his wet hair and opened the door.

Jasmin was in her blue jumpsuit uniform, with a full duty belt and sidearm. She looked pale, her hair disheveled, cap askew. The dark bags under her eyes seemed darker because of her glasses. She broke into a loud laugh as Mark awkwardly waddled toward her in his strange get-up. "You look like a clown."

Mark approached her, arms open, ready for an embrace. She stopped him. "No, don't!"

Murat observed the two in bewilderment.

"I've been up all night, at work. I smell bad." Delighted at the sight of Jasmin, Mark was disappointed with her rebuff, even though he understood.

They sat at the table in the office and sipped tea.

"Rudas will be closed for several days," Jasmin said. "It will take a while for the evidence teams to go through everything." She had helped with the arrests of Bognár's men, then assisted the evidence teams at the rooftop Jacuzzi and Turkish *hamam*.

"How did Kárpáty take it?" asked Mark.

"I didn't see him. He was whisked away by a team from Belsö Vizsgálati Osztály."

"What's that?"

"The Internal Investigation Department of Budapest police. They deal with errant officers."

Mustafa entered the room, hair wet, fresh out of the shower. He was shaved and wore crisp, clean, well-fitting clothes. "Jasmin, I presume." He shook Jasmin's hand. "We finally meet." His tone was respectful, one police officer to another.

"It's been a long night, but successful," she replied, holding his handshake. "Thank you for all your help."

Mustafa did not answer. He was looking at Mark's ridiculous outfit with a smirk. "We need to get your clothes from the Gresham hotel, soon." The respectful tone had vanished.

"I kind of like the look," Mark said with a grin. "Where's Turgut and Ergün?"

"Out getting the truck."

Mustafa ordered more tea and the three sat down at the table. Mark told them about Vadim Rusu's men and the violent scene in the warehouse near Ferihegy.

"They detained the flight crew that brought those two to Budapest," said Jasmin. "There's another big investigation going on out there."

"Those two Moldovans died in that warehouse," Mark said. "They were the ones who killed Ahmet. I met them. They interrogated me."

"How do you know that they were the killers? Did they tell you that?" Mustafa interjected.

"No. I learned that from Gérard, the French Interpol liaison. I met him in the field afterwards." Mark gave them an account of his encounter and Gérard's news that the Moldovans had been matched to footage from the hotel cameras.

Mustafa took a sip of tea and squeezed Mark's forearm. "See," he said to Jasmin sardonically. "You should make him an honorary Budapest police officer."

Jasmin smiled and nodded in agreement, eyeing Mark with admiration.

Mustafa wasn't finished. "But no, that can't be. He's already FBI."

Mark gave him a stern look, then continued. "It turns out that Ahmet's transplant business inadvertently stole a kidney from the wrong man."

This was news to Jasmin and Mustafa. They listened keenly. "The man was Rusu's son. He died."

"Wow," said Jasmin. "So this was a revenge killing."

"Yes," confirmed Mark. "Rusu wasn't just going after Ahmet. He was out to eliminate everyone involved in the transplant business that killed his son. That's why Iancu was also targeted."

"Where does that leave you?" asked Mustafa.

"Obviously I was not an initial target. But I came into their crosshairs when I stumbled into their operation."

"Like you did into mine," said Mustafa, shaking his head.

"Yes, but with worse consequences. I don't know what they would have done with me in Chisianu once they finished questioning me, but I can imagine." Mark stared into space in silence, contemplating a fate he had narrowly averted.

Jasmin interjected. "The evidence team that went through the plane found various weapons and some other items of interest."

"Like what?" Mark shuddered at the thought of himself on that plane, headed for Chisianu.

"They had portable canisters of argon gas with tubing and masks, and rolls of industrial tape appliers. Clear plastic tape, mounted on dispensers." She paused and checked Mark and Mustafa for reactions. They stared at her expectantly.

"Do you get it?" she finally asked.

The men shook their heads.

"Those curious marks on Radu's body."

"You mean they tied him up with industrial tape?" Mark asked.

"They have to wait for a final forensics analysis," Jasmin replied. "But from what I've heard, they're sure that it will be a match."

Mark recalled the peculiar lines on Ahmet's torso, arms, and legs. He imagined the terror and panic his old mate must have felt as he was handcuffed and wrapped up like a mummy. Revolted, he felt goosebumps down his spine.

Jasmin continued. "They think that he was asphyxiated with argon after he was tied up. Then they removed everything, the tape and handcuffs, before they left."

"That explains the mask bruises on Ahmet's cheeks," said Mark thoughtfully. "He must have struggled against the mask." He recalled his own terror the night before, when a SWAT officer had applied a mask on him and how he too had struggled. He thought of Ahmet immobilized and helpless, knowing that whatever that mask delivered would result in his last breath. His childhood friend had finally run out of luck.

Mustafa pulled him out of his thoughts. "What's argon?" he asked. "I've never heard of that. Is it some sort of poison?"

"It's an inert gas," Mark replied. "Common in the air we breathe. It's not a poison." Mark recalled his high school chemistry and the elements he knew so well in the Periodic Table. "They call it a noble gas."

"It asphyxiates by replacing oxygen," added Jasmin. "There is nothing noble in the way that it kills."

How ironic, Mark thought. Argon, the subject of a stolen test that Ahmet had procured in his first foray as a broker, had eventually come back to kill him in his full-blown, mature career. *And he thought he deftly evaded Mustafa Bey, the Headmaster, all those years ago.*

"Breathing inert gases that replace oxygen has become a popular suicide method in America," Mark told Jasmin and Mustafa. "People place a bag over their heads and run a gas line into it. Helium or nitrogen are more common than argon. They call it an 'exit bag.'"

Mustafa shook his head. "American humor," he said with disapproval.

"Someone from the forensic team told me," said Jasmin, "that these gases are not detectable in autopsy. Gas poisons like chloroform or organophosphates would be detected on analysis of air samples from the lungs. But gases like nitrogen or argon that occur naturally in the air are not."

"How does one get access to argon tanks?" Mustafa asked.

"It's used in various industrial applications, especially in welding," Mark answered. "In the U.S., anyone can buy argon from welding suppliers."

"These KGB guys would have had an easy time with it," added Jasmin.

"So," said Mark. "Had they not found those canisters, they would never have known how Ahmet was killed."

"Correct."

"Simple and effective," commented Mustafa. "No violence, no blood, no mess. No evidence."

Mark was deep in thought. Externally there may have been no violence, but Ahmet, fully aware that he was being murdered, must have been in much turmoil. Panicked as he had been about Rusu's threat, the assault must have come as a major surprise to him in what he considered a sanctuary in Budapest. Mark imagined his friend's final moments, craving for oxygen, unable to fight back.

"It's horrific," said Mark, responding to Mustafa's estimation. "It may have been smooth and efficient, but it *was* violent." Mark was emphatic. "And messy, too. Remember, he urinated on the carpet. It had to have happened as he was suffocating."

Mustafa contemplated Mark's words in silence. "Yes, you're right." He was uncharacteristically deferential. "I knew him well, as you did," he said somberly. "He helped me a great deal in my youth after taking over his father's business. He may have been mischievous, but he was a kind and gentle man. He did not deserve this."

They all felt silent, contemplating the tragedy.

Finally Mark spoke. "Will the Budapest police go after Vadim Rusu?"

Jasmin shook her head. "That is beyond our scope. More in Gérard's arena."

She took her cap and glasses off and rubbed her eyes. "I'm beat," she murmured. "I need a good shower and some sleep."

Mark walked her out. They stood at the door of the garage amid various paraphernalia strewn about. "I met your dad," he said.

"I know."

"Nice guy. He's very proud of you."

Jasmin looked down bashfully.

"He has every right to be." Mark approached closer. "He expects a swift promotion for you with what happened last night."

She looked up at him. "That was all thanks to you."

A loud grating noise startled them. The garage gate had come to life, revealing, as it ascended, a Mercedes truck that had backed up to it. Turgut and Ergün emerged from the cab at the sight of a *Rendőrség* uniform in their garage, looking nervous.

Mark greeted them in Turkish. "*Merhaba.*" He summoned them in, introducing them to Jasmin. "Remember her?"

The sleep-deprived, weary officer they met did not resemble the sexy young woman from Nyugati Station. Sensing their perplexity, Jasmin smiled. "I was about to leave," she told them.

She took off her glasses and turned to Mark, her auburn eyes revealing more than her fatigue. Mark opened his arms. This time she did not refuse. They held each other tight, with Turgut and Ergün watching bemusedly.

"I'm headed to Istanbul today," he said to her quietly.

"I'll miss you," she whispered in his ear. "I hope we meet again." She gave him a kiss on the cheek and released herself from the hug. Mark wished he could have another night with her, but he knew better.

"Thanks for saving my life," he said more loudly, audible to the Turkish mechanics.

She began walking away in confident steps. "Oh, it was nothing." She gave him a formal military salute. "Glad to do it any time."

She brushed by Turgut. "Nice garage you have here."

The two Turks watched her depart. When Jasmin disappeared, they turned to Mark, eyes wide, more mystified than ever about this unusual doctor.

Chapter 58

* * *

"That outfit looks good on you." Turgut smiled beneath weary, bloodshot eyes, showing discolored teeth between meaty, bearded cheeks. He was wearing a similar gray jumpsuit that tightly enclosed his large gut. It had fresh grease stains.

Mark looked himself up and down. "We'd better send Murat to Gresham to fetch my luggage."

Ergün approached Mark cautiously. "Was that the policewoman you were dating the other night?"

Mark nodded.

"I hope she doesn't make any trouble."

"Don't worry," Mark said, confidently. "She won't."

They walked together toward the garage office, Turgut ahead of them. "I didn't recognize her."

"She's tired. Worked all night." Mark stopped to look at the Turkish pair. "You look worn out, too."

"It took more work than we expected to prepare our cargo." Turgut eyed the teapot but did not pour himself any of its contents. "We'll clean up now and get some rest."

Mustafa came in and told them that Murat had left for Mark's hotel.

"When do we leave?"

"Four in the afternoon," answered Turgut. "If all goes well, we should be in Istanbul by seven or eight tomorrow morning."

"How do we cross the Turkish border?"

"You will be in the cargo area of the truck." Turgut chuckled. "Contraband, like everything else."

* * *

The blue Mercedes 410 D was at the cargo bay of the garage, its back doors open. It was a small truck, six-wheeler, with a tall cabin and a short, snub-nosed hood. Mark and Mustafa observed the interior of its cargo compartment full of car parts. Hoods, trunks, and quarter panels were stacked to the top toward the left. In the rear, toward the door, windshields and rear windows were carefully arrayed like giant platters in a kitchen strainer. To the right were several full engines and boxes of small car parts. Behind them, in the dim light of the windowless compartment, Mark made out the shadowy outlines of a recliner chair. He was finally out of Turgut's jumpsuit and in his regular clothes.

Murat shone a flashlight inside. "Look, *Doktor Bey*," he said proudly. "We rigged this just for you, so you can have a comfortable ride."

Ergün arrived carrying another box of car parts that was heavy, judging from the way he held it. He laid it down at the cargo bay and looked in. "Business class," he said, giggling.

Mustafa gave Ergün a slap on the back of his head, the way his uncle did. "How come you don't give *me* the VIP treatment?"

"Sorry," said Ergün teasingly, "but you're nothing but a small-time Turkish private eye." He pointed to Mark, his dirty index finger touching Mark's chest. "Now he—he is an important foreign agent. An American."

Ergün placed his arm around Mark's shoulders. Mark apprehensively eyed the spots where his hands landed, hoping that the fresh shirt he was finally wearing wouldn't meet the grease-smeared fate of most things in the garage.

"Ahmet traveled to Turkey in a fancy Mercedes," Mark told the group. "It had a high-tech secret compartment in the trunk for him to hide in, complete with air conditioning. Dumitru, his driver, showed me the whole thing when he took me to the Central Market."

"You rode in that Mercedes?" asked Murat, awestruck. "Wow!" He gushed. "Your life is so glamorous."

Mark had an instant flashback to the roof of Rudas: Iosif bludgeoned and dying; Iancu mutilated, floating in the enormous Jacuzzi. *Hardly glamorous,* he thought.

Mustafa broke the awkward silence. "Ahmet may have traveled in a better Mercedes," he said, "but he still had to hide." He slapped Mark's back. "Now you have to hide, too."

"I am becoming Ahmet," Mark exclaimed, alarmed by the thought.

"Not quite," said Mustafa consolingly. "You have a long way to go."

"Where will you be sitting?" Mark asked Mustafa.

"Up front. In that cramped cab. I'll make sure to make their drive hell for them."

After the final boxes were loaded, they all stared at the cargo compartment of the truck in silence.

"*Haydi*," said Turgut finally, *come along*.

Mustafa turned to Mark. "You know what you must do," he said quietly. "*Yolcu yolunda gerek.*"

It was an old Turkish saying: "The traveler must travel."

* * *

THE NEXT CHAPTER

This ends Book One in the Mark Kent series. In Book Two, Mark travels to Istanbul, where he meets his old flame, Günsu, and high school mate Leon Adler, now an Interpol liaison. He also meets Dr. Gazioğlu, the infamous Turkish transplant surgeon, and reunites with Latif Bey, Ahmet's father. As Mustafa predicted, Mark becomes embroiled in various troubles that eventually force him to go to Romania and Moldova, in the process experiencing a startling reunion with Olga, the masseuse. The mysteries surrounding Olga's husband, Cesar Kaminesky, including how his name came to appear on the radiology report that summoned Mark to Europe, are revealed.

* * *

Acknowledgments

This story is a product of requests from old friends in Istanbul, fellow English High School students, for a recollection of our old days. I hope that Cem Kocasoy, who was more emphatic than most, will find it to his liking.

A huge thank-you to another EHS classmate, Loni Arditi of Tel Aviv, for his technical assistance regarding police matters. Loni retired from a colorful career as an Israeli detective and later, Interpol liaison. Loni recruited a colleague, Aggie Lantai of Budapest, ex-Hungarian Interpol and bomb squad, whose additional assistance proved invaluable. My tour of Budapest with Loni and Aggie will remain one of the best memories of my writing career.

I was also fortunate in having Robert Lawrence, M.D., an extraordinary pathologist, as an advisor on forensic matters. His concise, creative ideas were crucial to the project.

A special note of gratitude to Fenari Narman of Hamburg, Germany, for introducing me to Rudas Thermal Bath, and to Doug O'Hair of Lodi, California, trusted radiology technician in my operating room, for acting as a sounding board for my endless plot ideas.

My old English High School classmate and best friend Selim Hacısalihzade, of Zurich and Istanbul, remains a dedicated and tireless reader, whose honest critiques were vital to the realization of the final story.

My editor, Mim Harrison, was a staunch pillar of support in what is now our third project together. Mim, more than anyone else, is responsible for catapulting me to the ranks professional authorship. *Merci beaucoup, mon cher ami Mim*, as Commissaire Gérard might say.

A final note of acknowledgment for yet another EHS classmate, Ahmet Biliktan. We were best friends in our teenage years. His mysterious disappearance in the 1990s and my persistent but futile searches for him inspired this story. As the early version of this novel was taking shape, my determined detective work at last bore fruit. My reunion with Ahmet in Bucharest, Romania, after four decades, was nothing short of a miracle. It will remain yet another indelible memory of this project.

* * *

ABOUT THE AUTHOR

In addition to being a writer and a neurosurgeon, Moris Senegor is an avid wine enthusiast, music educator, cyclist and photographer. In this, his third book and first novel, Senegor once again brings readers his talent for bridging the New World with the Old. His research took him to Hungary, where, while walking the streets of Budapest with police officers, he sampled Hungarian cuisine and wine, both vividly described in the narrative. Follow Moris Senegor's varied interests on www.morissenegor.com.

Made in the USA
Middletown, DE
01 February 2018